MW01171325

Book Cover by Jupiter @saintjupit3rgr4phic

Internal Art by @Gurge.Art

1st edition 2024

AMEFYRE

BOOK ONE

A POCKET OF LIES

R. A. SANDPIPER

1

I dreamt of Him tonight. I asked mother to send me away, where I may live in His worship. She refused.

Diary of C. Aubethaan, est. early 8th century

It wasn't fair to say that Suri was lonely. She was so used to solitude, it was knitted onto her soul.

The tavern door across the street swung open. A jaunty tune and a breath of warm air tumbled out into the winter night. Suri pulled her worn cloak tighter. Gods, it was freezing. How long had it been since her bones had felt that kind of heat? A roaring fire, a comfy seat, even a hot meal. Her stomach growled at the thought of actual food.

Suri's life was a series of unwritten judgements. Sometimes she could see the truth of a thing clear as day. Usually, she guessed. Tonight, she guessed that smell from the alley wall was a mixture of piss and rainwater. She knew the single coin she caressed wasn't hers.

Once more, she rubbed the whorled metal piece in her pocket. A single bit. The lowest coin in the Forgelands and about the size of her thumbnail. Enough to feed her for a day if she ate next to nothing.

Her whole damned fortune.

But Geren would find her tomorrow. She grimaced, touching her neck. Her fingertips traced the purple bruises he'd left the week before. It'd been her own stupid fault.

Suri had two choices. Pay off a gang each week in return for protection and the dim hope the others might leave her alone. Or don't pay, and wind up dead the next time she fucked up. The second option became more likely each day, and Suri's hunt for a third door had been crushed along with her windpipe last week.

She'd spent a week recovering, and her pockets were as empty as her stomach. Geren wouldn't let her off, though. She owed him five bits, due tomorrow. There would be no extra time. If she didn't pay him, he'd kill her.

Great.

So, the lonely bit she played with was not hers at all. It was his.

A voice laughed near the door. Suri's knees bent, her breath levelled, her hand readied in front of her.

The woman left first, stumbling out the tavern door. Her black skin glistened under the tavern light, a sheen of sweat from the many bodies inside. Suri scanned the woman's form. A sizable lump protruded from her left hip pocket. She could almost hear the ale sloshing around in her body. The woman glanced back at the man behind her, his hand encircling her arm.

"You were supposed to remind me not to play cards," the woman said with a cat-like grin.

The lantern hanging from the door illuminated his face as he smiled. He had tanned skin, kind eyes and sandy hair. He was tall, even by Suri's standards, who stood shoulder-to-shoulder with most men. "And you would have listened to me?"

They were outsiders, judging by their sturdy clothing and darker skin. Northerners were usually as pale as the snow dotting the roofs of the city, and Suri was no exception. She saw no purse-like lump in his trouser pockets, but considered the deep trenches of his overcoat as he swung it over his shoulders. The coat hit his side with a weighted thud.

The pair took their first steps away, both unstable on their feet. He murmured something in her ear, and she threw her head back in a laugh, her cropped black hair emphasising the curve of her neck.

There was a gleam in his eye, as he looked down at her. Suri didn't like it. She took a step to the edge of the shadows. He swept his hand through his hair. He seemed unthreatening, yet, as if he wanted to seem that way. Though maybe she wished for a flaw in her prey to cover her own.

Still, he would be her target that night.

The pair strolled together across the cobbles, and Suri moved from the true darkness of her alley spot to follow. The man's overcoat had deep pockets and, with every step, the material gaped and retracted, sighing a breath alongside his gait.

The city shone with Loris' moonlight, the windows of the bricked buildings closed firmly against the night. Devoid of life, like the Parched Lands to the south. Suri preferred to do dark deeds in the dark.

One beam of moonlight hit against a paper warrant nailed to the side of a building. An artist's reasonably accurate version of Geren's face stared back at her. Geren Sharpe. Wanted for petty theft and burglary. The poster was so weathered, the reward amount was illegible. But Suri knew it already. Three silver for information leading to his arrest.

Over thirty bits. A decent sum, probably enough to tempt his stupider friends to consider betraying him. And yet Suri had been richer than that last week, when Geren had caught up with her. Her own damn fault for trying to steal his number two. She deserved the beating. She would have done the same to him. Still, it stung, not just the bruises, her reputation was in tatters. No one would join her now, if she ever amassed the funds to try again. She focused on the word "petty" on the warrant to soothe the sparks of anger, knowing how much it annoyed him.

The pair turned again. It was a dead end. Either their destination was near, or they'd noticed a tail. Unlikely.

Still, she paused before following them, darting a look around the corner. The two still ambled forward with no urgency.

She never understood why her fellow thieves loved the idea of being wanted. Geren collected his posters like a badge of pride for evading the guards. New pups who'd barely taken a pear drop from a wet baby would sign their lives away to work in the infamous Geren's band. Suri didn't want infamy. If they asked her—which they didn't—any form of notoriety at all was a sign you were a damned awful thief.

Still, she wondered how her poster would look. Suri Hillsend, aged twenty, wanted for ten years of barely scraping by. What would the reward be? Would it even pay for the paper they printed it on?

She ducked round the corner, deep in shadow again. The two in front of her were almost impossible to see. She used her ears instead, following their footsteps. She could still hear the rhythmic movement of the steps in front of her.

Was that two sets? Or one? Surely it should be louder. Suri stopped, squinting. She could only see one set of shoulders.

Something was wrong.

Just as the thought came to her, a hand grabbed the back of her neck. The grip made her knees buckle, and Suri fell to the stones with a gasp.

Shit.

"Thought you were clever, huh?"

The voice was cold and cruel. Double shit.

She grabbed at the stones for purchase and made to launch herself away. As she pushed herself forward, that hand came back again. This time it hoisted her up by her shirt until she was dangling above the ground, her clothes a noose around her neck.

His strength sent a spike of genuine fear through her.

A tinkling laugh sounded in her ears, as the blood rushed to her head. The woman approached. There was mirth in those eyes, but it was not from joy. It was darker.

Suri wheezed in a pittance of breath. Just her luck.

"What's wrong, mouse? Cat got your tongue?" Her leg whipped up and slammed into Suri's side, knocking her out of the man's grip and back onto the ground.

She pulled herself to her hands and knees. Fire lanced through her side. Damn, that woman could kick. She needed to get out, make a dash for it. But she couldn't catch her breath.

"Wrath's doors! I honestly wouldn't have noticed her, Scilla. Northern wine, eh?" he said.

Suri clawed in a ragged gasp of air. "Look, I didn't mean—"

Another kick cut her attempt to speak short. Same side. Her shoulders hit the stones hard and the force of it flipped her onto her back. Son of a bitch.

The woman's face appeared over her, her cheekbones carved like a sculpture. Scilla. "I only barely noticed her. She almost robbed us blind. Kol would have killed us." She smirked. No kindness in her eyes. About to speak again. Or kick again.

Fuck that. Suri was done with this horror show right now.

She swept her leg round to snag against Scilla's, pulling her off-balance. Scilla stumbled to the side as Suri moved into a crouch. The man was almost on her. She leapt out of the way of his fist, dodging him. She scratched at his face as she launched herself to her feet. He groaned as she spun out of his reach.

Served him right, the prick.

Her eye fell on a small metal insignia attached to his collar. *Kol.* Oh fuck. She registered it just as Scilla moved towards her.

Suri ran.

She couldn't fight this, she knew that.

And now, she also knew where they were from. That empty golden sand timer pinned to him proved it. Desert dwellers from the Wrath-blighted land to the South. They called it the Parched Lands now, and it was a wasteland.

Which also meant the Kol they referred to was *the* Kol. Demon King of the Parched Lands.

But she knew the city. They didn't.

"You can't run, little mouse!" he said.

Oh, but she could.

She ran.

They followed, her stomach rolling with horrid anticipation of the heavy boots pounding behind her. She'd turned this into a game. A game she had to win.

Suri was fast. Even with the pain in her side, she still felt confident that she could outrun these two. But she didn't understand how they'd known she was there. She'd done it by the book, she was sure of it. Her footsteps slapped against the stone.

She hadn't even taken a damned bit from them. Why wouldn't they let her the fuck be?

Left down the side of the main road. Left down the next alley. This one wasn't a dead end. No people. That was good. People were obstacles. People wouldn't come to her aid. She pushed her legs faster, harder. She couldn't hear their footsteps anymore.

"Mousey? Where are you?"

The woman's voice. So close, almost like a breath in her ear.

What? Where were the footsteps? They couldn't be that close.

It must have been a trick. Adrenaline. She couldn't have heard that right. She propelled herself down to the next right, risking the smallest glance over her shoulder. No one, nothing. Just the darkness.

"Mousey, mousey, mousey!"

The words were a breath in her other ear. Scilla. She yanked her head around and looked as she ran. Wrath's balls. What was going on?

Still nothing. Just darkness.

She had enough faith in her sanity to know it wasn't her imagination. She heard it. It was them. She panted as she tried not to panic.

Where were they?

With a quick jolt of fear, she risked a look above her as she ran, but still nothing. She rounded the next left and ducked into a narrow alcove that housed a carved shrine to Queen Lera. She sent a quick mental apology to the Trio as she caught her breath, back pressed against the cold stone. Clearly, the Gods had a bone to pick with her this week.

A minute passed and nothing happened. She peered out of the alcove and the coast seemed clear. She darted round the corner, into a small private square. Empty. Residences with dark windows formed its perimeter.

She looked back to the alley. Still nothing. No one.

That she could see, anyway.

The pounding in her head faded to a dull pulsing as her breath came back to her. Quiet fell over the courtyard, the only sound a trickle of water from the stone basin in the centre.

Her mind told her she must have outrun them. But her gut told her that wasn't true. She was being watched.

She turned slowly, half-crouched, ready to run at a moment's notice.

A hand shot out of nothing, of nowhere, of the darkness itself, and gripped Suri's throat.

"Found you." He threw her body across the courtyard, as if she weighed the same as the one bit in her pocket. The wind ripped past her and she crashed into the stone basin. Pain reverberated across her back and down into her legs.

She screamed. And still she saw no-one.

No. It wasn't possible. She'd looked and they *weren't there.*

She knew she couldn't move. Yet she *had* to move. She pushed her arms down and tried to pull her legs up, but had only got to her knees before she heard them again.

Real footsteps this time. Two sets for sure.

And then, so quickly, she was wrenched up again. The man pulled her by her arms, twisting them behind her back. She tried to duck, arch her back, manoeuvre out of his grip.

Scilla slowly walked towards her with a look of mocking sadness. "Did you think you'd got away?"

Suri snarled a lip. "Leave me the fuck alone, you bitch!"

Then Scilla punched hard. Suri's head whipped to the side with the force of the impact against her face.

"I was just going to teach you a lesson," Scilla said. "But now. Now you've hurt my friend. And that won't do. He has a party tomorrow, you see. He won't look presentable." Scilla slapped her across the other cheek.

The force knocked Suri's face to the other side, and she felt a jolt in her neck. Scilla didn't just hurt her, she embarrassed her.

For fun. Was she out of her damned mind? She hadn't killed the woman's firstborn.

Suri turned her head once more. Looked into that face. She summoned the last of her strength. Then she spat.

Saliva, speckled with blood, hit Scilla in the face. The woman flinched in shock, raising her white sleeve to her face. "I'll slice your ear for that."

"Great. Your voice is giving me a headache," Suri said. The words hurt to push out, her cheeks already smarting. But they had the desired effect.

Scilla growled. Rage flashed in her eyes, and Suri smiled. "Hold her still, I'll crop her," she said to her companion.

Hold her still? She was already being held like a toy for the woman to torment. Yet the surrounding arms somehow tightened, and Suri had to choke back a scream.

Scilla's fingers grabbed at her ear, and she flinched.

"Wait, Scill. Look there!" he said.

Scilla turned around, following the man's gesture. Suri couldn't see anything. When the woman turned back, her eyes were full of mirth.

Oh, no.

"Even better," she said. "Take her money while I grab it."

He shoved Suri, and the floor collided with her body. It was so cold. And yet, everything burned. An extra level of pain set in when his groping fingers closed around that one bit, the one thing she had left, other than the clothes on her back. "Is that it?" he said. It didn't even feel like a taunt. Just a simple reaction, which made it so much worse.

Scilla returned, carrying a bucket. Its contents sloshed against the side, threatening to spill. "Move back, I don't want to get it on you," she said to him.

His hands left her body. Scilla threw the bucket.

Suri jammed her eyes shut as warm liquid hit her body. It seeped into her clothing immediately, sticking to her everywhere.

"Get a better profession, rat," Scilla said. Then they left, disappearing as fast as they'd arrived.

Suri lay there on the uneven cobbles, now covered in someone else's urine. She could taste the iron tang of her blood. She didn't even want to think about the smell.

Last week was a comeuppance. This was different.

She would kill them. Somehow, she would do it. She would tear them apart with her own hands if she needed to. Weapons be damned. She knew their faces. She had one of their names. Scilla. It was enough to find them. Do something—anything.

Her thoughts swirled with half-baked plans, her head pounding with a darkening fog. She had nothing left except boiling anger. Her desire consumed her in its awful simplicity.

Revenge.

2

*My sister has taken on her greatest challenge yet,
one that might prove difficult even for her. Setting
her sights on a Prince was one thing, but the King?*
Diary of C. Aubethaan, est. early 8th century

S weet Suri.

The deep voice washed over her body and her eyes burst
open. Were they back? How did they know her name? She
weakly lifted her head and scanned the courtyard.

The fire, dulled by her body's stillness, crackled across her
ribs. She hissed through her teeth at the pain and tried not
to move anything. If she didn't move, if she didn't breathe, it
didn't hurt. If she didn't breathe, she couldn't smell it.

Make them pay.

The noise made her jump, sending a fresh wave of pain jud-
dering through her.

It wasn't one of their voices. Even their disembodied whispers from the night before didn't reverberate and echo through her like this. Male, for certain. But it came from *inside* her, speaking into her thoughts, her very mind.

The only people that heard voices were chatterers and high priestesses, two categories Suri firmly did not want to be part of. She could only hope it was some temporary madness. She needed to speak to Mother Edi. Now.

Suri let the cobbles in front of her settle into focus. A pale light reflected in the dew that dampened the stone. Her still damp clothes peeled from the uneven stone beneath her as she sat up. She breathed through the pain and blinked again. A small green vine creeped down the side of the stone structure looming above her. Was it there last night?

She was cold. So cold.

The memory of the night broke over her like the dawn she must have slept through. She winced and crawled to her feet, using the stone basin to support some of her weight. Every part of her hurt, but her back and left side bore the worst of it.

The smell of the piss all over her had ripened overnight into something horrible and sour, and her clothes clung to her like fleas on a dog.

At least the courtyard was empty, thank the Gods.

Suri leaned over the basin. Its wide stone bowl featured a carving of Loris, God of the Moon and Tides. If Suri had to have a favourite diety, Loris would likely take the prize. She'd never spent much time in the water, but he seemed the closest of the Trio to a God of Night.

She looked at her reflected face and it wasn't pretty. She muttered a curse against those foreign desert bastards and their mothers.

Her nearly black hair pressed to her scalp in matted clumps, stuck to the blood oozing from her right temple. It didn't look like anything was broken, but her jaw blossomed with bruises all the way from her ear to her pointed chin.

A splatter of something brown dotted up her neck. She hoped it was mud.

The anger rose back up for a second and then lost out to fatigue.

It was that narrow chin and her slightly exaggerated cheekbones that gave any hint there was more to Suri's blood than just human. It wasn't much. The barest smidge of Fae blood somewhere in her distant line. Not enough to be remarked on. Half the people she knew had something to show a distant relation to a Fae: a single golden eye, longer fingers, a pointed ear, or narrow tongue. Sure, if she lived to old age, she might find herself with a handful more years than a pure blood human. But with her luck, she'd be lucky to even make it to the end of a human lifespan.

She dipped her hand in the water, warping her reflection to nothing. The barest act of drinking hurt, too. She wiped as much of the blood off as she could bear with the near frozen water, gritting her teeth against the sharp sting on the open wounds. Pink rivers of water moved down her hand as she grasped the side of the bowl.

It was time to move.

The first step she took made her worry she would collapse, but she had to keep moving. It was the only way to keep the cold away and she still had her pride, even if her torso was likely more blue than white right now.

She dragged her body down the streets of the Forgelands' capital, her shaking hand dragging along the freezing stone walls of the city of New Politan as she tried to provide herself with a tiny amount of support. After what felt like miles, she was at one of the many entrances to the narrow web of streets that separated the merchants from the filth. The Tangle: the poorest underbelly of New Politan, thrumming with the ugliest parts of both life and death.

The mess of the streets held the greatest hedonistic pleasures a human could encounter. It was where the worst of the North came to hide or drink and where the best of them never ventured.

Suri moved into the lane and took a moment to catch her breath. It was dangerous to show weakness here at the best of times, and she refused to look weak in her own home. She avoided leaning against the wall, which smelt of every type of waste, and straightened her shoulders. She didn't know why she bothered. In her current state, she matched the surroundings perfectly.

It was quiet, too. She was lucky the early hour of the day meant that most of the Tangle was unconscious. Still, she passed a man begging with a light manipulation trick and more than one peddler of dried plants that would apparently connect you to other worlds.

Every breath squeezed painfully through her body. She'd had worse. But she couldn't afford a setback. Geren might actually kill her this time.

Another turn. Nearly there.

She passed the first brothel. The flickering tallow candle, encased in red glass, showed the premises were still open for business. Guided by the dull, frequent red glare which lured with their sultry glow, Suri reached the fourth.

The fourth brothel on the street was unremarkable except for the carved sculpture of a defaced figure embedded into the stonework. At one time, long ago, this had been a holy house to the Old Gods. There had been two brothers, or lovers, and even on rare occasions both, depending on which storyteller told it. Diophage, the Old God of Life. Sotoledi, the Old God of Death. Now, it wasn't clear which of the two this was supposed to depict. Suri wouldn't have known it was even a pagan building if it weren't for the clear intentional battering the stony face had taken. No one would do that to the Trio.

And now, its door held a red entranceway. She passed by it and instead cut down the side of the building. She made sure no one was behind her before she entered the worn wooden door near the back. Dark steps led straight down to a weak yellow light. She made her way down the stairs like a cripple. She couldn't prevent a small grunt, as her hand slipped off one wall and her full weight went into her step.

Gods, she needed to lie down again.

"Who is it?" A high-pitched voice.

Suri rounded the corner and saw the young boy half-crouching, a blunt knife held out in front of him as if to defend himself. He wore a filthy shift that was perhaps once white, and some darker shorts. Suri noted the threadbare blanket caught around his ankles. A mop of dirty brown curls covered his dark eyes. Ren.

"Hey, kid."

She smiled as the boy relaxed. He was maybe eight. A couple of years younger than she'd been when she'd first come down here over a decade ago.

"You didn't do the knock. You have to do the knock."

She looked around the room. The dim light, cast off the candles on the worn table, was barely enough to make out the surroundings. Two kids lay in the back corner. Older than Ren. They were curled up next to each other, still asleep. One alone curled under the table itself, a foot poking under from what looked like a pile of old cloth.

"It's early. Didn't want to wake anyone," Suri said, and it wasn't entirely a lie. An attempt on her life right now would probably win points with Geren.

Ren himself was lucky she had come and not someone picking a fight. Even in her state, she could take out a kid like Ren in a few seconds.

You could kill them all.

The others might not even wake if she acted fast enough. Take his knife, slice his throat, and keep him quiet. Stick the others in the heart. All of them could be dead so easily. If only the two from last night were as easy prey as this.

Kill them all, sweet Suri...

Her head snapped round to look up the stairs as it sang in her head again. No one was there. A deep, wistful song of a voice. Maybe this was a new form of manipulation, some ability someone had discovered that allowed them to speak to people. But why her? Could he hear her thoughts back? Why would she even think about killing Ren? Any of them?

"Ma says you have to do it always."

Suri looked back at the boy. Ren played with his knife, toying with the edge. He looked unconcerned. He hadn't heard that voice calling to her.

Then his face wrinkled. "Ew, why do you smell so bad?"

She shuddered to shake the weird thoughts out of her mind. "You don't wanna know, kid."

Ren frowned. She asked where Ma was, and he pointed to her usual room.

Suri looked at the other two on the floor and then back to him. "Make sure you get some rest, eh?"

The boy grinned. "I'll kick one of 'em awake soon!"

She walked through Ma's door.

Masses of melted and dried tallow covered the surfaces, odd peaks rising from here and there, tufting warm light. A clay sculpture of two ambiguous figures embracing stood eroded by the side of a straw mattress in one corner. A figure hunched in the only chair next to a large table.

Ma, or Mother Edi, was awake. Awake and incredibly old.

The part-Fae took longer to age.

Many people here had some level of Fae blood from the time when Fae and humans had been far more intermingled, but for the last few generations the pure Fae had refused to leave the Glen. They now lived in isolation in their Glen in the North of Drangbor, ruled by the Fae King Xianyu. She wasn't sure exactly why this was, but she'd heard it was connected to some important Fae dying. Many still living had tenths or even a quarter of that blood within them. For those with trace levels like Suri, the Fae links in her heritage would only matter when she lived to a hearty seventy-five years, instead of sixty.

Mother Edi was part-Fae. Rumour had it she was a woman grown before the Wrath. Suri had done the maths. The Wrath occurred not long after the turn of the 8th century. So now, in the early 9th century, if it were true, that would make her at least one hundred and twenty. Though, unlike the eternally youthful part-Fae Queen of Drangbor, Mother Edi wore her one hundred years in grooves that ran deep in her skin.

She sat in a worn wooden chair, sewing a patch onto an even more worn shirt. The shirt was clearly that of a child's. She didn't look up when Suri walked in, but her slight change in posture showed she was aware she wasn't alone. Her eyes were bad, glazed over with milky white. After a couple of seconds, she put the sewing down, and turned to face Suri.

"Take those off," she said. Mother Edi's hair was a black and grey mess, tied with an old red string barely visible through the many snarled locks. Lines mapped a woman who had led a full life. As a child, Suri had feared her, seeing something dark in her crooked nose and chin. Now this was one of the few faces that made her feel like herself and not a desperate vessel of the night.

Suri tried to reply, but her throat felt stuck. She peeled off her clothes, down to her underwear, and stepped out of the pile.

Mother Edi watched her. "What happened, my girl?"

Suri's eyes filled with tears. The last bit of strength she had deflated. Suri leaned back into the door, shutting it, and swallowed. "Picked the wrong targets."

Mother Edi still didn't move from her seat. Her ankles were in worse condition than her eyes. "Come and lie here. Let's see."

She slapped the table in front of her with a firm, leathery hand. Suri took a few deeper breaths and hauled herself the last few steps to the table. She had bled on this table many times. As a child with a scraped knee, as an adult last week.

She pulled herself up and swung her legs around before lying back, defeated by that final use of her muscles. Mother Edi shuffled around the table, as she assessed Suri. She poked and prodded, sometimes cupping an arm, or moving a leg.

"You're too skinny."

"Yes," Suri said. It was a simple truth.

"These injuries are severe. You did well to get here."

Suri didn't respond.

"Have you felt the beats?"

Suri shook her head. "No time."

Mother Edi frowned. "Do it now."

"I need to ask you something. About the people—"

"Soon," she interrupted, raising a hand. "Now, beats."

Suri nodded. She started with the places that she wouldn't have to move too much to feel. That would stop her from sitting up for longer than she had to. She held her left hand just above her right, so close she could feel the fine hairs that rose from her right wrist tickling her palm, but she didn't touch. She took a deep breath and ignored the pain in her ribs. Instead, she concentrated on her heart beat. She drowned out everything else, until that thud was the only thing left.

This was always so much harder when she was in pain.

She kept her hand where it was, dismissing the flickering light against her now closed eyelids, ignoring the feeling of the uneven wooden planks beneath her, cancelling the smell of bodily fluids that wrinkled her nostrils.

Thud. Thud. Thud. Thud.

There, she had it. It took her half an hour to complete the loop of her body. The beat was now everywhere. Mother Edi would know if she tried to cheat.

"Well done," she said, as Suri's hand touched her heart one last time. "Now, questions?"

Suri kept her breathing steady, some of the pain ebbing from her body as she took a moment to decide how she wanted to word it. "Can people speak into the minds of others? Is this a manipulation skill?"

"What have you heard?" Mother Edi asked.

Suri explained the events of the night before, and the voice from this morning. She couldn't help but let her rage seep into her voice as she retold it. Yes, she had tried to rob them, but they had humiliated, and nearly killed her.

Make them pay.

She could feel his encouragement as she spoke, whomever it was. It seemed to tell her to seek revenge, and she wanted it. She wanted it so much. Mother Edi's face did not change throughout.

Half a minute of absolute silence passed before the wizened woman spoke. "Moving light and shadow, that's manipulation. Moving something from here to there. But to form it where none exists, or to move within it, that is beyond."

"How?" Suri asked without hesitation.

The question was risky.

Manipulation was the movement of worldly elements already present. Tricks of light, swirling patterns of dried leaves in the air, party tricks used for entertainment and impressing little children. But manipulation had initially come from the Old Gods, and was met with equal parts awe and fear. It was permitted within at a low level, and the learning of small tricks was common practice if one had a natural aptitude for it. To protect everyone, the knowledge of how to develop and strengthen these skills was closely guarded by the priesthood. Anyone attempting to go beyond the realms of small manipulation was punished.

She shook her head. "You cannot learn this thing. It is dark. Heresy."

"Through worship of the Old Gods?"

Mother Edi nodded.

Disappointment washed over her. The hope she might learn the skill died as quickly as it rose.

True magical creation and destruction of any kind was outlawed. To acquire that kind of power, people had to commit barbaric acts in the name of the Old Gods. Even teaching it would grant you a death sentence. It didn't surprise Suri to find out that her attackers from the night before were willing to tap into that amount of darkness.

"You say a different voice speaks to you today. Describe it to me, the exact words," Mother Edi said, her voice dropping until Suri could barely make it out.

"It's a deep voice. He knew my name, but I never told them it. He told me to make them pay."

Mother Edi blinked her milky eyes, then stood and shuffled into the darker reaches of the room. A drawer opened, accompanied by the rattles of too many items clattering into each other. When she returned, she held up a small piece of metal in front of Suri.

It was the size of the top section of a little finger, a narrow canine ending in a rounded tip. Suri had no clue what the silver piece was for. Mother Edi held either side of it, before pulling it apart. There were two halves of metal, with a needle between them that allowed it to slot together.

"Another earring?" Suri asked. Her right ear already had two piercings, both small metal studs that went through the lobes. The first given to her after... *After.* The second, around four years ago, when she was sixteen and the nightmares had come back.

"The metal disrupts the voices," Mother Edi said. She often spoke a language it seemed only she could understand. Almost before Suri was aware of it, she'd taken the needled end and pierced it through her right ear near the top, twisting the other side into place.

Suri clenched her jaw for a moment against the sharp sting as her eyes watered.

"Take some clothes from that drawer," Mother Edi said, picking up her sewing. "And rest."

Suri knew this meant she was dismissed. But she couldn't resist the questions that still bubbled up. "So I'm not going mad? I really did hear someone? How did it know my name?"

Mother Edi kept her head down and kept sewing. "You're not mad. But you are too angry. I can feel rage around you, inside you. You must learn to control it, or it will consume you."

Suri's breath caught for a second. The urge to retort, to tell Mother Edi she had no idea what she was talking about. Because why *shouldn't* she be angry? Everyone was out to get her. Geren, the city guards, anyone she came across. They deserved her rage. It had been nothing but cruel to her since the day she was born. This whole world—No.

She focused on the air pushing beneath her bruise-mottled chest, and calmed herself. She had trusted Mother Edi for most of her adolescence and now, into adulthood, she was the only person left in this city Suri still trusted. She would not disrespect her. She *was* angry. That much was true. She would try.

"Thank you."

Mother Edi watched her. "Are you still alone, girl?"

"What?" Suri replied.

"It isn't safe to be alone."

"I have you."

"I am old," Mother Edi said.

Suri blinked. She picked at a nail with a shaky hand, dropping the eye contact. Of course, she was old. She wasn't stupid.

Mother Edi wafted her hand. "Rest, girl."

Suri grunted a yes. A lie. As if she could rest. She had a debt to pay.

After dressing, she left the basement where she'd spent so many nights. Ren had gone somewhere. Suri opened the door fully into the morning. The day was usually when she slept, ate, and waited for the advantages of darkness. But Suri didn't have the luxury of time.

Geren would soon come for his payment. And she wanted to eat something. More than all of that, Suri needed the security of weight in her pocket.

She made her way to the Merchant's Quarter, her progress slowed by the pain in her body. She passed one of the larger carvings of the Trio standing in the lapping water. To some, with *a lot* of Fae blood, they were the New Gods. To Suri, they were the only Gods.

Atrius first sat astride a Roanhadham, the mythical Fae horses of old, with a crown of carved sunrays. Then triumphant Dvaius, God of War and Rebirth, his sword aloft. Finally Loris, on one knee, with his hand dipping into the waves. The three had appeared to the Drameir Queen in a moment of great need a century ago, and had been guiding figures for their world ever since.

The feet of Loris and Dvaius were empty of tribute. At the feet of Atrius, the Sun God, tens of weathered candles littered the floor. The city prayed for an early end to the bitter winter.

Suri gave a curt nod to Loris and carried on. Whilst summer guaranteed a warm place to sleep, it was no help to her profession. She preferred the darkness.

She weaved through to the busiest street, the only part of the whole blasted city which thrived in the morning. The markets.

Technically, she wasn't allowed in this area. It was Geren's hunting grounds. But she had little choice at the best of times, and this was far from that. The street widened to fit the number of bodies, yet they still packed in shoulder to shoulder. Merchants moved around their stalls as boys flogged wares in loud voices, ready to pounce if anyone passing by even glanced at the items. The street was a corridor of pure noise.

As a child, Suri lived in these markets. One hand in a pocket, while the other pilfered sweet treats. She would dance away with several bits and a full stomach.

Some things were easier when she was a child. Some things were harder. Especially after Esra.

Now older, she could protect herself from most. But she never went unnoticed in a crowd. Not only was Suri a head taller than most women, her clothing and near constant injuries made her immediately obvious to the many guards who patrolled the market. The guards had likely marked her already, and if not, she would draw their attention soon.

Plus, she had Geren's hounds to contend with, who were even worse than the guards. It made her job very difficult. Then she noticed there seemed to be more guards here than normal. Maybe double. She could see six on this side alone. That made her job nearly impossible.

But Suri was the best pickpocket in the city. And she was desperate.

She weaved through the bodies that crushed and swelled against her. She kept her head down as much as was possible, serving a double function as she looked down into the surrounding pockets.

Her first prey today was too easy. The pudgy-fisted child wandered a couple of steps from his mother. He hadn't gone hungry for a day in his life. It took a slight fake stumble to get a hand into, and out of, the child's pocket. Suri slid the coins into her pocket. She could feel from the size and the patterns pressed into the metal. Three bits. Nearly enough for one debt.

"What's with all the southerners arriving?" a voice said.

Suri would have liked to have been further from her initial target before she stopped, but curiosity got the best of her. She paused near a fish stall and listened.

The market wasn't just for money. New information could make the difference between life and death. And she had to admit, she wanted to know about the *southerners*. The word alone had reignited that bubble of rage at two specific *southerners*.

She knew she shouldn't be this angry. She should listen to Mother Edi and let it go. It was too soon, though, too fresh. And whilst that voice didn't whisper at her, telling her to kill them, she could still feel its intent inside her; driving her to eavesdrop, track them down, end them. She tried to rationalise it. Of course, she was mad. Revenge was a comfort. A companion when she was having a shitty day. Plus, it wouldn't hurt to know what was going on in her city.

"The Prince is having a ball tonight, they'll be coming for that."

She remembered the words from last night. Something about him having a party tonight. This ball? A ball was a blessing and a curse. Tourists were known to have a foolish disposition of generosity to the poor. Something about travelling gave them some odd desire to chuck coins in the way of the destitute.

A ball also meant more guards, which explained the presence here today.

"Did he invite every royal in Peregrinus?"

The merchant tried to speak to her, before he apparently assessed from either her clothing or demeanour that she wouldn't buy anything. She wouldn't have long before he forced her to leave.

"Everyone with a daughter, I think. He's looking to marry."

"Then why are the sand folk here?"

Her heart jolted. *Them.*

Most people hated the desert dwellers on principle, with the cruel Lord of Death as their ruler. They distrusted the land, too, cursed and barren forever in the devastation of the Wrath ignited by the Lord of Death himself. Suri now had a reason for her own brand of hatred. Scilla. She flexed her jaw to confirm that yes, it still hurt like a bitch.

"Are you scared?" the other man taunted.

"You're not? The Demon King has been wiping out traders on the Drameir Road for months. He leaves them blackened, shrivelled up like..."

Suri shivered at the reference to the Lord of Death's particular brand. Killing using death magic left the bodies empty and blackened, their very blood and essence gone from their bodies in an instant. It granted him his other name, the Demon King.

"There's no daughters in his lands, though."

"No life there at all."

Suri rolled her eyes. It was true nothing *grew* there. It couldn't. Life existed, though. People lived in the Parched Lands. Thieves and deserters mostly. Her kin. Suri knew people from the Tangle who had chosen a life of exile in the Parched Lands over a long death in jail. The unappetising courtiers of the Lord of Death.

"If they're here. It means trouble," the man replied.

She spotted the merchant coming over to her again, and quickly wove her way back into the crowd. She'd heard what she needed to hear. The ball wasn't worth the risk. Even if those scum were there, she had no way to get in there. Not one that wouldn't land her in a prison. The castle was through a Gate in the royal district, defended by even more guards. She only needed about eight bits to have enough to get through to tomorrow. She wouldn't risk her life for it.

As she scouted the area for her next victim, the crowd around her crushed backward.

The bodies crammed together, lifting Suri one foot off the ground. She kept one hand firmly locked on her three bits as she let the people sway her from side to side. Her added height allowed her to see what everyone backed away from.

A clearing had formed ten feet ahead.

Two women and a guard stood in the centre. The duo matched in pure silver robes. Priestesses of the Trio. The guard held something, and the priestesses were looking at it. Three more guards forced back the perimeter of bodies.

Priestesses and guards were never a good combination. At best, they were recruiting. The Tangle called them Snatchers for a reason. At worst, they were scouting for a heretic. Either way, Suri wanted none of it.

She pushed her way through to the edge of the thoroughfare, her eyes darting towards an alleyway. She watched as she moved. It took her a couple more seconds to realise the figure in the centre wasn't holding a bit of cloth, but a child. A cowering boy under a shrug of dirty red fabric.

Snatching was today's choice, then.

A priestess came forward and touched the boy's shoulder. He looked up at her face and Suri saw him in profile.

Ren.

Wrath's belly. Her stomach contracted as she steeled her jaw and kept moving. She couldn't do anything for him. She watched one of the priestesses take Ren by the hand and walk away with him.

She reached the alleyway, shoving past the last part of the crush, almost sprawling across the cobbles with her momentum. Her hood had fallen off in the crush, and she pulled it back up as she watched the guards start to allow the street to move again.

It wasn't like the priesthood was a terrible fate. Free lodgings and food for life. But they came unannounced, day and night, and took children off the streets. If tapped, there was no option to say no. If they thought they felt the Trio within you, to deny it was to deny their faith. Suri hated the idea. Trio or not, the lack of choice was suffocating. Plus, you had to live in the South. She was Northern, through and through. It was all she knew, all she needed to know. All Esra had taught her, all he needed her to be.

"Would you look who it is?"

That voice.

She knew who it was going to be before she'd even moved a muscle. Suri spun on her heel.

His wide face cracked ever wider with that smarmy smile.

Geren.

3

*I've taken to riding deep into the night. My Roan-
hadham whisks me to a life more exciting than my
own. There is wonder yet in this world.*
    Diary of C. Aubethaan, est. early 8th century

"What a pleasant surprise." Suri kept her tone neutral,
but her fingers twitched for a knife that wasn't there.
He wasn't alone. On his left, a new boy she hadn't seen
before, who couldn't be more than thirteen. On his right, an
older teen lurked like a shadow.

Her jaw tightened. Tufter had been one of Geren's party in
her kicking from last week. He'd created the irritating bruise
on her ribs, now multiplied by last night's battering. He'd been
there when Geren had stood over her and mocked her. She
wanted to punch him for that sin alone.

"You know these are my streets," Geren said, his smile still in
place.

It was big talk from a second-rate gang comprising of mainly kids. May's gang was the only one with any real claim to territory. No one fucked with May. Geren, however.

It made losing all the more embarrassing. Her rage at Tufter was nothing next to Geren. When he looked at her with his ugly tidewater eyes, she remembered all the ways he had hurt her. She could scrape them out.

"I got lost," Suri deadpanned.

"Always the joker," he said with a snarl. "Tufter, search her."

Suri took a step back and hit the wall. She raised her hands as Tufter moved forwards. "Be reasonable. I'm leaving. No harm, eh?"

Geren narrowed his eyes. "I could have killed you last week. You tried to start a fucking rival gang with my *own man*, you idiot."

Again, she flexed for a weapon she didn't have. Twenty years and she'd never learned to control her rage. Instead, she honed it, fed it, sharpened it. She let the anger transform into armour. Geren was maybe one year older, and a worse thief on almost every level. The thought that she had to pay *him* made her blood boil.

Suri felt a whisper of something inside of her again and tried not to think about it. She sucked a cheek in, releasing it with a pop. "I underestimated his loyalty."

Geren paused, then shook his head. "No. You underestimated me. Tufter, search her."

Tufter took another step towards her, and Suri glared at him. The shred of fear in his eyes made her smirk.

Geren pointed at her. "Move, or resist, and I swear to the Trio I will kill you right here."

Suri bit her tongue to hold back the threats that threatened to spill out.

The odds were not in her favour. They outnumbered her, and her body was half-broken. She might not walk away from a fight she started now.

Tufter grabbed at the pockets of her borrowed clothing. His breath was rank as he leaned around her. When he was done, he reached for her hands, peeling the three bits she'd grabbed from her sweaty palm. "Here you go, boss. Not much on her."

Geren held his hand out and glanced at the coins with a humiliating disinterest. That was her fortune. Now it was three more coins in the oaf's pocket. He tucked them into an oily little bag around his expanding waistline. He was growing wider and slower by the hour. That such a weasel was her enemy infuriated her.

He glanced back up at her. "You brag a lot for a girl with three coins to her name. That's not even enough for your measly debt."

She kept her face blank, masking the turmoil that threatened her whole body. She wanted to cry, to scream, to kill. The only reason he'd risen to any sort of power was because of the rumour that he broke his blood bond. Blood magic was the oldest kind of magic. Before even the Old Gods of Life and Death, there was blood. They caught Geren three years ago. They'd carved him a blood bond to spend five years in the mines. And yet, only a couple moons later, he'd come back, and the Seer of Blood's men had never sniffed him out. His band of children thought him some kind of hero. Suri figured they'd carved him with a duff bond, and he'd got lucky.

Geren shrugged at her silence. "You know what? I won't take your life today. But tomorrow you owe me a double debt. Ten bits."

An animal-like noise came out of Suri. "What? You just took all my money."

"How is that my problem? You broke the rules."

Suri took a breath in through flared nostrils, trying to cut some of the bite out of her words. "I broke the rules. You took my three bits. Fine, we're square. Why add more?"

Geren grinned. "Because I can. If you keep fighting me on it, maybe I'll triple it."

Suri almost snarled back at him.

Then he leaned in towards her. "Heard from your big brother recently? What was his name again? Esra?"

Suri snarled then.

She saw red.

No one talked about Esra.

Suri pushed forward and head-butted Geren square in the nose before he could blink. Esra was *her* brother, her protector, the only one she had. Geren had no right. She raised her fists to ram one in his gut and another in that ugly face, but then she felt it.

The knife at her neck. Tufter's steel. He'd moved faster than she expected.

She stilled, despite everything inside her wanting to kill the man-boy for even mentioning his name. Geren knew exactly how her brother was fucking doing. Where he was. Geren had evaded the blood bond while her brother had not.

Geren straightened, one hand covering his nose. She couldn't tell if she'd broken it, but it was bleeding. He took a step forward.

Suri let him square up to her. He was shorter than her, and she let him know it. Tufter's blade remained on her neck.

Geren stared up at her, unafraid. It was galling. "Fifteen bits. Tomorrow," he said, baring his browned teeth. "Or you're dead."

She swallowed. He turned to leave and then glanced back.

"Oh," he said, "and I never see you here again. "

He held her gaze, and she didn't flinch. She didn't reply.

She wanted to let out a million savage retorts, half of them about his mother and the other half about his tiny cock. But she couldn't.

He clicked his tongue and turned from her, strolling down the alleyway, hands in his pockets. A casual whistle sounded as his minions followed behind. She leaned against the wall as soon as they were out of eyeshot.

Shit.

Suri looked up at the mid-morning sky. One day. Fifteen bits.

It wasn't a crazy sum of money in her normal life, and if she was in a gang, it wouldn't be much of a stretch. But alone, and barred from the stalls and thoroughfare, she was restricted to pick-pocketing outside of taverns on the edge of the Merchant Quarter, or praying for a last minute announcement at the arena which always led to good pickings. There hadn't been a match in the Arena Quarter for weeks though, and she doubted it would come today.

If she got lucky, she'd live. If she got unlucky, she was going to die tomorrow. And that uncertainty twisted in her belly like a knife.

The thought flitted across her mind that she could run for it. Leave the city, go somewhere, anywhere else. But Esra was getting released *so* soon. Months now, maybe even less. She promised him she'd have something for him to come back to. That she'd be someone. She'd promised *herself* he wouldn't come back to the bottom of the heap once more. She sure as winter rain would never let him come home to her having run away.

Fuck that. She was staying.

But as soon as she paid this debt, there would be another. Then another. Geren would keep her on his leash. She would never get out of his cycle of debt. Esra would get roped into it, too. They'd be in a worse position than before. And it would be her *damn* fault.

Unless...

Unless she could get enough money to break the cycle. Unless she could steal so much, some value so obscene, that she could actually live again. That *they* could live again. Really live this time, not the shadow of an existence she'd had for a decade.

Wrath's fuckery. She was going to have to do it.

Suri had a ball to crash.

Suri watched the main square in the Royal Quarter through wooden slats. She'd found an open entrance to the sewers, and tried not to spend too long thinking about how her proximity to human filth was becoming a habit. It had taken her a full hour to work her way under the city. Eventually, she had pulled herself up a ladder to see a different view, home to impeccably painted people and buildings with beautiful, blue-tiled roofs.

She lay now in the wagon of an empty cart on a paved road, close to the mouth of the main plaza. Carved into the centre of the square was a rounded square moat, wide enough that any jump would fall short before the halfway point. Protected on the other side of the moat was a white marble tower. Three sides were walled, the stone rising flush from the centre of the moat. Even someone able to leap that distance would find no purchase on the tower walls. The one remaining side held the access point. White marble steps across the moat led into the tower and to the object it housed.

The Gate.

The Gates allowed for instant travel between two connected points. One step into it and you'd come through the paired one, miles away. But the world's rarest material, amefyre, powered them. So rare that Suri was pretty certain this was now the only working paired Gate on the Peregrinus mainland. Before the Wrath, there were a number apparently, but for reasons Suri hadn't overheard, they were all gone now. No other kingdom claimed to have one, no traveling troupes sang of another. The only rumours she'd clocked was from merchants, grumbling that the priesthood bought up every piece of amefyre that left their mines.

But that wasn't why she was here.

She knew that it was borderline suicidal. But, if she didn't try, Geren would kill her. If she tried and failed, the guards *might* kill her. Somehow, she calculated that the risk not worth taking a few hours ago was now her ticket out of probable death.

From Suri's vantage point at the far edge of the square, she could only see half of the staircase, and yet she could count over ten guards. Thirteen, to be specific.

It wasn't a surprise, but she didn't have to like it.

Her initial plan was to scout the Gate, the single entry point to the Forgelands' castle. She hoped that as the day wore on, she'd figure out a way to sneak in, posing as a guard. But now she could see how stupid that plan was. These were royal guards. They were dressed more finely than those that patrolled the rest of the city. They had fancy lapels and golden braiding across their chests. And they were all, as far as she could see, men. There was no way she could pose as a guard. They probably all knew each other by name, and one look at her in all that finery would get her laughed into a quick exile.

Her next plan to pose as castle staff, a serving maid or similar, also died as soon as she conceived it. She'd passed herself off as a maid in the Merchant Quarter before and assessed this couldn't be that much worse. Fancier furniture, more guards to avoid.

But stewards stood at the bottom of the stairs, checking every face that arrived.

Suri watched the square as she tried to think of any way out of this disaster. There was no way in without an invitation.

Oh, Wrath.

Was it riskier? Yes. Was it possible? Maybe.

Then, a guard walked past the mouth of her street and paused. She gritted her teeth praying he'd just continue past. He looked down the length, glanced at her wagon, then took a step in.

Wrath.

He approached and she ducked her head down, holding in a sigh. She breathed in shallow breaths, the thick brown cloth scratching at her cheek as she stared at the bottom of the wagon.

He was close now. Five paces. Four. Three.

His paces were steady, uniform. She thought for a second he might just walk right past her. Two. His footsteps slowed.

One.

He stopped. She didn't move a muscle. He was standing right next to her cart. Close enough to hear the individual links of his chain armour move. A hand brushed the cloth.

"Excuse me, sir."

The hand dropped.

The voice may as well have been Queen Lera herself. This Trio-sent woman saved her. The guard turned to face the voice, and Suri allowed herself to breathe a little.

"Yes, my lady?" he replied. He didn't move away.

"Could you give me directions to The Darkened Door?"

Suri's mouth dropped open.

The man choked. "You must be mistaken. That's..."

He moved a couple of steps in her direction, and Suri clawed in a deeper breath.

The Darkened Door was a brothel in the Tangle. It was the fourth brothel on the right. What on earth would this woman want with the brothel that sat on top of Mother Edi's?

As the guard was surely looking at the woman, Suri risked looking up through the slats. The woman was wearing a fine dress in opulent silk of shimmering emerald. She wore her hair up with ribbons of the darker auburn shade framing her face. Suri could tell that she was an elegant, high-ranking woman. Rich. She would have no reason to set foot in the Tangle.

The woman gave a weak smile. "It is no mistake. Are you able to direct me?"

A young white woman with dark hair. That was helpful. Much easier to pretend to be a person she at least had a passable likeliness to. Not that she'd ever tried to impersonate anyone specific before, but all she needed was the right name to get her through the door. Then she could be anyone.

"I could not... It would be..." He spluttered, then cleared his throat. "Miss. That establishment is not fit for a lady of your... It's not safe there."

Suri's mouth quirked, and she wished she could see the look on his face. Instead, she appraised the woman again. Her long silver neck chain dipped into the bodice of her dress, masking its pendant, if any. Her long sleeves extended beyond her hands. A small round bag swung from a metal string, nestled against the fabric of the giant dress.

It did not escape Suri just how pretty she was. Or how rich she must be.

"Fine," the noblewoman said. She looked almost otherworldly, and Suri wondered if she might have a touch of the Fae enhancing her features.

She also wondered if he'd have the nerve to tell her it was a whorehouse. It seemed unlikely.

After an awkward pause, the woman sighed. "That is all."

"Yes, miss," he replied. Now dismissed, he walked past her and back into the plaza. Suri noted the redness of his cheeks.

The woman carried on down the street, towards Suri. She ducked her head back down. After the footsteps faded back, Suri pushed the blanket away then dropped down from the wagon with barely a noise. She moved in the shadows of the edge of the street, following the woman at a distance.

As she pondered her next move, a child swooped past. She was an urchin, maybe only eight years old, with dirty blonde hair and grubby feet. She stopped just short of the woman's dress.

"Miss! Please, miss!"

The woman turned. The girl held out nail-bitten hands with grime in every line of her small palms.

"Please!"

To Suri's surprise, the woman opened her small bag and took out a coin. She placed it into the kid's awaiting clutches and matched her waifish grin with a demure smirk. The kid dashed back past Suri, and she almost reacted too late, pushing herself back into the shadows as the woman's eyes followed the child.

A sixpence. That's what she had given.

The equivalent of six bits.

Like it was nothing. Like it was a little game to play with this child. And that wasn't the only thing Suri had noticed when that clean and dainty hand had reached out from under those silk sleeves. The woman wore a ring. Clustered purple gems that caught the afternoon light.

Amefyre.

The purple gemstones could be nothing else. And the amefyre she wore was not that of a priestess, a band of steel with a tiny shard of amefyre locked in its centre. No, this was the ring of royalty, with a cluster of several larger amefyre stones studded in a pattern. It marked the wearer as the ruler or heir of some part of Greater Peregrinus.

This woman was a princess.

Suri didn't know how to feel. The generosity of the woman made her feel sick. The amount was meaningless to her. How many bits did she have in there? Fifty, perhaps? Probably more. How many months could she live off the contents of that one purse?

A thickness lodged in her throat. She couldn't fight the sensation that she was yet another pitiful dog in the street waiting for a thrown bone.

She followed the lady for the better part of an hour, analysing the auburn-haired beauty's way of walking, her manner of speech, her confidence. When she was ready, she ducked around some side streets to wind up ahead of where she guessed the lady's steps would take her, pausing by a narrow lane. There were no guards that could see down this one. Plus, it had a sewage grate.

Perfect.

Suri pulled the grate open and sat at its mouth. She ripped a square from her cloak and positioned it to cover her face, resting just below her eyes. The clops of ridiculous shoes approached, and Suri coughed a few times. As soon as the woman passed by, she croaked out the word of entreaty that she hoped would turn the silly creature's head. "Please."

Please come here, she thought. Please let me rob that purse.

"Please." Suri tried to look as frail as she could, which was easy to do. The woman looked over at her, bent over, clutching her genuine aching ribs. She saw the pity, and it made her angry. The ethereal voice from that morning whispered again, and the noise distracted from the remains of her guilt.

Suri dashed forward and grabbed the woman, pulling her to the floor. One of her hands held the lady's arm behind her back as the other smothered the scream that tried to escape. "If you're quiet, I won't have to hurt you."

The woman stopped struggling for a moment and Suri used the opportunity to move her squirming body towards the hole which would lead them to the sewers. The woman's dress bunched against the opening, and the fabric consumed Suri as she pushed her through. Something ripped, then they were on the putrid side.

She pulled the woman to her, her hand back across that pretty mouth. With her free hand, she snapped the bag open, revealing the ticket to the much grander prize.

She had a princess. She had a dress.

And now she had an invitation.

Game on.

4

My father states he has found a match for me. I
tell him I have already found my life's purpose. He
struck me soundly. Mother did nothing.
Diary of C. Aubethaan, est. early 8th century

T he dress didn't have any blasted pockets.

Well, that would have to be fixed. Along with the tear
on the hem.

They were in a small stone alcove, a single raised section
separating them from the city's waste. Suri was almost used to
the stench by this point.

The lady somehow still looked elegant, even tied up against
the wall in her undergarments in this filthy place. Her face was
painted in the way rich ladies favoured it, with her eyes and
cheeks darkened, her lips curved into a yet more perfect bow.
Suri's eyes dipped to the curve of her neck and the neckline

of the cream dress that clung to her. She saw the hint of a full breast under the fabric and looked away, embarrassment flushing through her.

Suri looked instead at the bag resting on the floor. Before she'd opened it, there were two paths open. The first, where there was enough money to give her a new start. She wouldn't need the ball after all, and there would be plenty just lying around for the taking. Any easy start into her future. Her own gang. No paying anyone else ever again. The second was much harder. Impersonating a noble lady at a ball. She didn't know if she could do it.

Then she saw the contents. The single sixpence within, lying flat against that ornate piece of paper. The ball it was.

Six bits. Better than nothing, yet nine short of her debt.

If Suri were to let her go and make up that remaining nine by selling the dress, she would have problems. For one, finding a fence willing to take a risk on it, and one that wouldn't sell her down the river the instant the guards came sniffing around about the kidnapped princess in the green dress.

The ball gave her an opportunity to get more than just what was on the lady's back. It put an entire castle's worth of wealth at her fingertips. She would get enough money to pay her debt, and other items to sell over months, which would keep her comfortable for a long time. Maybe she could stay alive *and* out of prison. And then, when Esra returned, she'd have something to show him. A new life for them both.

She'd gagged the woman, of course. Suri didn't want to listen to the wailing or the pleading. But the woman wasn't fighting her bonds. The princess was watching her with those dark eyes partially shielded by auburn hair. The only time she'd protested was when Suri took her necklace. She'd yelled then, muffled by the cloth at her mouth.

She had a name now, written in a handsome script on the invitation.

Viantha Waterborne.

Suri didn't recognise the name, which probably meant she was a daughter of someone in the Pail. There were too many of them, with their region run by several Guild Leaders and not one monarch. It was too far away for Suri to care before this moment. She cursed herself. She could walk right up to her parents without the smallest clue.

After a moment of reluctant pondering, she grumbled and removed the gag from her captive princess. She surprised Suri by not crying out like a pup at first breath. "Your parents? What are their names? What do they look like?"

Viantha answered her questions in a calm voice.

Suri listened to her lilting accent. The vowels were longer, the consonants more defined. Suri was never one for accents, she didn't have a natural ear for them, but she'd have a stab at it, if only to save her own skin.

"May I have my necklace back?" Viantha asked, staring at Suri's hand where the chain spilled over.

Suri snorted. "What?"

"My necklace. Please," she said. "I don't care about the dress, the shoes, the money. Even the ring. But the necklace, I—"

"Why were you asking about the brothel?" Suri asked, interrupting her.

Viantha flinched. Barely, but it was there. "Excuse me?" she said, her voice soft like petals.

"Earlier," Suri said. "You asked a guard about The Darkened Door."

Viantha's brow creased.

Suri pressed on, impatience leaking into her tone. "That is a brothel. Why were you trying to find it?"

"The same reason anyone else would—want to find such a place."

"You can't even say the word. Did you even know what it was?"

Viantha swallowed and made no reply.

"Why?" Suri asked, crouching down beside her. She pulled at the edge of the cloth covering her face, making sure it was still in place.

"I was supposed to meet someone there," she said.

"Who?"

Viantha didn't respond.

With the questions about her family, Viantha had answered what she asked and then stopped talking. She'd been curt and to the point. But this time, she was hiding the truth.

"Who?" Suri asked again.

Viantha stared down at her hands. "There was a book I was going to collect."

Suri stood back up to her full height. "You were going to a brothel? To pick up a book?"

"Yes," Viantha said, a blush now reaching her ears.

Suri sighed. She considered yet again what strange prey she had caught. She opened her palm and eyed the silver chain. The bottom of it held a small carved flower, one she did not recognise. It didn't look particularly fancy. If anything the metal looked as inexpensive as her own earrings. "What's special about this necklace?"

Viantha's wide eyed stare was full of need. "It's... sentimental."

Suri sighed, then stepped over to the noble lady, dropping the chain over her head.

"Thank you."

The sincerity in her voice made Suri's skin itch. She wasn't doing her a fucking favour; she'd just robbed her blind.

Viantha said nothing else. No cries for help, no assurances of rewards for giving her up.

It was odd. But Suri didn't have time to care about the oddities of Viantha Waterborne. She gagged her again. She had neither the time nor the inclination to press the woman further about jewellery or stocking her personal library. Perhaps it was one of those crude books with every fathomable position displayed in pictures.

The heiress regarded her as Suri finished dressing and rifled through her things. The last thing she took from Viantha was her ring, her fingers trembling as they traced the purple gemstones encased by golden claws.

Suri didn't trust amefyre. It was a godly substance, used by the Priestesses to keep the Gate running and who knew what else. She put it on, almost expecting some holy fire to strike her down as she did. There was nothing. The metal was a dull weight against her finger, cold and heavy, with no real difference to the feel of the metal in Suri's ear.

A moment later, she took it off again and put it into that infuriating bag. She would have to wear it tonight. It would be too much of a giveaway if she didn't. But Suri knew she couldn't keep this trinket past tonight. She could never sell it. There were less than twenty in all of Peregrinus. She'd have to be careful enough selling the other wares she hoped to pick up tonight, let alone an amefyre ring. Maybe she'd leave it in the sewer.

When she had the dress mostly on, and had twisted her hair around the sleek clips that had held Viantha's in poor imitation, Suri was as ready as she could be.

She checked Viantha's bonds. They should hold. They would have to. She turned to leave and then looked back at the princess. "I'll be back with food and water."

Viantha simply stared back at her, unmoving. Suri left the alcove with a shrug, moving through the underbelly to the Merchant Quarter with practised precision.

She'd been nice to the girl. She would be fed and watered and shouldn't be disturbed. That was more than Suri had some days. The princess would have gone to the ball, drunk silly drinks, and maybe danced with the Prince. Then she would have left, full but otherwise empty-handed.

Suri would not leave empty-handed.

And those things were worth much more than a noble-woman's discomfort for one night.

She fell into the role as she walked through that dank, filthy place, wrinkling her nose and lifting her chin. The smell would cling once she'd left, but she hoped that would add to the performance she was going to have to sell.

A rich woman, a noble woman, set upon by thieves. A woman who was supposed to be at the ball tonight. She was *expected*. Suri told herself this mantra, convincing herself of her rightful place. She tried to emulate that elegant head tilt and slope of the shoulders.

Her life might depend on her selling this.

Suri crouched, her hand against the wooden door. This time, though, she was the one in the horrible silky contraption. It was so heavy; she felt the weight of the skirt digging into her hip bones.

She listened for a moment, took a deep breath, and removed her improvised face guard. It was time.

This part of the Merchant Quarter was new to Suri. There were only shops here, no outside market or obvious game for her. But it was an area where a fine woman might come to get her dress fixed.

She was careful to exit the sewers and shut the door behind her, distancing herself from the area. Not a moment later, she saw a guard. She'd hoped that she would have a couple of moments to learn how to walk in these angled slippers, but no such luck.

She masked her face into some imitation of anguish and cried out in his direction as he turned to look into the alley. "Mercy! I am saved! Please help!"

He hesitated for a fleeting moment before jumping to her aid.

She told him thieves had *ruined* her dress and *stolen* her necklace.

Within minutes, he had given Suri his handkerchief and was escorting her to the nearest seamstress. She held onto his arm like a lifeline, only partly acting. These shoes sucked. The guard did not utter a single complaint, believing her a vulnerable damsel, even when she turned her ankle on a cobble and sprawled half into his arms.

When they arrived at the shop, Suri doubted they'd believe her, but the guard relayed her tale to the owner and he fell for it. With a pitiful look, he waved her through to the back room, where a seamstress sat on a stool.

Her eyes went wide as she turned to take Suri in. The dress was dirty and tattered and her face was not in much better shape, probably still with a nasty gash on her right temple. Her hair had fallen out of her attempts to pin it. It was lucky she wasn't able to see the bruises that lay beneath this grim facade, or the woman might have fainted.

"My lady…" she said, trailing off.

Suri jutted out her chin, head held high. She would act the perfect lady even if her appearance was far from it.

"I was set upon by some vagrants. You will make me presentable for tonight's ball."

The seamstress ducked her head slightly. "Of course, my lady."

"I'd like the dress to be adjusted too. I've grown bored of this colour."

One, or both, of her captive's parents would be there tonight. She hoped that if she masked the dress, it would not be obvious she was wearing the same one as their missing daughter. That would be a shit way to get caught.

"Of course, my lady. Perhaps first, though, we can get you cleaned up?"

Ah, of course. So much for sparing the seamstress the sight of her broken body. Suri kept her posture straight. "That's fine."

The seamstress nodded and came around her, undoing the laces with much more ease than she'd initially tightened them. She'd nearly broken her arms lacing herself up. The seamstress's hands paused against the fabric as the dress came away from her back.

Her bare back.

Suri deemed it a step too far to leave Viantha in nothing. She'd discarded her own borrowed ones on the off-chance this would happen. The threadbare, ill-fitting material would have been a dead giveaway.

"My lady..."

Suri almost laughed. At this moment, she was so far from being a lady.

"It's all the rage in the Pail," she lied. "Please, continue."

The seamstress unfastened the rest, and a moment later the dress fell from her body, pooling at her feet. Other than her shoes, or rather, Viantha's shoes, Suri was naked.

"And one more thing," Suri said, whirling around to look at the seamstress, whose eyes shot up to meet hers.

"Yes, my lady?" The woman sounded utterly lost.

"Pockets. Lots of pockets."

The procession of nobility felt endless on those marble steps. The women looked ethereal. Suri had never seen so many rich shades before, nor had the luxury to stare at the rich without fear of retribution.

Tonight she had the best protection you could have in this city: wealth. Or at least, the illusion of it.

She paused at the edge of the Royal Quarter and couldn't help her eyes wandering to the trinkets adorning the men and women, catching and reflecting the light. They were advertising their greed, and Suri was happy to take some of it from them.

She had taken the time to feed Viantha, throwing her a bread roll and a leather flask. She hoped that all Viantha recalled after she released her was that a tall, pale-skinned woman with dark hair had taken her clothes and ticket.

She walked into the square, caught off-guard by the weight of the dress.

The seamstress had overlaid the emerald green silk with a spider's web of black lace, covering the whole bodice, with crystals pulling together strands of string into little clusters. The starry netting changed the look of the dress, which Suri sorely needed.

The seamstress had also placed six pockets into the dress, burying them into the folds. She hoped that the woman rarely travelled out of the Forgelands, because the amount of requests Suri had disguised as Southern custom bordered on the ridiculous. She acquired it all on the promise that she would come back in the morning to pay them, which was something that would never happen.

Suri walked with small bird-like steps. She reached into the round bag and took out the ring. She paused, and looked at the gemstones for just a moment, before slipping it onto her finger.

Part of her head that had been humming stopped. It had been a low drone and, until it was gone, Suri hadn't noticed its presence.

Strange.

Mother Edi's words from earlier about the metal helping with the voices came back to her, and Suri glanced down at the ring adorning her left index finger.

From that same finger, a loop of black string held in place the black netting that covered Suri's arms until just below the sleeves; an attempt to cover her injuries sustained in the 'robbery'.

The guards amassed at the bottom of the steps did not stop her, though she felt their gazes on her. She moved past them to the foot of the stairs, trying to ignore that tickling tension at the back of her neck.

It went against everything she knew to keep her back to guards. She tried to steel herself, play the part. Relax. She watched in front of her instead, where three or four courtiers formed a dwindling queue near a footman.

The only people she could recognise here, beyond her own city's king and heir, were the parents whose daughter she'd locked up and the villains who had beaten her to a pulp the night before. As much as she burned for revenge, she knew her plan was much more likely to succeed if she saw none of them.

Beyond those waiting to go in was the Gate itself. The structure was forged with amefyre, a beautifully carved stone trellis with the gems embedded somewhere inside. Confined within its bounds was a pitch black void. Beside the Gate stood a priestess. When they weren't busy snatching children, they were the missionaries of the Trio, trusted with the upkeep and sanctity of the Gates.

One courtier took a lumbering stride through the Gate. The darkness swallowed him and he was gone. Gods, she had to go through *that*.

Darkness she could deal with. But usually she had a decent guess about what was on the other side. Here, she was walking into the unknown, into some contraption of ancient gods and men.

She didn't trust it.

Suri hoped that those around her perceived her slow silence as a quiet mystery. She was trying to stay upright in her *cursed* shoes.

She reached the footman. as the Gate consumed the last courtier in the gaggle.

"Your ticket, my lady."

She handed him the invitation. Red paper, edged in gold, with black and gold calligraphy spelling out the name Viantha Waterborne. The man glanced at it, then looked up at Suri. The clipped smile he wore fell from his face as a shadow passed behind Suri.

An edge of dark fabric brushed against her leg. She turned to see the back of a broad man striding up the stairs, his dark hair and black cloak all that was visible of him.

"My lord! Your ticket!"

The male turned at the footman's call.

His face, for a moment, was thunderous. Then a smirk formed, painted across a chiselled jaw. He raised a thick, dark eyebrow.

She followed his face down past his dark eyes, to a prominent nose and full mouth. Her eyes dropped to his neck and then below. A decorative silver breastplate lay against the black jerkin which hugged his broad shoulders. His legs were clad in a black leather and a cloak swept against his black shoes.

Her eyes moved back up to his, and she found them locked on her. For a moment, he too looked stunned. Though his gaze was more of a man who had seen a ghost, and not the ogling stare she had given him. Then he blinked, and the look faded. He winked at her, and Suri clenched her jaw.

"You wish to see my ticket?" he asked the footman. His voice was a liquid honey drawl. It was hypnotic, nothing like Suri had heard before. But then, she'd never seen a man that looked like that either. Suri felt a twist in her stomach, the tightness of desire. A shortness of breath, as if momentarily choked.

The footman made some sort of sputtering noise, and Suri could not blame him. She dragged her gaze back to the footman, who looked terrified. "No, no. Of course not. My lord. I mean, your—"

The voice cut in, interrupting him. "How gracious. But you don't need to change the rules on my account."

Suri kept her eyes fixed on the footman, ignoring the silken voice now only a couple of steps behind her. She gulped in a quick breath. How hadn't she heard him move? She heard everything. Surely she couldn't be that distracted by a man's looks. She felt her cheeks warm.

Damn it, she needed to move. This man was going to cause nothing but problems.

She looked straight ahead up the stairs, keeping the movement of the gorgeous figure out of her eye line, as she began the ascent towards the Gate.

She'd not climbed three steps when the footman called out to her.

"My lady, do you not want your invitation?"

She turned and saw two pairs of eyes watching her, the blue eyes of the aged footman and the dark eyes of this stranger. "Keep it," she said, turning back to the stairs.

She pulled up her skirts this time and climbed with more speed, meeting the Priestess's stare as she reached the top of the stairs. The Priestess nodded but didn't otherwise acknowledge her. This was it. She was here. It was time for her to take what this world owed her from those who did not treasure it.

Then she felt it. Fingers against her right arm, just above her elbow, touching bare skin. The covering must have slipped down.

She looked up at the man whose thumb grazed her flesh. With that smouldering gaze, he looked down at her.

Gods, he was tall.

"Now, where does a girl like you get a bruise like that?" he asked.

His fucking voice.

In his other hand was the invitation she'd left behind.

"Thanks," she said, her voice tight. She took the invitation from him, but he kept his grip on it before releasing it.

His gaze fell to her name and his eyes widened. That wasn't good.

"Viantha," he said, drawing the name out. "A pleasure to make your acquaintance."

No one was supposed to attach that name to her face once she'd got past the footman. This was going to be an even bigger problem.

And there was something about being near him, almost an aura around his body that hummed with the same frequency as that droning she sometimes felt in her head. It was intoxicating and distracting. Everything she didn't need right now. She had a plan. She wouldn't let him screw it up. "And yours, stranger."

He smiled, wider now, with genuine mirth.

He looked like he would speak again, but Suri moved. She took the two steps that would separate them, at least for a moment. His fingers dropped from her arm as she stepped into the Gate.

5

The local tournament came and went. I ignored what I could about the event. My sister attended every day. She brags about making eyes at the King. I think only of Him.

Diary of C. Aubethaan, est. early 8th century

Suri's skin grew cold.

Her body—Weightless.

There were indistinct sounds in her head, trying to form words. The echo of an echo of a scream. A small tug.

Then, in what could have been half a second, or half a minute, she completed the step she had taken back on the cold marble steps and stepped onto a plush carpet.

She glanced behind her. There was nothing but blackness again and she took a step forward, further into the light and away from the threatening vertigo.

She stood at the top of a staircase. Music filled the room around her, bleeding merriment. Deep red carpet abutted a mahogany bannister overlooking an opulent ballroom. Red and golden fabrics hung down on either side of the grand hall, embossed with the flame and anvil sigil of the Forgelands. *We are the flame.* The motto was quite literal, with both King Thandul and Prince Shaedon able to manipulate fire. King Thandul's flame was gold, like Atrius' sun above. The Crown Prince, however, was rumoured to control a blue flame. Ren was convinced it was because blue was his favourite colour, which was as solid a theory as any other Suri had heard.

Gold metal sconces nestled into stone arched walls, and a giant golden chandelier hung from the highest point of the ballroom's ceiling.

The staircase flared out from both sides of Suri. She reflected for a moment on just how stupid this plan was, and the risk she had taken by coming here. The Gate led to only one place, the Grand Palace of the Forgelands. It was the only way in and out of the Palace, as the building was on a small rocky island somewhere north of the northernmost reaches of the land. Suri didn't know exactly where, how many miles it was to the coastline, or if it was even accessible by boat. She had never seen the sea, let alone experienced the rise and fall of a boat. So if anything went wrong here, she could only leave by this one, guarded Gate.

A thief had to have an exit strategy. Usually multiple exit strategies. But here she was. Powered by her greed.

She took one further step forward and paused for a moment, appraising the mass below her.

At the far end of the ballroom was a raised area with two giant thrones facing toward the floor. Both were dark brown contraptions of metal and wood inlaid with gold.

On the larger throne sat an ageing man, his dark brown hair peppered with grey. King Thandul was not a man prone to joy. He dripped with wealth, his slim frame leading to slim hands where many giant rings almost blocked his fingers from view. From this distance, Suri couldn't guess which was the amefyre one, each new one as obscene as the last. The purple of the tunic itself was almost the colour of amefyre, that medium shade with a lilac refraction. If anyone needed a reminder of the Forgelands' control of the gemstone, they would need look no further than their king.

The smaller throne was empty. The Queen was a recluse, not seen in public since Shaedon's younger brother died years ago. Suri's eyes moved from the raised plinth down to the noble horde below. She scanned the people, most of whom were talking, drinking and laughing.

It wasn't long before she spotted the prince.

Prince Shaedon wore gold, his crown sitting lopsided on his red locks. He stood with a group. She noted his easy posture, shoulders shaking with laughter, but he did not turn in her direction. She was almost disappointed she couldn't study him further. Her King she had seen in pictures, and once or twice from his occasional speeches. Her Prince she knew nothing of beyond rumour. He was young, handsome, and ambitious. Suri disliked him, on principle, for his wealth, but she was curious to see if the comments on his looks were true.

Her breathing lurched as she saw something else. Wings. She had seen them in carvings, in tributes. Never outside of stone, never in the flesh. There were three sets of wings in the room below her.

One was a pale green, another a pale purple, the third set almost white. She'd heard some true Fae, the pure-blooded who lived in the Fae Glen in Drangbor, could fly. She didn't know if this was true, and she was too distant to see much more of their bearers.

She walked to one side, conscious that she was in full sight of the entire ballroom right now if they looked up. It was better to get down into the thick of it.

Before she reached the footman, however, she felt that presence again. Him. He'd come through the Gate.

"Pray tell," came the voice again. Too close again, almost at her ear.

She did not turn, despite every hair on her arm standing at full attention.

"Where is your accent from? I'll admit it's been a while since I ventured into the Pail, but I cannot recall its likeness."

What was that sensation? She couldn't place it. It was almost like heat coming off him, but it was more a tone, a vibration.

Then she focused on his words and realised she had made yet another error. Would she have to leave before she'd even begun? This man was becoming a nuisance.

"I'm not in the habit of talking to men I haven't been formally introduced to, my lord," she said, turning her head fractionally in his direction. She tried to imitate Viantha's manner of speaking, but it sounded wrong even to her.

He chuckled.

Suri moved out of his influence and reached the staircase. The footman reached for her invitation.

"Why do you need it?" she asked, her voice quiet.

The footman looked puzzled. "For your introduction, my lady."

Suri smiled with all the sweetness her body could muster. "That won't be necessary."

"My lady?" the footman asked, his eyebrows pulling together further. "It's my duty to announce all the Prince's guests."

Her heartbeat throbbed in her mouth. This was not going according to plan at all.

She took the man's still outstretched hand and pressed the sixpence into it. She widened her smile as she closed her hand over his. She hoped it would be enough. "I would like to surprise my parents. I have been away for a long time."

His eyes widened, and he nodded. "Uh, of course, my lady."

She released his hand and moved downwards into the fray of the ballroom, not looking back at the footman or the mysterious man in black.

Suri removed the amefyre ring from her finger and dropped it into her bag. She didn't want anyone else connecting her to a missing princess. So long as she avoided that irritating man for the evening, no one else would be any wiser.

That throbbing in her head came back. Subdued, but present. She would ask Mother Edi about it soon.

Suri was halfway down the stairs when there was a loud knocking. Half the eyes from the room looked up to the other side of the bannister, and Suri's eyes followed. He stood, awaiting his announcement. She heard more than one gasp from the beautiful crowd below before a word was even spoken.

"Announcing," came the wavering voice of the footman. "Lord Kol of Tartarus."

Ice spiked across Suri's body.

She watched the man she'd been speaking with descend the opposite staircase. His face had lost some of its humour, though a twinkle of it still existed as he strode towards the revellers.

This was Kol. Kol was here.

The floor below fell silent.

The footman's voice had stumbled over the title, uncertain what to call him.

Kol was a Lord, but he was also more than that. And less than that. Kol was a plague, a darkness. People in the Forge-lands called him the Lord of Death.

The Wrath had occurred at the moment of Kol's birth. In the Old World, before the Wrath, there were only two Gods. Sotoledi, the God of Death. Diophage, the God of Life.

One hundred years ago, the Wrath had changed everything.

A Fae witch led a pagan ritual to the Death God, Sotoledi. She delivered her child of trickery upon Diophage's sacred Life Altar, tarring it with ruin. Death was empowered, and bestowed His Wrath upon the world. He laid waste to most of the Eastern lands. A beautiful land, and a thriving city once known as Ucraipha, was stripped to nothing. The area was still unrecovered. The Parched Lands. The Wrath destroyed every man, woman, living creature, and plant in an instant.

It was a desert now, a cursed barren wasteland.

Queen Lera stopped the ceremony before every person in Peregrinus died. She slew the Fae witch. The only life to survive in the lands surrounding the Altar was the Queen herself, the pagans, and the witch's infant son, Kol. Death spared them from the suffering he inflicted on everyone else.

Over the century, Kol had festered in that wasteland, naming his city Tartarus, risen from the bones of the ghost city of Ucraipha. Or, as people now called it—the City of the Damned.

Kol was its de facto King. And a mass murderer in his own right, just like his mother and his Death God.

The man Suri had just spoken to. The man descending into the ballroom alongside her, almost matching her pace. They were both predators here, but the magnitudes could not be further apart.

His delivery into this world caused the shattering of half of Greater Peregrinus, Suri's delivery had caused the death of one fatigued woman. Suri's prey was shiny metal. This man's prey was the world.

On some level, she was afraid of him.

But Suri had lived her life in fear, and the decades between his atrocities and this present moment made her quickly move onto more practical concerns. She resented him for his decision to come to this ball tonight. Her own prey would be nervous and on edge. Her hunting ground was no longer going to be the drunken wealthy but a scattering of frightened animals. She would have to be even more careful. She refused to choose the wrong targets again.

The crowd had formed into little clusters, casting furtive glances towards the staircase that Kol now moved down. Prince Shaedon bent over the King's throne, muttering something in his father's ear. Suri noted the tension in the Prince's shoulders and the static expression on their faces. Even with that gold dust warming his features, the face held a cold distance.

It was clear that one, they had not invited Lord Kol to this ball and two, no one would remember her arrival.

She reached the ballroom floor without a social or heel related incident. Moving her purse strings into one hand, she took a glass of shimmering liquid from a footman. Whatever it was, it smelt expensive. She held the glass as a prop as she appraised the unfamiliar landscape.

Suri couldn't see anyone matching Viantha's mother's description around her. Ressa Waterborne, Suri had discovered, was the Guild Leader of the Water Guild in the Pail. The Pail was the southernmost tip of Greater Peregrinus and was ruled by five guilds. Ressa was the leader of one of them. Viantha was Ressa's chosen successor, her second child.

She saw the Seer of Blood, though. He stood like a skin statue in the corner—bald, with papery skin and a lifeless white gaze. Like the Gate, this was the only alive Blood Seer Suri had ever heard of. She had no clue from staring at his strange alabaster face how old he might be. She had a crawling sensation which led her to believe it was far older than she wanted to believe possible.

Blood magic was ancient. He carved symbols into the skin which locked the bearer into a promise or condition. It could be a contract of riches, or a punishment. Nearly ten years ago, that same Seer had carved a bond into Esra. If her brother left his sentence even a day early, or attempted to escape his fate, the blood bond would burn, and the Bloodhounds would come running.

What an insidious, pale worm of a man.

Kol reached the end of his staircase. Suri matched his steps toward the thrones with steps of her own away from it. She would move in whatever way possible to keep as much distance between herself, Ressa Waterborne, and the Lord of Death.

Her feet moved across the slippery varnished floor with limited grace.

She tried to focus on her task.

She would steal whatever she could mask. Fine glass and metals, cutlery and baubles, even a string of pearls or a golden chain, so long as they were not embossed with a sigil or otherwise of unique quality.

Her movement toward the back of the room brought her to a table filled with food. Her mouth watered as a groan in her stomach sounded at the sight of so much food.

Several courtiers lingered beside the obscene spread of culinary delights, occasionally taking a serving of some sweet or savoury choice with no discernment or separation. This decadence was a disease upon the world.

Suri found herself caught between wanting to eat everything on the table and wanting to destroy it. She figured she might as well sample the food first. Destruction could come later.

She placed her glass on the table as she appraised her options. A gold forked serving tool lay over some purple vegetable, and large silver spoons dipped into some other sweet thing. She lumped a few items onto her plate, licked it off, then pocketed the spoon.

A glance on either side showed no one looking in her direction. She moaned around her first full bite of food, before cleaning her plate in a matter of moments. Her pace was far from regal but, at least she used a fork.

When she returned to the table for seconds, she noticed a serrated square knife. It had a golden handle and looked to be worth a pretty penny, stuck halfway into a slice of some whole roasted bird. She had taken one step when she heard it: the female voice that stood out from the inane chatter of those around her.

Suri's shoulders stiffened.

"Did you see the look on Thandul's face?" the woman said.

The gruff male voice that responded sent a coldness over her body.

"He knows how to make an entrance," he said.

Both were here. Together. Behind her, right now.

Her tormentors from less than a day ago. She had been expecting them, but she hadn't seen them. Kol had distracted her.

"It hasn't changed much, has it? Three years since the last one and they haven't even bought a new rug. Where's all that money going?" Scilla asked.

That icy feeling burned, her blood heating as the echoing in her head from before returned. Suri's anger had always been hard to contain, yet this felt more than ever. The hint of a *whisper* moved her down the table to that knife.

"Definitely not a new cook. I can't tell if those are stewed peaches or if one of their Bloodhounds had an accident," he said.

Scilla laughed, and the sound made Suri flinch.

Bloodhounds. The nickname given to the men in the Seer of Blood's employ, who hunted down anyone in breach of their bond. Suri had only seen them a handful of times, and she was smart enough to get well away. They were lethal.

"A reputable source told me there would be goat," he continued.

"Your definition of reputable needs work," Scilla said.

The man sniggered as he moved closer to the table, closer to the food. His hand came down beside her to grab a roll and Suri froze before taking a spoon of whatever was in front of her with mechanical movements. She was confident there was nothing to identify her as the girl from last night. She checked her laced arms, there was no bruised flesh showing this time.

The same would not be true if they were to see her face. The seamstress had taken pains to paint her in the court style, but beneath it were her features, her silver eyes, her rage. She reached for the blade as the man took a skewered piece of meat and leaned back to his companion.

"And Shaedon is to pick one of these?" Scilla asked.

Suri could taste her derision as she closed her hand over the knife's hilt. The feeling of cool metal in her palm did nothing to calm her.

"I overheard some mother whining about how this was a farce. He's already made his choice," the man said. "Kol won't be happy."

Suri cut slices of meat, dragging the knife back and forth through. It was not the right grip to inflict the greatest damage, but they would not catch her unarmed.

"Surely he hasn't picked *her*?" Scilla asked, turning away. Their footsteps took them away from the table.

Suri did not hear his murmured response. They were out of earshot. She took a couple of deep breaths, steadying her heartbeat as the tension in her shoulders ebbed a little. She released the knife, her hand was white. She hadn't realised how tightly she'd been gripping it. Flexing her fingers, she glanced behind her to confirm that the two shadow dancers had left.

Suri stabbed the three slices of meat she'd cut with the knife and placed them on a plate. Keeping up appearances, after all. As she picked up the plate, she slipped the knife and two forks she'd noticed earlier into one of her pockets.

She then turned around to face the ballroom anew.

Ten minutes in, and she felt a breath away from disaster, with little to show for it. She had some items, but not much. And more than that, she needed at least fifteen bits. Tonight. She would need to carry on, and she would need to do so whilst avoiding four people who circled the same room as her.

She moved to an alcove near the back of the ballroom to take stock, noting those terrible two: Scilla and the man.

Then she spotted another. Viantha had not lied. The exact woman she had described stood near the centre of the room. A gap in the crowd allowed Suri to observe her fully.

Ressa Waterborne was beautiful. Her hair was a white-ish silver, long and pinned straight down her back. She wore a weaving sapphire circlet and her cerulean gown slit up to a height on her thigh, which should have looked scandalous on a woman her age and position, but somehow flowed off her like her namesake. She wore a stern expression, at odds with her otherwise enchanting appearance.

Not what Suri would have expected from a Guild Leader, had she thought to form expectations at all.

She scanned the crowd now to find her newest problem, the one who knew her fake name and could expose her lies to this court.

Though she needn't have looked for Kol.

He was coming straight for her.

6

Oh! joyous day. I saw Him today. Not in dream, in waking. My sister spoke of a courtly invitation, and behind her, Him. Only for a second did He show himself to me. Why must He leave?
Diary of C. Aubethaan, est. early 8th century

Her blood thrummed again before he spoke a word to her.

That feeling spread across her body. A swelling cold. A dark, pulsing voice. *Sweet...*

His frame blocked her view of the ballroom, his black locks of hair framed by the chandelier. She noticed now that his skin had a slightly pearlescent shine to it. It was like marble, the light bouncing off it unnaturally.

As he approached, she looked at him in his entirety. He was beyond handsome. The most handsome man she had ever seen.

As much Fae as he was a man, surely, to be one hundred years old and to look only a handful of years beyond Suri's own age.

"How lucky I've been to run into you, when you are the object of me coming to this ball," he said with a smirk. "Viantha."

Suri swallowed. The words were thick and drawn out. The very way he said the name was teasing, a gauntlet being laid before her. "You've found me," she said. "And I'd rather not discuss anything alone."

There, that sounded a bit more like a Pail accent. At least, more than her last butchered attempt.

He didn't take the hint to leave, cocking his head with that same smirk. "There is much concern for your whereabouts, my lady."

Shit. Did he know she wasn't who she said she was? Or was he simply messing with her? She cursed the Trio. Perhaps he thought her truly a princess and meant to extort something. Well, there was nothing he could gain from blackmailing her. She had nothing. Unless he wanted a dirty knife or a couple of forks.

"Is that so?" she asked.

Kol nodded. "It is so. Shall I inform our guests that there is no need for such worry, and that you are, in fact, here, skulking in this corner?"

Suri raised an eyebrow. "I'm sure the scandal you have created by speaking to me alone in this corner may cause more concern than it would resolve," she said, grazing her forefinger around the rim of the glass flute. An idle gesture that she hoped would come across as bored and unaffected.

Kol looked down at her hand for a moment, then met her eyes again. "You have an unrivalled concern for my reputation, fair lady."

Her eyes roamed over his broad chest, catching on a beautiful silver brooch. The metal work was so fine it was almost like strands of hair, a network of metal laced into a spiralling sun.

She looked back up at his face, annoyed that she had to tilt her neck to do so. His eyes were so dark, she couldn't tell at that moment if they were brown or black. If his intention was merely to taunt her, she wouldn't let him.

"You mistake me. I think only of myself," Suri said.

Kol flicked his eyes down her dress and back up. There was no smile on his wide mouth now as he spoke in a low voice. "I do not doubt it."

Before she could respond, he closed the gap between them to a single step. He touched her right hand, the one holding the glass. She nearly dropped it as his finger tapped against hers. That cold pulse that she felt in the very air of his presence now burned through her body at his touch. Could he feel it? Or was this some remnant of that thing, that voice? *Sweet Suri...*

"I see you've misplaced your ring, princess," he said. "Grave, indeed."

His own fingers were empty of amefyre. A sign that he was not, in this society, acknowledged as a King. His finger hovered next to her ring finger for a moment, then he dropped his hand back to his side. Suri took a breath and quelled the burning in her veins.

She was through with being toyed with like a plaything by this powerful man. "What is it you want from me?"

Kol tilted his head. "How direct. That's no fun."

Suri scowled for a second, and Kol's smile returned.

He wanted to play games? Fine. She looked down at her gown for a moment; the hand holding her purse strings toying with her skirt. Then she met his eyes, looking at him from under her lashes. "Would you prefer me to be coy?" she asked, before adding sharply, "Your *highness*?"

Kol's jaw tightened, and she watched as his hands flexed into fists at his side. The bubble of air around them felt more intense, thick with that echoing pulse. For a fraction of a second, Suri swore she saw a black mist swirling behind him. "Careful, little thief. That tongue will get you in trouble."

Suri's stomach flipped. *Thief.* She couldn't help but flit her eyes around her, but no one else was in earshot.

He stood, his expression unfathomable. She calculated fast. Had he seen something, or just guessed at her purpose? Her delayed response would have likely already confirmed any doubt he might be holding. He knew she was a thief. But she knew he was unwanted here. He was no friend of Thandul or Shaedon.

"That would be a welcome break for my hands," she said, assessing his reaction.

Kol hesitated for a second, then he chuckled. "So you are not Viantha. But I'm betting you know where she is..."

Suri said nothing.

"You'll tell me," Kol said. Commanded, more like.

"No," Suri replied. "I won't."

Kol smiled. "You are something new. I'm not in the habit of people saying no. Tell me your true name."

Engaging with him was the right play, then. Perhaps he wouldn't expose her secret to the ballroom just yet. But his words. *Something new.* He saw her as a novelty, a token amusing pauper who had snuck into his world. A thing to be laughed at.

She would teach this foreigner a little lesson about Northern hospitality. She closed the gap, leaning in, her mouth moving towards his ear. Kol matched her movement, and she pressed her hand against his chest to keep a breath's distance between them. The surface was unyielding.

The smell of him was intoxicating; rain after a drought, the coals of a long dead fire. Relief, and longing, of something there and nothing there at all. *Sweet.*

Her mouth was inches from his ear and the black locks that curled around it. She opened her mouth and let out a breath. He stiffened. She said that one word again. "No."

As soon as the word escaped her lips, she leaned back again, removing her hand and moving back a few steps from the pulsating influence that seemed to ripple off him in waves. She did not meet Kol's gaze, as she turned from him, the thundering in her blood and head reduced to a dull roar.

She strode away from the alcove and rejoined the room, aware of some eyes on her as she left the Lord of Death behind. Suri focused on two things. Avoiding the three remaining people in the room that could break the remnants of her cover, and the small object that lay in her palm.

As soon as she was surrounded by unfamiliar faces again, she took half a moment to glance down at her latest prize, before placing the silver brooch into her purse with a less than demure smile.

Suri was being watched. She stood in the circle of onlookers watching the couples dancing across the floor, feeling the heat of the eyes. She kept her eyes focused on the kaleidoscope of silk and satin that flowed around her. Prince Shaedon danced with a woman in a golden dress. The steps traced something on the floor with their feet, but they could only move in certain directions. The woman was as unrecognisable as the dance, but Suri's eyes were more drawn to her glittering tiara, rather than any identifiable features.

The attempt at subtlety in the courtiers' furtive glances was laughable. They wouldn't last a second in Suri's world, if this was how they tried to avoid detection. Hushed conversation followed looks from across the room, occasionally interrupted by the swirl of a gown.

She needed to leave soon. Her tower of deception was one blow from complete collapse. But even with the brooch she'd just taken, Suri had so little to show for this risk. She wanted more, feeling the greed down into her blood.

Maybe just one or two more things. *Yes.*

Wait it out, until those around her had lost interest in her, and then she could leave with no one noticing. If, in the meantime, she slipped that gold bangle from that woman in the magenta dress, then it was her fault for leaving it hanging off her wrist.

Ressa Waterborne moved onto the dancefloor, going straight to Prince Shaedon. She tapped him on the shoulder, stopping him in his graceful, but pointless, movements. The Guild Leader of the Water Guild spoke a few words to the Prince, then the two of them traipsed again in that strange formation.

Suri glanced up at the Gate. Ressa might be telling the Prince now about how her lovely daughter had never arrived at the ball. They could be seconds away from announcing a search party. The eyes that lingered on her were now being drawn towards Viantha's silver-haired mother and the heir to this nation.

Bangle be damned. She was leaving now.

Then, as she turned, she saw them again, the two dressed in black.

Scilla and her male companion to her left. They watched the dancefloor as they drank. The man pointed something out, and Scilla laughed.

Suddenly, the area behind the duo cleared, the rows of courtiers positioned behind them shifting to either side. Kol's dark hair pushed through the gap made for him, his head well above the height of those around him. He clapped a hand on the shoulder of each of Suri's tormentors, smiling as he whispered to them. A smile that twisted like a knife in Suri's gut. He even ruffled the man's hair.

She'd known they were desert dwellers. Who their... master was. She hadn't quite realised they were best fucking friends. This was the company the Lord of Death kept. It figured.

They acted like nothing could touch them. They were immune from challenge, from fear. Kol was their security. They could stroll through a city, shitting on its people, and no one would do anything because everyone feared the Wrath, Kol's Wrath.

Make them pay...

As that eerie voice whispered again in her head, she imagined walking over there, pushing through the dance floor. Her hands around Scilla's neck. Gripping. Squeezing. Tendons bulging. Her dark eyes bugged in her sharp face. She could see it. She could almost *feel* the flesh beneath her skin.

Then Kol's eyes flashed towards her. Straight to her. His face was a mask.

That feeling, that need to kill Scilla, did not dissipate as he held her gaze. But she looked away first.

Breathing. Flexing her hands.

A couple of seconds later, she flitted her eyes back towards the space he had been standing and saw nothing. The two villains in grey looked over their shoulders with confused expressions, but he was gone already.

"My lady."

Suri almost jumped as the voice came from her right. Her heart seized for a split second before she realised it was not his voice.

But her heart didn't calm when she turned and saw who was standing before her.

"Prince Shaedon," she said, almost falling over in her terrible imitation of a curtsey.

The Prince bowed to her. Bowed to *her*.

His red hair was darker than she realised, without the direct glare of the chandelier on it, as he bent towards her. The straight locks were oiled and combed back.

"May I?" he asked. Shaedon reached out his hand.

Suri hesitated. To accept would mean she would have to speak to the Prince. He would ask questions of her and expect her to know how to dance. Her ignorance of the world might become clear to all. To refuse would be to draw more attention, to risk offending the Prince in front of all his courtiers. To be watched as she exited.

She smiled in a placid way, and placed her hand into his. "I must admit," she said, as Shaedon pulled her onto the dance-floor. "I am a very poor dancer."

With Suri's slippers giving her that extra height, they were almost matched eye to eye.

His eyes were a pale blue and crinkled in a kind way when he smiled at her. "That is no concern, my lady," he replied. "I can lead."

He swept her round by the hand, holding it aloft as he placed his other hand where her waist met her hip. She settled her other hand on his shoulder, copying the posture she had seen on the other couples. Shaedon took a step, and Suri stepped back a fraction too late, trying to match his movements. She stared down at the floor, watching their moving feet intensely.

"Your mother did not wish you to learn?"

Suri cracked a genuine smile at the lack of subtlety once again. She glanced up at her Prince. "She did not, your highness."

She hoped that was the correct address. The Prince didn't seem to react to it, so she went back to concentrating on the pattern of their feet.

Her feet always seemed to be behind. For a moment she would get the rhythm, but then they would turn in another direction and she would lose it completely. They had not built these damned shoes for dancing.

"I must admit something to you too, my lady," he said, causing Suri to almost lose her footing. "There are many fine ladies here, and I have found myself quite at a loss. Pray, what is your name?"

And there it was. This time, inescapable. A no would not suffice to the Prince.

Suri had asked Viantha for this. For the names of other fine ladies in her kingdom, her acquaintances and fellow courtiers from the Pail. She had hoped not to use it. It was fallible, a lie as thin as paper. There was nothing for it. She would have to hope it would stick long enough to finish this farcical dance.

But as Suri raised her eyes to meet the Prince's, she saw them again.

The three of them were laughing. At her. She was certain of it. Her three tormentors flocked like vultures. She was the corpse they were picking at. Maybe they had recognised her. Maybe they were all laughing as Scilla recounted that night. How she'd lain in filth at their feet.

So, instead of gifting Shaedon with a full lie, she gave him a half-truth. "I'm sorry, your highness," she said. "What was it you said? After—well—I'm a little out of sorts."

The Prince Shaedon furrowed his brow, pausing their steps. Suri's feet thanked him for it. "Are you alright, my lady?"

Suri bit her lip. "It is nothing I would wish to trouble you about, your highness. They're your guests, after all."

The Prince moved closer, gripping Suri's waist tighter. "I can assure you it is no trouble," he said. "If anything has happened to you here, I demand to know it."

Suri shook her head, but then looked deliberately towards the three. The two minions were still chuckling, Kol stony-faced. She looked back at the Prince. "I should not have said anything. I do not wish to make a fuss."

He followed her eyes and found their destination. The concern shifted to anger.

Perfect.

With him distracted, she could soon leave this awful evening. Suri hung her head. "I feel a little faint, your highness. Might I leave to get a refreshment?"

The Prince dropped her hand, still holding her waist, and touched her cheek. She looked up at him. Boy, he was mad. What a lucky coincidence that they had the same enemy tonight. "Of course, my lady," he said.

Suri moved out of his remaining hand, relieved to have that claiming grip gone from her body. She didn't enjoy playing the damsel. She was powerless enough in her own life to want to be powerless in this lie, too. She dropped into another terrible curtsey.

"Can I escort—"

Suri had already turned. She'd moved a single step when someone grabbed her wrist from behind. She glanced back and saw Prince Shaedon's eyes locked on her arm. Locked onto the large purple bruise that she'd been trying quite hard to keep covered since Kol had noticed it.

Her sleeve must have fallen as they danced. Another reason to hate dancing.

"What happened?"

Damn.

Fine. More theatrics.

The Prince dropped her arm as she turned fully back towards him. He didn't meet her eyes, though. "Was it—?"

She wanted him to know it was them. For someone else to know a sliver of what had happened to her and try to do something about it. More than that though, she needed to survive. And if this situation got any bigger, it would ruin everything. She was on the precipice of self-destruction as it was. "Please, your highness. The last thing I want is to cause a problem," she said.

"An assault on one of my guests isn't something I can look away from, I fear," he said.

Suri held back the instant urge to roll her eyes, then her stomach coiled. It was back. That crackling air. Heating her blood. Stirring that rage within her.

Him.

Kol was there, on the dancefloor, behind Prince Shaedon. He tapped the Prince on the shoulder. He turned, dropping his loose grip on her wrist.

She could leave. In this one moment, before it came crashing down. She could leave.

Suri didn't move. She watched, rooted in that intangible energy, as the Prince of the Forgelands and the Lord of Death stood chest to chest.

"May I cut in?" Kol asked, with a look at Suri.

Was he unaware of the tension? Or simply used to being received this way?

"You will not touch her," the Prince said.

Kol raised an eyebrow at the Prince. He leaned back. "Shaedon, you need to loosen up. I'm after a dance, not her hand."

The Prince didn't move a muscle. The other dancers near them had stopped moving, too. "You will not touch her," he repeated.

A brief scan of the room confirmed all eyes were on them.

Kol smiled. It was not a kind smile. "And who are you, Fire Prince, to tell me what I cannot do?"

The air around them felt darker. The Prince's shoulders shook, his fists clenched at his side. Kol watched him, his posture easy.

When Prince Shaedon spoke next, it boomed across the room. "You have come here. To *my* ball. Uninvited. We have granted you our hospitality. You and your... emissaries have drank our wine and eaten our food. And now you mock me. Assault *my* guests."

Kol flicked his eyes to her and then the Prince again. "And?"

His lack of denial radiated through her. He knew then of the torment at the hands of his envoys. He didn't care. Why would he?

Prince Shaedon raised a hand, then lowered it. With barely contained rage, he continued. "*And* there is the other matter. Robberies on the Drameir Road."

Kol clenched his jaw. "If you believe that to be *my* work, then you are far stupider than I gave you credit for."

"You will leave. At once," he said. His voice shook with anger.

Kol spun in a slow circle, ignoring the spectators as he looked only to the throne. "King Thandul. Do you echo your pup's sentiments?"

The King was standing, his perfectly tailored clothing creased from his long-seated position. "I'm sure that there has been some mistake."

The Prince took a step towards the throne. "Father—"

Kol swung round and pressed his hand against the Prince's chest. "You see, *Prince*," he said, pushing him back. "There has been some mistake."

Anyone would think 'prince' a curse word, the way Kol spat it.

The Prince stumbled back before righting himself, raising his right hand. One chandelier went dark, the fires of fifty individual candles winking out, to reform as a ball of flame in his hand. And the fire was blue. Then he threw it.

The manipulated fire flew at Kol. The Lord of Death swept his hand, and the flame was gone. Extinguished in a swirl of black mist.

Suri's heart pounded. Fire manipulation was rare, and Shaedon had performed it with such ease.

Kol clicked his tongue. "Now that. That was truly a mistake. Let the record show that your Prince attacked first."

A clamour rose in the ballroom. Kol's answering smile was as icy as the flame. Guards from around the ballroom surged forwards, more than Suri had even realised were there. Four rushed into the circle.

Swords unsheathed, and Kol's expression shifted.

"My lords, end this madness!"

Screams drowned the King's voice as Kol twisted his left hand in a tight spiral, the guards falling to the floor.

Dead. He had just used death magic. Creation and destruction of shadow was one thing, but to have the power to destroy life itself with the flick of a hand. The acts he must have performed to tap into that type of power terrified her.

The crowd scattered and fell back, but Suri's eyes had not left Kol. She saw it. The next move. His right hand flexed at his side, and he made a slight gesture with his fingers. Different. A signal.

She swung her head around. Scilla and the other one broke forward from the circle of onlookers. Towards Shaedon. For a moment, Suri thought about running.

But then she stepped to the side and into the path of Scilla.

Sweet Suri.

She spun into the path of Scilla as the voice stroked her like a cat. Suri's foot caught her shin and she grabbed Scilla's wrist as the woman stumbled, pulling her arm until it was about to snap. Scilla reached for a knife at her calf and wrenched her arm to slice at Suri's ankle. Suri stamped down on her hand, driving her pointed heel into the woman's hand until she screamed and dropped the blade.

Make. Them. Pay.

The man found his target and grappled Shaedon from behind, taking the Prince by surprise. He looked round and his eyes found Scilla on her knees in front of Suri. He paused, looking at Kol who hadn't moved since his signal.

"Teach the boy a lesson, Barsen," Scilla said as she struggled against Suri's grip. "I'll deal with this one."

The partner—Barsen—looked back to his conquest and shoved Shaedon onto the floor.

Yes.

Three more guards had come forward, surging past the bodies pushing up the stairs and out the Gate. Kol killed them in an instant.

The King's voice cried out, barely audible over the thrum in her head. "Stop this charade at once!"

Suri pulled at Scilla's arm, forcing her to kneel up to avoid a fracture, her heel still digging into her hand. The contortion satisfied something dark inside her, and she bent her head towards the villain, spitting her words.

"That's the second time you've underestimated me, *Scilla*."

Scilla pulled round in her grip, but Suri twisted her arm back harder, causing the other woman to cry out in pain.

Barsen slammed his fist into Shaedon's face. She could feel that hand, remembering it holding her, immobilising her, so Scilla could punish her for a crime she never even had the chance to commit.

Make them pay.

Kol only watched, his eyes flitting between his emissaries. He made no steps to intervene.

"Who—?" Scilla choked out.

So they didn't know who she was.

The squeal in Scilla's question satisfied her hunger somewhat.

Suri moved her foot off Scilla's hand, then grabbed her neck, wrenching her head up and back, until her body was flush against Suri's.

"What's wrong, *mouse*? Cat got your tongue?" Suri whispered, pulling her head to one side and speaking into her ear.

Scilla gasped.

She pushed a hand into Scilla's pocket and pulled out a handful of coins. She quickly scanned them and pocketed them.

Still shy of Geren's debt. But a life debt sang at her fingertips. *Kill her.*

"Kol—"

She cut off Scilla's choked plea with a clench of her hair. Suri whipped her head up to look at Kol. His eyes met hers. Before he flexed his hand, Suri dropped Scilla's arm and had the meat knife pressed against her neck. It was still damp with the blood of the wrong creature.

"I wouldn't, if I were you," she said.

Kol tilted his head and opened his mouth as if to respond, but Shaedon had pulled free, Kol turning to him as the Fire Prince pushed his now blue ignited hand into Barsen's jaw.

Suri didn't loosen her blade from the woman's neck as the smell of melting flesh met the man's scream.

"Barsen—"

Scilla's cry caused her throat to press against the metal.

Mmm...

Barsen wrenched himself away from Shaedon. He moved his hands in a quick gesture and vanished into nothing.

Somehow, Suri must have been stopping Scilla from performing the same trick. And more than that, she knew now how to hurt Scilla the most. The pulse in her head didn't feel like a headache or a distraction any longer. Instead, it was the beat of her personal war.

Shaedon stumbled to his feet. He looked around with wild eyes, searching for the nearby shadow. His red hair had fallen from its slicked perfection and now fell over his eyes, his lip split and bleeding.

He saw Suri with a meat knife to his uninvited guest, and his confusion was palpable. She winked at him, a smile playing at her lips. Maybe she could use this to her advantage; claim some reward for defending the Prince.

Barsen appeared from the darkness, directly behind Shaedon, his leg sweeping in a kick that knocked the Prince's knees from under him. The left side of his face mottled red, the burnt flesh hanging strangely on his lower cheek.

As soon as Barsen had grabbed him again, Kol raised a hand. Barsen stopped, holding the Prince's wrists, but not moving further. The Lord of Death looked between Suri and Barsen, the two jailors.

"I grow bored of this," he said. "I'll spare your pup if you spare my emissary."

Shaedon spat on the wooden floor in front of Kol.

"I can change my mind in an instant, little Prince," Kol sneered at the kneeling royalty.

"Let us leave it here, Lords, we need no further bloodshed tonight."

Suri wanted to laugh at the King's weak proclamation as everything inside her raged to the opposite tune. Not needed? Far from it, it was necessary.

"Release the Prince," Kol said. Barsen did so, dropping his grip and moving to stand next to Kol. Shaedon stood, but made no move to pursue. Probably wise. He'd been beaten twice.

Kol looked at Suri. "Your turn."

Suri paused, playing with the knife. She didn't work for Thandul or Shaedon and hadn't agreed to this swap. Kol looked calm, as if believing her to be linked in by this same strange honour system they played to.

She cocked her head. "But of course, your *highness*."

He clenched his jaw as she flicked the knife away from Scilla's pulsing neck. Suri dropped into an exaggerated curtsy as she watched her prey scramble to her feet and move to her protector.

The three of them stood, facing a near empty ballroom.

"Well, this has been interesting," Kol said. "Always a pleasure, Thandul."

Thandul looked ready to faint, the bulging vein in his forehead far from relaxed, even with his heir now freed. Scilla stared daggers at Suri. They were twins, in this one regard.

Kol nodded to Shaedon. "I look forward to the wedding."

Shaedon sneered, but wisely made no reply.

Kol flicked his hand, and the two emissaries held his shoulder.

He had miscalculated. He must have believed her to be some Forgelands agent, wanting to help Shaedon, faithful to the future heir. A girl bound by high society, and that unspoken rule that you did not kill outside of a fair match. You did not take advantage of weakness.

Suri's rules were different. She survived on the weakness of others. She had nearly died due to her own weaknesses many times, and there was no loyalty beyond the blood in her veins. She had never been helped; not by her people, or by her city, much less by her King or Prince.

Hurt them back.

They had humiliated her, cruelly, but she had the chance to fix it. Opportunities like this didn't come round often.

Even as she justified it, even as the dark thoughts chimed against that hushed voice inside her spurring her on... She *knew* she was about to do something stupid, something she might not be able to take back.

She guessed she didn't care right now.

So, as Kol moved his hands, Suri moved hers.

Yes.

The knife flashed as it left her grip. It spun in the air, catching the light of the chandelier as it spun towards its target.

Kol's eyes widened, but it was too late. His hands had completed their gesture, and a shadow was forming around them.

Scilla screamed, as the knife found its target in warm flesh.

Barsen gasped, the blade lodging into his heart.

Sweet Suri, my child.

They disappeared.

7

Mother and father forced me to attend the ball. I danced with many, but none were Him. I imagined His arms. Sister danced twice with the King. I do not like his eyes.

Diary of C. Aubethaan, est. early 8th century

"That was nowhere near," the young man said. "Are you even trying?"

Suri had stuck out her lip, staring at the knife lodged four feet wide of the painted target.

"Why do I need to learn this?" she asked.

Esra scratched at the scruff on his neck. He was around twenty then and had only just grown into the now consistent cover of stubby brown hair.

"You're nearly grown. You need to learn to look after yourself."

"I'm only ten, Esra!"

"You'll be eleven in a week," he replied. "Too old to be whining like a brat. Again."

She grumbled, but did as she was told, testing the weight with little throws in her right hand. Similar knife wounds covered the crates in the single-room abandoned building at the western edge of the Tangle they'd been sleeping in for two years. Esra practised every day, and spent the rest of his time spinning tales of future riches. When they would have their own gang, sleep on mountains of sweet cakes, and not answer to anyone.

Suri raised the knife and threw it.

"Better," he said, as the knife sank only two feet off the target this time. "You need to commit more. You're losing accuracy."

He nudged her out of the way and threw a knife. It slammed into the centre of their makeshift wooden target, almost breaking it.

"Show off."

He smiled, but it faded. "Is there anyone else you trust?"

Suri stared up at him. "Why?"

"Because," Esra said. "It's good to have allies. They can keep you alive."

Suri poked him in the ribs. "That's what you're for."

Esra simply stared at the target.

"Show me again," she said. Her brother was acting weird.

He picked up two more knives, and again threw one straight into the centre, so it nestled right beside the first.

A slow clap sounded from behind them. Esra whipped round, so fast, his second knife already raised. He moved in front of Suri, shielding her.

Suri turned, too. A boy stood at the entrance to their home.

"You haven't lost your touch, Esra," he laughed, glancing at Suri. "How's tricks?"

Suri frowned. Why wasn't Esra relaxing? It was just Clacker. They were part of the same gang, both reporting to the Tanner.

"What do you want?" Esra lowered the knife a finger's width.

"Me?" he asked, gesturing at himself. The gaudy orange shirt he wore looked new. Things rarely looked new in the Tangle. "Nothing, man. I'm here for your debt."

"What are you talking about?" Esra asked. "What debt?"

"Word is you scored big. May wants her cut."

Esra's eyes darted to a bag in the corner. "She already got it."

"Well, she wants more," Clacker said, not missing the look.

Esra scoffed. "And she sent you to come claim it?"

He shrugged. "Guess so."

"And if I refuse?" Esra stepped, blocking Suri from view.

Clacker narrowed his eyes. "Then I'll take your little sister. As collateral."

"The fuck did you just say?"

Esra threw the knife, and somehow Clacker dodged it. Esra shoved Suri away and she rolled against the floor and into her dirty straw bed. She flipped onto her belly to see Clacker leap onto her brother.

Esra was unarmed. Clacker drew his weapon. A crude but sharp blade, curved slightly. Clacker drove it down, and Esra only just caught it.

She screamed, pushing herself up and ignoring the scrape on her knee. Esra held Clacker's forearm, stopping the knife from moving closer to his neck.

She ran without thinking, grabbing a throwing knife from the floor. Then she jumped onto Clacker's back.

She stabbed until he fell off her brother and sagged onto the floor with a wheezing gasp. She stabbed until Esra yelled at her to stop. That it was done.

Esra stared up at her, as Clacker bled through that horrid orange shirt.

"Are you quite sure this is where you want to stay, my lady?" the barman asked, his voice confused. Suri blinked at him, the memory of where she was and what she'd just done still fresh.

After the knife had flown into Barsen's chest, and the three had disappeared, the fallout of the situation hit home with those who hadn't yet fled the ball.

The braver courtiers had moved in to check on the guards. They were dead, but it was a nice thought. Amidst the cries and confusion, and brief dearth of guards, Suri ran up the stairs and through the Gate, without being stopped.

She'd walked as fast as she could risk, both for her ankles and the suspicion of the remaining guards, to the Merchant Quarter. She hoped that the hubbub of the streets at this late hour would mask her whereabouts, if only for a little while.

She'd picked this inn almost at random, checking over her shoulder as she'd walked until she was convinced that she was free of a tail. This inn, The Wooden Penny, was the next she came across.

What in Wrath's name had come over her? She'd killed him. *Killed again*, an awful part of her thought. She'd killed the man in front of everyone. They were *leaving*. They had provided the perfect distraction.

Now she'd put a target on her back.

She painted a strained smile on her face. "I'm quite sure."

The inn was loud.

Behind her, most of the patrons were watching a bawdy troupe enact the drama of Queen Lera and the Wrath. She glanced back to see a young boy with a long blonde wig and gauzy fabric wings pretending to search a painted landscape.

Suri was certain the half-Fae Queen would not approve of this depiction of her formative moment.

"What sort of room do ye want, then?"

Suri smiled and tried her best to look weary, which wasn't hard. "Whatever you have that's best will do fine."

The barman nodded, twiddling two fingers in his beard.

"Of course. I'll have my wife take you up to the top floor. No one will bother you there."

"Thank you. If your wife would let me borrow some other garment, that would be greatly appreciated. I don't have my chest with me, you see."

The barman looked uncertain again. "I'm not sure we have anything that is fit—"

"I need nothing fancy, just anything that is less... grand than this," Suri said, leaning towards him. "I'll pay you for your assistance."

The barman looked around his clientele, then nodded.

She couldn't pay him, of course. She had a few bits from Scilla, but needed every one of them. If he insisted on any payment upfront, she could stall by leaving Kol's brooch as some form of collateral. And then steal it back.

It was all so stupid. That thrumming echo in her, whatever it was, that wanted her to throw that knife... that horrible and all-consuming need for revenge. It had dissipated as she left, as if the frosty night air had extinguished the heat inside her.

Suri was escorted by the barman's wife up some stairs as those behind her exploded in raucous laughter. They'd reached the stage in their play where 'Queen Lera' had fought with the pagans, four men wearing all black with their skin painted red. In this version, the Queen fought them off by distracting them with her breasts, before stabbing them.

It was a wonder this troupe was still alive.

Part of her wanted to stay to see how much more ridiculous the play would get. At this rate, a goat might play the witch. But she knew it would raise suspicion. They had to perceive her as being far above the company that would frequent this place. The real her wouldn't even be allowed through the door.

It would not take long for the people at the ball to ask one another who she was, and realise no one, from any place, could say. Plus, she'd killed an emissary.

Kol's emissary. Would anyone even miss him? She almost groaned at herself in her attempt to hope that she wouldn't be on every poster from the Arena Quarter to the Tangle.

Infamy was coming for her. Maybe her ridiculous exploits would help her recruit her rival crew once Geren was off her back.

Suri felt like an imbecile for putting herself in the limelight. But if she was honest with herself, she delighted in the memory of Scilla's scream as it had filled the half-empty ballroom. She'd wanted revenge, and she'd got it. It was a colossal mess, yet Suri couldn't stop a small smile from spreading.

The lady of the house led her to her room and assured her she would look for something alternative for her to wear. As the door opened, Suri focused her eyes on the small wooden bath on the side of the room.

She asked the woman for hot water, mumbled a thanks, and closed the door. The bag dropped to the floor and her shoes followed it. The sheer pleasure of bare feet was unmatched and she flexed her toes against the thin red rug that lined the old warping wood.

In the five steps that it took for her to cross the floor to the sturdy wooden framed bed, with its equally sturdy cotton sheets, she was undressed. She pulled at the threaded knots at her back until they loosened, and the contraption fell off her slight curves. The weight of her dress, and the stolen trinkets

R A SANDPIPER

that still lined its pockets, now pooled in the centre of the room, its unwieldy mass of fabric so large that she marvelled she'd held it up for that long.

Lying back on the bed, some of the tension from her body spilled out. She peeled the black netting off her arms, until she was once again a woman of just flesh.

She lay across the comfortable surface for a moment but she couldn't relax for too long. A couple of hours, perhaps, to let the heat of the guards on the streets die down and get a moment of needed rest in a comfortable bed. Once she was back to her real self, she wouldn't be able to blag her way into a fine room like this again.

When the wife returned with a couple of steaming buckets, she averted her eyes from Suri's nakedness. Suri watched with a half-lidded gaze as the innkeeper's wife returned to fill the bath to the brim, before putting down a pile of items, and leaving.

Suri made a quick appraisal. A thin cotton towel, soap, a sponge, and a dress. A simple ankle-length yellow one, with a brown waist tied, looped round it. It was nice, probably one of this woman's best dresses. To a lady like Viantha Waterborne, however, it would likely be a dress only suitable for a chamber. For a thief like Suri, it was far too nice to blend in well in the Tangle. She should have asked the innkeeper for trousers and an old shirt instead. Far more practical, and she could have made them fit with some small amendments. But it would have been a strange request for a lady to make, so she would have to make this work.

With the barest hesitation, she dipped a toe and then a leg into the bath. A shudder ran through her body as she sank into it, propping her legs on the edge as she submerged her head.

The water drowned out the sounds of the revelry from the bottom floor, the liquid grounding her. Suri held her breath as long as she could, feeling the swirling water pull and loosen the fastenings in her hair. She dragged her fingertips through it, shaking it until it fanned around her in the water. The earrings were the next to go, and she cleaned them, too, washing the gold dusting off her shoulders and down her chest. The same hands, the only hands she trusted, ran over her entire self.

When she pulled herself from that water and dried off, she was wholly herself again. Only cleaner.

She sat on the bed in the empty room and found she didn't feel alone. That was strange.

Mmm.

No one could see her. But something still thrummed there, both inside and outside her, this force that felt like it had bonded to her very self.

Sweet Suri.

The voice, the one that had been so frequently rolling around in her mind for the last two days. It had been there in the ballroom. She had heard it, *felt* it. Deep, rumbling, persistent. He had focused her on her revenge, and she had taken the encouragement in her stride.

But now.

It was different.

Sweet.

It wasn't pushing her. It was praising her.

You made them pay.

Each word was like a finger licking up her spine. She arched her back as she sat, heat flushing down inside her.

Good, sweet girl.

She pulled the towel tighter around her body. The cotton caused friction against her breasts. She stood, the pace of the thrum rising in her head.

Mother Edi had told her the earrings would help. She put them back in, but was still vibrating with energy. Oh Wrath, she needed a distraction.

Something to stave off this burning feeling. It crept across her skin, making it nearly impossible to keep her thoughts away from the dark eyes of a certain Lord from that night.

She grabbed the huge green dress from the floor and bundled it, along with the contents of the pockets and the round bag, into the wooden wardrobe. Suri pulled the simple yellow dress over her naked form and tied the rope tight around her, before slipping those evil shoes back on.

It was a risk to go downstairs, but her whole body felt charged up. Pulsing. And damn it, she might find some more practical clothing.

In a moment, she was downstairs, seeking a whole new type of prey. Far easier to identify and trap. The play had ended during her bath, which was a shame. She moved her way to the side of the bar and scanned the players, who now mingled with the patrons. One was quite handsome, despite the red paint still clinging to the side of his face.

She gazed at him, and it took less than a minute for him to catch her eyes, move through the crowded room, and offer to buy her an ale.

She had one mug. Then a second. Free for the favours he hoped she would grant him.

"We've played all over Peregrinus," he lied.

"Oh, really?" she asked. "Where was best?"

"The Pail, I'm sure," he replied.

"Gods, that's so far," she said. "Why there?"

He leaned in, and she ducked her head closer. "One night, I went out walking. And there, in the moonlight, under Loris' own moonbeams, I tell you. I saw it. A Roanhadham."

"No," Suri said, pressing her hand to her mouth.

It sounded fake even to her ears, but he seemed encouraged, nodding. "Yes. Led by a beautiful maiden. A true Fae, no doubt. Wings and all."

"How big was it?" she asked.

He smirked. "The size of three horses, I'm sure."

She clenched her fist to keep the laughter from escaping. The Roanhadham were legendary horses ridden by the Fae of old, rumoured to have special abilities. They were also a complete myth, or at least long gone. There was a different tale every week about what they looked like, what they could do.

"She wasn't even leading it with a rein. She didn't need to, I'm sure. Them Roanhadham can hear your thoughts."

He wasn't all that cute. But he was keen, and her body felt electrified, still. The whispering voice kept coming back.

Sweet Suri, well done.

The purr crept up her back, stroking her senses.

And so, less than half an hour had passed since their greeting, yet her next words worked as magically as any Fae trick. "I wish I could hear you better. It's so loud."

At his suggestion, they moved to her chambers. In the end, though, the pleasure was all hers.

Suri took from him what she needed, rocking across his damp body as she found temporary release from that inner voice that tugged at her.

As her conquered prey slept, she rose from the bed and gathered everything from the room, also grabbing his trousers and shirt. They were pretty good quality, and this alone would have been a good haul on a normal night. Now, after hours in heavy dresses, they were a gift from the Trio.

She wrapped the ornate dress up and tied everything into the towel, taking the soap, even the candlestick. She put the yellow dress back on. She was still in the Merchant Quarter, so needed to look somewhat presentable.

Suri stepped into the hallway, taking care to close the door quietly behind her. Perhaps he would think her a drunken dream. She would not think of him at all.

She found a window that opened out across a roof down the back of the building. Easy. She slipped her shoes off, placing them in the bundle, before climbing through it and scrambling to the edge, trying to keep her precious bundle off the wet tiles as much as possible.

It was a storey drop to the floor. Suri lowered herself as far as possible, with her arms and fell into a crouch. She stumbled a little with her bundle, but didn't fall, slipping the heeled shoes back on.

Other than her towel bundle, half-dried hair, and lack of cloak, Suri looked almost ladylike. She walked at a comfortable pace towards her captive. The girl had been down there less than a day, so Suri wasn't sure why she felt guilty about it, but leaving her there all night felt wrong, for whatever reason.

Suri hoped that those who sought to track her movements would find their trail running cold at this inn. She had covered her tracks and, once she'd freed the princess and found a safe place for her items, she could lie low for a while until the heat around the ball died down.

She weaved her way through the streets, back to the street with the little door, checking over her shoulder before ducking through.

It was damper and more disgusting down here than it had been before, like someone had thrown a bucket of piss down the corridor itself. She breathed through her mouth and tried as hard as she could to ignore the foul scents around her.

She needed her hands free for this encounter, in case Viantha tried anything, so before she got near the alcove where she'd left the princess, she knelt on the grim floor and found one of her old spots. She pulled at the dank brickwork, a few bricks up from the floor, and it crumbled out, two rats jumping out of the gap behind it and past Suri.

It was a cramped fit to shove the full bundle into the wall, but she managed. She replaced the brickwork as best she could.

The only thing she took with her was the ring. Suri rubbed at the rough gems that adorned it as she walked. She couldn't sell amefyre. Even if she could break the ring into its tiniest fragments, no one in their right mind would buy amefyre from a thief. It was too much of a risk. She had to give it back.

Her footsteps joined the quiet soundscape of dripping walls and scurrying rats.

Just before she reached where she'd left the princess, she tore a patch of fabric from the brown gauze underlayer of the dress. Another mask. Another lie.

A shuffling from the alcove. The tearing noise must have alerted the princess.

With the ring clenched in her palm, Suri rounded the corner into the alcove.

Empty.

The rope was a limp snake on the floor. No prisoner. The flask lay beside it, no bread. Nothing else. Viantha had escaped. How?

Suri took another step and looked around the room, searching for any clues.

She jumped and spun as she heard a man's voice.

"Missing something?" Two guards stood in the arch behind her. Armed with short swords, they blocked her path.

Fuck.

Suri swept her hands behind her back, hiding them so she could move the ring.

"By the order of King Thandul," the older guard said. "You are under arrest. For the kidnap of Lady Viantha Waterborne, the theft of her person, false impersonation, and unlawful entry into the Palace."

8

They have requested us to attend the King's court for the season. I see Him more and more. He comforts me.
Diary of C. Aubethaan, est. early 8th century

She was screwed.

Her eyes flitted between the two, but she knew it was hopeless. She couldn't get past two armed guards. Not when their only goal was to stop her from getting through. Her only hope was finding some later opportunity for escape.

As they moved to bind her, she spun, as if to struggle. They dashed forward to grab her and pulled her arms back, clasping her wrists together. But she'd already made the move. The amefyre ring now lay in her mouth.

The guards pulled the cloth from her face. They searched her body and told her to walk, before marching her up and out of the sewer, as two more guards came around the corner.

Four now. Almost impossible for her to escape. How had Viantha got out? The knots were tight. She couldn't have slipped free without help. Got lucky with a guard roaming the sewers maybe? Unlikely. She must have convinced a passing urchin of some future payment for freeing her. It was the only feasible option.

Damn.

She cursed herself over and over as they marched her back through the Merchant Quarter. It was the dead of night now, maybe a couple hours before the yoke of dawn. Suri hadn't slept properly in days. She pondered the list of her offences. Kidnap and theft of Viantha, impersonation, and unlawful entry.

They hadn't connected her to the greater thefts at the ball itself. People probably hadn't realised items were missing yet. However, the omission of the murder was glaring. Perhaps she hadn't killed him.

But through that thing inside her, that calling thrum, she knew. He was dead. She felt it.

So why had they left it out?

It was a small matter now, she considered, faced with her own death. At least if she was dead, she wouldn't be in debt.

The guards threw her, with no explanation, into a cell in a guardhouse. It was clean. There was even a straw cot in the corner. Whilst not the warm bed she had claimed for the night and hated herself for leaving, this cell was still intended for those far above her station. Abusive drunk nobles, not Tangle urchins. The cot was a darn sight nicer than many alleys she'd spent nights in. She fell into it and, despite the constant light overhead and the clanging of the baton as the guard passed her cell, even despite her knowledge this might be her last night alive, she managed to sleep.

They dragged her from her slumber soon after. This time, in the icy morning air, the pass through the Gate felt worse. Colder than ever, stripped bare and then reformed. It was over before it began though, and she soon stumbled back into the throne room she'd fled from not ten hours prior.

The guards pushed her to the top of the stairs. When Suri saw her audience, she froze for a moment. Another shove nearly made her careen down the staircase. She had expected a noble to preside over her 'hearing', but the thrones were full.

King Thandul sat on the largest throne. Prince Shaedon sat on the other. Both looked at her as she descended. The Seer of Blood stood beside them, a ceremonial knife laid on a piece of red cloth before him.

But it wasn't the presence of those three that surprised Suri the most, even if the Seer made her skin crawl. It was her. The woman in the blue dress.

Viantha.

She had come, in spite surely, to watch Suri brought to justice. The morning light filtered through the frosted glass and its brightness cast lazy patterns over her watchers. Looking at her now, warmed under the rays of dawn, it was apparent how terrible of an imitator she had been. The dress clung to her soft and generous curves, with a neckline that dipped slightly in the centre of her chest. The shade of the blue sat sweet on her unmarked alabaster skin, topped by the long silver chain. Her cheeks were so rosy it must have been artificial. Her eyes told Suri nothing.

Suri was lucky the truth of the woman's beauty had not fully spread to the far North, or the footmen may have never let her in. That luck had now run out.

She would face her death with the scraps of dignity she still held. She held her head up high. The troop of guards led the thief down the stairs, her feet sinking into the plush carpeted fabric with each step.

Far nicer to be barefoot when being executed, Suri decided. She reached the bottom and the guards directed her to the centre of the ballroom.

There was a moment where no one spoke.

"You've searched her?" the King said, breaking the silence. A fair concern.

A guard spoke. "Yes, your grace. We caught her in the sewers, where, uh, Lady Viantha stated she was being kept. She must be the captor."

King Thandul held up a hand. "Yes, thank you. Viantha? Can you confirm your captor's identity?"

Suri's eyes shot to the princess.

"It is her, your grace."

There was no room for doubt in Viantha's words. Suri wondered how she could be so sure. She'd worn a mask when speaking to her, and her dress was different. Sure, she was tall with dark hair, but you would think there would have been a moment of uncertainty.

Well. That was a short end to a fruitless life.

The King leant back on his throne and stared at the thief.

"So, girl. Who do you work for?"

Suri didn't expect conversation, much less one she would have to engage in. The ring sat heavy on her tongue. She swirled it around until it was sitting in her right cheek pocket. "I work for no one, your grace."

The King snorted. "You work for no one? This is your claim?"

"Yes."

The Prince stood. "So you claim you stole the heir to the Water Guild's seat off the street, stole her invitation, all so you could get into a ball where you killed an agent of the Lord of Death... because *you* wanted to?"

Suri considered his words for a moment. "Yes."

The King laughed. It was not a kind laugh. "Do you think us fools, child?"

Suri tilted her head. "May I speak, your Grace?"

Thandul threw his hand in a callous gesture.

"This mark here was from when they held me by my neck in a back alley," she said, pointing to her neck. "This mark," she continued, motioning to her face. "Is where they hit me across the face."

"What is the meaning of this charade?" the King asked.

"Here is where his *agent* nearly broke my arm," she said, tapping her elbow. Then, she twisted and showed the bruised back of her arm. "This is from when they threw me into the gutter."

The King looked bemused.

Suri met his gaze without flinching. "My reason for wanting to kill that shadow demon had nothing to do with your politics."

The King said nothing.

She nodded to the Prince. "He asked me who caused this bruise. I didn't lie. It *was* them. I wanted revenge."

She figured it was better to omit her intention to rob the ball blind. If they hadn't missed anything, it couldn't hurt them.

The King leaned back. "What's your name, girl?"

"Edi, your Grace."

She wasn't sure why she lied. Perhaps for some sort of protection. She'd just told these men the truth. The whole truth was too much.

"And where are you from?" the King asked.

"The Tangle, your Grace," she said.

The King laughed.

"A backwater thief. One of *our* bloody backwater thieves," he said, addressing Prince Shaedon. "This nothing girl killed a shadow!"

The Prince shrugged. "She got lucky."

Thandul tutted. "Don't be sour. You've been scuffling with them for years, son."

Shaedon scowled.

"Girl," he said, looking back at her. "What of the other shadow?"

Suri narrowed her eyes. "She lives, your Grace."

"I know that. What do you mean to do about it?"

"Nothing, your Grace," she said. It was the truth. His death was the only punishment she intended. It was probably overkill already.

"And the master?"

"Nothing."

"Disappointing," he said.

Suri looked across the three royals, unsure if they expected her to speak.

"Well, we must punish you. What you did to Viantha Waterborne is an unforgivable offence."

Shaedon's scowl faded. The words were a blow, even though they were all she could have expected.

"You have broken many laws, and you have caused distress to a noble house in the Pail," he said, before pausing. "But your actions, intended or not, were a blessing to Greater Peregrinus."

The whiplash of the conversation made her tremble.

"It would seem a waste to kill you. But it would be an act of aggression both against the Parched Lands and the Pail to not punish you. It would be cruel to Lady Viantha to not see you removed," he added, smiling at Viantha. "So, I have decided."

She was so tense she could feel her muscles on the edge of seizing. The King flicked a hand, and the Seer picked up the knife and moved towards her.

"You will be exiled forthwith for a period of twenty years. You will be sold to the Southern slavers. If you return to this city before twenty years, you will be executed."

Suri's breath fell from her. Sharp relief met with instant fear. Exile? This was all she had ever known. The city, the Tangle. Everything about her, everything she knew about the world could be found within these walls. Without New Politan, without the Forgelands, who was she?

And Esra. Esra's sentence was weeks from being complete. He was about to be free, if he had lived through the back-breaking ten years. He would come back here, come back to her. He'd promised her. And she'd promised he would have something to come back to. He was going to arrive back here alone. The gangs would eat him alive.

What if he thought she'd left him behind? What if he thought she didn't care?

The Seer stopped in front of her. He was the same height as her and smelt of old paper and perfumed powder. He raised the knife towards her neck, causing Suri to flinch, but only cut into the fabric neckline of her dress, before pulling it away from her body, exposing the swell of flesh near her heart.

He poised the knife's edge against her flesh.

"There is one condition," the King said.

Suri looked up.

He smiled. "I will allow you to return early if you kill Scilla of the Parched Lands."

Suri sucked in a breath. That voice, that beat, started a pattern in her heart. Tapping. Pattering. So low, but so clear.

Shaedon held up a hand. "Father—"

The King interrupted. "You must prove this, Edi, Shadowkiller of the Tangle. You must come bearing some fruit of the kill. Then I'll allow you to walk these streets again. If you're seen here without that proof, the Bloodhounds will execute you in whichever manner they see fit."

The thrum got louder, the rhythm in her hands, her ears.

The Seer dragged the knife into her flesh and she clenched her fists as she felt the pull of the cold blade. It wasn't as painful as she thought it would be. She glanced down. The Seer's knife cut true, but, as soon as it had cut a path, the carved path went black. It took thirty seconds for him to carve the symbols, and she didn't cry out once. A chevron pointing down. A sand timer, the symbol of both time, death and the Parched Lands; a collection of tiny dashes formed into two concentric circles. He tapped three drops of her blood, dripping from the knife, into a vial.

Then he shuffled over to the King, who worked a giant blue ring off of his finger. With the same, still dripping, knife, the Seer cut a small incision on the side of his finger, next to several similar tiny scars. One drop of blood caught on the knife, and was dropped into the same vial. The Seer stoppered the vial, putting it into his pocket with a shaking grip.

Once done, the King flicked his hand at her. "You are dismissed."

The Prince stood to leave, as the guards grabbed her arms.

"Your Grace?" she called.

A guard yanked her arm. "Who said you could speak, *girl*?"

She paid him no mind, as the King had turned to look at her. His eyes were curious.

Sweet Suri...

"What if I kill *him*?" she asked. Her voice held nothing. No tone or emotion.

"Who?" he replied.

"Kol."

There was no challenge. It was a statement, nothing more.

The King's eyes sparkled as he smiled. "If you kill the Lord of Death, girl, you can name your prize."

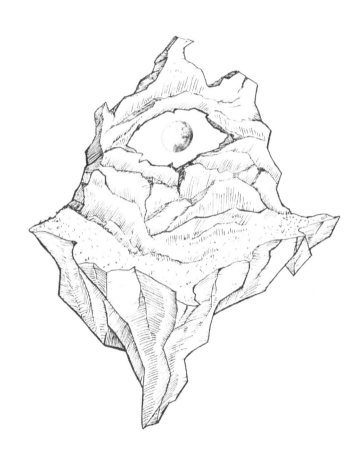

9

My sister is gone nights as well as days. My parents hope for an announcement. I despair. The paved Drameir is nothing to the hills of home. I miss the grass, the trees, the flowers. We revelled in life there. I can only feel Him in dreams now.
Diary of C. Aubethaan, est. early 8th century

T he cart hit another rock and Suri's bones rattled as she rubbed at the carved black symbols under her dress.

The Seer had added a new bond beside the first. A sand timer again, and a gemstone. King Thandul laid the new conditions. If she killed Kol, she may request anything in his power to give, other than that bestowed on him by blood. So, other than birthright, kin or further bonds, anything was fair game. The Seer nicked the King's wrist, and the ritual was complete. Not that she had any hope of using it.

The landscape changed with each passing day. From forests, outside the city walls, to become sparser green plains. For a while in the distance she would see clusters of woodland, and then those too went. The grass was the last life to go, the sprouting green trying to claw its way through drier and drier soil. Now, the soil was sand. Suri hadn't seen green for two days.

The sun wasn't high in the sky yet and already Suri was too warm. There was an oppressive stillness to the heat, her arms coated in dust.

It had been five days total, and the scenery wasn't all that had changed.

The smell, too, had ripened from a low level waft of unwashed recent exiles to a stench that rivalled her sewers. There was nothing for it, they were never let out of their cage. Dirt and filth covered Suri's dress. She wondered what the innkeeper's wife would make of her, the fine lady she'd given her dress to now sitting in the sweat and piss of seven people.

That first night, when the slaver had taken two buckets of ice cold water and sloshed them across the floor of the cage, the icy chill had left Suri shivering the whole night, her teeth chattering against the bite of the Northern winter night. She had cursed the slavers, her hands pushed into her armpits for the smallest amount of remaining body warmth. Now Suri craved the tepid bucket of water that would hit her skin later this evening. But there was a long time to wait.

She readjusted her position, the ache in her knees and legs unbearable. The need to stand and stretch filled her so completely that only sheer force of will stopped her from kicking at that cart door until she, or it, broke.

Deep into that first night, with numb fingers, when everyone had fallen into fitful sleep, she had taken the ring from her mouth and knotted it into her hair. She'd placed it near the bottom of her scalp and wrapped pieces of her hair from the nape around its band and gemstones until it was stuck. The rest of her hair fell over the top of it. The following days had only matted her hair more, lodging the jewellery into its position more firmly.

Most of her fellow exiles didn't speak.

Two teen boys, a few years younger than Suri, sat in the back. They could have been brothers, but their matching missing hands twinned them as blood never could. Thieves, like her.

She flexed her hands now, feeling a phantom pain and a tug at her stomach as she imagined that experience. The boys cradled the stumps day and night, the blood-soaked rags long dried and browned. The second day, one of them had a sweat on his skin that wouldn't leave. Now, on day five, he was barely conscious. His friend had taken his food the last two nights.

Then there was the old man, his eyes bulging with a watery sheen as he gazed at nothing. His gums slapped when he ate, and his breath whistled through his remaining teeth at night.

The only other woman sat with her calves poking out of the slats of the cage. She hadn't spoken a single word. Her hair sat in looped braids interwoven with wooden beads, her nails long and curved. She wore a single golden band around one wrist. Why hadn't the slavers taken it from her? They had deemed Suri's own plain metal earrings of no value and left them in place, but that looked far more precious.

To her right was a large, muscular man. He must be three times her width and nearly half again her height. Someone, or multiple someones, had broken his nose many times. He had warm brown eyes deep set into warm brown skin, framed by eyebrows that were too thin. He seemed fine. But he took up too much space, which meant less space for her. And that alone was enough to sour Suri against him.

Finally to her left, a skinny man, dressed in ill-fitting clothes.

"The name's Maggory," he had said on the second day. "What cause of will has shepherded you to this resplendent facility?"

She had studied him from head to toe and ignored him.

The long black coat with its red tails hung loosely over a baggy, lurid purple waistcoat. The golden handkerchief which draped from the pocket was now soaked through with sweat from his brow. A trickster perhaps, one who would convince her to enter some seemingly simple game of chance she could never win. "At least we are not condemned to the Storm Pan, eh!"

This time Suri did not even look at him.

The Storm Pan. A prison of almost legendary status. It existed somewhere south of the Forgelands, which to a Northerner was everywhere. It was an enormous plate of metal, some said almost as large as the Great North Lake. They would force the prisoners onto it, come rain or shine. Suri didn't really understand why it was so bad. A large metal plate didn't seem any worse than this carriage ride.

Maggory was met with repeated silence from the others, except for the old man, who had replied to him in an unintelligible mess of words.

Suri saw no need to form a friendship with her cage mates. They existed in the same space. There were no shared stories. Their silence was not companionable.

On the fourth night, the woman had killed the old man. She accused him of stealing her bangle and then strangled him to death. It didn't take very long. Perhaps this was why the slavers hadn't taken it from her. The slavers pulled him out in the morning and left his body in the desert.

Her only true company was that feeling. That thrum that she found again in the true cold of the first night. It was quiet. But it was there. She found if she concentrated on it, she could almost lose herself in it. The meter was so different from her pulse. It rubbed discordantly against her heart. Some nights she felt the voice too. The barest of whispers. A familiar comfort now. *Sweet Suri*, the lullaby would repeat. Calling her, embracing her.

Sometimes the noise would flicker across her skin like a small flame, startling her nerves. Sometimes a cold fingertip, dragging and pulling at her.

She dreamt of it, a formless shadow wrapping around her, tighter and tighter. She'd woken that morning before dawn with a gasp, the shadow of her dream holding her so firmly she felt she was losing the very breath from her body. Yet still she looked forward to the night. The thrill of the whispers was the only time when she could tune out this world. This foul smelling, endlessly jarring, and dream-crushing world.

Suri was grimly aware of her reality.

She had made enemies. Powerful enemies.

In three of Pereginus' four courts.

The Forgelands had exiled her. They had ripped her from the only home she had ever known. She was to be a stranger to the only city she understood for the rest of her life. If she returned with her conditions unfulfilled, the Bloodhounds would know. They would hang her if they were feeling kind.

The Guilds of the Pail would hear of Viantha's troubles. She would find no solace there.

And the Parched Lands, which grew ever closer under the unstable wheels below her. The King of this wasteland was not her biggest fan.

The weight of the hatred against her had Suri moving backwards a little into the shadowed middle of the cage, when she felt it slowing.

Careful, little thief.

Remembering Kol's words sent a shiver through her, despite the heat. She smiled. She had followed his instruction, to an extent. Her aim had been careful.

The only court she had yet to offend was that of Drangbor, the court where Queen Lera sat. The half-Fae woman was a legend and a paragon of faith. Not somewhere Suri could fit in. The Fae Glen didn't yet hate her specifically. But given their love of the ancient magics of blood and souls, going there wasn't an appealing thought. Rumour had it the Fae turned anyone who stepped in the forest uninvited into some unsavoury beast, from a roach to a vulture harpy. Those who avoided that fate were bound to dance until their deaths.

She looked out from her spot, hoping to see what had caused them to stop.

Made of sandstone and wooden balustrades, the guard tower was around three stories high. Suri squinted at the new building on her landscape, noticing that on top there were three guards, standing under the shade of some orange fabric pulled against the heat of the late morning sun.

At the bottom of the tower stood another guard, dressed all in white instead of the red of those at the top, who strode over to the slavers. She saw his weapon first, a short sword sheathed on his hip.

The clothing covered almost all the guard's skin, and had to be uncomfortable in the warmth. His tight-fitting, white long-sleeved top matched the baggy white trousers which creased into a tighter cuff at the ankle. A billowing white tunic had a brown sash and he wore a white hood. Only his hands and eyes were visible.

The wagon jolted forwards, before settling into its normal speed. As they rolled away from him, the guard murmured. "Welcome to your new home."

This was it, then. She was in the Parched Lands, lands that were as unfriendly as their pseudo-King.

They continued for a few hours more, passing guard towers with increased frequency. They must have passed at least eight within a few hours. Some were directly on the road. Some Suri saw in the distance, towers surrounded by a sea of nothing. What did they have to guard against?

Every swallow scratched at her throat like nails. They hadn't given her any water yet today. As she sat with her eyes closed against the oppressive warm air, she imagined the weight of a leather flask in her hands, bringing it to her cracked lips and pouring its contents down her throat. She would squeeze it as she lowered it and feel cold water overflow from the top. She pictured it pouring in trickling streams down her dirty fingers.

With a croaked sigh, she opened her eyes.

Looking down at her hands, it surprised her to see a couple of drops of moisture. She looked up, hoping the supplies strapped to the top of the cage had somehow leaked through. Nothing. It must have been sweat. The disappointment didn't have time to fully settle in, as Suri was once more distracted by the horizon.

In the distance, she saw two towers. One on either side of the path this time. And behind them, squat sandstone buildings in the distance.

The slavers stopped again. They jumped down and sauntered round to the cage, appraising their stock. One of them, the shorter man, pointed to one slave. The boy, the one with the fever.

He was dead.

Two down in a handful of days.

"Push him to the door," the man said. The larger slaver brandished his dull sword, as if they needed another threat. Where could they run to? The world around them was death itself.

The other boy and the woman dragged his dead body to the door. Suri moved out of their way as the corpse passed. His eyes were open and glazed over. When had he died? Had anyone noticed his passing?

With speed that belied the jowls under their chins, the slavers opened the door and removed the boy, before closing it again. The slavers examined their remaining cargo and threw several stale bread rolls into the cart. They then passed round flasks and Suri drank until he ripped hers from her grasp.

Not enough, not nearly. But the fire in her throat had lessened.

Finally, they brought the buckets out.

When they went in for a second round with the buckets, Suri felt lucky. When they came back for a third, throwing water on each captive's body, her sense of dread came back. The water hit her face and hair and chest, her hands and body. She rubbed her hands over her face, pushing the water against the grime and crusted salt. She squeezed the excess moisture out of her dark hair and into her hands, running the already dirty water across her arms.

A final round of water hit each of them. What profit was there in this, save to make the slaves more presentable?

They were priming their livestock.

She looked at the town in the distance with fresh eyes. Dragged once more towards some unknown fate. Who in this forsaken graveyard would find use for her?

10

*Sister tells me he plans to wed her. I must run
away. Be with Him and nature once more.*
Diary of C. Aubethaan, est. early 8th century

"Quite charming, is it not?" Maggory said to no one in
particular.

The town was small. A jumble of low lying structures, with
a couple of larger stone structures that rose higher into the
blistering air.

The road beneath them had changed to swept rock.
Coloured fabric in warm hues of red, burnt oranges and browns
hung from windows and across empty doorways, billowing out
onto the street.

The cart rumbled into a square and came to a stop. The
slavers jumped down and placed weights behind the cage
wheels, a move that felt final. Suri's dress and hair were dry
already.

A handful of people were setting up wooden stalls. Their arrival drew a couple of curious looks, but they soon looked away.

It was desolate. A ghost town. Surely they would find no trade here, there was no demand, no anything. They sat, their manacles clinking in the scorching breeze that teased respite, and they waited. Suri glanced at the stone building across from her, which had a carving across its exterior wall of a winged beast with a woman's head holding a knife. Her face contorted in some ugly way, and Suri wondered if it was a poor artistic impression of a winged Fae. Soon, the temperature dropped. The air eased to it, not quite a chill, but a blessed neutrality.

The ghost town came alive as the sun dipped lower.

A few people at first, joining the square and filtering into the larger buildings. Their fashions were much the same as the guards but less defined, airy tunics over leggings. There were other fashions too. Thicker, wider styles. Northern silhouettes with narrow waists. Streams of people started moving around the market stalls. A young woman lit a lamp hanging over the inn, The Cursed Sister, as waiting patrons filed in after her.

The people ignored their cage at first.

Suri had always enjoyed watching the flow of people, examining the ways they walked, moved, and spoke. The mannerisms that betrayed class or wealth, occasionally both. Postures that were relaxed or uncomfortable. Nervous ticks betraying the location of that which they didn't want to lose.

She tracked the movement of one woman weaving through the now busy square. She could tell she was coming towards their cage long before the woman raised her eyes to nod at the slavers. She looked to be in her forties. She wore the dress of the local people, but adapted. Over her cream shirt with flowing sleeves, she wore a cinched, dark blue corset. Her shirt parted at the neck, the top of the corset creating a full cleavage which was decorated with heavy gold necklaces in a variety of sizes. Gold bangles adorned her cuffed wrists and ankles. She wore no face covering. As she approached, Suri noted she had lined her eyes with blue and had three gold rings pierced through her bottom lip.

"You look well, Jom."

Her voice was husky. Practised, a cute ploy.

"As do you, Daiyu," the slaver replied, his voice wavering a fraction. She held him in hand, then.

Daiyu winked at him, then looked to the cage. Her subsequent examination was as thorough as eyes alone could be. She looked at every individual, eyes flitting, measuring against unknown metrics. When her eyes snapped to Suri, pausing on her eyes for a couple of seconds, then flitting to her narrow nose, thin mouth, cheekbones, dark hair, shoulders, chest, hands, hips, legs, and feet. A full inventory.

She then looked back at Jom. "I'll offer a good price for the two women and the big one," Daiyu said. "I'll even throw you a penance for the cripple boy."

Jom lounged on a faded draped chair to the side of the wagon and waved a bored hand at her. "I can't promise you nothing before the auction."

Daiyu smiled at him. "By the book, I like that about you."

Behind her, more lights turned on, lamps of yellow light that hung on strings across the square. The warmth of the golden artificial light duelled with the waning orange sun which had fallen to the tips of the rooftops.

Daiyu looked around and back at the slavers. "It would seem it is time."

More people filtered into the square, some walking in their direction. Half were guards, dressed in red. Half richly dressed: the would-be buyers of flesh. One by one, Jom dragged them out of the cage and chained them to posts.

Suri's legs stretched with a delicious pain.

But the sheer, simple delight of standing for the first time in days was soon lost. The crippled boy was sold first. Jom asked about his skills and the boy said nothing. The bidding started at two silver. He was sold for three silver and three.

She quickly did the maths in her head. Twelve bits in a silver. Thirty-nine bits.

She couldn't decide if that was a good price. Suri herself had amassed over forty at one point, so that must be low if even *she* could have *owned* a person. Humanity was worth so little in the end. What a life could give another, what they could take from each other. It was the way of things.

Daiyu had bought him. She smiled, and Suri couldn't decide if the woman reminded her more of a cat or a snake. She suspected Daiyu ran a whorehouse. A guard had bid against her. Buying slaves to use as guards? Surely, she thought, they could never be trusted. But then the population of the Parched Lands were all off-cuts. No one chose to come here. Perhaps the honourable *Lord* prevented them from leaving too, Suri thought. Owned for life.

A different person bought Maggory. An innkeeper? Something else? He was sold for four silver, even. He claimed some skill, but Suri couldn't make sense of his flowery response.

The burly man sold for six silvers to a matching large man.

Then, a disturbance caught her attention. Some figure in black rode into the square on a huge black horse. People jumped out of the way as he thundered to the centre and dismounted the horse. She couldn't make out his face.

Jom moved to Suri. "Now we have this lovely lady," he announced, with a hint of a jeer. "A beauty, eh, gentlemen? A *Northern* beauty at that, too."

She resisted the urge to spit on his foot.

He granted her a lascivious wink. "Just look at her fair skin. Dark, luscious hair. Those slate eyes could knock a grown man dead! Bit of a wash and she'd be a real treasure."

Suri had never in her life felt less treasured—less human—than in this moment.

Jom nudged her arm, and she sucked in a breath. The thrum in her blood pounded to the surface. She glanced at the guards, then down at the floor, releasing the breath. She couldn't kill him. They would execute her.

She couldn't kill him.

"What else can you offer to these fine folk?" he said.

She met his eyes and he perked up. She wondered what he expected her to say. Some choice words came to mind. None that would see her walking out alive, however.

With her chin raised, she looked away from him, staring out into the gathered crowd with venom.

After a moment, the slaver forced a laugh. "A silent woman! Never heard a complaint about that, eh?"

The crowd didn't respond to his attempt at a joke. She noticed they'd been largely silent, except for the bidding.

"Shall we start at four silvers for this little princess?"

Princess.

She almost choked on the irony of his pet name. Trying to be a princess had got her exiled here to begin with.

Daiyu took the opening bid, watching Suri as she raised her hand. "Four silvers."

Four silvers. A single bit more than the value she had amassed over weeks and months to change her life. And within a second, it was freely and casually offered. Offered in exchange for *owning* her.

She couldn't kill him. Or her. She couldn't do anything at all. She was powerless. A thing to be acquired. Nothing. No one. A body and a face.

What had been the point of every one of her struggles? Every day, she'd hurt others and herself just to stay alive? Her fists clenched as the reality of her situation set in.

She was being *sold*. There was no recourse for her. This was allowed, expected. In the eyes of the law, she deserved this. She was cattle.

"Any further on four?" Jom asked. She barely heard the disappointment in his voice as her ears rang.

Was she overvalued here? Undervalued? Did this woman know what she truly bought? A girl a few years into womanhood. An exile. Sister. Murderer. Fighter.

A failure.

Jom raised his hand, but movement came before he spoke again.

A man, the tanned, short one who had bought Maggory, stepped forward. "Four and a half."

Suri assessed him. Would it be a better fate than what Daiyu offered? Or far worse? She would struggle at every step, she told herself. She would not go gently into her new life. The most tiresome woman in this whole Trio-forsaken desert.

Daiyu rolled her eyes and played with one of her necklaces. "Give this one to me, Kurchin. Five silvers."

"Five silvers and a half."

The woman sighed. "Six."

Jom pointed eagerly. "That's six silvers for the lady. Do I hear a response, good sir?"

Kurchin grumbled a little but nodded. "Six and two."

"Seven."

"Going for seven. Any more?"

Jom's question rang out to a silent audience. The bidding swam behind Suri's ringing ears. She glanced up to confirm that yes, her would-be owner was Daiyu. A pleasure house, then.

An acid-like pain stung at Suri when she recalled two years prior, when another woman had offered her a whore's life. Not forced. A choice. She *knew* life in one of the many Tangle brothels. Many of the girls she'd grown up with had chosen it. The priesthood and prostitution. Two very different places with a near identical offering. A roof, a bed, some food, a few bits to spend. In exchange for worshipping some trumped up male a few nights a week. A great offer for a girl like her. And still a choice she had turned down without hesitation.

"No?" Jom checked.

It was never what she had wanted. It never would be. And now she had no choice in the matter. At least before, she might have had some agency. Some means of refusing a customer, some money of her own to spend. This was infinitely worse. Enslaved to a bed.

A thought slipped through the cracks of her fraying mind. She could end it all, before it destroyed her. Who she was. What she was.

"Alright, then this princess is s—"

"Eight."

The deep voice cut in from the back of the group.

The buyers turned. Her mind felt noisy and dark. A covered well in a thunderous storm. She blinked and looked up, eyes dry from her unblinking stare at the dusty floor.

She noticed his height first. When the buyers parted, he towered across the space, stepping to the front of the group of buyers.

He wore a black variant on the guard's clothing, the tight fabric on his arms doing little to mask the muscles underneath. He clenched his jaw, the line of bone carving out his face, his wide nose and dark eyes now boring into hers.

He was the rider. But that was not the title that mattered.

Jom stumbled over his words. "Your Grace, what a pleasure."

Kol's black eyes did not leave Suri's.

Jom tried again. "My most gracious welcome to our humble gathering. Did I hear you correctly, my lord?"

The Lord of Death's full mouth spread into a feral grin, but his gaze did not break. "You heard correctly. Eight silvers. For the *little princess*."

She was truly drowning now.

Careful, little thief.

He was the man who cursed this very land. She had forced him into a fight with the Northern Prince. And she had killed his man. And if she killed him... she could name her price.

The rage was coming off him like waves, as though she could feel the heat of it in her airways, suffocating her.

"My apologies, your Grace, I would not have tried to buy the girl if I knew you wanted her for yourself," Daiyu said.

Suri almost choked. For himself—?

No.

Kol's eyes finally moved away. He looked at Daiyu with a warmth he had not held for Suri. "Do not fret, Daiyu. I do not want her."

The statement landed on Suri, but she didn't react. What would he do to her? What *could* he do to her? She thought she had hit her very lowest, and he was digging beneath her feet.

Daiyu clucked her tongue. "Then why—"

Kol's dark eyes danced. He was enjoying this. "I bought her for Gwin."

"What?" Daiyu replied, her voice incredulous.

The large man hadn't moved since he'd bought her burly cage mate. But now he jolted. "My Lord—your Grace—you are serious?"

Kol smiled. "Deadly."

The scarred man looked confused. Suri watched, spending most of her energy trying to stay upright. She felt herself swaying. Who was Gwin? What path had he set her on?

Daiyu spoke again. "Your Grace, will you not reconsider? Don't throw her to Gwin and his dogs. She could do good work here."

Daiyu's concern did nothing to help Suri. Clearly, the whorehouse was nothing compared to this new horror. She couldn't stop the slight sway in her steps as she swallowed with a dry mouth.

Kol's smile dropped a fraction. "I disagree."

Gwin shook his head. "But sir, she is thin. Weak, ya see? I don't have any use for her."

Suri breathed in. Out.

"I can assure you," Kol said, with something close to a snarl. "She is not weak. Use her as you would any other recruit. No special treatment."

Use her. In. Out. Cattle. Nothing. No one.

"Yes, sir."

Kol reached into his pocket and threw a small pouch of coins at Jom. "She goes with Gwin."

Jom jangled the coins, and Suri caught the pleased line of his mouth as he felt the weight. "Of course, your highness."

With that, Kol turned his back and walked away from the rest of the auction.

A pause. A lull.

The auction then continued around her as Suri's blood pounded around her skull. Breathing proved to be almost too difficult for her. She tried to focus on it and nothing else.

In. Out.

She needed a plan.

Sold.

Kol had intervened to throw her to an even worse fate. The act of a royal, to come to a small trading post to crush the pitiful life she had left. Her anger and hate towards him bloomed so quickly, and so fully, that it distracted from the despair in her soul. She clutched onto it, holding that hate in her heart. It might be the only thing holding her soul together, keeping her human.

The echo of that voice from before. She clung to that too, its odd whispering her only solace. In. Out.

Swirling. Swaying.

Then Jom moved her, along with the larger prisoner, into a new cage. The others were all taken away. So her journey would continue, on towards wherever Gwin needed her to be.

Time passed. She was fed a plate of something mealy. The cage was washed.

She stayed in it all night. Watching the revellers in the square, not speaking a word. At one point, when it was clear no one was paying any attention to them, she took out the golden bangle she had stolen from the woman. She twirled it, watching it catch in the light, but could not think for the thrum and the rage.

She thought she slept at one point, but when she opened her eyes into the empty gauzy dawn air, she found that her nightmare was not over.

He was walking towards her.

He wore the same black outfit, but looked rough, his hair poking out at odd angles. As he strode towards the cage in that still crisp and dewy air, soon before the sun would chase it away, he looked debauched. Behind her the giant slept soundly, evidenced by a low rumble of a snore.

Kol stopped without ceremony, a couple of steps from her.

The proximity made her skin thrum with that same dark anger as before. The rage that had dissipated with exhaustion flew back into her and she struggled not to curse every facet of his being.

"You," he said.

"Me," she said.

Kol's gaze roamed lazily across her body and face, then settled back to her eyes. "So they caught you."

She nodded, scared of the venom of her response.

"They didn't execute you," he said. He had the gall to sound tired. Tired as *he* came to gloat over *her* slavery.

And that's what tipped her over the edge, sweeping her into the tidal wave of anger. He would not silence her. She was a person. A fucking person, not a thing to be bought and sold. "I too am surprised."

Kol stared at her. She didn't flinch.

"Why?" he asked, breaking the eye contact and pacing across the sandy floor. "What was the deal? Spy on me? Sell them information?"

The only reason he fathomed they could have let her live was to cause a problem to him, of course. And yet, it was true. She watched him and answered honestly. "Kill you."

Kol laughed. The chuckle that escaped him was real and yet so furious. He looked at her again, the weight of it like the desert sun, scorching and uncomfortable. "When my spies told me that you had been exiled, I couldn't believe it. I had to see it for myself. They didn't even *whip you* for it."

He spat the words with such venom, that for a moment Suri didn't know how to reply.

"I knew Shaedon was a witless worm, but I thought at least Thandul had an ounce of respect. But to find out that he sent you to kill me? The world has gone mad."

"Stranger things have happened," Suri said.

Kol's answering smile was dismissive. "So you intend to try?"

"Not right now."

His hand flexed at his side. "And why's that?"

Because they had chained her in a cage. Because she had no weapon. "I have no fight with you, your highness."

It was a lie. Before, her fight had been with Scilla and Barsen but that was now over. She'd killed him, and she'd paid for it with exile. It was done. She hadn't planned on finding Scilla or Kol and winning her freedom. It was next to impossible. Until Kol stepped into her already destroyed life with the sole intention of pushing her further into the dust. Oh yes, she had a fight with him.

The Lord chuckled again. The surrounding air hummed with a darkness that swore off the coming dawn. "No fight with me, just my closest allies."

Suri said nothing.

Kol paced the sandstone blocks. When he stopped, he dragged his hand through his black hair. Something dark tugged at Suri.

She would tear him apart. Just set her free and she would destroy him.

"Scilla told me. What they did to you," Kol said.

His voice was more measured. His eyes were blank. Why would he bring this up? Would he torment her by taking her through the brutal tale of their assault? Maybe he would tell her how they revelled in it.

"It was wrong," he said. "She had her reasons. But it was wrong."

Suri blinked.

"But, what you did? Killing him. That was wrong, too."

Well, at least that confirmed one thing. The guy was definitely dead. She noticed that the control he had over his voice wavered when he mentioned the death of his emissary. She had hurt him by hurting his *friend*. Should she feel remorse? She didn't.

This man was part-Fae, a Lord and Prince. People called him the Demon King. Living Death. Wrath's Body. And he wanted to speak to her about right and wrong?

It was an eye for an eye. Justice was never truer than that.

She had nothing to say to this tortured man. She did not grieve for his minion, and she would not give him the satisfaction of justifying her actions. If taken back to the same moment, she would throw the knife again. She thought she heard its voice, then. Louder than the thrumming whisper. It seemed to say, *And you will.*

Kol must have realised she would not reply, as he spoke again. "What is your name?"

Suri did not respond.

"Your name, girl. I know it is not Viantha."

"Edi."

Kol made a choking noise somewhere between a laugh and a cough. "You are determined to lie to me, then."

Her eyes flashed up at him. Her lie had fooled the King. How could he tell? A bluff, maybe.

Kol put his hand to the bar of the cage. "Tell me one thing."

Suri waited.

His voice was lower. "No lies."

Suri made no promise, instead staring at the tanned hand he had clenched so hard it whitened.

"When you threw your knife. At Bar—at him," Kol stuttered a little, and Suri enjoyed it. "Tell me. Did you intend to injure or to kill?"

She licked her dry lips, raking her eyes over the tension that was stamped across him. "Does it matter?"

Kol noticed her eyes, and his jaw clenched. "It matters."

Suri paused for a moment, staring at his black and soulless eyes. "I wanted to kill him."

As he dropped his grip, she saw them. Shadows. They stretched into the air in dark tendrils. Almost like vines. *Almost like hands,* another part of her thought. Then they were gone.

He spoke again, in a whisper. "Was it just you? Or were you—told to?"

Told to? She took no orders. She was part of no gang. That thrum moved inside her, caressed her, *tasted* her. Unless he meant—the voice? No. "My actions are my own."

Kol growled and reached his hand up, clenching it in the air before him, towards her.

She felt it, the shadow of his hand. Gripping, his thumbs and fingers pushing into her windpipe. She couldn't. Breathe. She clawed in the tiniest amount of air, but he squeezed it from her throat again. She pulled at the hand. Air. Nothing there. The pressure, she couldn't breathe. She. Couldn't. Her eyes bulged.

Then, nothing. She gasped, hunching on the deck of the cage, pulling in ragged gasps.

She rubbed her throat, as she looked at him with fog in her eyes. It wasn't the first time someone had strangled her and she doubted it would be the last. She refused to let him win.

So when he made eye contact again, she did not break it.

Again, he looked away first. "This conversation is over."

"Seeing as I can't leave," she said. "I'd consider it an interrogation, *your highness.*"

Kol glanced at her neck. "She will come for you. If the desert doesn't kill you first."

She could only assume he meant the other one. Scilla.

Bitch.

He clearly wanted that to be the final word, a lovely parting dagger thrown at her. Intended to scare her, silence her. Make her obey, perhaps.

Suri smiled. "So much to look forward to. The hospitality of your court has truly lived up to expectation, Lord Kol."

Kol's eyes darkened. "I could kill you. Right now."

Death. It was always death. The one big threat, given out more freely than any compliment. She lived each day on the edge of death. Since her exile, she had been a dead woman walking. She had contemplated her death a million different ways from when she was a child. Today, she had contemplated it coming at her own hands. What did he think his words would do?

A phantom of his hand touched her throat, stroking across the white skin. "It would be as easy as breathing," he said, with that hint of dark mirth again.

"Why don't you?" she replied. Suri leaned into the hand. It disappeared.

Kol's face lost all expression. Blank. Nothing. Something about that sent a chill down her spine. When he spoke again, his words were a poison, set to kill over hours and days and weeks. "Because you are alone. You are thirsty. You are hungry. You have no friends. You have no family. No one is coming to save you."

Suri did not move.

Kol did not stop. "You are death. You are nothingness and joylessness. Killing you would be a blessing. It would give you *meaning*." He glanced at her, her wooden cage, the buildings in the square. "But this, your suffering, your slow disintegration. This is your death. You're living it right now. Hour by hour."

Suri was as still as the bars that caged her.

Kol leaned closer. "And when you eventually die. Days from the place you called home. Days from the place that exiled you and cast you out." The Lord of Death sneered, delivering his parting blow. "No one will remember you."

That was a lie. She could feel it.

Did he feel it too?

11

Another ball. Mother and father insist I must go.
I will do my duty to them. I pray each hour to my
Diophage. He whispers back, and I feel stronger
with His voice.
    Diary of C. Aubethaan, est. early 8th century

T he first blessing was that Gwin gave them double rations.

    Suri wolfed them down, trying to ignore what this must mean for their end destination. They needed to be strong, for whatever it was.

The second, the cage had wooden beams protruding from the roof with lengths of fabric tied between them. It cast the floor in a glorious shade.

The big man's name was Narth. He was a murderer, too.

On the second day since leaving the outpost, the midday heat left them both lying on their backs, panting. Sweat dripped on

Suri's brow and pooled in her armpits. She didn't dare move. Here, if she stayed still, she couldn't feel the way her clothes stuck to the wooden slats, the way her hair itself was wet against her neck.

Her anger at Kol had faded after he'd left. She had tried to put that down to exhaustion, or simply that looking at his face was the primary reason for her anger. But it was more than that. It was him, his shadowed darkness that had called to her own darkness.

Whatever will for revenge burned inside her. Maybe it burned in him, too. The hatred felt less strong now, like she'd burned through all the fuel he'd given her, and now the fire was just smoking embers in her mind.

"Did you leave people up there?"

She had taken to replying to Narth now. There was nothing else to do.

"No," she said, not moving anything but her mouth.

The slightest fraction of a breeze passed over her. The cool air touched her face, highlighting the moisture covering her from her bottom lip down to her ankles.

"Did you?" Suri asked, delayed.

"Yeah," he said.

She found her eyes glazing over as she focused on the air itself. Sometimes there were swirls, like she could see the heat sitting and moving through the invisible spaces. Her eyes focused in and out of the absent spaces.

"Do they have someone?" she asked.

"My sister is there. She might help," he replied.

"Good."

She closed her eyes against the endless nothing.

"He doesn't like you very much, does he?" Narth said.

She blinked her eyes back open. "Who?"

"The Death Lord."

Suri snorted. "No, he doesn't."

Narth clicked his tongue. "That's bad luck."

Suri laughed, a single bark. "Yes. Yes, it is."

Another warm breeze swept across their bodies. "He killed my parents."

"What?" Suri said. She turned to look at him, propping her head on her damp arm.

He stared up at the cloth roof. "Fifteen years ago. They ran spices from Drameir to New Politan. He executed their group. Nearly twenty people."

"I'm sorry," Suri said.

"It was a long time ago."

"You're certain it was him?" she asked.

"The eyes," he said. "They were black. Just black."

She didn't ask him to explain. She didn't have to.

Death magic. The signature for killing with that kind of magic. It did something to the bodies when a shadow killed them. Kol was known for it. He was the only one barbaric enough for the practice. She was lucky that she would at least die by her own toil far from him, rather than become another one of his shadowed corpses.

Her mouth was stale. She reached out and grabbed the flask that Gwin had left in their cage, replenishing it every few hours. She poured a mouthful of hot water into her mouth and tried to feel relief from it.

The call from Gwin made Suri sit up, her dress peeling from the cart. "Ho!"

The call wasn't irregular. Neither was the way the wheels slowed to a stop. Gwin usually stopped to speak to any passing caravans. For Suri, it was something, anything, to break up her day. Something new to hear, see, someone new to analyse.

But what she saw *was* something irregular.

The caravan itself, or convoy—since there were three—was not novel to Suri. She'd seen this style before, in New Politan. Silvery wooden beams bolstered the caravans. The wooden sides of the carts were painted in shades of grey and muted purple.

Priestesses of the New Gods.

These were their colours, and on the fronts of the approaching vehicles was their symbol. The diamond shape hovering above a cupped bowl.

They were so out of place here, rumbling down the swept stone road, surrounded on every side by a bleached wasteland.

Lord Kol allowed the Priestesses here? He was a pagan. His very birth was in worship of Sotoledi, the Old God of Death. He *created* this wasteland, and now he allowed the Priestesses of the Trio here. To do what? Fix his mess?

For a moment, Suri thought the priestesses weren't going to stop.

They did, though, the first wagon coming to a halt just past their cage. Out of the second carriage, a woman opened a small door set into the side. Her priestess robes were immaculate, her face fresh. She smiled.

"Good afternoon, traveller."

"Good afternoon, Priestess," Gwin replied. "How fare ya?"

The Priestess nodded. "Our party fares well, thank you. And yourself?"

Gwin's gruff voice came back. "Well enough. Not sure these two would agree."

The Priestess glanced at the cage then. Suri caught her eye for a fraction.

"Are you headed to the iron mines?" The Priestess said.

The iron mines? The Parched Lands had mines?

"Aye, lady. Any news?"

Fuck.

That's what Gwin did. That's where they were going. Mines. That was why Gwin didn't want her. He knew it would break her in a matter of days. Working hours and hours in this heat. Day after day, until her back broke or her lungs gave out. No, that was what Kol wanted for her.

Suffering and slow disintegration.

She hadn't given enough thought to where she was going. Mining was a painful and slow death, the primary form of punishment in the Forgelands. Most of them never came back. Esra hadn't, and it had been ten years.

Here she was, in a cage, being pulled towards a fate worse than that. Not only the mines, but the mines *here*, in the land where nothing lived. Where any hope of escape would mean dying of thirst instead.

"More sandstorms, traveller. We could not get near. I bid you better fortune."

Or death by sandstorm, in a mine, apparently. The Lord of Death had done his job well.

"Thank you, Priestess."

She refused to admit it was over. She wouldn't submit to the path of her destruction he had laid for her.

The Priestess nodded and moved to close the door.

"Priestess!" Suri called out. She tried to not be embarrassed by how her voice rasped.

The elegant woman looked at her, then back to Gwin.

"Shut it, girl!" Gwin called.

"Please Priestess," she called. "I am a Princess!"

The Priestess looked at Suri with a quizzical brow, appraising. "What is the meaning of this?"

"Ignore the girl," Gwin said, thumping the roof of the cage. "Last warning, or I'll gag ya."

Suri pulled herself to the front of the cage. She slipped the golden bangle onto her wrist, hoping it would somehow help her case. "I am Princess Viantha Waterborne! I was betrayed in the North."

Gwin jumped down from the front of the cart. "That's it!"

"Viantha? Of the Pail? What is the meaning of this claim?"

Suri kept speaking, barely thinking ahead of the words that spewed out of her. "I am promised to the Priesthood. Please. Take me with you. Ask your Queen. Ask Queen Lera! She is expecting me in Drameir! If you leave me here, she will know. I will send word from the mines. There will be consequences!"

Gwin grabbed Suri's arm and pulled her, wrenching her hands from her grip on the bars. Raising one ham fist, he slapped her across the face. "There will be consequences indeed, girl."

The slap made Suri's eyes water, yet Gwin was holding back. There would be far worse to come when her charade was dismissed. But she had to try. It was a chance of death here or a certainty of death there.

She called out again. "I am Viantha. Your duty calls on you to help me. I am promised!"

Gwin slapped her again. "Shut your mouth, girl."

Suri blinked through the shock of pain in her face and jaw.

"What do you say of this, keeper?" The Priestess called out.

"Move along. This is nothing but a stupid girl playing make believe. I will deal with her."

The Priestess had turned to look behind her, speaking in hushed tones.

"Ask them, ask them," Suri cried, getting the priestess' attention once more. She pointed to Narth, who was sitting up watching her with wide eyes. "He saw me brought to the cage by the royal guard. The Lord, the Lord Kol! He called me princess. He knows me."

Suri flinched for a slap that didn't come. Gwin did not loosen his vice grip on her arm, but he did not hit her again.

Narth coughed. "The royal guard brought her, Mister Gwin."

Gwin groaned. "Not you, too."

The Priestess hesitated. "You," she addressed Gwin. "What do you know about this? Is she what she claims?"

"Unlikely, my lady. His Lordship *did* speak to the girl, but why would he sell a princess to me? Must be a pack of lies."

The Priestess nodded. "Well, we have tarried long enough. Since the girl has no further proof, then we must be o—"

"And what of my ring?" Suri called. "If I could show you my ring, would that prove my identity?"

"What ring, girl? You have no such trinkets," Gwin said.

The woman's eyes focused on Suri's hands, then went to her neck. "It would help. But I see no ring."

"Girl has nothing on her but this filthy dress and her very skin," Gwin called back.

Suri breathed in and then out. She tried to remember how Viantha would speak. Slower. More deliberate. "My amefyre ring. The only one of its kind. Forged specifically for the heir of the Water Guild. Would you believe me then?"

The Priestess turned back for a moment, speaking a few words, then turned and nodded. "If you have it, I will believe your story."

Gwin let go of her arm. "Go on, show her."

Gwin's voice was not unkind. It was pure frustration and disbelief. Frustration at having to deal with a lying girl and maybe disbelief that the same lying girl was about to conjure something from nothing but skin and hair.

And conjure she did.

With weak hands, Suri pushed her fingers into the knots of her hair, feeling past the matted exterior. She wiggled her index finger until she felt it hook into that loop of metal. She twisted and tugged and eventually ripped, feeling some strands of her hand tear from their roots in her impatience.

Gwin saw it first and gasped, stumbling back.

Narth saw it next, his look of total shock only lessened by his lack of eyebrows.

The priestess saw it finally, and her eyes gleamed. Another face, the person the priestess had been speaking to, looked out of the window. He was handsome, with long silver hair hanging straight down. His eyes roamed over her, before squinting at the ring.

Suri held it, pinched between her forefinger and thumb, and stared at the pair.

The man spoke a few words under his breath, before the priestess cleared her throat and addressed Gwin. "Traveller, you are illegally harbouring a woman of royal birth, intended for the Priesthood. I demand you release her into our care immediately."

"Yes, Priestess," Gwin said, his voice not as firm as it had been.

Suri put the ring back on her finger. It brought with it the chill that belied the surrounding air, a weight to it that its mass did not explain. She held her hands out to Gwin to undo the chains. He clacked the key in the lock and the manacles fell from Suri's wrists and clattered onto the floor of the cage. His small pig-like eyes lingered on the ring.

"Sorry," he said. No title, no grovelling. More than she expected.

He opened the cage, watching Narth warily as Suri climbed out. She wanted to run, leap, stretch. She wanted to dive into the carriage, in case they changed their minds. Instead, she tried to carry herself as a lady, keeping her chin high and her eyes level.

It was only when she caught Narth's eye, and he granted her a companionable wink, that she felt something true. A pang in her chest.

Suri did not have friends. She was alone, and she liked it that way. But Narth had been kind to her, had spoken to her with an equality and simplicity she enjoyed.

"And my bodyguard?" she said, throwing the question to the priestess.

"What now, lady?" the priestess said.

It was a risk; she knew that. But she had to try.

"This man is my hired protection," she said, waving a shaky hand to Narth. "He will come, too."

Gwin growled. "He will not!"

The priestess held up a hand. "Surely, he is being held for his own crime."

"Only the crime of being associated with myself."

Gwin made a noise, which was half barked laughter and half choke. "I bought this man with my coin. Take the girl, fine. You cannot take him!"

The priestess turned away, again in some silent and unseen consultation. "She has proven her identity. The man we cannot vouch for or feed. He will remain."

Suri looked at Narth. She'd been avoiding his eyes since the moment she'd lied on his behalf. His eyes were warm, surprise coating his expression.

"Leave, princess," he said.

Suri understood, but it didn't lessen the pain. She turned back to the priestess. "Surely—"

"No," she said. "Time marches on, and the sun is hot. Let us be on our way. Come."

There was no room for negotiation. That was it. It was as if she had sealed his fate herself, as Kol had sealed hers.

He would die in the mines. She hadn't done enough.

A wave of emotion threatened her, and she suppressed it, pushed it down beneath the thrum. She clenched her fists so tightly that the crescents of her nails carved into her flesh. She breathed. "Thank you for your help, Priestess," she said, as she reached the little door.

This was who she was. A liar and a thief. She could only try to keep herself alive. This flesh and bones. This breath. The only things she was responsible for. She could pretend to be someone else for a time, try on a mask or two. But she would never be a saviour. Not to Narth. Not to anyone.

"Welcome aboard, my lady."

12

*The King's eyes followed me all night. My sister
has not spoken to me since.*
Diary of C. Aubethaan, est. early 8th century

Suri climbed the two wooden steps and entered the carriage. As the door closed, a cold wave passed over her. She couldn't fathom as to the source.

"My name is Priestess Manira," said the Priestess, the holy woman's gaze taking her in from her hair to her dirty, bare feet.

Priestess Manira was the tallest woman Suri had ever met.

The carriage was opulence itself. It moved, and the motion was smooth. Purple and grey rugs covered the floor of the cabin, and they blinded the windows against the warmth of the day with fabric curtains.

"Viantha Waterborne," she said, with a curtsey. "Where does your party travel to?"

"We are making our way back to Drameir. It is a few days' ride from here," Manira replied.

She was blessed then. A few days later, she would find herself safely transported to the one place that didn't seek her death. She would sneak out somewhere near the border of Drangbor, long before they reached Drameir.

She would live, after all. Kol was wrong.

Suri looked at her surroundings again. A network of narrow brass pipes lined the room. They had a white film to them, and her gaze traced them around the compartment.

"The pipes are lined with ice, Princess Viantha."

The man stood just behind her right shoulder and smiled when she turned to him. He was shorter than the Priestess and a little taller than her. "To keep the carriage at a pleasant temperature."

His silvery hair was so shiny it caught her eyes like a piece of finely crafted jewellery. He was as pale as the grave, but somehow it looked other, ethereal, not corpse-like. His eyes were brown and his features delicate. Fitted maroon and grey tailored trousers clung to him, and a black cravat was tucked around his neck, which Suri found obscene given their environment.

"But how? How do they stay cold?" Her curiosity was genuine. There was no way they could have been in these parts for days and had anything approaching cold, let alone frosted, pipes.

He grinned and pulled off an elegant grey suede glove, holding his clean hand out to her. Was this some invitation to go elsewhere? To their store of ice? Was she to kiss it? Curtsey?

He winked. "If you would touch my hand, *Viantha*."

He'd said her name like it was a secret, a promise. Perhaps he knew something or suspected something. She reached towards his hand, her clammy and dirty hand looking terrible in comparison. She hesitated at the perfection of his skin.

"Please," he said.

And since he'd asked again, and he was clearly a man of some status to be accompanying this troupe of priestesses, she pressed her hand to his.

It was cool to the touch and soothed the clammy warmth of her own hand, which had felt itchy in the heat.

"Remarkable," she said, because she felt she should. Though she knew little of what she was supposed to take from this.

The man suddenly moved his other hand, trapping her small grimy hand between his palms. Before she could protest, she felt it.

True cold ice on her hands.

His icy cold grip stripped the heat from her hand, from her very blood. Her hand went from chilled to painfully cold in an instant. He didn't stop, the ice freezing her from the fingertip to the wrist. She gasped, feeling the chill up to her elbow and barely stopping her knees from buckling under the cold. She almost cried out, biting her lip to keep the shriek in.

Then he let go.

She pulled her frozen hand back to herself, rubbing some warmth into it. It wasn't blue, thankfully.

He laughed. A deep laugh. The Priestess didn't smile or laugh.

"You see? I'm the how."

Suri appraised him once more as he put the glove back on. She tried to give no sign of her pain. "You're a water manipulator?"

He met her eyes and tilted his head with a smaller smile. "That's the boring way to describe it."

When she'd seen him before, she hadn't seen him truly. She'd seen that his shoulders were narrow, his frame wiry. She'd seen his handsome and unscathed face. This was a face that was not battle weary, skin that had not been drawn haggard by starvation. She'd seen a powerful, but weak, man.

She had been wrong. The backs of his hands had drops of sweat, now frozen in place after the pain he had knowingly inflicted.

"And anyway," he said to her. "From what I hear of Ressa's heir... so are you."

This man was no prey. He was a predator like her.

Viantha Waterborne was a water manipulator, then. She hadn't told her.

She realised at that moment how stupid she'd been. Of *course,* Viantha hadn't told her she was a water manipulator. Suri had locked her up in a damn sewer. She probably knew she could use that ability to escape as soon as Suri turned her back. Damn it all.

Yet this man knew. Or perhaps, was trying to catch her out by admitting to a power Viantha did not in fact possess.

She would have to be careful. "You must allow a woman her secrets. Lord...?"

He bowed, not breaking eye contact. "My deepest apologies for not introducing myself, princess. I am a special advisor to Her Grace, Queen Lera of Drangbor."

Suri nodded. He had not given her his name. Only his title. Whether this was deliberate, she couldn't say. "A pleasure. What brings you to the Parched Lands?"

"Diplomacy," he said.

She held his gaze. "It must be so diverting to visit new places."

"Indeed, princess."

Suri looked at the Priestess, who was watching them impassively. "Priestess, I hate to press on your generosity further, but you see my appearance...?"

Manira blinked and then smiled. "Of course. Follow me."

Suri was led into a smaller compartment of the same carriage.

There were two wooden cots fastened to the floor with simple wooden chests at their feet. More rugs cushioned the floor and two circular windows let in light from behind purple gauzy curtains.

"This is my sleeping quarters," the priestess said before pointing to the chest in the small, but densely furnished, area. "There is spare clothing in there."

Priestess Manira waited in the doorway. Behind her, Suri saw the advisor had moved to sprawl across one chair in the corner of the other compartment. He dragged his fingertip along a brass pipe as he watched them.

She knelt beside the chest, looking at the folded clothing inside. Garbs of the Priesthood. She'd never had the time or patience for belief in something bigger. There never seemed much point and now it was just a means to an end. Another mask to keep her alive.

"We travel fast, and off the roads. We will stop at an inn for a proper rest once we reach Drangbor," the priestess said.

"Thank you," she replied, still on her knees.

"We are at your service, Princess," Manira said with a smile.

Suri made a habit of watching people. Perceiving their emotions, their mannerisms, their tells. Him, she could tell, he was dangerous. She could tell nothing of Manira.

"And I yours," she replied, not knowing if that was the right response. She knew so little, yet her life depended on it.

The Priestess left the compartment, closing the padded wooden door behind her. Suri fell back into a comfier sprawl and let herself breathe as she felt the smooth movements of the wheels beneath her.

Off the roads. Why? She would spend no more time here than she had to, if given the option. Perhaps they didn't want to pick up any more strays like her between here and Drangbor.

And the advisor. He could kill her with a touch. She remembered Kol, and how he could kill with a twist of his fingers. Maybe this advisor could kill her without touching too. Could he kill her without seeing her? Could he feel her warmth from here?

Suri pushed herself to her feet and moved to the pail of water in the corner. It could very well be poisoned. She had no way of telling. She dipped a finger in the water, followed by her hand. It was cool, soothing. Not icy. When she brought her hand out, the water looked clear. There was a faint smell of rose.

She cleaned herself as thoroughly as she could from head to toe and, when she got to her wrist, she paused, feeling her pulse scatter under the thin skin. She breathed in and out.

Nothing.

She hadn't practised. She hadn't had time. There was still that other beat, that other thrum that she always felt, that made her question what she was reaching for. But there. She picked out the string that was her, her heartbeat. So faint, she could barely hear it. She focused on it and tried to follow Mother Edi's advice.

Lose it all. Stop thinking so much. Feel.

Remembering the words cast a pang of longing through her chest. She realised then how much she relied on Mother Edi, how much she took her presence for granted. Mother Edi was always just there, in that basement, with her taciturn support and old bandages. Family, in a way. The only one she had now after Esra. Esra...

Lose it all. Stop thinking so much. Feel.

She stopped thinking about her family, or what might remain of it. Stopped paying attention to her sopping hair, as it dripped cold water onto her thighs. She stopped thinking about the many people trying to kill her.

Instead, she thought of Mother Edi. Narth. Esra. She was Suri. This was her body. She was alive and she would survive this. Minutes passed before the beat was strong enough to risk tracing. She moved her hand in a touchless caress up her arm, to the corner of her elbow. Soon she reached her heart, still feeling it, and let herself relax, pressing her hand to her chest.

She washed until the water in the pail was dirtier than she was before dressing in the clothing of the Gods.

The thought came to her so suddenly then—almost a prayer. She would not die in the Parched Lands.

It was a promise. Borne of pure stubbornness maybe. But she whispered to herself, nonetheless. "I will not die here."

If she were to die, so be it. But not here, not in the dunes of this forsaken wasteland. Anywhere else, anywhere at all. She would not let him be right.

Not here.

13

The Kingsguard found me in the shrine. They bade me report to the castle this night. I will not go.

Diary of C. Aubethaan, est. early 8th century

"What are they doing?" Suri asked.

In front of her, in the waning light of dusk, four priestesses swayed in a loose formation. Manira stood to the side, reading a small silver-backed book. Suri stood next to her. The three carriages had come to a stop an hour or two prior, deep into the afternoon and past the hottest point of the day. One held the priestesses, another guards.

"They are worshipping, Princess," Manira replied, snapping the book closed. Suri glanced at the cover. *Creatures of Greater Peregrinus.* An interesting choice for a priestess, Suri would have expected some holy text.

She looked past the swirling women for a moment to focus on the guards. Their clothes were similar to the guards in the North, except the stiff uniforms were silver instead of red. She'd noticed earlier that all the carriage drivers were guards, too. Eight guards accompanied the party of five priestesses and the advisor. Considering the advisor was a force to be reckoned with in his own right, this seemed an overly large amount of security.

She was missing something. Then there were the wary looks from the guards. They were not happy to have found her, that much was certain. Why? One more to protect? One more to feed? She moved her eyes back to the dancing priestesses and fiddled with Viantha's ring. *Worshipping*.

They'd taken their head veils and gloves off first, and stood with heads bowed in low conversation. Then, from nothing, something flowed. Watching them now felt private, their bouncing locks seemed indecent. She almost looked away, but the rhythm of their movements was fascinating.

They would take it in turns to spin at the centre as the other three stepped around them. Then, the one in the centre took from her bodice a small knife with a white handle before pressing the blade to her bare palm. That thrum in Suri's body thudded at the cut. The priestess removed the knife to show a small laceration, a red line which blossomed into a flowering puddle of blood. She outstretched her hand, spinning in opposing motion to the rest, and brushed her bleeding hand against the hand of the others.

"Why do they bleed themselves?" she asked the Priestess, unable to stop herself.

The priestess, with the cut hand, swapped with another who performed the same movements. As the woman cut into her palm, Suri *tasted* the metallic tang of the blood in her mouth. She'd bitten into her own lip as she watched and was tasting her own blood.

"Our blood is life, salt, truth," Manira said, not looking away from the worship. "We bleed for our Gods as a symbol that we are all nothing but flesh."

Nothing but flesh. It was a truth that she knew well. But, it was not so for all. The advisor, Kol, Queen Lera. What were they? Flesh was not all. Fae blood, magic from the Gods. They were not all equal.

"We show our weakness," Manira continued. "And in turn, we ask for strength."

Suri watched Manira. "And do the Gods reply?"

At this, Manira looked down at Suri. "There are many ways to reply."

And that was one of the most evasive ways to reply. It sounded exhausting, to spend a life chasing signs, deciphering a meaning in something so intangible. If Suri couldn't spend it, eat it, or kill it, she didn't know what to do with it.

"I am surprised that Lord Kol allows you to pass through his lands, Priestess," she said.

"Are you acquainted with his Lordship?"

Suri shrugged, realising too late that was probably not something princesses did. "Very little. I speak only of his... reputation."

Manira nodded, looking back in front of her. "Leaders from every part of Greater Peregrinus have signed the Holy Treatise. To allow us to move through the lands uninhibited, to promote good and root out evil," she said. "The Parched Lands are no exception."

"You are treated well here, then?"

Manira smiled, but there was a hint of tension there. "We may move through the lands uninhibited."

So that was a no. Suddenly, Suri felt everything slip into place. The group had stopped in the middle of the day, rather than overnight. They travelled heavily guarded and had been reluctant to stop for Gwin. The Priesthood were scared. Scared of Kol.

"Is that why you do not wear your rings?" Suri questioned, pieces dropping in line as she thought through their strange methodologies. "Why you've diverted from the roads? The guards? You feel you'll be attacked, robbed?"

He was a bully. A tyrant. These priestesses couldn't even use the roads. Because of him.

Manira's expression barely shifted. "Your curiosity does you credit, princess."

Suri's frustration rose. Why wouldn't they speak straight to her? It was clear they were fearful. Why would they not admit it to her? They must believe who she was, or why would they have taken her in? So then, why would they not trust her? It's not like Viantha Waterborne had any allegiances to the Lord of Death. As far as they were aware, he had sentenced her to the mines. "I want to help."

"The best way you can help us is by staying safe. You've had an ordeal. Rest for a while."

A firm refusal. Of course, they believed she was Viantha. A double-edged sword. She had to convince them she was capable. She didn't need to be coddled away like a useless princess. "Priestess, I am sure that I—"

Manira interrupted her, before she could get any further. "You have been shown your quarters, yes?"

"I have," Suri responded, confused by the shift.

Once they had set up for their rest, one priestess had pointed out a whole compartment in the third carriage that she was to use. By herself. It was obscene.

"Are they comfortable?" Manira asked.

"They are very comfortable, Priestess," Suri answered.

"That is good. Let's speak when you have rested."

Worse than a refusal. It was a dismissal.

Suri tried to keep her cool as she walked with the little grace she could muster into the third carriage. She closed the outer door with care, before stomping through to her compartment and shoving the interior door closed behind her.

She was to be treated like a princess in every way then. A useless prize to be protected for a Queen that wasn't really expecting her. If she could just get them to see the injustice themselves. If she could get them to act against Kol and his men, she could help them. Maybe as a group, they could have a fighting chance of killing one of them.

If you kill the Lord of Death, girl, you can name your prize.

King Thandul's words came back to her, swirling. It felt impossible then. What chance could an exiled slave have to even meet him again? As a princess, however, in a well-armed caravan...

Manira would not listen to her today, so she would have to consider how she might make a stronger appeal tomorrow. Suri sat heavily on the bed with a huffed sigh. She looked up and caught her reflection in the round, mirrored metal across the compartment.

Her dark hair was clean, even neat. She had found a bristled brush to drag through her matted locks as she washed, and now it hung in a sleek, dark bob, just past her shoulders. She wore gloves, bearing the impression of the ring beneath. The soft and loose clothes hid the worst of her, the injuries and the skinniness.

She looked like a lady. And the lady's eyes were filling.

She pulled the clothing off her body, until she stood in nothing but a thin chemise and underwear. She tugged the ring from her finger and slammed it down on the nearest table.

Ragged breaths filled and left her as she found herself in the mirror. Found herself, as she stroked her along still visible ribs. Found herself in the rainbow of bruises on her arms and legs.

She drifted forward, until she was standing an arm's length in front of her reflection. She found herself in her silver eyes, her thin mouth. That thing was back, that thrumming. That felt like her too—comforting, something she'd had before.

She closed her eyes and let herself feel it.

Days from the place that cast you out.

Being ripped from her home. Mother Edi, the only person left she cared about.

You are alone.

That boy's stony expression as he lay dead a foot away from her.

You have no friends.

Narth.

No one is coming to save you.

And him, of course, in all of it. Kol's words.

She clenched both hands into her hair. He saw her as a child. A pathetic girl who didn't know what she was doing. What was she supposed to do next? She wanted to plead, to scream, to cry. But he was right. She had no one to turn to, no one to trust. If only Esra was back. He would know what to do. But he was still in the mines. Or worse, he was out, and he thought she'd left him. He was all alone, like she was. Like she'd been for nearly a decade.

Please, she thought.

She didn't know what she needed. But she wanted, more than anything, to feel less alone, for even a second.

Please, she thought again.

Suri.

She opened her eyes at the deep murmur.

In her reflection, she saw something. Darkness, but formed. Her heart juddered, the blackness like ropes of shadow coalescing. Into a person. No?

She turned. There was nothing there. She looked back into the mirror, but nothing was behind her. It was the voice. She felt sure of it. It had spoken to her. It had some physical form. What was it?

"Who are you?" she asked aloud, wiping the tears from her face.

All.

The deep reply seemed to reverberate in her head. The sensation was strange.

She took a couple of uncertain steps and sat back on the bed, pushing herself into the corner of the cabin, so she could watch the whole compartment.

"All of what?" she murmured.

I will not hurt you, sweet Suri.

His voice, for now it seemed like a *him*, reminded her of a void. The kind she had made as a child by pressing the heels of her palms into her closed eyes. That slightly painful and yet comforting swirling darkness. It spoke and echoed in her head, leaving an aftertaste of nothingness.

"How do you know me?" she asked.

I watch.

She was underwater, unhearing, unfeeling.

"You wanted me to kill him," she said.

The voice at the ball had encouraged her and enjoyed it.

And you did, he said.

The voice was a purr, a compliment.

"I don't know what I'm doing," she said.

A noise from near the carriage. The exterior door opening. It was quiet. It was likely one priestess, trying not to wake her. She watched the door, regardless, as she listened for a response.

A couple of footsteps from outside the compartment.

Find a weapon. The door. Now.

There was an urgency in the voice, no room to argue. She scampered to the edge of the bed and looked for a weapon, anything she could use. There was nothing, nothing sharp, nothing.

Fuck.

She saw the handle of the door move just a fraction. With the lightest steps she could, she moved to stand behind the door as whoever was coming lowered the handle with extreme care.

The door was pushed wider as Suri let out shallow breaths.

A shoulder moved into the room. A guard's uniform.

He must have seen into the room and realised that there was no princess lying on the bed. He hesitated and she thought, for a moment, that he might leave altogether, until he pushed further and wedged her behind the door. He strode into the room, looking at the closed window and empty bed, but she didn't recognise him.

He was holding a knife.

So, they wanted to kill her. The Priestesses wanted to kill her. Why? Had they worked out she was an imposter? Still, to send a guard to murder her while she rested. Could she not have even a moment?

Damn it all.

Suri threw the door closed, slamming it on its hinges and the shock of the noise made the guard jump and turn. He raised the knife, but Suri was already on him. She leapt and thrust her elbow down on his wrist, making him drop the knife. It clattered to the wooden floor.

Yes, my sweet.

She shoved the heel of her left palm up into his face and felt the impact, as she crushed it against his nose. The bones broke and the man screamed in anguish. Suri screamed back, raging against this fucking world that wouldn't let her exist. Then she dived away from him, back onto the floor.

Her eyes pinned on the glinting white knife, as she crawled along the floor. Her hand stretched out to reach it, but he grabbed her ankle, pulling her back. She clawed her hands into the wood as he yanked her backwards, twisting onto her front, just as the guard straddled her body and pinned her hands to the floor.

She wriggled and tried to escape, gasping under the sheer weight of him. The guard looked at the knife, then back to her. He moved his hands from hers and grabbed her throat. He pushed hard, but she had her hands.

She could punch him, pinch him. Surely. Something.

She punched him in the gut.

Once. Twice.

Nothing. He continued to press on her. The pressure on her throat, her head, was going to explode. She needed air. She would not die here. Suri pulled up his padded tunic and jabbed her fingers at his sides.

For a moment, his grip around her neck loosened.

She gasped in a strangled breath and thrust her hips upward, the motion making the guard lose his balance and topple across her. She wrenched herself from his grip and pushed herself along the floor, as he regained his balance. He clutched the back of her chemise and pulled her back. She spun and watched his face as she pushed the knife deep into his flesh, just below the ribs.

She rammed the knife upwards, to the hilt. To his heart.

Well done.

The voice comforted her as she watched him die. Three. Three people. She'd killed three people now. A breath hitched in her throat as she tried and failed to keep her shit together. His eyes didn't close. They never did.

Breathe in. Breathe out. Now think.

She pushed off the dead guard and sat on the edge of the bed, looking at the pool of red liquid as it seeped into the purple rug. A shame. It was a nice rug.

His blood covered her underthings. The low rumblings of noise outside the carriage had stopped. It was eerily quiet as the orange light of sunset bathed the carriage.

She had killed a guard. There were seven more, plus the advisor and all the priestesses.

She couldn't run. They had the numbers and the horses to track and kill her. They didn't even need to do that. She was miles from the road, and didn't even know how to go about finding it. She would likely die in the desert.

Death at every angle.

So, she had to risk speaking to them, convince them that whatever had made them want to kill her was wrong. And she had to do it now, before they sent three more guards to check on this one.

The robes she had been wearing before were in the corner of the room, having snagged on a small stone bust. She hadn't noticed it before and took a step back when she realised it was of the God Atrius, the blade of his tiny sword holding her robe aloft from the table. A thread of superstition or faith caused her to leave them there. It felt wrong somehow, to kill a man and immediately put on the clothing of the Gods.

Instead, she pulled the guard's bloodied trousers from his body and shimmied them over her, fastening the belt as tight as it went, and then tighter still, before tying off the leather. She prised the knife back out of the guard's body and wiped both the hilt and her hands on his tunic.

She stood and took four deep breaths. In. Out.

Holding the knife in one hand, Suri opened the door to her compartment. The belly of the carriage was empty. Suri looked for hidden attackers, but all was silent. She reached the outer door and kicked it open. The sand triangle, where not an hour ago the priestesses had danced and the guards relaxed, was now empty. She considered how many knew about the plot to assassinate her. Of Manira and the advisor, she was certain. Of the others, how many were waiting in line should the first fail?

The sun was setting above the far carriage as Suri stepped down the carriage stairs and onto the soft sanded ground below. She closed the door behind her and moved, so that she could see all three doors at the same time. She swallowed past the gut feeling that told her to protect her body above all else, her hand shaking as she held the knife up.

"Priestess Manira," Suri called out. "I wish to speak with you."

Then she waited.

She trusted they had heard her and breathed in and out as she waited for the response. A door opened.

She half expected five guards to come rushing out of it towards her, but she saw the robes of the priesthood swish into view instead. Manira came first, exiting what had been the first carriage to her right. Behind Manira, the silver-haired advisor stepped onto the sand.

They stood, watching her, not moving any further in her direction. From the left door, stepped three guards. Both closed the doors behind them, and the arena was set. Her against five.

Manira nodded to her. "Princess."

Suri swallowed, still holding the knife aloft.

"I need somewhere else to rest, Priestess," she said, her eyes not wavering from the woman's. "My room has a dead man in it."

Manira's lack of reaction cemented it. She was the one who had spoken the order. "Is that so? How curious."

Suri clenched her jaw. "Why do you want me dead?"

Manira sighed and raised her hand towards the guards. "I do not need to engage with you, girl."

The guards unsheathed their swords but took no move forward.

"If it is the Lord Kol you fear, I can help you," Suri said.

Manira kept her hand there, keeping the guards locked in their position. "And what would drive us to accept the aid of a liar and a thief?"

Suri lowered her hand. A trick? Or did they know. She furrowed her brow in a mockery of confusion. "I don't—"

Manira cut her off. "You are not Princess Viantha."

Her firm conviction left no room for doubt. Suri saw Manira's hand and the positioning of the guards. To disagree here might be fatal.

"And yet I have far more reason to side with you than the scum that live in this cursed land," Suri said.

Manira's fingers twitched. "So, you admit it. What reason would we have to believe you?"

Suri grasped at one of the few tools she had left. "Did you hear about Prince Shaedon's ball?"

Now she permitted herself to look between her opponents, as she noted flickers of interest on their faces. They had heard something. News travelled fast, and it might save her life. This was the thing she hated to use. There was no way to hide in it. It was raw. It was her own self.

The truth.

"I was the one who killed Barsen," she said, stepping forward. Her voice rang loud and clear, as she shouted the confession. Manira said nothing. The advisor bore a small smile, one of twisting greed. This might be her only moment of having their attention. She took another step forward, her eyes locked on Manira's unwavering hand. "Perhaps you also heard that a certain lady never made it to the ball that night. I impersonated

Viantha Waterborne and killed Lord Kol's personal guard. I would do it again."

Warm wind swirled in between the carriages, picking up loose sand and buffering it against her sweat-soaked skin. No one replied to her.

Suri tried again. "Take me with you, and I will stand with you. Against Kol."

The advisor's serpentine smile had grown. He took a step forward now, moving past the motionless Manira. "Why did you kill Barsen?"

Suri looked him up and down, dragging her eyes from the tips of his silver clasped boots, up past his ever-present cravat, to the immaculate head of hair. "They hurt me. Him and Scilla. I had the opportunity for revenge, and I took it."

He nodded. "And Viantha? Tell me exactly what you did with her."

His voice was conspiratorial, like a friend sharing stories in the dead of night.

"I waited until she was alone. I tied her up in a sewer, took her dress and ring, and went to the ball in her place. She escaped somehow in the night."

Manira dropped her hand to her side and walked towards Suri, stopping a few steps short. Suri did not move, as the guards shuffled forward too, swords drawn, with uncertain glances at the priestess. "You would propose we forgive you, take you in as one of our own?" Manira spat. "You have admitted at least two grievous wrongs here, and you expect us to trust you."

"You're already one guard down. Take me on, and you're back to eight," she said, forcing a nonchalant wave of her knife at the guards. "Or you can click your fingers and send them to me. You'll lose one, maybe even two, before you kill me. Then you're three down."

Manira's eyes blazed with fury. She was close enough that Suri had to look up at her, and she tried not to be intimidated by the strength she saw in that iron gaze. Manira would probably rather lose two of her men than trust her with anything.

She had so little left to bargain with. It couldn't end like this. She tried to slow her speech, not sound too desperate. "Whatever your reason, you fear Kol. You evade him. I hate him. He sold me to the mines. He gave me a death sentence. I will fight him and that prick Scilla with everything I have. With my life."

She might as well have been standing in this warm twilight naked, as she felt more vulnerable now than she had been in all her time in that cage.

This was it, her only card left. She unbuttoned the shirt and dragged it to the side, revealing the blood bond carved into the skin atop her breast. "If you don't believe it, read it. I am bound in blood to kill them."

The diplomat took a step forward, staring at the markings on her chest.

It was not exactly the truth. She would fight Kol with every-thing she had, and she *was* angry at him for what he had done to her, how he had tried to seal her into a shallow miner's grave. Part of her wanted to bring *him* to his knees, to destroy his life as readily as he had tried to destroy hers. But it wasn't just hate that drove her. A larger part of her knew the man was far more than an enemy. He was her lifeline; her shot at returning to the life that felt aeons away—only better, stronger—with any prize she wanted to name. The blood bond went both ways. Whilst it bound her to her exile, it also bound the King to his promise.

"If you fear him, then you think he's coming after you. This is where I *need* to be," she said. That thing inside her hummed. It was mute now, only as strong as a stroke down her back. Yet it strengthened her, even as the guards drew closer. "I don't ask forgiveness. Keep me as a guard, as bait, whatever you want. Until we're out of this desert. Then let me go, and then neither of us have to see each other again."

Manira stood in silence, the wind tugging against her hood. She raised her hand again, and this time she had used up every one of her lies and truths. If this was the end, so be it. She had tried everything, and would fight until her blood spilled under the desert moonlight.

The advisor gripped Manira's hand, lowering it as he passed. He stood before Suri, then strode around her in a slow circle. Her bones stiffened as she tried not to move.

As he passed her left elbow, he dragged a finger, laced with ice, up her forearm. She shuddered as the cold spiked up her arm, then left just as suddenly. It took everything in her not to strike at him.

His voice was glass and silk. "Viantha Waterborne, de facto Princess and heir to the Water Guild of Lartosh. You tied her up. In a sewer?"

He rounded back to the front of her, glancing at her neck, which likely bore the new reddish bruising of her recent strangulation, then looked at her face. He waited for her reply.

Suri gave a curt nod. "Yes."

The advisor grinned and then cackled. He bent over, gripping his thighs as the laughter erupted from him. Suri's grip spasmed against the hilt of the knife, as she watched for a new trick. The guards, too, looked unsure.

Was he mad?

A moment later, he straightened and wiped a non-existent tear from his cheek, before stepping back to be in line with Manira. "I say we take her. But I'll be having her ring."

Manira looked at the advisor, then back at Suri.

Suri saw the weight of so many calculations whirring under the mask of the Priestess's faith.

No one moved. Manira and the advisor stood appraising her, the guards waiting to be told their next step. Would it be a three against one deathmatch? Or would it be salvation?

Manira let out a huff. "You will be under constant watch. One step out of line, you die."

It was something. It was life. For now.

Suri nodded. "Deal."

"You wanted her," Manira snapped at the man still standing beside her. "She's your problem now."

Manira spun on her heel and mounted the stairs, slamming the door behind her.

The tension still lay thick. Suri's heart was fit to burst against her ribs.

Was this real? Could she truly live?

Why had he allowed it?

The advisor smiled and held his palm out to Suri, gesturing to the knife she still held. She breathed out. This was it, then. Life, perhaps, if she could trust.

They had told her they would trust her. And if she believed that, and trusted them in return, she would have to surrender her last defence. She raised the knife. Taking a breath, she spun it, catching the blade. She pressed it into the advisor's palm and dropped her grip.

His hand closed around it and, for a second, he held it out, blade pointed to her. Her stomach twisted at an awful speed, the sensation of making a horrible mistake.

Then he twisted the blade, before tucking it into his jacket.

Out of sight.

The guards relaxed. She couldn't believe her luck, not realising until that moment how certain she had been that she was about to die.

He reached out his empty hand. In entreaty, in greeting. The smile that now played on his mouth seemed more genuine. "Pleased to meet you in your true form, miss?"

The silent desert paused for her answer. There was trust and there was truth. Entirely separate concepts to Suri. So, she wrapped herself in the only blanket she had left. A mask, another lie.

"Edi."

He nodded. "The ring?"

She took it off without a thought. It was almost a relief, removing it from her finger. Like a dead weight taken off her heart, her soul. For such a light item, it felt heavy, numbing almost. She looked at it, sat in her hand for a moment, then passed it into his waiting one.

He smiled. "Edi... Remind me to give you something pretty if we survive this."

He turned to leave, but Suri spoke. She hated the nervous strain in the rhythm of her voice. "I don't think I ever did catch your name."

"Oh yes. How rude of me," he replied.

The advisor straightened his neck scarf as he pondered his reply. He dropped into a low bow, his silver hair looking blonder, as the last golden light of the day hit the crown of his head.

"Rasel Waterborne, at your service."

Rasel Waterborne.

The shock of it hit her like a first breath of frigid air.

Viantha's brother.

It was one of the few questions Suri had asked her. Her family. Rasel was not only her brother. He was her *older* brother. He thought he would be named heir, but Viantha had been named in his place.

And now, here he stood bowing before her.

Rasel had known she was a lying thief from the moment he had seen her, chained in that cage. He had *allowed* her aboard. She saw now the similarities, his hair the same silver hue as his mother's. His rose petal mouth, the same as Viantha's.

A powerful water manipulator. Passed over by Ressa in favour of the daughter. And now here. An advisor, not to the Pail or the Council of Lartosh, but to Queen Lera of Drangbor, the regnant of another land altogether.

He swept out of his bow and winked to Suri, gesturing to the first carriage. "Show's over," he shouted. "Let's show Edi here why we're all quaking in our boots."

14

A letter came from the King. My sister's rage at finding the words addressed to my name instead was terrible. I am invited to a private dinner. She insists I stay, my parents insist I go. I disappoint all in every step.

Diary of C. Aubethaan, est. early 8th century

The first carriage wasn't like the others, the whole shell was one large space. There were two armchairs and benches under the four windows. The floor was familiar, silver lacquered wood covered with plush rugs.

Manira and two guards were already inside when they entered, staring at a wooden chest , shackled to the floor, in the centre of the space.

Rasel motioned to one of the guards, flicking his hand. "Open it."

The guard hesitated.

"She can't help protect something if she doesn't know what it is," Rasel said, his voice raised. "Open it."

This time, the guard didn't hesitate. He removed the first padlock hanging from the front of the chest, then the second, before opening the lid of the chest to reveal a smaller, intricately crafted silverwood chest inside it. Its metal fastenings looked new and housed a set of three small locks, each of which had room for a tiny key.

Rasel moved behind the chest to the armchair and took a seat. "This wasn't a routine visit. We were sent to recover something stolen," he said. "Several weeks ago, the treasury of Drangbor made an alarming discovery. A quantity of amefyre had gone missing."

Suri stared at the silverwood chest, wondering who held the keys and how much the chest itself was worth.

Rasel reached under the chair and pulled out a bottle of a dark spirit. He held up the bottle in the small remnants of the day's light. "It didn't take long to trace its whereabouts to the Parched Lands."

"Kol stole amefyre?" she asked.

Rasel opened the bottle and ran his finger down it. Suri saw the glass frost, the icy cold of the bottle now giving off steam. "From the Grand Temple itself."

She swallowed as she watched him tip the bottle back and take a drink. "And you're here to take it back?"

He lowered the bottle. "We already have."

Suri's eyes went to the chest again. There, through that small amount of wood, held the world's most expensive commodity.

Rasel spoke again. "Priestess Manira alone holds the keys to this chest. Within it are several small lockboxes. I filled one with the amefyre. The others, with lead and iron of equal weight. Only I know which holds the bounty."

A whole lockbox of amefyre. The wealth that was just inches from her was astounding. World changing. But his words were a warning to her. A triple lock, that she would have to get past if she wanted to steal from them.

Not only to steal the guard's keys, but to steal Manira's, and then fathom which lockbox held the gemstones and somehow steal whatever unlocking tool Rasel carried.

She drew her eyes away from the silver wooden box and looked at the advisor. "How did you find it?"

Rasel walked over to the outer chest, the bottle swinging from his hand, and kicked it closed. "He was storing it near his iron mines. It won't be long until they realise we've taken it."

He motioned to the guard, who knelt to refasten the exterior locks.

"You think they're going to follow you?" Suri asked.

He smiled. "If they're not already, they're fools."

This was much worse that Suri could have imagined. Not simply the fears of wanderers in hostile lands, but they had taken something of extreme value, something that Kol undoubtedly wanted to use as a chip against Queen Lera. They were running for their lives.

"You believe the Lord would kill you? A group of priestesses?" she asked.

Rasel shrugged. "The Demon King has shown he cares little for the lives of others. Kill us? No. I fear that his retribution would be worse than a swift death."

A shudder rippled up her spine. "So you ride through the night and barely stop, hoping to make it to the borders of Drangbor before they catch you?"

"Watch your tone," Manira said.

"Wouldn't it be faster for someone to take the single lockbox and ride alone?"

Rasel looked at the Priestess. "That is a matter we—"

"It is too risky to allow someone to travel alone with such a burden. Someone could easily kill a lone rider. If they catch us as a group, we can fight," Manira said, cutting across his words.

Ah, Suri thought. They did not trust each other.

She wondered which of them was truly in charge of this mission. Who was the Queen's favourite pet? The triple lock was not solely a warning to her. It was protection against themselves.

Before, it had been her only way to survive. Now, the chance to hurt Scilla or Kol was a near certainty. This was where she needed to be. Even if she wasn't able to kill Scilla or Kol, the Queen of Drangbor might throw in some coins if she assisted in the recovery of the precious amefyre.

"Let me help you," Suri said.

Manira seemed bored. "Obviously, you will help. We have no need for dead weight."

"What can I do?"

She pointed to a bench. "Sit and watch. There are pagans in the dunes out here. You see anything, knock twice hard on the roof."

Suri nodded and moved to perch at her post. Outside, the sky was purpling.

Manira directed two of the guards to take the first watch, then directed a further two to take the second. Those on the first watch sat on two of the benches. She then looked at Rasel, who still lounged in an armchair, looking at his fingernails.

"Of course, the girl goes nowhere without your escort, Prince," she said, the words almost hissing through her teeth.

Rasel met her eyes, his own colder than Suri had ever seen. He exuded winter through his entire body. "Naturally, High Priestess. We wouldn't want her stumbling into the Healing Fields."

The Priestess looked like she wanted to say more, staring at the sprawled man, but nodded and strode out of the carriage.

Suri flexed her fingers. "What are the Healing Fields?"

Rasel turned his icy look to her now. He smiled, just barely, the open bottle still swinging from one hand. "Another lovely obstacle. A mist-covered expanse of the desert just to the south. Anyone who walks in suffers some horrible disease-ridden death."

Suri swallowed. She'd heard of it, but she thought it was a story. The ancient blood witch who killed any man or beast who entered her mists, bursting their organs from the inside, and raising their body in terrible boils. "The Blood Mists? They're real?"

"So, you *have* heard of them. They are definitely real, princess."

She shuddered. This was a waking nightmare.

"Are you going to be trouble?" he asked.

Suri opened her mouth. Closed it. Then shook her head.

"Shame," he said, then stood up and snapped his fingers. "If my new guest moves from that window at any point tonight, kill her. I'll pick her up in the morning."

He left with the bottle swinging from two fingers.

A noise hit the side of the carriage and they lurched forward. They couldn't have stopped for more than an hour. In that time, she'd killed another person. And somehow, she was still alive.

The first watch passed easily. She ignored the guards and stared out the hatched window. Her eyes glazed, her vision fading in and out of focus as the lavender sky darkened through the shades to a deep indigo. The guards sometimes passed her a waterskin. It was cold and refreshing. For the first time since arriving in this desolate land, she could study the sky.

Here, away from all the lights, the stars burned brighter than ever. She saw other colours in the edges of their light, blue and golden swirls encircling the white pinpricks that dotted the nighttime canvas.

The second watch was harder.

They stopped for a couple of minutes whilst the guards changed around. The guards she had been with for the first few hours left and two others replaced them. These did not give her water. They were angry. Friends of the guard she'd killed, maybe.

Staring out into the never ending darkness, with its dunes that barely shadowed against the night's backdrop, became a chore. It was cold in the carriage at night, especially in a thin top. The blood on her trousers had long since dried and now sat rough against her thighs. Not moving from the bench, she pulled her legs up and held them.

She cradled herself as she watched. For a time, in the darkness, the wetness of tears leaked down her cheeks. She'd come so far and had so little to show for it.

She had no one.

Whilst not a new fact, it felt bigger here, her emptiness reaching out and finding no walls to bounce off. No sound to mask it.

Suri played with her earrings, the cheap metal spikes through her ear the only things that reminded her of home. She wondered if Esra would find out she had been exiled when he got back. If he'd come looking for her. If there would even be anything to find.

Her eyes drooped, her blinks lengthening.

Then, she jolted her head up from the comfy crook of her knees. The carriages had stopped once more. Dawn was breaking.

When the door opened, Suri expected more guards. But it was Rasel. He looked like he'd only just woken up, his silver-white hair loose around his shoulders. Her eyes, tired as they were, took in his appearance. He'd clearly just woken up, and yet he had carefully arranged the same silken black cravat he had been wearing before around his neck.

Odd. Was he hiding something? A valuable necklace? He glanced around the carriage and, a moment later, his cold eyes found hers.

"Come on then," he said, waving her over.

She stood, her limbs so stiff they felt wooden, her body drifting through the motions of walking.

When she stepped out of the carriage, the light all around nearly blinded her. She pulled an arm over her face to block the sun, then immediately stumbled against a clump of sand underfoot. She scuffed a couple of steps and steadied herself with a hand to the already warming ground.

Rasel pulled her to the door of another carriage, wrenching her up the stairs before releasing her. It was one of the priestesses' wagons. He pointed to the longer padded divan against the wall.

"Sleep," he said, as he fell into an armchair.

Suri stood still as he sat bent over with his head cradled in his hands. She swallowed against a dry mouth. "Where are the priestesses?"

Rasel glared at her. "Asleep. As I would like to be. So keep it down."

Suri moved to the padded lounger and sat, pulling off her footwear. She lay down and stared up at the carriage roof, as her trousers scraped against her legs. A moment later, she sat up again. She removed the belt of her trousers, then paused, looking up at the older Waterborne. He looked away as she met his gaze.

She removed the trousers and lay back down, using the trousers as a sort of blanket to cover her underwear, and was asleep within seconds.

What felt like moments later, he shook her awake. "You're back on watch."

The sun was high in the sky and Rasel stood over her, his white hair falling almost into her face. The familiar rumble of the carriage beneath her had stalled again. They must have paused for a break in highest heat of the day.

"Choose your poison, kidnapper," he said.

In one hand he held a waterskin, in the other a carved glass of whatever brown liquid he appeared to live on. He seemed much more awake, the taunt back in his voice. He leaned back as Suri sat up.

Fuck, she was still so tired. She grabbed the water skin.

He shrugged. "Your loss."

After she'd guzzled down half the skin and paused for breath, Rasel pointed to a folded pile of clothes. Grey ones. Great. Priestesses robes again. She was hoping for some guard clothing with actual trousers. Pockets, maybe. Wishful damn thinking.

But she was still alive.

Her tired hands pulled the robes on with the dexterity of a child.

"Ready?" he asked.

She replied she was and followed him out of the carriage. But, instead of leading her to the other carriage, he started walking out of the huddle of stalled carriages. She paused.

He turned back to her. "Come on."

She followed, catching up to him as he strode into the dunes. "I thought I was back on watch," she said, her breathing a little strained in the unfamiliar terrain.

He shrugged. "Well, that seemed pretty boring."

"Isn't Manira g—"

"Fuck Manira," Rasel snarled.

Suri followed the pace of his steps, silently agreeing with him. "Where are we going?"

They'd only been walking a minute and already, all around them, was a sea of sand as far as the eye could see. She'd already lost sight of the carriages behind, and a lance of fear broke through her groggy mind.

"Somewhere more fun."

They were walking towards nothing. She wondered if this was some plot, but what could they do to her out here that they couldn't already do to her back at the carriages? But what would be the point? She was at their total mercy already.

And then the landscape changed.

She thought it was a trick of the light at first, when she stepped over a dune top and saw a hazy reflection. But soon it was clear.

It was water.

"What is this place?" she asked.

The dunes swept down into a basin of sand, where nearly clear water formed a lake within it. There was no life next to the water. No pockets of green, no trees. Just water lying on the sand.

"It's our own personal bath," Rasel said, with a genuine smile. It made him look more unhinged than she's ever seen him.

"How does this exist?"

"The rain has to go somewhere, I suppose." Rasel dragged his cuirass over his head and stepped down towards the oasis, his feet sinking deep into the sand. He threw the leather garment to the side and started unfastening his trousers. He was soon butt-naked, except for the scarf around his neck, and stepped into the water, the garment still on. When the water covered his ass, he turned back to Suri. "Are you getting in, Edi? Or have your priestess robes turned you into a prude already?"

Suri gaped at him. She hadn't looked away, never wanting to turn her eyes from a threat. But heat rose in her cheeks then, as she took in his sculpted white torso and shoulders. He wasn't wide, but he was lithe. Attractive, even.

He smiled. "Suit yourself."

He turned back and dived under the water.

Oh, screw that. She was getting in. She strode down the sand and, once she reached the water's edge, pulled off the robes. Unlike Rasel, she kept her underthings on.

The water was warm, almost uncomfortably so. Regardless, it felt nice, and by the time she was submerged, it was quite peaceful, as she felt herself again for a fraction of a moment.

She'd never learnt to swim, so she stayed where she could touch the sand beneath her. Rasel floated on his back in the deeper water, wafting himself around in a lazy circle. She tried to only watch him from the corner of her eye, too conscious of how every part of him floated at the water's surface. She was no prude, she didn't have the luxury to be so. But the idea of him catching her ogling him made her nervous.

Then he started singing a melancholy tune.

> "Yonder she goes, to the eye of the storm,
> Lo, lo, the eye of the storm.
> Life will she meet, his wisdom she'll scorn,
> Lo, lo, in the eye of the storm.
> Death will she greet, in his twisted form,
> Lo, lo, in the eye of the storm.
> The lovers are warring, she's caught in the storm,
> Lo, lo, the eye of the storm."

He stopped singing.

"What was that?"

Rasel looked at her, like he'd almost forgotten she was there, his smile razor-sharp. "Did you like it?"

"Yes," she replied.

He tutted. "You shouldn't. It's a pagan song."

He started floating again, humming to himself.

Again, she averted her eyes. But the question bubbled. "What happens to her?"

Rasel righted himself again at her question, shaking water out of an ear. "What?"

Suri's cheeks flushed with embarrassment. "The woman in the song?"

She should have just said it was nothing, it was dumb to have even asked.

Rasel swam towards her and, when he got close, Suri shivered. Not from fear or nervousness this time, but from cold. A delicious, cool patch of water emanated from the ice prince. It wasn't freezing; it was just right. She leant into his space. Gods, that was refreshing.

He smiled at her, as he stood beside her. "She got what she deserved."

Suri swallowed. It was blissful, yet she couldn't relax around this man. He put her on edge. She felt that thrum from him, the one calling her to kill and take her place in the world. As she'd felt it near Kol, so she felt it now.

Rasel tensed. "Look, there," he whispered.

She followed his gaze toward the dune at the far side of the oasis. She thought she saw a flicker of something but wasn't sure. "What is—"

An arrow pierced through the air. It was coming for them.

Rasel splashed up the water.

Fuck.

She didn't even have half a moment to drag in a breath, before the arrow stopped. Trapped in a frozen splash of water, lodged in place. She stared at the arrow as it locked, frozen in the air for a split second. Then it fell.

It was less than a hand's width from spearing through Rasel's head.

Shit.

"Run, Edi."

She thrashed against the water as she battled to shore. She grabbed her stuff and scrambled up and over the dune. Once she was over it, she ducked and gave herself two seconds to breathe.

Then she ran back the way they had come as fast as she could, making it to the edge of the camp, gulping in breath after breath. Rasel arrived a minute behind her in similar condition.

"What was that?" she asked, as soon as her breath was back. "Who was that?"

He shook his head. "One of our desert friends, I expect."

She pulled on her clothes. "Are they coming after us?"

"If they do, I'll kill them."

She nodded, staring back at the dunes in their wake. She couldn't see anything. If they were out there, it looked like they weren't in immediate pursuit. "I'm going to my watch."

He nodded, still breathing hard. Still staring back out.

The rest of the day was nothing but watching. Manira was livid and everyone was on high alert. They moved slower than before, risking the slight time loss in the hope of a better chance of spotting their attackers precious moments earlier.

Suri watched so keenly her eyes stopped feeling like eyes. The dunes stopped looking like dunes. She flinched at every infinitesimal movement of sand. By the time Rasel came to fetch her, no one was any the wiser about what had happened out there. Everyone had their theories, of course, but it boiled down to nothing.

This time Rasel escorted her without force. He led her to an actual sleeping compartment. She didn't hesitate, pulling off her robes, shedding the clothes down to her undershirt and short underwear, before falling into a bed.

Her eyes drifted shut as Rasel pulled off his boots. His dead eyes met hers as she fell asleep.

She woke up before him.

Rasel was sitting up on the bed across from hers. He was asleep. It was still dark. The pulse under her skin, somehow stronger again over the last day, had sent her dreams of indigo-hazed delight. The voice had come with actual words. They still thrummed in her core, the lull of sleep not fully gone.

She sat up and watched the southern Prince's face. From his complexion, you would think him Northern. Pale as a winter's morning. And still that cravat. He never took the damn thing off.

Sweet girl.

The voice was not an *it* any more. The voice was a *him*. She had seen him last night. The dark silhouette. She could still hear the murmurings echoing in her head. Calling her *sweet*. Calling her *his*.

Not just a call to arms. It was a call to *her*. It was personal. Intimate. A play at seduction. It swirled in her with a potency that addled her half-awake brain.

Her handful of sexual encounters had one thing in common. There was always some transaction. She traded her intimacy for a night of feeling protected and secure, when she'd slept in the sailor's arms. She'd traded it for a feeling of excitement, when she'd slept with that shopgirl.

And now, she watched Rasel.

Suri moved to the edge of the bed, placing a hand on Rasel's knee. He blinked awake and flinched away from her, standing. His breaths came in quick pants, before he realised it was just her, dragging his fingers through his white hair with a scowl.

She raised her hands in mock surrender.

"What do you want?" he asked.

Suri stared at him and raised herself to her knees.

It wasn't that she desired *him*, but what she desired *from* him. A feeling that she was a person in this world. That she was a woman. That she was not alone. A relief from the crawling itch of pleasure almost granted to her in her dreams and a distraction from her likely impending death. A good trade.

She reached for his hand. She brought it part way towards her, watching his eyes as they darkened. He didn't move his hand back, so she brought it to her breast and dropped her grip. His hand remained.

He blinked at her, his brow furrowed. He still didn't move.

She waited, and he moved, his thumb caressing her nipple over her undershirt.

Suri reached up, meaning to remove the black cravat. Her fingertips had barely grazed it, when his hands snapped up to grab hers by the wrist. Tight, but not painful.

"No," he said.

Then he pushed her down onto the bed, following her until he was on top. One of his thighs sank between her legs. Her breath caught.

"Is this?" he asked.

She nodded.

It was almost funny. Suri felt the strangeness of the situation with a bubble of emotion. Pain, anxiety, mirth, desire, all mixed with a melting pot of absurdity. She smiled.

A laugh might have broken free, if not for the noise.

The sounds of two loud thumps against a carriage wall. A scream. Dread rippled through her.

They were here.

15

I will go to the King. I will tell him of my love
for His Godliness, Diophage. He will send me to
worship, and all will be resolved.
Diary of C. Aubethaan, est. early 8th century

T he scream cut short. The moment hanging between
them broke in an instant as Rasel pushed away from
her.

They were here. Kol's men had found them.

Fear swept across Suri's body like a stiff wind. Anticipation accompanied it. And as much as she tried to dampen
it, those knocks resonated deep within her. A tuning fork to
the voice in her head. Yes, there was excitement, too.

Make them pay.

Suri pulled on her outer robe and pushed herself from the
bed, as the wagons jolted to a stop. She glanced back, and
saw Rasel pull on his boots.

They held half a moment's eye contact before she pulled the door open, barefoot. Two priestesses sat, clinging to each other in the main compartment.

They jumped as she pushed into the room. Suri lifted her finger to her mouth.

Quickly, quietly, she opened the main door to the outside. It was pitch black.

The knocks had come from the first carriage in front of them, where the guards watched the precious cargo. The scream was harder to place. She wanted a weapon, but mostly, she needed to be out of the box with only one exit.

She jumped, landing in the sand. Her toes sank into the grains as she dropped to the ground, rolling her body under the belly of the carriage. She breathed, waiting for her eyes to adjust to the dim light.

It took her a few seconds to see the contrast between the bottom of the wagon and the top of the sand. A few more to note the outline of the front wagon. Then she saw the body. Lying limp on the floor by the first wagon. It must have been the guard driving the carriage. Pulled from his seat. Suri saw no attackers, nothing but a pair of ankles beside the carriage she'd just left. It must have been Rasel's. He moved off immediately.

She listened as more boots hit the ground outside the carriage doors. The four guards exchanged hurried, half-whispered commands.

One lit a torch, the light illuminating the sand in broken ripples of golden and black. She saw the four of them spread into a semi-circle, their feet pointing outwards.

A whistle of metal sounded from her right, where the dunes stretched out into the endless night. A thunk as the knife sank deep. Into leather. Into flesh. A gurgled gasp from its target.

Her limited sight caught up, as one pair of boots stumbled forwards, crumbling to his knees. His torso slammed down with its full weight, lodging the weapon deeper. The face, not fully dead. Brown eyes, staring. Staring at her. Mouth gaping as sand cradled his head.

Suri blinked.

The ghastly light of the torch cast his face in strange planes. He died moments later, as the three remaining guards scattered.

She had no idea what his name was. He'd given her water not four hours ago.

"Protect the priestesses!" The strangled cry of a guard echoed around the dunes.

Suri watched the other boots scurry back to the carriages. In a single movement, she pulled herself forward on her elbows, out of the shelter of the carriage.

She pushed the guard onto his back. Avoiding his eternal gaze, she wrenched the knife free, prying it from his chest, before grabbing his short sword with her other hand, and pushing herself up.

She kept her back to the carriage, knife in one hand and short sword in the other. Her fingers clenched and unclenched against the hilts as she waited with the other guards.

She paid no attention to the corpse at her feet, no attention to the darkening sand to his side.

When she breathed, it was not air. It was that other thing. That dark and cold reassurance that whispered through her hair like a shivering breeze. She didn't hide from the sensation. The thrum that had been rising in her blood since she first heard those two thunks in the night.

She allowed it to rise. She didn't stop it when it enveloped her.

Sweet Suri. Avenge everything. Everyone.

Suri let it, *him,* guide her hands. The knife was fine craftsmanship. It was curved slightly, with one edge wicked sharp and the other with two serrated hooks.

She let *him* push her with his cool caress into that crouched stance.

Bring them death, my sweet warrior.

When the shadows arrived in force, she did not fear.

Her knees did not feel like they would buckle. They were ready to pounce.

The shadowed figures stepped into that range of half-light. Feet wrapped in cloth, not boots, moving with the ripples of the sand rather than staking an impression on the top of it.

Five of them moved from the right of the carriage behind her.

The silence lasted a fraction of a second.

She spun with an inhuman cry towards them and descended on them, as if she had come from the depths of night itself.

She killed the first with a shortsword to the gut, kicking him away from her as she whirled. The second as she stabbed the knife into his jugular. The dark thrum inside her sang a praising war cry through her bloodstream.

The three remaining had time to raise their weapons.

Cruel and curved scimitars.

Two men, one woman.

Suri feinted, ripping her knife free as she whipped her short-sword to clatter against the woman's scimitar. Her knife embedded into the woman's chest as their swords willed against one another. As the attacker fell, she noticed another blade lunging towards her and danced backwards.

The tip of the scimitar grazed her stomach as she dodged back a couple of steps. Three lay unmoving. Two moved toward her with deadly expressions.

Suri glanced over her shoulder.

Five more attackers had moved into the clearing on the other side. Two guards crouched in defensive stances in front of them. Another lay dead.

The horses whinnied and bucked.

She existed now in the eye of the storm. Her limbs were still moving back, dodging those in front of her, caught in the vortex of the thrum.

But her heart was steady.

It was clear that they were outnumbered. But the darkness she pulled on didn't care.

One of the guards moved across the sand to aid her. This one had also given her water. His name was Gorsh.

The blood in her veins screamed at her to kill him too, to kill everything that moved near her. The little part of her that still felt herself stopped just shy of stabbing him when he came within an arm length.

Gorsh launched himself at one of the two desert dwellers still breathing.

Some part of her twisted then and wanted to stay still. To watch the inevitability of these two against one. To watch him die like the rest, like they all probably would in this terrible place.

She intercepted the killing blow of the other as he engaged the first, their backs pressed into one as they fought. One of the attackers dropped low to the floor, sweeping Gorsh's knees out from under him, knocking him prone.

She shoved her opponent back and swerved to block a descending scimitar from impaling Gorsh's chest. But as the attacker straightened, he threw sand in her face.

Suri flinched, tossing her head to the side, as she raised an arm to guard against it. Half a moment later, she lowered it with a growl. Ready to kill. Ready to punish.

The wide blade of a scimitar was a hair's breadth from her neck, a hand gripped her upper arm. That thrum beat like a drum and part of her almost wanted to test it. To taste death. Lean in. Destroy herself along with everything else.

"Drop your weapons," came a voice.

A second passed. Two. The blade pressed to her neck.

She dropped the knife and shortsword into the sand.

"Can I kill her?" the one holding her life asked.

"No. She's a priestess," said the one in front as he caught his breath.

His accent surprised Suri. This man was from the north. Then she realised, everyone here was no one. All the desert dwellers were just citizens who had messed up badly enough to be confined here for eternity.

"She doesn't fight like a priestess."

"How would you know?" the one in front replied.

Her scalp wrenched, as she was suddenly dragged backwards. Her eyes lingered on Gorsh's body as she watched the attacker pull the scimitar from him, blood gurgling from the side of his mouth.

Whoever held the torch dropped it, and she was plunged once more into the depths of shadow.

She could only hear.

The grunts of the attackers, and the gasps of the defenders. Doors wrenched open, their hinges whined, and the wood slammed into the carriage walls. The stumble of blind feet on the steps. Sniffling from the priestesses. A muttered threat. One of them cried out.

And then the horses.

The fucking horses.

Their panicked braying cut through the noise of men. Their terror, a mirror held up to the horrors inflicted on the innocence of their world.

Above it all. Between it all. Filling the very air. That thrum. It kept her sane. It kept those noises from consuming her. Kept her from panicking. Swaddled her. As if the darkness was not apart from her, but a part of her.

When again a torch was lit, the scene was very different.

The battle was over. They had lost.

The priestesses kneeled in the sand around her. All but Manira.

She had yet to see Manira or Rasel since the fighting broke out. All the guards lay dead. The sand-borne captors, six of them still alive, walked around them.

They were not bound, not gagged. In another situation, she might have thought that they had a chance, the five of them dressed in priesthood robes, against the six. But they were not only unarmed, but unorganised. And the fear, in their desperate whimpers, stopped her from even attempting anything.

Any remaining hope died when she saw another walk into the clearing. A woman, clothed in navy that flickered royal blue as she stepped into the torch light. The golden light hit the high points of her cheekbones as she looked down at the women crouched on the floor.

Suri ducked her head down, pulling the gown tighter around her. She regretted the lack of a hood.

She could see Scilla's clothed footpads stepping amongst them.

"Have you found it?" Scilla asked. Her feet paused next to Suri's bowed head.

"We found it. But there's something you're going to want to see, General," one of the attackers replied.

General. General Scilla. No lady then. A person of war. Suri supposed it made sense. Scilla still stood beside her, her warm breath tickling Suri's neck.

Then she stepped away, and Suri exhaled.

"Show me."

Suri risked glancing up, keeping a watch on Scilla's back. The attackers laid open the door to the first carriage. First, they pulled out the chest. The outer and inner chest lay open, the second chest brimming with small steel lockboxes.

"You got into it?" Scilla asked.

"Open when we found it."

"Who—"

Behind the chest, a guard was pulled out. His body hit the sand below and the sack of flesh rolled over, a pale-hilted knife pointing out of his chest.

The white handled knife was Manira's blade. The only one able to open the second chest. Had she killed her own guard?

Then a second body was pulled out of the carriage. This one didn't create the same noise. Instead of a deep spreading of weight across the sand, the sound was a metallic thunk. There was no movement in the body.

"That snake," Scilla growled.

It was Manira. Frozen solid.

She was caught in suspended animation, her hand reaching out, finger pointed. Her face was twisted in horror and pain.

Perhaps Manira had killed the guard. Perhaps Rasel had killed them both.

It didn't matter, she supposed. The priestess was dead.

The screams from the priestesses around her went unpunished. Suri's own stomach was close to losing what little food remained in it. Only Scilla seemed unfazed by the terrible sight.

Suri ducked her head again.

"There's only five horses," one of the attackers said.

Scilla pointed to two of her men. "Chase that rat to the border."

"Yes, General."

She wanted to spit on the sand when Scilla's boots, wandering again in laps in and around them, passed near her robes.

"What to do with you?" Scilla said. The voice was quieter, but not softer.

One by one, she pulled the hoods of the priestesses back. Suri cursed at herself. There was no way out of this.

"The treaty says we have to let you go. Even if you are dirty thieves."

Scilla stopped next to each priestess, dragging an idle hand through their hair.

She paused next to Suri. "No hood, priestess?"

"That one is vicious. Killed two of ours," said the one with the northern accent.

Scilla crouched. "Is that so?"

Suri kept her head fixed on the ground. She could feel the woman's hot breath against her face. It brushed against that thrum inside her and sparked the hatred deeper and deeper inside her.

Scilla's fingers lifted her chin. How dare she touch her?

Make them pay...

This was it then, no rest for the wicked.

Suri grabbed Scilla's fingers and jerked, twisting as hard as she could. The bones snapped. Scilla screamed. The guard Suri hadn't realised was right behind her yanked her backwards. The blade was at her neck before she'd gasped in a breath.

"Shall I kill her?"

The dark lord's general was bent over, cursing. She waved her uninjured hand towards the guard. "No," she said through gritted teeth. "I'll deal with her."

The guard didn't move the weapon even a tenth of an inch. Scilla held her hand, cradled in the other. Then she looked back to Suri.

"You." The voice was pure in its vehemence. "How in all shittery are *you* here?"

Suri chose not to respond. The nick of the blade pressed still.

Scilla stared at her. A moment later, she broke eye contact with the killer, barking orders. "Strip the carriages. Give the barest one to the priestesses. Give them one horse."

"This one stays," she continued, pointing to Suri with a smile. "Because you are no priestess, are you? You're the dirtiest thief of them all."

The only pleasure Suri could derive from the minutes that followed was the obvious pain that Scilla was in.

For all her hatred, she noted Scilla was the same creature as her in one respect. She wanted revenge and would stop at nothing to get it. And here, lying helplessly, was Suri. The subject of her vengeful waking dreams.

If the roles were reversed, Suri would kill Scilla.

So, she was to die in the desert after all.

At least Scilla's plan had been thwarted. Rasel had taken the amefyre and run off, just as Suri had suggested. Suri hoped he would make it to the border of Drangbor.

Three of the priestesses were pushed into the carriage. Another was pushed up onto the driver's seat. The reins were placed in her shaking hands. At Scilla's order, the horse was spurred, and the carriage started a slow rumble.

And then it was just the empty carriages, Scilla, her band of carrion feeders and Suri.

Scilla bound her fingers straight in some kind of rough bandaging. Suri had broken her fingers before. She knew how painful that was, despite Scilla's cool and collected expression. She watched only the woman's fingers as Scilla walked to where she crouched bound on the floor.

Her first words were a surprise.

"I won't kill you. That would be too easy."

Suri should have been afraid, but she only felt relief.

Scilla sat down before her.

The gag was untied. A moment later the blade returned to her neck.

"What would *you* say is a fair trade? For killing a good man. For risking the sanity of another?" Scilla asked.

The thief watched as the general considered what *punishment* she should have. Punishment for the justice she gave to the world. She'd killed a man. Only the Gods could judge if he was a *good* man, Suri sure as dirt had judged him otherwise.

Scilla's lip curled. "You have no idea what this has done to him."

Suri thought this odd. She did know what she'd done. She'd killed him. Then she took in Scilla's expression, allowed the words to sink in. Did she mean Kol? Risking his sanity? Had she hurt the powerful half-Fae's feelings?

"What would you say is fair?" Scilla repeated.

Suri stared at the general, unblinking.

Scilla smiled. "Cat got your tongue?"

She almost didn't react, but she felt her eyes tense, as she watched Scilla's smile grow.

"Hold her up."

Her guard pulled Suri to her feet.

"Let's leave your fate in the hands of the Gods. Life and death. The two eternal truths."

So, Scilla was a pagan. Suri found she wasn't surprised.

Diophage, Life. Sotoledi, Death.

The Trio who had appeared at the Wrath, those who were worshipped by Lera's Priesthood, were a bit more varied. War, rebirth, plants, the moon, the tides. They weren't connected to barbaric acts, or dark heretical magics, they were points of guidance. They had nuance, colour.

Scilla however saw the world in black and white. The simplicity of thinking only in terms of Life and Death was oddly tempting to Suri. The dance of Diophage and Sotoledi, the old pictures of them showing them forever intertwined. Some idols showed Death with a knife to Diophage, sometimes they were shown in almost a lover's embrace.

Suri did not move as she let Scilla dictate her likely death.

"Some street tramp gave you life. I'll give you pain. The desert will bring you death." A slow death, then, as he had promised. Her next word was not addressed to Suri, but to the stars in the night's sky. "Justice."

Suri found herself thinking they were like two sides of a single bit. That same burning thrum echoed back from Scilla. The same one she had felt from Kol, when they had stood close.

The general touched her bound hands. Unravelled the bindings.

The guards moved their grip on her arms to her hands, pulling them to either side.

Scilla trailed her finger down Suri's left arm, encircling her hand with a softness. Her hands were rough. Calloused. "You steal. So really, I should take your hand."

The guard held her hand aloft like the tail of a dead dog. Suri tried not to shudder at the thought.

Scilla trailed her hand back and gripped Suri's jaw. "But you also lie. Somehow you convinced these sacks to trust you," she said. "Maybe I should take your tongue."

Suri felt tendrils of real fear. Pain was an old friend. But to sever something from her, to live without the only things that gave her a chance in this world. To die a shadow of herself. She would prefer any other torture.

Scilla looked into her eyes then and must have caught, for a moment, the panic they betrayed.

Suri saw the revelry in the general's dark eyes, as they pierced into her own grey eyes. "It seems you have decided for me."

The emissary, the general, the attacker in the night, backed up a couple of steps. She stared at Suri, holding her gaze, her dark eyes twinkling in the low firelight of the torch.

"Take one of her eyes."

16

The King is an evil man. My family is deaf to the
injuries hidden inside me. I leave tonight.
Diary of C. Aubethaan, est. early 8th century

The pain was all consuming. Immeasurable. Suri could not move. She could not think.

Her eye. Her *eye.*

The urge to hold, to soothe. But her sandy hands would hold no salvation, only further torment and pain.

Her Eye.

She pinned her hands to the floor as she lay. She writhed. She *felt.*

Suri had nothing.

She screamed into the void. And screamed. And screamed.

17

The shrinefolk have taken me in. His people are kind, they love Him too. They don't know Him as I do, but they understand.

Diary of C. Aubethaan, est. early 8th century

The pain was eternal.

The wind had pushed the sand around her. It piled up on her right side, half submerging her body. She stared up to a noon sun through an eye that barely understood the world.

She knew that she needed to get out of the sun. Her skin was too hot, too tight across her body. It would be burnt already, doubtless.

The half-blinded thief crawled her body towards a hazy structure.

Soon, she lay under the shade of one of the ransacked carriages.

Here, she fell back into that trance-like state. It was not sleep, it was not nearly that restful. There was no peace in it. But it was a lack of movement, a lack of something. All she was able to do was take from everything else, everything else that she was. Then, maybe there would be something to give back to that gaping hole. Some strength to lend to that horrible pain.

Time passed.

The sun was setting, the light hitting her face from beneath the carriage floor. She opened her left eye. She imagined her other eye should open too, and all she would see would be an endless red. Blood and horror.

Instead—it was nothing. Not even the blackness of a closed lid. Just nothing.

Her world was off kilter. Everything looked too close, or too far.

She had a pounding headache, which she was only just able to feel around the swirling pain in her face.

Suri was aware that she was in a desert, alone. She was vulnerable. She hadn't drunk water since the early hours of the night. Just after...

It had been hours.

She crawled herself to the edge of sunlight, pulling herself back out.

The corpses remained where they were.

The smell had not yet set in, but the view of them made her stomach turn. In the light of day, the dead lay as equals. Just bodies now. Men, mostly, and a couple of women. Knives and swords laid their insides bare. Pain left their faces contorted.

Suri looked away, before the water left in her body tried to leave it.

Inside the carriage, everything of any value was gone. Worse, they had taken the buckets of cool water that lay in each room.

Thankfully, they had not known to take the water from the pipes. In the daytime, Rasel would freeze the pipes, keeping the worst of the temperature at bay. But at night, the pipes would unfreeze. The valves that held the water and allowed some to drip forth were in the bedchambers at either end. She mimicked the action she had seen Rasel use the morning earlier.

Climbing onto a bed, she sat upright and twisted the still cool metal.

There was a moment when she thought she was wrong. They had taken this too. Or poured it out for the sake of it. But no. There was a whirring noise and a soft clank, then a small consistent flow of water poured free. It wasn't cold, but it was heaven.

She drank her fill, half-lying on the bed underneath the nozzle. For a minute or two after she had drank, she let the water pour over her, unmoving.

Suri considered that Scilla had won.

Yes, she had water. Maybe two carriages worth of water in these pipes.

How long would that last her? Days?

What then?

She was alone, unarmed, injured. In the middle of a desert, surrounded by people who wanted her dead. What chance did she have?

The priestesses were long on their way. Rasel was either dead, or in Drangbor already. They would never return for her.

Her next sleep was fitful. She'd wake up, drink a bit of water, and sleep again. The pain went from a screaming cacophony to a shout.

After what might have been an entire day, she realised the water was running low.

She took a sip, as the afternoon light crept in.

This was Scilla's gift. A slow and humiliating death, where she lost what was left of her pride. Lost all hope.

It was Kol's dream for her, manifested.

That thought drove a spike of anger through her. An anger that somehow felt loud even amongst the pain.

She clung to her anger.

The anger propelled her to move. She ripped her robes and soaked the fabric in some of the remaining water, squeezing it through again and again until the cloth was as clean as she could make it.

She took the soaked material and wrapped it diagonally around her face, taking care to have it touch her eye as little as possible, not wanting to think about what was underneath. She tied it firmly at the back of her head, the makeshift bandage covering half her face. It was ugly, but it was less ugly than sand in the half open wound.

Suri turned the water off. She stood, holding her anger like a crutch to keep her upright, to stop herself from lying back again from the pain.

Moving slowly, she walked around the wreckage of the camp, finding every flask she could. She found eight. She also took footwraps and a hood. Then, amongst the bodies festering in the late afternoon heat, she managed to find a dagger.

Scilla had done her job well, but not well enough.

Scilla had tried to break her, but every step that woman took gave her more of a reason to keep moving. To walk her own path until theirs could cross again.

Her looting complete, she filled each flask to the brim using the water from the other carriage and stored them in a bag.

Then she waited, drinking her fill from the remaining water in the pipes. It was warm now, the never-ending heat of the day turning the shaded carriages into sweat boxes. She was bathing in the heat of the air.

When the sun dropped along with the temperature, Suri fastened the hood in place, donned the footwraps and her bag, and left.

The only plan she had was to walk in the direction the carriages were headed, for as long as she could. Their party was attacked within a day's ride from the edge of Drangbor. She might be able to reach it on foot.

Suri had been left with two crucial things. Her life, for one. The only thing she truly prized. And the other, her red hot desire for revenge.

But she also had three big problems.

First, the terrain. Every step on the sand took the energy of four on a normal path. Second, it was dark. She stumbled often, using valuable energy to right herself.

And the pain.

It was a river of endless, knowable pain. Her head screamed at her. Suri ground her teeth. Her hands clenched open and shut, as she warred with a horrible and overwhelming urge to clutch at her face, to hold the wound.

The worst was the disbelief. She wanted to pull the bandage from her face. Maybe it had healed, maybe they hadn't gone through with it. Maybe now it would be fine. Maybe *now*. Her hands grabbed her head and then she pulled them back.

The hope was everything. The hope kept her moving. If she took off the bandage and felt the same blank nothingness. The same emptiness. Could she carry on?

She tried to counter her rising and volatile hopelessness with that thrum of anger. The shadow that had caressed her in the darkness and moved her body in that dance of death last night.

It was so faint. Barely there. The roar that had consumed her last night was gone. But finding it was a distraction. It got a little louder, when she imagined how she might kill Scilla. The justice she would serve upon her.

Sometimes he whispered, the barest hint of his voice. But it was encouragement. She knew he supported her.

Pain.

And another step.

Pain.

More steps.

More pain.

Her thighs burned, as she scaled and descended the small dunes and the indigo of twilight descended into complete blackness.

She heard nothing but the skittering flurries of sand, as her boots pulled into a new step. She saw nothing. The feeling that she may as well now be blind filled her with immense terror.

The waves of nausea started in the early hours. The liquid had sat like a rock in her stomach and now it was laid onto the sand.

She couldn't bring herself to feel sorry for herself, she could only feel relief that she could still see her own vomit.

More steps.

More pain.

Her pace was slow. Painful and slow. But she kept moving. To stop was to decide Kol was right.

The monotony of the horrible landscape was broken once in the morning when Suri noticed two new features to her environment.

The first was a tower to her right. Nervousness hit her first. A twist of unease and fear, watching the base and top of the tower for any movement.

The second was a weird haze to her left. It clung to the air near the sand, like the night hadn't quite left that space. The dawn wouldn't penetrate it. It took her too long to realise that it wasn't a strange haze, or some trick of the eye.

It was mist.

The edge of the Healing Fields, or the Blood Mists, lay only thirty paces to her left. She could have stumbled in the night, or turned a fraction, and she would have walked into them without even knowing it.

She kept moving, for lack of anything else to do, anywhere else to go. She kept striding through the endless sandy purgatory.

The tower was almost a confirmation that she was real. That this was all real. Other people were feeling the first uncomfortable heat of the sun that now hit against her back.

It was something.

The Blood Mists were something else. All she had to do was move a few paces left and it would all be over within a minute. She'd shrivel up or burst open and then she would be nothing. The sand would flow over her. Everyone would forget her.

More steps.

More pain.

She didn't move further from the Mists. She kept them close to her, like a knife she could fall on. It was some way of knowing that she was choosing her fate.

She kept thinking that pain would lessen, but it never did.

When the heat came for real, when it started to pour on her, the pain felt worse. The wound itself —hot. Protecting it from the sand was needed, but it added a cloying warmth to the skin over and above the warmth that was now everywhere.

Sun.

Steps.

Pain.

Hotter and hotter, as the sun rose towards its peak.

She drank two of the flasks of water, but still felt shrivelled. Her skin, leathery.

The day rolled past in a blur of pain. She didn't know how far she'd gone. It had taken hours for the tower to pass from view, and the Mists had curled away to the left and now sat long behind her. In the mid afternoon, she curled into a ball and slept.

When she awoke, the sun was dipping beneath the horizon. There was a moment, so brief, that she forgot herself. Forgot where she was, what had happened to her. Then it came back to her, the memories pouring over her like the sand, as she sat up.

She dragged herself to her feet, then set a similarly dragging pace through the night.

Steps.

Pain.

The landscape did not change. Her anger hung threadbare in the face of the void around her. By the morning, she still saw no sign in the distance. No towers, demarcations, walls. Nothing other than more rolling sand. Perhaps, she'd walked the wrong way.

She had nearly run out of water. She had one flask left and the morning heat was beginning. She knew that one flask of hot water, walking all day across a desert, was not enough, but refused to accept it.

She had stopped hearing the thrum in the night. He had left her. She did not begrudge it, though it hurt, a cool blanket ripped from beneath her.

There was hope, however. But this hope was grounded in her very self. This hope was grounded in her blood, her real beating heart.

As she moved, she would count her heartbeats. She didn't stop or trace her skin, but, as she walked, she tried to imagine the feel of her heart. Suri recalled Mother Edi's words and guidance and tried to guide herself through the motions as she moved endlessly, painfully, slowly.

Thud. Thud.

She focused on her throat. She imagined she could visualise the inside, see where it was dry, and feel her heart carry that beat of life through it, around in, down inside her.

Thud. Thud.

The sun was now deep in the sky. She reached for her flask. It was still full.

She hadn't touched it since the morning.

Suri had not had a sip of water, walking through the midday heat. She was thirsty, yes. But the thirst of minutes, not hours. She had a little to drink. It tasted the same.

It was unfathomable, and so Suri did not fathom it. It meant only that she could survive longer.

Once more, she lay in the sand, counting the beats of her heart as she drifted into slumber.

Thud. Thud.

A murmuring voice wavered in and out of her head. It was almost like that voice. Male, deep, close. But it sounded warped, as if coming from outside her.

"—the Daughter. Cannot... Who..."

She tried to ignore it, until a shuffling of sand made her jolt upwards, blinking in the sun. She felt a tap on her shoulder.

"Here."

This time, she recognised the voice in an instant. Suri blinked and scrambled a few steps back. She fell back into the sand, creating distance between them.

He was crouched next to where she'd been lying, his hand brushing something in the sand she couldn't see. His expression was unfathomable—some mixture of confusion, delight, and utter torment.

"Get away from me," she said, her voice scratched to a husk.

He straightened out of a crouch, standing to his full height. He was dressed in all white. The clothing of his people, the full length arms and trousers with the white belted tunic tied to his wide torso with the hood and a full length cape. His dark eyes burned through her.

The Lord Kol raised his hands. In one, he held a flask. In the other, the reins leading to the same huge horse he had ridden into the outpost all those days ago. "Fine, just take it."

He threw the flask to her. Suri flinched as it landed in the sand by her knee.

Black leather with a fine braided strap. She picked it up, twisting the cap. The inside was the same colour, so she could not make out the contents. She sniffed and a little sugary scent hit her nose.

She watched Kol, waiting. The shadowed lord still had his hands held up, and he sighed in exasperation.

"It's not poisoned," he said.

Suri still did not move.

"What would be the point? If I wanted to kill you, I'd just need to poke you with a small stick," he growled.

Suri scowled at him. "Why draw it out?"

Her anger was definitely still there. Buried, but there. He had brought it to the surface within a minute.

"I've decided I'd rather you live," he said. It was nonchalant. Enigmatic.

"Why?"

He didn't respond for a moment, again staring at the sand beneath his feet. Then he shook his head. "Call it a whim."

A whim? A choking noise clawed out of her dry throat.

It was hateful. It was the errant thought of one man whether or not she would die. It was not her steps, her pain. Her choices and her struggle were irrelevant in the face of his *whim*.

She couldn't tear her eye away—but she also didn't know how to handle the unimaginable rage.

"You stumbled pretty far, considering," he said, in the face of her silence.

Suri jutted her chin out, feeling the hot cloth that wrapped her festering eye shift as she moved. "Not far enough. I'm still in this shithole."

The man in white pointed to her face. "I have something for that. May I?"

Kol took a step forward, and Suri pushed herself back. He paused.

"No. Stay away," she replied.

He knelt to the floor. The Lord reached into his tunic, and Suri tensed. He pulled out a small jar.

Kol chose his words, his voice slow and deliberate. "It will help your eye. You've come this far. Don't lose to something ridiculous."

This too, he threw towards her. She picked it up, looked at the jar of white gloop for a moment, and then looked back at him.

"How did you find me?" she asked.

He shrugged. "Scilla told me where she'd left you. I figured you'd have walked in this direction. I found the footprints."

Suri suspected it was a lie, at least in part. There was something convenient and nonchalant about it. And footsteps faded so fast on these sands. But his mention of *her* had set her blood boiling.

"Does Scilla know you're here?" she asked, struggling to even say it. The name felt like a curse, acknowledging how close to death Scilla had brought her. A waking nightmare that was far from over.

Kol looked down. "She does. I doubt she'll be happy with my change of heart."

Suri snickered. "Because you've decided you want to torment me a while longer."

"Exactly."

She opened the flask and drank deep. She couldn't help but close her eye from the relief that passed, as she swallowed the cold liquid quelling the fire in her throat.

She opened her eye to see Kol staring at her. "I can't decide which of you I hate more."

Kol clenched his jaw, digging his hand into the sand at his feet. She watched the veins pulse. "Ah yes, a hard decision. On one hand, someone who beat you, took your eye, and left you for dead. On the other... me."

His eyes burned through her, but she lacked the energy to consider being intimidated. "Yes. You," she replied. "You, who wanted me to be nothing. You, who gives the orders. Her actions are your actions."

Her voice was simple. She had no need to exaggerate. She spoke only the truth.

"As I said, I changed my mind."

On a whim, she thought.

Kol dropped the sand he clenched in his hand and sat back. He sighed and pulled his face guard down. His wide mouth was so unfairly pretty, even now, in this horrible place.

Suri leaned back, drinking the liquid. She quenched her initial thirst before realising that it didn't taste entirely like water. There was some other sweetness or flavouring to it. If it was poisoned, then she was already dead given the amount she'd drunk. But he had a point. She was sat a couple feet from the most dangerous man in all of Greater Peregrinus. If he wanted her dead, he wouldn't need poison.

He watched her. She watched him.

"What do you want, Kol?" she asked.

The Lord of the Parched Lands did not change his gaze. "I want to make you an offer."

18

He joins with me in dream. His spirit inside heals
every part of me. I am euphoric.
     Diary of C. Aubethaan, est. early 8th century

"An offer."

She repeated Kol's words, unable to hold back her scepticism.

"Yes," he said.

"You want to make me an offer?" She echoed him like a dullard. But she didn't understand. What could she have to trade?

A hint of a smile ghosted on his lips. "That's what I said."

Suri was unable to hold back the bite in her words. "Have you seen me? How is it an offer, when I am unable to refuse?"

Kol shrugged. "Still."

"What is it you want from me?" she asked.

"How about I tell you what I will give you first?"

She didn't like this. The way he controlled her very life and the conversation. She was powerless, always so damn powerless.

"Fine."

Kol reached out his arms, gesturing to all the space around him.

"Your life. You are lost in my lands. If I leave here, you die."

Suri frowned, about to argue, but Kol cut in.

"And you are going the wrong way," he said. "I will grant you safe and fast passage to the edge of my lands, where you can cross the border to Drangbor and then go wherever it is you wish."

Suri considered it as Kol lowered his arms. It could be true, or it could be a lie. She had no clue where she was going, that was for sure. She'd been sure she'd walked in a straight line... She tried to look where she'd come from, only the sand had shifted as she slept and she couldn't now see her footsteps.

His huge bastard steps were all she could see.

Even if she knew the right direction before, she certainly didn't know it now.

Damn it all.

She chewed her chapped lip, then looked at him. "And?"

Kol gave a wry grin. "There is something else you desire? More than your life?"

She pointed at him. "Don't play with me."

Kol raised a thick eyebrow.

"I'm not stupid. This offer grants you something in return. I would expect some element of payment, or else you are not offering me anything at all, you're just sparing me from death. You're offering a beggar's mercy and call it compensation."

Kol nodded.

"A fair point. How about this? I will give you your mercy, but I will also give you three more things."

Suri could tell from his mocking tone that he had always intended to offer her more. He was baiting her.

"What do you want me to do?" she asked again.

He ignored her question.

"First, I will give you some gold. Spend it on food, inns, whores. It is not my concern."

Gold? He offered her gold. She was an escaped convict, a murdering slave. Offering her bits would have been too much. Silver would be generous, but he offered her gold?

Suri had never seen a gold piece before. She didn't even know how many bits a gold piece was worth. Twenty five? Fifty. Maybe even a hundred.

She could do so much. She could finally start her own gang.

Her mind whirred. That was thinking small, even. Two gold was likely enough to buy muscle and a couple pickpockets over to her side. *Some* gold he said. Multiple gold.

Obscene.

Some had to be at least three. What if it was five? Ten?

Shit, she might be able to buy out Geren's whole operation and eat real hot meals for months.

She truly tried to feign disinterest. But she couldn't help her eye scanning his horse's saddlebags. How much did he carry on him now? If she were only stronger. If he were only weaker.

"Second, I will give you this."

She watched him like a hawk, as he reached into his tunic and pulled out what looked like a black square of cloth, with some sort of string.

He threw it to her. She did not flinch. She caught it in one hand as her other still held the half empty drink.

She appraised it and, for a moment, it made her breath catch painfully in his chest. It was a mockery of a thing. It was so cruel.

An eyepatch.

A black soft fabric eyepatch, with a soft strap around it which would fasten it to her head. It was well made. It was nice fabric.

It was the worst thing she'd ever seen.

She hadn't let herself think about it until then and the pain of it made her want to cry. When the barest of a tear formed in her eye. In her *one* eye, in her *only* eye, it took everything, everything she had, to blink it back. To see the object as an object. It was a thing. Things do not hurt you. People hurt you. Do not let him hurt you.

She flipped the fabric over in her palm and saw a silver pattern painted over the opaque fabric. It only went from bad to worse, as she took in the pretty drawing of an eye.

Suri lifted her one blazing eye, in all its fury, up to him. "Really? An eye?"

Her voice did not shake.

Kol had the gall to look a little pale. "It is spelled with Fae magic. I will be your sight where there is blindness."

Her voice shook now. It was not grief, but anger behind it. "What?"

Kol explained in a calm voice that warred against the hot pain like a poker in her heart. "It is *seeing silk*. I can use the same silk and see through mine, to yours. I can see as if I am you."

She would never look like Suri again. Never *see* like herself again. She was a thief. And she was half-blind. It had been taken from her. By him, by *his proxy*. "Why would I ever let you see what I see?" she asked, allowing every trace of venom to pour from her.

Kol rocked back ever so slightly. He recoiled from her, from her broken face. "It is a gift, not an obligation."

It was not a gift. It was a taunt.

Look what I did to you. Look what I could do again.

She hated him. She *hated* him.

Suri placed the eyepatch on the sand in front of her. She refused to look at it. Swallowing past that lump in her throat, she asked. "And third?"

Kol did not move, did not make some sweeping gesture or even look behind him. He sat, hands on his knees as he watched her. "Third, I will give you my horse."

At that, the horse made a huffing sound. Suri could have sworn it *understood*.

His horse.

She took in the sight. The huge stallion. Shining mane, gleaming coat. It was darkness itself, it was beautiful. She had thought it black before, but she saw now it was a very dark brown. Giant. Terrifying in its greatness.

Interesting.

Unexpected.

A handful of gold. Life-changing for her, but for him? Not important. His spying silk was little more than a taunt.

This was curious. This was something he cared about. A creature he respected. Given to a creature he wanted dead.

Suri pursed her lips. "Why me?"

Kol played with the sand again. Everything about his physique and his face screamed danger to her. But this movement, picking up the sand and letting it stream between his fingers. It was so oddly childlike.

"Lera's lot trust you, sort of," he said, as the sand fell between his fingers. "We hate each other. They would not suspect you to be working with me."

And here it was then.

"And if I refuse?"

Her mouth felt instantly dry again, as she waited for his reply.

"If you refuse my offer, you will still leave with your beggar's mercy. But nothing else."

She breathed out.

She was shocked. She would refuse him, and he would let her live. He would give her back her life, deliver her from his evil land. For nothing.

Gold. A horse. Whatever the silk was worth. Incredibly tempting. Ridiculous, even. Surely nothing she could provide could ever match what he had just offered her.

Suri only paused for a few seconds before replying. "Then I refuse."

Kol huffed. "You will not even listen to my request?"

She shrugged, drinking more of the liquid. Some of the pounding in her head had dissipated. She felt better. Weak. But definitely better. "You may tell it to me," she said. She still had both her ears, after all. Scilla had not taken them yet.

Kol stared at her again. "But you will not consider it?"

She looked at the patch on the sand. She looked at the majestic beast standing against that endless repeating backdrop. Then she looked back at him. The Lord of the Sands. The Lord of Nothing.

She was sorely tempted, her fingers almost itched to hold that life-changing sum. But it was never going to happen. The gold could get her a new life, but it was a weight around her neck. She had gone from a Northern slave, to almost being condemned to a die in a cursed mine, to essentially a prisoner of the priestesses. To agree to this, would be to bind herself into some contract with a man who had told her in no uncertain terms that he wanted her to die a long and excruciating death.

She did not trust him as far as she could throw him. As soon as their business was concluded, if she even managed to perform whatever ridiculous task he wanted, there was nothing to stop him from taking his precious gold and throwing her right back into the slave cart.

She shook her head. "You offer me freedom, or a golden cage."

Kol didn't reply for a moment. When he spoke, his words were careful. "In return for my three gifts. I ask only two things from you."

"What two things could you possibly want?" she asked, curiosity getting the better of her.

"Answers. I have two questions I need answers to. The first being, where is the amefyre?"

Suri scoffed. Politics and money. Of course. It was boring in its simplicity. "So, you stole from them, they stole it back, and now you're bitter?"

Kol's mouth locked into a grim expression. "The amefyre was mine."

She fathomed that it was impossible for her to care less about the health of the sandman's coffers. She smiled in a patronising way. "I'm sure it's already on its way to the treasury. Somewhere safer. Away from grabbing hands."

Kol glowered at her for half a moment, then recovered his expression. He spoke slowly again. "If so, that is what I wish to know. Find the location of the amefyre. Show me some proof of its whereabouts. And that would be all I ask from you."

Suri looked at him with no small suspicion.

"That's it. You'll give me the silk, the money, and your horse. All you want me to do is to prove that they've put the amefyre back in the treasury?"

Kol nodded. "Yes."

She couldn't stop the question that rose despite it all. She might not take the offer, but she wanted to understand just how stupid this man was.

"Why?"

He watched her mouth as he spoke. "Because I don't think they are putting it in the treasury. I think they are using it to create a new Gate."

Suri folded her arms.

"And that concerns you," she stated.

"Yes."

She gave it a few seconds of thought.

"I refuse your offer."

Nothing had changed. He seemed to ask so little of her, which could only mean that agreeing to whatever this plot might be was dangerous and too good to be true. She refused to be a pet to this man. To be at his beck and call. To accept his demands.

Suri couldn't make out his expression. He was silent for a time. Perhaps regretting his decision to allow her an option to live. Perhaps he would change his mind again. On a whim.

Kill her after all.

Suri staked her life on the honour of an honourless pagan. The baby of the Wrath. She ought to be ashamed.

"What would you request from me?" he asked. "I can take you to the outpost, give you fine wines and rooms. Name your price. Ask it of me."

Suri thought this was another joke. His expression made her uncertain. There was something there.

She did not believe it. He would not open up himself, lay himself bare to her requests. To *her* whims. He could not be this desperate.

This man, who had taken so much from her, teased her with the offering of whatever she desired. Funny now that the thing she wanted most in the world was that which she'd taken for granted for twenty years of her life. A simple thieving life in the cold, barren North.

"I want nothing from you."

Kol's eyes flashed and she thought the lash of his tongue was coming. But he said nothing.

He stood and she thought the steel of his sword might come instead. But again nothing.

Still, he towered there, silhouetted in white against that beautiful horse.

"You are resolved," he said. "Let us leave, then. Are you able to stand?"

Suri pulled herself to her feet without a second's hesitation. The burn in her legs was so severe, and her knees so weak, that she nearly buckled straight back into the sand. This damned sand.

She brought herself up to stand at her full height. She held the flask in one hand and grabbed the silk eyepatch in the other. She threw the eyepatch at Kol. He caught it, deftly, and did not respond. She would not keep anything he gave her. She wanted no bonds to him, no debt beyond the heavy weight of her life.

Kol gave her a hesitant look. "Can I ask—?"

"What?" she replied.

He stared at her, his gaze thoughtful. "Do you still have my sun brooch?"

Suri had a half second of confusion before it came back to her. His brooch. The beautiful pin, designed to look like a spiralling sun of thin silver strands. She'd stolen it at the ball.

"No," she replied. His eyes tightened at the edges, and she felt a weird urge to elaborate. "I didn't sell it. I didn't have time. I left it with the other stuff. In the sewers."

Kol nodded. He held her gaze for a moment and her cheeks reddened. She couldn't explain it. A moment later, he moved to stand beside his horse.

She realised now that this was his intention. To ride them together to the border of his lands. She had never ridden a horse. The thought was alarming, but she refused to let it show. If he could ride as well as he did, then she had the dexterity to at least stay on the damn thing.

He watched her, reaching out his hand towards her.

As she stepped forward, a hand's width from her toe, something poked out of the sand. It nestled out of the exact place she had been sleeping minutes earlier before Kol arrived.

It was also where she'd seen his hand hovering. Where he'd been staring.

A tiny, green plant.

It was a narrow vine, spearing out through the yellowed sand. Two tiny dry leaves sprouted from its wiry stem. It was about the length of her index finger. Frail.

Yet alive.

Life. Here. Almost under her very foot.

How had she not seen it when she lay down? She must have been more exhausted than she realised.

"What is that?" Suri asked, looking back up to Kol.

The Lord had followed her gaze and was staring down at the plant with what she could only assume was the same expression she wore. A lack of understanding. Wonder, maybe.

At her question he lifted his gaze back to her.

"That," Kol replied. "Is why I didn't kill you."

She raised an eyebrow.

He didn't kill Suri, because she was near a plant.

She considered that maybe he thought she'd squish the thing fighting him off. Maybe it was sacred to whatever his pagan beliefs were. She decided that the most likely possibility was insanity.

"I didn't know you even had plants," she said.

Kol stared at her, then reached his hand back out to her.

He would not tell her. He would not tell her anything. Her curiosity burned. Life was possible in these dead lands after all then. What did that mean? Was it widely known?

Doubtless even if she did ask, it would not help. He would give her some enigmatic response that would not help her at all.

Besides, she didn't want him to know she cared, that she was curious. She'd already given enough interest away. The more she asked, the more he would look for ways to involve her in his schemes.

Perhaps she could find answers elsewhere, from anyone but him.

Suri stepped forward. She looked at his outreached hand. She looked up at the beast, now only a small distance from her.

It was so tall. She'd never seen a horse this size before. The grey mares and stallions pulling the priestesses wagon had been fine specimens, but this horse was something else. She ignored his hand and took another step forward, moving slowly, so the beast could watch her movements if he wanted. Her hand shook slightly, as she reached out and brushed her fingers over its neck.

The beast made a small noise and she forced herself not to flinch. He was firm and muscular, there was no give under her fingers. He felt solid, unbreakable. She stroked her fingers down a little, then retracted her hand.

Suri appraised the stirrups. Did they have to be so damn high?

"Wait," she said. She spun around to look at the Lord of Death. Her head pounded with the speed of her movement.

He had reraised his mouth guard. His dark eyes bore into her, watching her every move. In case she tried to run for it.

"You said you wanted two answers from me. What was the other?" she asked.

Kol moved past her, and his clothed arm brushed her robed arm. Her skin pimpled from the contact as he patted the horse's saddle. "You would not agree to the first, is there any point in asking you the second?"

She narrowed her gaze at his back. Evasion again. "What was it?"

"Get up first try, and I'll tell you," he goaded.

Suri stepped forward. Without hesitation she thrust her left foot up, hooking it into the stirrup with as little grace as a baby animal and decidedly less charm. She almost lost her balance, but pushed her weight forward and gripped as high up on the saddle as she could.

She heaved.

She felt then how much of her strength she'd lost in the past week, how she had clung to the scraps of it. It was tenacity alone that had hauled her up and over and now into an unfamiliar saddle.

She was so high up. Suri looked down at Kol, hoping to give him a pointed look, but his eyes were on the horse's mane.

He stroked the horse's back, then looked up at her. "I wanted to know your name. Your real name."

"Oh." That threw her off guard. She opened her mouth and then closed it.

Her silence had already confirmed his suspicion from the cage, that Edi was a lie. She still didn't know how he'd worked that out. What mask would she wear instead?

Kol watched her, his face impassive. Then he looked down and started detaching the saddlebags from the horse.

"What are you doing?"

He continued. "I'm not letting you run off with all my stuff, little thief."

She furrowed her brow. "You are not coming?"

Kol looked up and smirked. "Disappointed?"

She scowled.

He moved around the beast and detached the other set of saddlebags, swinging them around his shoulders. He moved to the front of the horse and said something under his breath.

"Ruben is a relic of the past. He knows the way," he said, stroking the horse's nose. He looked up at her. "And the way back."

Suri scowled at his pointed comment. "I'm not going to steal your damned oversized horse."

She could have sworn she saw something akin to mirth in his eyes. He looked down, before she could study it further.

"He will stop near the Pananti Foothills. They will look different from the dunes and are the informal border between us and Drangbor," he said, as he passed back around to the side. "If you're going to breathe death, at least take it where you might do some good."

As she tried to make sense of his words, Kol touched two fingers to Suri's calf, just for a second. She flinched from the touch as he removed his fingers. He whispered again. "*Asari ith vulturis.*"

"What's that?" she asked.

He took a few steps back, giving her and Ruben a wide berth. "It is a saying of my people. It means... try not to die, little thief."

He clicked his tongue and the horse moved underneath her. She scrambled to grab onto the reins and hold them firmly against the handle of the saddle.

Suri looked to Kol, as the horse plodded its first couple of steps.

"Suri."

She didn't know what compelled her to say it.

He cocked his head. "What?"

She swallowed. She'd cast the stone now, might as well see it to its conclusion. "My name is Suri."

Kol stared at her. She stared back. He nodded.

"Suri?" he asked.

She cocked her head.

"Hold on tight."

Then he whistled, a low and quick sound. She barely had time to grab on as Ruben shot from underneath her. She let out a yelp, as they galloped off into the growing dusk. Behind her, a man's laughter.

As she rode, she thought of him. She thought of the offer he had made her. His horse—one of his three gifts—pounded across the sand underneath her as if it were flat sturdy ground. She thought of his request, his belief that Queen Lera might be building a new Gate.

But her thoughts kept coming back to that plant. The one that would have been nestled beside her head as she slept.

If a thing like that could survive in a place like this, then maybe there was hope for a half-blind wretch like her.

She would make her own money, free of any chains. and then she would return to the North. Disguised, wiser, richer. Ready to start her life again.

Hours later, Ruben slowed to a stop. She'd finished the drink Kol had given her long ago and was sipping at the one flask she had left. She tightened the stopper back on, before looking down at the horse, then around her more closely.

"Are we here?" she asked. She wasn't sure why she'd asked it out loud, as if the horse would hear her.

But the horse snorted. And it almost felt like a response.

In the distance, she saw it in the growing grey light of dawn. Hills, different hills. A variation to this torment of a landscape. The relief she felt, the feeling that this place did end, nearly overwhelmed her.

She swung her leg up and over, landing deeply. A whole new kind of ache made her thighs and stomach feel like jelly. She hadn't realised how much she'd been working just to stay on and upright.

Suri noticed then that the saddle was not empty. Where the saddlebags should have been was a small tied black pouch.

She untied the bag from the seat and opened the drawstring. Inside was two silver. In the Tangle, a small fortune. It would feed her for a month. He'd likely forgotten he'd even left it there. Pocket change compared to the gold he'd offered before.

The silk eyepatch was folded up next to it.

She pulled it out and looked at it for a moment, before tutting and putting it back into the pouch. Maybe she could sell it. She tied the pouch to her waist.

She patted Ruben's neck. "Your master is trying to spy on me."

Again, almost in response, Ruben moved his front left hoof, pawing it against the sand.

With no small amount of fear, Suri walked around to the front of the horse. As he had done. She looked at the horse and the horse looked back at her.

She reached her hand out flat, stopping short of the creature's long face. He was a huge beast, midnight black. His eyes were gentle though, his manner calm. He moved predictably, not skitting around like other horses.

"He said you know the way back, sweet giant. How can you find anything in this nothing?" she asked softly.

Ruben moved his nose into her hand. His hot breath tickled her skin. She held her breath, not wanting to scare him, and he moved his nose back.

"Thank you for taking me. I'm sorry I have nothing to give you."

The horse moved away from her then, and she stayed stock still. The wildness of living creatures was terrifying to her. The randomness of the world outside of man, the lack of understanding of everything in it that could kill her; winds, sun, and beasts. She did not know the tricks. The horse turned and whinnied at her.

She waved her hand at him. "Alright, alright, I'm going."

Suri looked back towards the foothills and started walking. It had been her most pleasant interaction in days.

In the hour that followed, the sand dunes' pure shades started to mix with brown. Soon the ground underfoot was a bit firmer, now dried sunbaked soil. The foothills grew closer and, at their small peaks, she could see the scrub of some half dead bushes that dropped along their horizons.

When she reached the top of one of the small hills, she breathed in, tasting moisture, dirt, and life in the air.

The weak dirt underfoot quickly turned into dark soil and green grass. Rolling hills of thick emerald grass rose and fell. Nestled in, and around, were hills formed entirely of slate grey tiered rock. Even on these though there was life, with cascading purple flowering bushes pushing through the rock faces. Small settlements arose here and there, puffs of smoke emitting from chimneys. Wildflowers scattered the fields.

For a moment, she looked back. Surveyed the endless stretch of sand and nothingness behind her.

She thought she could still see, in the distance, the shape of a large black horse.

Waiting.

Watching.

Then she looked forward and took her first steps into Drang-bor.

19

Mother found me. She says I must return home. I will not. I will not.
    Diary of C. Aubethaan, est. early 8th century

"Do you have an audience with the Queen, priestess?" the guard asked.

Suri had reached Drangbor's capitol, Drameir, only hours prior. Her journey had been a fast one, once her clothing had been recognised at the first village she passed, and she was then ferried on nothing but goodwill towards her priestly robes. After two comfortable days, she stood at the foot of the castle. The Seat of Drameir.

The city was beautiful. Dark slate roofs matched the outcroppings of rocks dotting the landscape. The clean cobbles of the streets glistened with rainwater. The flower boxes adorning the windows of the city's houses were filled, even in the wintering months, with blossoms of various shades.

The streets were calm. The darkness of the Tangle was missing. The nights were somehow quiet, clear of drunkards and terror. A large number of priestesses roamed in groups, usually accompanied by one or two guards, and people moved out of their way.

The cityscape was finished by its twin pinnacles. The wider of the two, and the newer, was the cathedral. Its towering four minarets spiked into the sky. It too, was made of grey slate. The windows held stained purple glass.

Opposite it, was the older and narrower, but noticeably taller, Seat of Drameir. Suri now stood at its foot, in front of a guard.

The castle had been a vestige from the time of Diophage and Sotoledi. For hundreds of years, the King of all Greater Peregrinus sat at Drameir. When the last King—Volker—died shortly after the Wrath, he left no heirs and a terrible legacy. His was a reign of true and fervent belief in the Old Gods. When King Volker died, the belief in the Old Gods had already turned. Lera's vision of the Trio had already launched the first of many pilgrimages to the Altar, some of whom would soon become the first priestesses of the realm. The living nobles were left with a choice. Name Volker's widow, Queen Consort Lera, the Queen of all, or split the realms with each fiefdom becoming a Kingdom in its own right.

The Seat of Drameir still stood, but now it only ruled over Drangbor. Queen Lera had reigned here, and only here, for the last one hundred years. It had been a period of peace, religious growth, and understanding. The priestesses of the New Gods had brought harmony to not just Drangbor, but all of Peregrinus.

It was not spoken, but it was known. The true power of the land had never left. It still sat in Drangbor. At the Seat of Drameir.

Suri nodded to the guard. "I have an audience with her advisor, Prince Rasel."

The guard knocked on a hatch embedded into the silver birch wood door. The door was styled like the Gate at the Forgelands, with its stone columns at either side carved with creeping symmetrical ivy.

The hatch opened and a man's head popped out. He was well groomed, with tanned skin and midnight black hair. He looked her up and down.

Suri tried not to feel self conscious about her eye, the one now absent and forever dormant under her recently acquired brown leather eyepatch. Whilst it was worse quality by far than the silk in her pocket, anything was better than wearing his little spying cloth.

She had, however, lowered herself to using his other gift, applying the white goop sparingly morning and night. The relief it provided was immense. The skin remained taut and ugly under her touch, but it wasn't hot anymore.

The medicine might have saved her life. But it was his fault she had needed it in the first place.

The man narrowed his eyes. "What is your name?"

"Edi," she replied.

He looked to the guard. "I do not know the girl's face and we have no appointments. Send her to the cathedral."

Suri cleared her throat and took a step forward. The guard moved his hand to his oversized sword. She couldn't help but think how slow that weapon must be. The sheer weight of it alone. The man in the hatch looked at her with a withering scowl, but Suri stated in clear words. "I have an audience with Prince Rasel, I accompanied him on his recent venture east."

The man's face changed in an instant, his scowl melting into a thin line. "One moment."

The hatch closed and Suri tried not to fidget, as she felt the weight of both guards' eyes on her.

Minutes passed, and Suri debated if she should leave altogether, then the hatch reopened. The man looked a little frustrated.

"Open the doors," he said to the guards.

They followed his instruction, both pulling at the same time to open the beautifully carved huge wooden doors. In the gap between them was a large hall, with parquet flooring in precise black and white diamonds. Lanterns ensconced in more purple glass lit the marble walls.

The man, who Suri could now see was dressed in a sleek black suit, wafted his hand towards the inside.

"The Queen demands your presence in the throne room. Follow me."

Suri stepped forward, into the Seat of Drameir.

It hadn't been her plan to come here.

Not initially anyway.

She'd formed her new plan only a couple of days prior when she'd arrived in the city of Drameir. The goodwill of her peers had got her this far, as she was travelling only half a day behind the priestesses and the truth that she'd got separated was easily believed.

That had served Suri. Her travel was pleasant, a padded front seat on carts laden with wool or hay. When she arrived in the city though, she found herself at a loose end. It was expected she would have the protection and sanctuary of the cathedral. That was something she could not claim.

So, she'd decided to find Prince Rasel. Because she knew something he probably didn't want the Queen finding out. He'd killed Manira. That was surely worth something to him. Maybe it could buy her enough time to work out what the fuck to do next.

But if the man in front of her was to be believed, a man who kept turning back to check on her with irritating frequency, they were not heading for the Prince.

A personal audience with the most powerful woman in all Greater Peregrinus. This had to be a bad thing.

Her squirrelly escort reached a further grand silver door, flanked by two guards. The doors opened for them.

Inside, the parquet flooring changed to pure white marble. The chandeliers filled the room with a warm white glow. Hanging from the painted ceiling were almost invisible strings of different lengths holding tiny purple glass baubles which bounced off the light, creating little dots of purple on the walls and floor.

She counted six guards. And one queen.

At the end of the room stood a single throne. It was made of silver wood carved into vines which tangled and interlocked into a sprawling chair. Several silver cushions padded the seat.

Upon it, perched with delectable poise, was Queen Lera. The half-Fae woman was around a hundred and thirty years old. It was hard to believe she could be older than forty.

She wore a pale pink gown, with a metal lattice bodice covering the top half, an imitation of chainmail. Her skin was pale but rosy, her hair light brown and straight. Her crown was a delicate mesh of silver, with the largest amefyre Suri had ever seen locked in its silver clasps.

A narrow silver sword rested against the throne. It gleamed with a purity that made the thief doubtful it had ever been used.

What stood out the most, though, were the large delicate wings at her back. They extended out, tucking into gaps in the vines at the back of the throne. They were a pale translucent shade, the colour hard to fathom. A bauble's glare bounced off them and reflected back tiny rainbows of purple prismatic light.

It was rare indeed, for a part Fae to be blessed with wings. They probably didn't work, though that didn't make them any less intimidating. It was a reminder of everything the Fae blood brought. Long life and beauty and, with that, power and wealth.

The man took a couple of steps, before dropping into a low and sweeping bow. Suri provided her best imitation of a curtsey, keeping her head bowed.

"Please, rise." The voice was commanding, yet feminine and assured.

She raised her head and moved out of the awkward posture.

"Approach," the Queen said.

They did, the man still leading her towards whatever this was.

She felt *Him* then. She felt the thrum of it coming off the Queen like a drum beat, the same one she'd felt around Rasel and Kol. With them, she'd felt it when they were close by, but with the Queen, even at this distance, it pumped through her veins.

Sweet Suri, united with my Lera.

She suppressed a shudder at the voice.

The man opened his mouth to speak. "Your Gra—"

The Queen raised her hand and he closed his mouth, her gaze falling on Suri. Not a cursory glance. But a full appraisal, head to toe. "You are no priestess."

Suri didn't know if she was expected to speak. If she were, she would not disagree. Queen Lera was the leader of the Priestesses, the leader of the Faith of the New Gods.

"Yet you wear the garb of my people, my priestesses of the new Gods. Some might consider that an act of heresy."

Ice swept over Suri's body.

"Your name is Edi?"

It was another statement, but the intonation requested a response. Suri swallowed.

"Yes, your Grace," she said, dropping her gaze.

"Call me Lera, please." *Sweet Lera.* She glanced up and saw a smile playing on the Queen's lips. "I have heard a lot about you."

She couldn't gauge the tone. What had she heard?

"My poor priestesses, the ones who survived that horrible encounter," the Queen continued, her voice warm as it trailed into nothing. "They told me you were kept back. That you were likely dead."

Still statements. There was no question. She waited.

Queen Lera leant forward, her hair falling over one shoulder. "How did you survive?"

The priestesses had heard Scilla. Heard her venomous tone and intent. And now, she was here.

"Not without hardship, your Grace," she said. She gestured to her face.

Her hazel eyes zeroed in on Suri's eyepatch.

"They did that to you?" she asked.

Suri nodded. "Scilla."

"Witch," Queen Lera said, a spark of anger flickering like a match onto her face. Suri couldn't help the small crack of a smile from flitting across her face. It was nice to know at least one other person felt the same way. "My advisor tells me you killed Barsen."

So she had heard from Rasel too, Suri mused. She wondered what that meant for her chances here.

Tell the truth.

The voice was so loud, echoing in her head.

"Yes, your Grace," she replied.

"Why did she not kill you?" the queen asked.

It was blunt. The directness of the question struck Suri with something akin to respect. "She thought the wound or the desert would kill me instead."

The Queen cocked her head, again sweeping her eyes over Suri. "And yet it didn't. You made it through the desert on foot, made it to my lands. Some might say you were very lucky."

Her gaze flashed up again, a hot spike of irritation flaring. "They should see the blisters on my feet and the burns on my body, then determine how lucky I am."

She could hear the voice purr in approval, or laughter.

Queen Lera paused and Suri regretted her words. A quick glance to the man on her right confirmed she had scandalised him. Then the half-Fae royalty leaned back, a smile again on her mouth. Something about the smile aged her. Suri couldn't figure out why, but thought it was something in the tiredness of it. The expression looked worn, like a shirt worn until the holes were more than the fabric.

"You speak with confidence," the queen said.

Suri ducked her head, trying to show some attempt at humility. "I beg your pardon, your Grace. I speak with exhaustion."

It was easier to apologise, in the face of actual power. She could feel the awe plucking at her heart. She wanted, for some unknown reason, to *impress* this Queen. To be interesting, useful. And she hated that feeling.

"Of course," the Queen said. "And what of Kol?"

She darted her eyes up. "What of him, your Grace?"

"Yes. Are you aware his demon horse has been spotted in my lands?"

Suri swallowed, her mouth dry. "No. No, your Grace. I had no idea."

The Queen studied her face for a span of seconds, Suri paling under the weight of the gaze, before she glanced away, and Suri managed to breathe. "A pity."

"Your Grace?" she asked.

"I was hoping Kol was following you."

Suri spluttered.

"It's no matter," the Queen said. "I will find some other route to catch him." She drummed her fingers against her throne. "I would like to invite you to stay here at the palace, as my personal guest."

Suri didn't know what to say. She gaped her mouth and then closed it, clenching her empty fists as she struggled to maintain her composure. The voice was purring in her ear, and its soothing coolness helped her to calm down.

A guest? Of the Queen?

The man to her side started. "Your Gra—"

Again, the Queen cut him off. "Rasel will return later today. You will dine with us tonight. I look forward to hearing more about your trip."

It was an odd feeling, a fluttering inside her that made her feel off balance. She wanted to smile, it almost rose unbidden to her face but pushed the feeling down. She was aware of her awkwardness in the face of the Queen's grace.

The Queen gestured to her shocked escort. "Take her to the Third Span. Ensure she is provided with a change of clothes."

"Yes, your Grace," the man responded.

The Queen waved her hand, and they were dismissed. The man started walking away from the throne room, and Suri had to trot to catch up to his furious pace. The voice quietened to a satisfied hum again.

She couldn't help but wonder if she had traded Kol's golden cage for Lera's silver one. But she decided that maybe she was happy to play the role of the captive. Suri knew what real power was. Real power was to be so fearsome, all would obey you. Real power was to be so dangerous, none would oppose you.

Queen Lera had held onto this throne for one hundred years. She held the key to power somehow. Be it through truth or lies, wisdom or treachery. If Suri could linger in this place, perhaps she could unlock herself from her own constraints. Perhaps, she too could become something to be feared. Something powerful.

Beyond that, as they took hurried steps up the wide marble staircases, there were more practical considerations. Like why she had risked coming here in the first place.

It was time to blackmail a prince.

20

The King has found me. The man now knows my condition, and believes the babe growing inside me to be his own. I tried to tell him the truth, he did not listen.

Diary of C. Aubethaan, est. early 8th century

The Seat of Drameir was a square tower, tapering narrower at each floor until its point at the top, obscured by the low cloud.

The stairs were in the centre of the building. Suri stared upwards, seeing each progressive set of stairs getting narrower. She couldn't fathom how many floors there might be. They climbed only to the third floor, the Third Span, which appeared to be some sort of guest wing. A giant portrait of Queen Lera and King Volker hung against a white marble wall. Having spent her whole life hearing of him as a piece of history, it was odd to see him painted in vivid colour. He was an attractive middle-aged

man with a square jaw, with Lera poised in a beautiful lavender gown—a vision of youthful beauty. She must have been
no more than thirty when they married and, as a half-Fae, she
looked closer to Suri's own twenty years. What really struck her
through, was how cold Volker's eyes were.

The man opened a door and gestured for her to go inside.

"Change your clothes at once. Dinner will be served at the
sixth bell."

Suri walked into the room.

It was the finest bedchamber she had ever seen. Much like the
carriages, the floors and walls were laden with thick cloth and
rugged fur in shades of purple and grey. In the near stonewall
was a small fireplace. A chambermaid sat back on her heels, interrupted by their entry. She nodded, then went back to stoking
the fire.

A huge bed centred against the far wall. It was postered, with
thick cloth swooping between its boughs. A hefty wardrobe and
chest also furnished the room, alongside a wide dressing table.

"Is there anything else you require...?"

Suri swivelled to the man standing in the doorway. He clearly
didn't know how to address her. Neither did she.

"No, that will be all," she said.

He nodded and left. The chambermaid, having got the fire
alight, left too, scurrying out before he closed the door.

She pulled off the robes almost immediately.

Not because she had been asked to, but because she'd been
wearing them for days. She tried to rinse them each night, but
it was cold and the robe never fully dried, never lost that scent
of damp and desert and dirt.

Once stripped, Suri washed herself as best she could with the
ewer and the basin.

She sat down on the stool beside the dressing table and looked
into the mirror.

With the eye patch on, her face didn't look too different. But, at the edges of the fabric, she could see the skin on her cheek start to pinch.

Suri took a couple of deep breaths, then removed the eyepatch.

The skin around where her eye should have been, was angry and red. The eyelid hung down over the bloodied void like a perpetual wink.

It took several minutes for her to look at herself without feeling disgusted, without that feeling of twisting horror in her belly.

More minutes passed before she could see anything else but the fury. Before she could be grateful that, despite it all, she was still alive. At least the socket did not look swollen and it wasn't weeping any nasty fluid. That was all the light she could muster.

She put the eyepatch back on and went back to the basin to tidy her appearance. She took her time washing the remaining dirt from her face, scalp, and nails, before pulling a brush through her hair. Rouge, kohl, and other substances were scattered across the table, but she did not paint on a mask today. She did not know what mask they would want to see. So she would present them with herself, until she learned how to manipulate them.

She went to the wardrobe and found a few dresses that she could understand how to fasten without help. She picked a mauve one, hoping that wearing purple would come across as some sort of peace offering. She pulled the dress over her head, and it fell almost to the floor. The mauve had a faint diamond pattern across it, cream cuffs, and a cream underlayer which showed slightly when she walked. She fastened the belted fabric at the waist. Mother Edi would be disappointed in her. She wasn't much more than skin and bone. She let the belt out a fraction, to give the illusion of some non-existent weight.

She found some light house shoes, which were comfortable and completely impractical. Once she was dressed, the third bell had yet to ring.

For the first hour, she lay on the bed. She fidgeted, nervous energy making her unable to rest. At the tolling of the fourth bell, she sighed and pulled herself to the door.

She was in the Seat of Drameir. Not only that, she was a *guest* of the Seat of Drameir. That meant that surely she was allowed to roam, in at least a limited area. If ever there was a time to snoop, it was now.

Suri headed straight for the stairs. At every other passing Span, she paused to look out of the window, noting how everything in the city below kept getting smaller. When she got to the Seventh Span, she was higher than every rooftop, bar the minarets of the cathedral. At the Eleventh Span, she was almost on par with them, and the people in the square below looked like bugs. It caused an odd thrill in her, her heart racing as she excitedly rounded each new set of stairs, imagining what vista she might see next.

But it was at the Twelfth Span that she could travel no higher.

The marble staircases had got narrower, as she had climbed. At the first staircase, you could have had twelve men standing shoulder to shoulder climbing up. Now, maybe three across would fit.

Where the stairs would continue there was a locked silver door. She frowned and opened a small window. She stuck her head out and looked up. Yes, it continued, for several more Spans. Now that she was closer, it looked like the very top was not roofed, just several columns that stretched upwards into the sky. For a second, she was sure she saw something move. A fluttering of fabric near the top. A flag, perhaps.

And yet, there was no way up. None that she was permitted, anyway.

Perhaps she would ask the Queen about it. She ducked her head back in and started her descent.

She was around the Ninth Span when the sound of low music drifted up through the stairs. She followed the sound down. It started fading again, as she descended to the Seventh Span. She turned and went back up, roaming the hall of the Eighth Span.

The music stopped, breaking off in a jagged pull. She was certain the sound had drifted from a door sat ajar on the eastern wall. Suri pushed it open. Inside was a library.

A large desk sat in the centre of the room, with an oil lamp burning. Already the light outside the floor to ceiling windows was fading fast. Winter stole the sun here too. She wished it had been the case in the Parched Lands. That wasteland seemed to turn the day slower, like a boulder dragging against the sun's journey.

The walls were lined with books and short ladders were positioned to help readers reach the many spines. Suri had never seen so many books in her life, let alone in one place. Sure, she had peered into the glass windows of bookshops in the Merchant Quarter of New Politan, but she had been looking for prey, and their shelves were largely bare at the best of times.

Here, there were no gaps in the walls of paper.

She walked to the desk. On it, sat a painting. A painting of rolling green hills and slate crests, where the tiniest strokes seemed to paint the wind itself. Suri was no artist, but she could tell it was a good likeness for the wilds of Drangbor.

It was, however, ruined.

Hastily scrawled words in dark brown lettering covered the canvas. Suri only knew the common letters, this was something else. More curved, less formulaic. The letters lifted high and low, swirling back and around each other.

In another context, if the script was less rushed, would have looked elegant. But here, it was a sprawling chaotic mess.

"Repulsive, isn't it?"

Suri jumped. She spun around, gripping the desk behind her. Prince Rasel stood not three steps away.

He smiled at her reaction and took another step closer. She had no idea where he had come from. How had she not noticed him? Were her senses really that dulled?

It was a relief to see him alive.

He was dressed more finely than before. He wore a blood red dress shirt, cuffed at the wrist with silver, and slack dark trousers. The black cravat was present as ever, but this time tucked almost casually into his wide shirt. His long white hair was tied into a low bun and pushed from his face by a woven mesh of silver. His eyes were lined with kohl. He smelt of lavender and charcoal.

Rasel had unlocked that noise in her head, unlocked *Him* once more. Her back arched under His welcoming mental caress.

Rasel looked down at the painting behind her and his smile dropped a little. "To spoil something so beautiful."

"Your Grace," she murmured, ducking into another shit curtsey.

He tutted, and she looked up. He flicked his head upwards. She rose.

"Can I see it?" he asked.

It was clear what he meant. His steely eyes were trained not on her good eye, but on where the other lay.

She swallowed. "Why?"

He shrugged. "Curiosity."

Suri paused for a second, then reached up and pulled the eyepatch off. Rasel didn't flinch. If anything, he leaned forward, staring at the space where her eye should have been. He raised a hand, then lowered it.

She could feel his eyes searching her face. Empathy did not drive him, not even sympathy. He simply wanted to see it. He wanted to look at the disfigured girl. Maybe this was a novel injury, one he hadn't caused or seen before.

Part of her respected him for calling it as it was. Curiosity. The other part felt disgusted.

"Does it hurt?" he whispered. She shivered.

She could tell he wanted to touch it. He wanted to reach up and prod at the dead skin, at the hurt, with an almost childlike sadism.

She pulled the eye patch back on and turned.

Before he could ask again, she changed the subject. "What does it say?"

She pointed to the dried writing.

Prince Rasel moved around to the other side of the desk. She caught his gaze for half a second. He did not look at the painting. He looked only at her.

"It's in the pagan language," he said.

"Oh," she said.

The Old Tongue then. The language from before the Wrath, the language of old scripture and of Old Gods. Looking closer, she realised she recognised one symbol. A circle with a triangle on the left and the three dots to the right. It was carved in the Tangle, under the half decapitated carving of the Old Life God. It was the symbol of *Diophage*.

"It's funny, really. Those words say, *'Asari ith vulturis'*."

Suri's heart leapt in her chest as the Prince traced some of the writing below the symbol. The words were one and the same, she was sure of it. The only words in the Old Tongue ever spoken to her and now spoken twice.

'Try not to die, little thief.'

"It's a warning of some kind," he mused, smirking a little. "The modern day translation means 'beware the witch'. Ironic, if you think about it. Maybe, if they'd been more wary of their own pagan witches, a third of our entire land wouldn't be scorched to dust."

Beware the witch, Suri mused. Kol had told her it meant she should try not to die. Some ancient way of saying 'be careful', perhaps? Rasel was right. It seemed stupid that their motto for keeping safe was about avoiding witches. Maybe, if they'd all been more careful of the Fae witch under their noses, the ritual of Death would never have happened, and their lands wouldn't have been scorched.

"They did this? The pagans?"

He nodded. "Sometimes pagans break into the cathedral or the castle. They're silenced before they can do too much damage."

Suri didn't think there were more than a handful of pagans left. There had been the cultists who had raised the infant Lord of Death but, since then, how had they gathered a following? Had the Lord of Death spent his last one hundred years converting the dregs of the world into his own pitiful missionaries?

"What does this one mean?" she asked, pointing to the symbol directly next to the one she thought referred to Diophage.

Rasel glanced at it. "It means Revenge."

Diophage. Revenge.

Suri frowned, trying to figure out any meaning. 'Diophage's Revenge'? 'Life of Revenge'?

The voice in her head seemed to find her musings funny. That same purr of laughter reverberated in her head.

But it meant nothing, not without the rest of the context. Rasel's scowl prevented her from asking for the full translation.

"Those earrings are incredibly ugly," the Prince said, staring at her right lobe.

"What?" she said.

He smiled. "Those earrings. It looks like someone found a few old bits on the floor, smashed them up, and then stuck them through your ear."

She jutted her chin out. It probably wasn't too far from the truth, but she felt rebuffed. Her only possession, only claim to her past, was nothing. "And?"

The Prince looked at her as if she had asked the stupidest question in the world. "You are dining with the Queen. They are hideous."

He held his hand out.

Trust him, sweet Suri.

In the desert, He had saved her life. He so rarely gave instructions, that Suri found herself curious as to why He would weigh in now. Here. In this inconsequential moment.

Suri sighed and pulled each spike out in turn. They weighed next to nothing, but still her ear felt lighter with each removal. She felt humiliated.

There was only a small moment of hesitation, before she dropped the three spikes into his waiting hand. He put them straight into his pocket.

That was it then. Now all she had of Edi was her name.

And her words. *The metal helps with the voices.*

The truth of it hit her again now. With no earrings, He swirled in her head. The noise and presence of him took up so much space in her mind. There was room for her thoughts, but she was sharing them with Him, and His thoughts were louder still than her own.

And He was delighted.

Good Suri. You're doing so well.

Rasel moved away from the desk, settling into a plush armchair. He picked up a glass of the familiar brown drink from the table and gulped down a large mouthful.

She tried to get used to the feeling of sharing her head. If she relaxed, it was fine. He was noisy, but He was the same. Purring, humming, and thrumming inside of her mind, but she could handle it. He was nice to her, He made her feel valued.

Sweet Suri.

She saw then the small instrument made of shining deep wood which was propped against the other seat. He must have been the musician she had heard.

"If I knew I was about to die, I can't say I'd scrawl a few words onto a painting with the blood from my gaping wounds," he said, swirling the glass. "But maybe that's just me."

If his words were intended to shock her, he failed. She looked closer at the painting with this new lens. Painted in blood. Fascinating.

She stepped away from it, around the desk, before perching on the arm rest of the seat next to him. Her leg brushed his as she reached over, taking the glass from his hand.

He did not protest. He stared at her, watching her mouth and neck, as she took a sip of the liquid and swallowed. His gaze burned into her as the liquid burned down her throat.

Her discordant thrum matched his.

Suri didn't know what it meant. She didn't know what commonality they shared. This thrum had a shape, had a form. It had saved her life in the desert. It swirled around Kol, and around Rasel. It clung to the Queen. Did it protect them too? What force could cling to her and Kol though? To help one was surely to hurt the other.

They are of us.

She threw a question back in her mind. What does that mean? But He simply repeated himself, then went back to His hum.

She swirled the glass a couple of times, in a mockery of Rasel's action. "What would you do instead?" she asked, not looking away.

She passed the glass back to him, brushing his fingers with hers. As she moved her hand back, his hand lashed out to grab her wrist. A whisper of a chill passed up her arm.

"Edi, Edi, Edi," he said slowly. "Are you flirting with me?"

She smiled. It was a smile of conspiracy, of deceit. So that was one thing she knew united them. Maybe she would find more.

She leaned in towards him, determined to show him that she was not scared of him. She lowered her voice. "If I was, you would know."

His grip loosened, circling her wrist in a caress instead of a shackle. "Is that so?"

Suri stood, pulling her arm free of his grip.

She sat in the chair opposite him.

"I don't like to play with my food, unlike some," she said, throwing the comment out lazily.

He quirked an eyebrow.

"And who would you be referring to?"

Here goes nothing, she thought.

"Don't you think freezing her was a bit obvious?" she asked. She feigned nonchalance, pretending to brush a piece of lint from her lap.

"I don't follow your meaning?" he said. So, he did want to play.

She caught his eyes again now. His expression was loose, comfortable. Non-threatened. That was good, she supposed. Men did stupid things when they felt threatened. But she needed him to understand her.

"It was a risk, surely. To freeze the High Priestess to death."

He didn't say anything, just continued to stare at her as he drank.

She pursed her lips. "You must have realised there was a chance the priestesses would survive to tell on you. The Treaty—"

"And what does a thief know of treaties?" he cut in.

Good, she'd baited him.

"Little," she said. "What does the Queen know of the untimely death of her favourite priestess?"

He leaned forward. "Enough."

Rasel didn't take kindly to her game. It was time to throw him a bone.

With a dramatic flourish, she put her hand to her forehead as she had seen ladies do. "It was horrible to see Scilla slit her throat like that." He watched her as she moved her hand to her collarbone, as if faint. "She made such a mess. It was very ugly."

His tendrils caressed her mind. He was happy. Enjoying her show.

Rasel leaned back. "Indeed."

She kept going, her voice as whiny as any highborn she had ever met. "And to witness it, with my own two... well, one, eye. It will live with me forever."

She'd really sold that last line, hamming it up with the perfect level of self-obsession. The white haired Prince rolled his eyes.

"What do you want, Edi?" he asked.

She stood and walked around the back of his chair. He didn't move from his seat, but stiffened as she drifted a finger across one of his silken-covered shoulders.

"Oh, nothing," she said, still affecting that voice. The voice of the feeble woman. "I only wish for a friend who will help me navigate this new world."

He laughed, a short bark. He still looked straight ahead, not turning to look at her as her finger drifted to the nape of his neck, causing him to shiver.

"You want us to be friends?" he asked, his voice strained.

She leaned in closer now, her lips almost at his ear. "We could start there."

He shuddered at her breath tickling his ear, before turning his head and looking at her. He grabbed the back of her neck with his free hand and pulled her to him.

She did not protest as he pressed his lips to hers. The thrum slammed loudly in her ears. The sensation was overwhelming. His lips were punishing as his mouth moved against hers, taking and giving little.

The kiss lasted no more than a handful of seconds. He bit her lower lip as he pulled back. His teeth were sharp, and she could taste the metal of her blood budding on her mouth.

The voice was quieter now, so she had room in her head to take a breath.

She smiled, not wiping her mouth.

"See, I told you."

He watched her mouth with hunger. "What?"

She winked at him and walked towards the door.

"What did you tell me?" His voice was petulant.

"I told you you'd know when I'm flirting," she said, over her shoulder.

He laughed once more, another short chuckle that lost volume immediately.

She had reached the door before she heard his voice again.

"But you lied."

Suri paused in the door, her breath lodged in her throat. She clenched her fist tighter, as she felt that urge to give away her crime and look instantly to the source.

Did he know what she had just done?

If not, what lie had he found this time? She held too many to count.

She turned back. He sat at the edge of the seat, looking ready to pounce. A strand of hair had fallen in front of his silver band.

She waited.

His mouth curved upwards. "You do like playing with your food."

She smiled and breathed a sigh of relief as she moved out of the doorway.

Suri didn't go far. In the hall, she scanned the room, finding a small alcove of curved marble where a carved facade melded into the wall. She walked to it, scouting the area for any guards and finding none. Behind it, there was a space cast in shadow. No one leaving this room would notice her unless they were looking. She hoped they wouldn't be looking.

In the alcove, now safe from the eyes of all, she opened her fist. In it, lay the earrings she'd watched Prince Rasel drop into his pockets minutes earlier.

Suri had found his request odd.

Yes, looking at them, they were unseemly. Pieces of cheap metal. But, to look upon her this day and decide now that these were unfit for her to wear, when they never had been before?

Her hair was rinsed, but not clean nor styled. Her body had lost the worst of its daily grime, but she doubted she smelt anything approaching fresh. Her face was bare, her skin dull. But the earrings, they had to go.

She could be wrong. It happened. But she knew what hunger looked like. She had seen a flash of that hunger in Rasel's eyes when he had kissed her. She had seen more of it when he peered at her healing eye and looked to her bleeding lip. But his eyes, when he asked so casually for her earrings. They were ravenous.

He wanted them. She wanted to know why.

She stood still for a few minutes. Steady and unflinching.

And then the white haired Prince strode out of the room. In a hurry, clearly. He scanned the hall, then made for the stairs.

She smirked.

This too, was a manner she recognised. This was the movement of a man who had lost something. And not only that, there was someone else that needed to know he didn't have it.

Where was the Prince off to? Why did he want her earrings? Did it have something to do with the voice?

And who did he report to?

The thief moved after him, her silken steps as silent as the grave.

21

My sister writes. I have betrayed her. She thinks I
must have sought to trap her betrothed all along.
She sends leaves. I will not brew them, she is wrong.
This child is not of blood, but of the glory of Him.
    Diary of C. Aubethaan, est. early 8th century

The white-haired Prince broke off at the Third Span. Suri
followed, keeping at least one wall between them.

This was her assigned floor. She thought for a moment he
was making for her door, but instead he carried on down the
corridor and slipped through a door at the end.

When Suri reached the door, she listened for a moment. It
wasn't distinct from the rest of the doors on the corridor. A
simple wooden door of the same silver wood. She heard nothing.

If this was another bedroom, she couldn't risk just walking in.
Then footsteps approached the door from the other side. She

leapt back down the corridor, tempering her pace to a normal walk just as the door opened.

Suri didn't look back and kept walking steadily. The footsteps were quick and light. Faster than hers. Catching up to her.

The footsteps were upon her.

She whirled round to look at the source.

A girl. A chambermaid. She looked up, alarmed at Suri's quick movement and almost dropped the silver tray she held, before bobbing into a curtsey.

"Good day, miss."

Suri nodded, trying to come across less panicked. "Good day to you."

The chambermaid moved a few steps past her, then paused and turned back.

A feeling of dread crept across her. She was about to get questioned on what she was doing, where she was going.

"Excuse me, miss."

Suri turned slowly, a fake smile covering the grimace beneath. "Yes?"

The chambermaid looked shy. She stared at the letter on the tray in front of her. "Are you Lady Edi?"

"Yes," Suri replied.

The chambermaid looked relieved. "Then this is for you."

She picked up the letter and handed it to her. Suri read the front of the letter. *To the Lady Edi.*

How strange.

She looked up to see the chambermaid walking away. "Hey."

The chambermaid froze. "Yes, my lady?" the girl asked. Meek as a mouse, this one.

"Who is this from?" she asked.

The chambermaid blushed. "I'm sorry, my lady. I don't know. It just came in."

Even stranger. Surely the only person it could be from was in this building.

"What's your name?" Suri asked.

"Gill, my lady."

Suri nodded and pointed to the door at the end of the hall. "Gill, whose room is that?"

The chambermaid followed her point. "The door at the end?"

"Yes."

"It's not a room, my lady. It's the stairs to the servant's parlour."

That was where the Prince had rushed off to? But why? It made no sense to her. Someone had to be down there.

Gill was still hovering, waiting for a response.

"Thanks, Gill," she said. "Um. That will be all."

Gill bobbed into a small, but elegant, curtsey that put hers to shame and dashed off. Suri pretended to stroll in the same direction towards her room, as she waited for yet more agonising seconds to pass, before Gill ducked into another room and out of sight.

Then Suri was moving back, down the corridor, with the letter in one hand. She reached the door, again heard nothing, and opened it.

A staircase lay before her. A narrow, stone staircase not lit through any windows. Only a couple of infrequent sconces lit the path before her. It twisted round, but she couldn't see the bottom.

Her first hurried step echoed, and she was careful then to make her steps lighter.

When she reached the bottom, a narrow corridor crept out. A couple of stout doors punctuated either side, with a further one was at the end.

She had no idea where the Prince might have gone.

Defeated, Suri retreated up the stairs and went into her room. She ripped a piece of fabric from the hem of one of the dresses in the wardrobe and tucked the earrings into it, before tucking them into her clothing, next to her heart.

Someone was interested in these earrings. Maybe it was Rasel, maybe it was someone else. She wouldn't let anyone take them again until she knew who it was and what they wanted.

Then she opened the letter.

Honest Edi,

It bothered me that you never heard the end.

She doesn't belong here, to me she is sworn,
Lo, lo, in the eye of the storm.
Please let her stay, let me keep her warm,
Lo, lo, in the eye of the storm.

He's taking her under, my rose is a thorn,
Lo, lo, in the eye of the storm.
She cannot respond, cannot hear me mourn.
No, no, in the eye of the storm.
Her body is cold, but I keep her warm,
Lo, lo, in the eye of the storm.
In the eye of the storm.

Try not to die.

There was no signature below. She thought it was Rasel at first.

But that last line.

'Try not to die, little thief.'

It was Kol. It had to be.

Questions circled in her mind. How did he know she hadn't heard the end?

He'd been there that day at the oasis. The day before the attack. He'd been there. Had he shot that arrow at Rasel?

He was sending her letters now. He knew she was here, in the castle. He knew she was going by the name Edi. Had he followed her after all?

The sixth bell tolled.

Fuck.

Low chatter quelled to silence as Suri walked into the dining hall.

Groans of wood grating back from stone echoed around the room, as many people stood at once. Suri met six pairs of eyes, not even counting the armed guards spread at intervals around the room.

The Queen wore a new dress. A deep blue, with seafoam green lace panelling. It lacked that chainmail appearance from earlier and she had left the sword behind. But that didn't make her any less dangerous.

They were on the Second Span, in a wide marble hall. White flowering ivy hung in manicured bunches around the room. The Queen stood at the far end at the head of the table. At one of the places closest to the Queen was Prince Rasel. He looked calm, jovial even. The other four diners Suri had never seen before, but it was easy for her to deduce they were rich.

She was out of her depth, and trying to get her thoughts off Kol and his damned letter.

All the faces looked at her expectantly, as the Queen gestured to the other empty seat beside her. Was she late? She had left her room as soon as the bell sounded. She held her back ramrod straight as she walked to the table, standing in the free space.

The Queen nodded to her, and she bobbed her head back. "Everyone, I would like you to warmly welcome Edi to my court. She is here for a time as a guest."

There was a low murmuring of greetings in response. Suri tried to keep her hands from shaking. With both the Queen and Rasel in proximity, the voice was purring once more. His cool tendrils steadied her scattering nerves somewhat, but she still felt ill at ease.

She looked to Rasel, who seemed to be enjoying her discomfort. She had to focus on not embarrassing herself.

"Please, let's be seated."

Suri sat down at the same time as the other guests. She watched the empty plate in front of her with rapture, afraid to meet anyone's gaze. How had Kol got a letter to her?

Those around her drank from their glasses at will. She took a sip of her own. Wine. The extent of her knowledge. She had tried a couple in the past, cheap bottles she'd stolen or that the others had fetched and allowed her a swig of.

This was far nicer. She sipped as she listened, anything to distract her from thoughts of the Demon King.

"Lord Dellon," the Queen said. "How are the harvests this year?"

The second finest dressed man at the table cleared his throat. He sat across from Suri to her left and noticeably held the largest waistline.

"Yes, yes, all as to be expected," he replied gruffly. He then, as gestured to the finest dressed man at the table sitting next to Suri. "On both sides of the Shale, of course."

The other man, clad in orange and gold, nodded. He was of olive complexion. Both sides of the Shale. That was the sea that separated Peregrinus from Kans. Was this man from Kans? She'd never met anyone from there.

He glanced at her and quirked a small smirk. His eyes were a touch feline, his skin flawless.

"Business is good this year," the man agreed. His accent stuck to his throat with an uncertain wobble. "And you, Lera'yon? How fare your exports?"

He addressed the Queen directly.

Lera'yon? What was that? No title. Suri darted her eye between the man at the table, whose manner was relaxed, and to the Queen, who did not react at all. No one at the table seemed to find it odd. Were they so well acquainted? Was this some custom she knew nothing of?

The Queen only laughed. "Oh, I pay little mind to such transactions, Yori'don. My priestesses are making such strides that I have little time for other matters."

"Dabri'yon awaits your delegation."

Queen Lera smiled. "It is a shame we could not be there to witness your Gate's reincarnation in person."

Kans had a Gate? Weren't they all long dead?

Yori'don's smile wavered. "Quite."

The Queen clapped her hands and attendants, laden with food, arrived.

The others seemed not to even see it, as though the spread was invisible. Their eyes were instead focused on Queen Lera, as she looked back to the portly man named Dellon. "Have my advisors informed you of my needs, Lord Dellon?"

Suri recognised only some of the dishes before her, but even this was guesswork. There was rice and bread. *That* she knew, even if everything was enhanced.

The bread was wide and fluffy, as if inflated with the breath of the Trio. It was moist, covered with some kind of oiled glaze. Herbs rested atop it and steam rose faintly from it. The rice was white as snow and smelt like nothing she had ever experienced.

And then for the dishes she didn't recognise. Pink meats on beds of some exotic fruit or vegetable. Orange fish coated with red sauce. Rubbery ringed flesh of some kind with a yellow glaze.

No one moved to serve themselves.

No one had even inhaled deeply, taken in the aromas. Suri's urge to take her cutlery and start loading up her plate was almost unmanageable. She forced herself to focus on Lord Dellon, as she swallowed the anticipatory saliva.

Lord Dellon frowned. "I have been informed, your Grace. I must state, though, that there will be some delay in the stock."

Queen Lera's smile didn't fade. "You're here now, aren't you? Travelling up with the last Southern produce delivery."

The attendants started making their way around the room, offering dishes to the guests. The first dish near her was the fish. She nodded, and a small amount was placed with care onto her plate.

Dellon squirmed. "That is true, your Grace. Though what I have not already passed on to yourselves is destined for the North."

Suri again nodded as a hunk of bread was placed on her plate. Still, no one had moved to eat.

"For the Forgelands?" she replied, with a wave of her hand. "They can wait. I need this now. Thandul will understand."

Suri agreed to a helping of the red meat, as she watched on.

Dellon paused. "Your Grace, I understand you have an increased need. I do note, though, that last week you also requested the rest of the stock from the Metal Guild—"

Queen Lera laughed. "I did not realise you were a book-keeper for the other guilds too, now. How busy you must be!"

Rasel laughed first, and the others joined in almost instantly. Soon all except Suri were heartily chuckling.

Dellon too laughed, albeit weakly. "Of course not, how silly. A good jest, your Grace."

Suri agreed to three more dishes, completely filling her plate.

Sod it.

They knew she was no lady. She didn't know when her next meal was coming and her curiosity to try everything was too strong.

The queen waved her hand at Dellon. "Do not worry yourself, we can discuss this further later. We have a guest here, it would be rude to discuss business all evening."

She raised her fork and the others followed suit.

Finally, they were allowed to eat.

Suri used the dainty cutlery with decent enough dexterity, trying everything in turn, and then together. She tried not to moan around the flavours, which burst and played on her tongue like the Moon God's fireworks in the night sky.

The main courses had rotated and left, then various sweets were placed on the table. The only thing Suri thought she could place were the apples, which were stewed and baked into a dish. The others, fruits and cakes and pies, were meaningless, but mouthwatering, to her.

She was full, but she agreed again to most of the dishes.

The conversation had lulled as people ate, but that silence didn't last long.

"Your Grace," Lord Dellon started. His voice was nervous, frayed, even to Suri's ears which were less trained regarding that Lartosh accent.

"Yes, Lord Dellon?"

He swallowed. "There is a matter of some sensitivity I would like to discuss with you after dinner, your Grace."

"We are amongst friends, Dellon," she said in response. Suri took a bite of a brown cake. It was sweet and melted in her mouth. She stifled a smile as she stabbed her tiny and impractical fork in for another mouthful.

"The Lady Ressa has asked all of the Guild leaders to assist her in locating her daughter."

Queen Lera tilted her head. "Locating her daughter? Is this her famous heir, Viantha?"

Rasel's jaw clenched.

Dellon looked vaguely ill as he nodded. "Indeed, your Grace. She is missing."

His skin was a greenish white against his jowls, giving him the impression of a bloated, rotting fish.

Queen Lera smiled. "Missing? I've heard the girl is betrothed to our dear Prince Shaedon! Perhaps there is a more logical reason for her absence? Wedding shopping, an elopement, even!"

Atrius above. *Viantha* was Shaedon's betrothed? Was this in place when she herself was in the palace? She had impersonated Prince's intended?

She must be cursed. To have stolen the identity of the princess Shaedon wished to marry and put her in a *sewer*. It was almost funny.

Dellon nodded again, vigorously. "Of course, your Grace. I am certain the girl is merely lost."

She fought back a snort and caught Rasel's eye. He too seemed to be fighting some expression, his face studiously frozen. If Suri was cursed, so must be Viantha. Lost? What sewer was she in now?

The Queen was all solemnity. "If I hear anything, I will send a messenger to Lartosh immediately."

Dellon shifted in his chair and gave a pallid smile. "Much obliged, your Grace."

Through the evening, Suri got a sense of why she had been invited. Whilst she was never spoken to directly, she was talked of often. The Queen would follow a pattern, start to discuss business of some kind, reach a half agreement, and then decide that it would be rude to linger on the matter further with a guest present.

It was a lesson in diplomacy and one Suri did not want to repeat. It was stifling, the atmosphere they lived in. The food and wine were delicious, but she couldn't escape the feeling that everyone was a single poorly-timed word away from war.

After the dinner had ended, and the last plate had been cleared, Queen Lera stood. She announced she was tired from the evening's festivities and would be retiring. The lords fell into practised bows as Suri stumbled into a curtsey. She watched the Queen glide away, her gleaming white hem brushing the floor as she departed.

With the Queen gone, the others sat. Except for Rasel.

Rasel gestured to her with a pointed finger. She looked around her at the others who had started low conversations. His entreaty could have only been to her.

He left the room, catching her eye again as he moved. Suri followed, glancing back to the table. No one watched her. She was as invisible as the attendants, as the food. Rasel paused at the foot of the marble staircase leading upwards.

He smiled at her and held his hand out. An invitation. "Do you want to see something?"

Suri hesitated for a second.

I want to see it...

The voice crept over her once more. If she didn't go, all she'd do was pace her room re-reading that damned letter. So, she placed her hand on his pale and freezing palm.

He led her up the stairs.

The former heir said nothing else as they ascended, staring straight ahead. His steps were slow and hers kept up with ease.

When they reached the Twelfth Span, he was slightly out of breath. Her own breathing had not changed.

The door beyond still lay closed. But he walked up without a thought and unlocked it, dropping the key back into his top left inside jacket pocket. Suri noted its size, shape, and material as quickly as any jewellery. Always know your escape route.

Rasel pushed the door. Beyond was indeed steps, far narrower and darker. The windows let in no light at this hour.

He looked back at her.

Suri moved forward a couple of steps, nearer to him. She looked up at the staircase, then looked back at him.

"My Lord—"

"Did you not want to come up here?"

His tone, his knowing look. Had he seen her earlier when she climbed? No, he was in his study, playing that music. Then someone else. Someone else watched her, reported on her. One of the guards, one of the maids. It could have been any of them. All of them.

"After you," he said with a smirk.

Her lone eye searched across his face again, then she moved past him and up the steps. He was right. She did want to go up there.

The steps were narrower for certain. They were also steeper, with each step perhaps double the height of the sloping steps of the earlier Spans.

It was impossible for Suri to judge their height. Instead of two distinct staircases that wound up to the next Span, there was just the one staircase, winding upwards without break. Occasionally there would be a small wooden door, but it held little correlation to the distance they climbed.

After minutes had passed, she paused by a window. Out of it she could see the tops of the spires of the Church. They were underneath her. She was higher than even the Priestesses, nearly as high as the clouds themselves.

She looked back down the stairs as Rasel came up behind her. He was fully out of breath now as he leaned against the curved wall.

He flicked one finger upwards in a lazy movement. "That's it, all the way to the top."

Suri considered again if this could be some sort of trap. Then she realised that no matter what action she took here, she was still a guest in this castle. If this was a trap, there was nowhere safe for her in Drameir. She had to trust in something.

She continued the walk upwards, her legs starting to burn as the walls got closer and closer. It got so narrow that as she walked she was inches away from brushing both sides at once. She mused that Lord Dellon would likely get stuck, if he even made it up to the Twelfth Span.

She reached another silverwood door, this time one that blocked her path. Rasel stepped up beside her. She tried to make room for him but, even sideways, he could not move past her without pressing the entire length of his body past hers.

She sucked in a breath as his body lingered against hers.

Once past, he knocked on the door. Two knocks, three knocks, one knock.

The door opened.

The ice lord stepped through, and Suri followed. Here, it opened out. The room had a small circular hall, with four thicker silverwood doors with metal work latticed across the pane of the door and around the edges. The low walls tapered inwards, and the ceiling was a much narrower circle.

In that small hall were two guards, one who had opened the door to them and another sat on an unpadded stool near to another door. His back was close to the walls, positioned in such a way that, if he stood, his head would hit the slanted surface before he was even half extended. They both bowed.

Rasel ignored them, moving to the small gap in one wall where there was an opening. Through it, the ascent could only barely be counted as stairs. The knee-high slabs were as much stairs as she was a lady.

He led the way, climbing the monstrosities for about five steps before he reached, and unlatched a panel overhead. He pushed it open and the wind swept in, slamming the panel down on the other side.

It howled through the small space they occupied and brought with it a horrible chill. Suri clenched her hands, as the frigid air hit her thin clothing and cut through her in an instant. Rasel seemed unaffected as he climbed through the hatch.

She followed, staring up at the hole that showed the dark night sky and the cloud. Suri used her hands on the freezing floor to push herself out.

Rasel grabbed her arm as she exited, helping her upright as the wind threatened to push her off the edge.

Her eye blurred from the wind. She blinked, studying her surroundings.

The roof.

There was no handrail, no guarding stone wall to catch her. There was only the edge, and several narrow columns which provided only the smallest amount of reassurance. The columns converged above her into a point. Between that was just air. Air that whipped and whistled.

The castle's top was maybe only twenty feet across. They stood on the outside edge, a stone border three or four feet wide. The inside of the circle dipped into a concave dome.

The inverted dome was floored entirely of some silver metal.

It dropped down quite suddenly, with the base of the semi sphere around five feet below them. It was half filled now with rainwater.

Suri viewed it all through her chattering teeth, her breath forming white clouds. Here she was, standing on the precipice of the land's most notorious prison. "The Storm Pan," she breathed.

The wind sucked her voice into a whisper. He still held her arm in support, his own posture remarkably secure for a man that was a step away from tumbling hundreds of feet to his death.

The cold was so harsh, her very bones shaken and brittle.

Rasel smiled. "Thunder Bed, Storm Pan, Dead Basin. It has many names."

The rumoured Drangborian prison was not only in its capital, Drameir, but at the very top of the Seat itself. She struggled to hold her shivers in, as she spoke. "Where are the cells?"

Rasel released her arm and strolled around the outside of the pan. He gestured for her to follow as he moved away from the entrance hatch. His arms were behind him as he wandered around the side of it with the calm of a nobleman on a summer's promenade.

"Just underneath," he said with a casual air, even though he had to half shout across the screaming of the wind. She took small steps, the damp cold of the stone underfoot seeping into her pitifully thin shoes.

Rasel nodded back to the entrance hole they had clambered out of.

"They're brought up for a spell whenever the weather gets bad. And would you hear that?"

He grinned as a huge crack of thunder sounded.

Suri jumped, her heart thudding painfully in her chest.

Only a second later, the city around them was lit up by a huge crack of lightning. For half a second, she could see all the roofs, glistening and damp far below. The crack speared down, lancing into a mountain top on the horizon. Its white tendrils clawed through the dark.

A guard moved out of the entrance, sure and steady despite the wind.

Rasel's tone was that of a gleeful child when he spoke into Suri's ear. "Here she comes."

Suri's unbraided dark brown hair lashed her face, as she felt the first spit of rain hit the bridge of her nose. The clouds above her hummed with an imminent downpour.

"Who is it?" Suri asked. Part of her already knew the answer.

"Can't you guess?" he replied, nudging her arm. "You'll get a kick out of this."

The guard moved out of the way. He held a chain which connected onto a pair of reinforced silverwood shackles.

She emerged, still somehow graceful. Her dark hair was a crow's nest of snarled locks, plastered in a damp matted mess to her face and neck. Her dress was a dark grey, and Suri was unable to determine if it had originally been silver, pale grey, or even blue. It was clearly still damp from the last time and clung to her thighs as she climbed the final step.

The prisoner looked up, curving her elegant neck to meet the gaze of Rasel and Suri. Her necklace was gone. To her brother, her eyes were dull. On meeting Suri's gaze, the thief thought she saw a flicker of recognition in those smudged eyes.

Then the guard pushed her without ceremony into the Storm Pan and that tiny moment of connection disappeared. The princess and heiress's limbs flailed as she was shoved into the glacial water.

Rasel laughed, and Suri shuddered. Dellon's line of questioning, his fear. It made sense. For the Guilds did have something to worry about.

Queen Lera had imprisoned Viantha Waterborne.

22

The King says I am to marry him. That he will name the child heir to all. No. He cannot claim me. It is His. I am His!

Diary of C. Aubethaan, est. early 8th century

"Why?" Suri asked, keeping her voice flat.

Rasel stared at his sister as she stood up to her thighs in the rainwater. "Treason. Betrayal. Siding with the enemy."

"Which enemy?" Suri asked.

Rasel smiled. "Not your concern. I brought you here to revel in the sheer fact of it."

As he was. And so was the voice. It seemed to hiss with glee.

"Isn't she a water manipulator?" Suri said. Rasel turned his gaze to her, and the edge in his eyes chilled her further still. "The water?"

Rasel turned back to look at his sister. Viantha shivered. She looked like she was trying not to move.

"Silverwood compresses power," Rasel said. "Being around it makes you less powerful. Wearing it almost nullifies it entirely." Then he smiled, his mouth curving upwards like a scimitar. "And *those* manacles. Well."

Suri looked again at the manacles around Viantha's wrists. Made of wood. She assumed it was this silverwood. This time she noticed the inside of the circlet was spiked. Her wrists were dark with dried brown blood from where the wood had sliced into her flesh.

"How long will she be here?" Suri asked.

"As long as she needs to be."

As long as she deserves.

The voice seemed so sure. So clear.

Suri watched, as Viantha stood in the Storm Pan. Her face was so blank. She couldn't help remembering it was the same when she had taken Viantha. The memory of the blank stare rose unbidden, causing Suri to swallow. She let out an exaggerated sigh. "This was fun. But it's cold. I'm bored. Let's go."

Rasel didn't look at her. "You go. I'm not quite finished."

The thief took careful steps back to the hatch, leaving the royals on the roof.

It took her some time to get back to her room. On the way down it seemed like there were even more steps than before. Her steps were heavy, weighted by what she had seen. It twisted her stomach.

All is well, sweet Suri.

The voice tried to reassure her, a cold stroke down her back. But she couldn't help replaying the moment when Viantha's cold, dead eyes had flashed up to meet her own.

She is not of us. She is ours to play with.

It's no different, she thought. Suri herself had done the same thing. Imprisoned Viantha, and for even less reason. Out of pure greed. Their reasoning was likely stronger than hers had been. But she found herself still unable to fully shake it off.

Do not fret.

The voice was right. It was not her concern. She had no morals to fall back on. She let its voice and rhythm settle her stomach and calm her nerves. She walked through the door of her bedroom and stopped.

Someone had been in her room.

It was almost unnoticeable.

They had tried to be careful, to cover their tracks. But Suri had left tiny snags, a single strand of hair wrapped around the doorknobs, tucked into the drawers. They were largely snapped or on the floor. The careful but precise disarray she had left the items in on the dressing table had been disturbed. The rouge's clasp now faced a few degrees more towards the mirror than it had when she'd left.

They had been searching through her few belongings.

And for what. She had arrived with little more than the skin on her back.

Unless.

She felt her chest and yes, they were still there. The earrings. Pulling them from their tiny bundle, she appraised them again. Dull metal, one of them seven or eight years old now and almost black from lack of polishing. Even the newest one was worn and beaten.

Rasel had said they were worthless and ugly.

Had someone come for them? Or something else? She had no clue what their value was. But maybe it was time to find out.

Light poured through the Fifth Span windows as Suri knocked on Rasel's door. It was early, only a couple hours after dawn. She knew she should likely wait for a better hour, but correctness had never been her forte.

She'd barely slept a wink. It was clear she was being watched and now someone had searched her room. The sooner she resolved this and left, the better.

After a grunt from inside, she pushed the door open to find Rasel shirtless. His hair was pulled back into a hasty ponytail, a thin glaze of sweat covering his toned chest. Still, as ever, the black cravat encircled his neck, its ends trailing his naked torso.

Exactly as she had hoped.

He stood at the edge of a full bed, maybe three times the size of her own.

"Bad time?" she asked.

He cracked half a lifeless smile. "It's fine. What do you want?"

She took a couple of steps forward and opened her palm.

She kept her focus pinned on his face as she revealed the three studs of boring looking metal. His face didn't change. "I came to offer you these."

He furrowed his brow. "Those ugly things? I thought I'd thrown them out already."

Rasel dropped his eyes from the earrings and wandered back to his bed, taking a seat. He was doing a very good job of acting disinterested, she had to give him that.

Suri smiled at him. "Oh, so you don't mind if I throw them out?"

Rasel shrugged. "Go for it."

"Catch you later, then," Suri said, turning on her heel. She made it to the door before…"Wait."

Suri smiled, a real smile this time, as she faced the door. She swivelled back, giving him a questioning look.

He stood again, coming towards her with his hand open. "Let me do it."

She sniffed. "Why?"

Rasel rolled his eyes. He stopped barely a step from her, and she could smell the raw scent of him. Fennel and spices. Some small part of her compared it to Kol's scent. She hated herself when the comparison came up short. "Look, Edi. You're smart. You know that. I know that. But you're involving yourself in something you know nothing about. Just give me the earrings, and you don't have to worry about any of it."

Suri placed her hands behind her back and squared her footing. She tilted her head. "Actually, I am involving myself in something very simple. A trade."

Rasel purred, leaning closer to her. "Is that so?"

If he thought seduction would work, he had timed his moment poorly. She was not immune to him, but there were more important things on the line. Her fortune, and thus, her future.

She ran a tongue over her front teeth. "For whatever reason, you want these earrings. I have them. You have something I want."

"Do I now?" he asked, with a playful edge.

She leaned in too, her other hand coming up as she swept her hand across his cravat. She tucked a piece of fabric into it and purred back. "Your purse."

Rasel took a step back, feigning disappointment. "How common of you. Desiring currency."

She shrugged. "It is a means to an end."

He looked her up and down. "You can't run. You can't go South, Ressa hates you. You can't go East, Kol will end you. You can't return North, your blood bond prevents it. So, what end would that be?"

Suri deflated at the mention of the bond. She'd been thinking about it all night, how she could possibly get around it. "That is not part of our bargain."

He stepped back into her space. "And what's to stop me taking the earrings from you?"

She didn't move. "I am the Queen's guest. And... I don't think you want me as an enemy."

"Would we be enemies if you're dead?" he asked with a husky breath.

She clucked her tongue and stepped around him, further into his room, clutching the earrings in her fist. He did not stop her. His gaze followed her, or rather her hand. "The sum I'm asking is probably less than what it would cost to clean my blood off these rugs," she said, gesturing to the opulence around her.

Rasel licked his lips, a dart of a serpentine tongue over his thin mouth. His hands clenched and unclenched.

Suri counted ten full seconds before he opened his mouth. "Fair. Name your price."

She lifted her face, looking to the painted ceiling as if pondering. They both knew she had a sum in mind from her entry. Suri played the timeless game she had played many times. Overvalue her goods by a factor of perhaps ten to one and hope to settle somewhere in the middle. "Five gold."

Rasel didn't even hesitate. "Done."

Suri only just about held herself back from gaping in shock. Her fingers tensed around the prize she had bartered with as she tried to breathe normally.

Five gold. Five. Gold.

Either the man had more money than she realised. Far more. Or he was right. She didn't know what she was getting herself into.

Rasel walked past her to a dark-stained wooden desk. He opened a black leather bag resting on the top of it and counted out some coins. He came back to her and opened his hand.

She opened her other hand. "You first," she said.

He sighed, but did as she asked, pouring the coins into her hand. Just five coins. But those five coins were likely several times the most amount of money she'd ever had. She closed her hand over them.

She shook the earrings which had stuck to her sweaty palm, into his waiting hand. She swallowed as she struggled once more to accommodate Him in her head. He was so present, consuming every thought, caressing her very being.

Rasel had lost all his earlier charms as he appraised her. "Now go."

She did not think twice before following his instruction. Suri wondered if he knew what he had done, in his trade. Perhaps it was consciously done.

After she found out why he wanted her damn earrings, she would be gone. She would be so very gone. And none of these courtiers, none of these Lords, would ever see her again.

The voice didn't like that. It whined at her.

Stay, sweet Suri.

On her way back to her room, she found it harder to walk—unsteady, every step trying to slow her down. She shook herself, hoping it was her lack of sleep that pulled at her movement, but guessing it was something more. Something darker. She made it back and shut the door. She knew now that people might be watching her, following her. To follow him was a risk she would not take again.

She didn't know if her plan would work, but it was the best one she had.

Suri grabbed the piece of *seeing silk* from her shoe and jumped onto her bed. She lay her back and placed the silk over her dead eye socket.

Nothing happened.

The disappointment waved over her, as her good eye stared up at the carved ceiling. Of course, she'd see nothing through this, there was no eye to see. Magic cloth, or no, it wasn't going to work.

She breathed for a moment, once again experiencing that sinking sensation as she tried to come to terms with her own blindness. She calmed herself with deep breaths.

She cursed Scilla and thought of Kol, the one who had gifted her this spying piece of cloth. As she felt that familiar rage come over her, a fuzzy image scattered into her eye.

A green hill overlooking a small grey town next to a wood. A familiar broad hand resting on a wide knee. Then the image changed, as if she herself had turned away. She saw the grass, and then nothing as the image went black.

A tut.

"Now, now, Suri," Kol said. "Did no one ever tell you it was rude to spy?"

She gasped and pulled the cloth from her face in an instant, looking around. Nothing. No one. Kol wasn't standing in her bedroom. She could hear through this darn thing, too? Had she tapped into Kol somehow?

She stared at the cloth for a second, watching it in the palm of her hand. She put it back on and there was nothing, no voice, no sound.

Had he disabled it somehow? Irritating man. Calling her nothing, selling her, offering her anything she wanted. Cruel, confusing man.

"Were you trying to think of me this time or am I just that irresistible?" he asked.

"Insufferable," she murmured to herself as she tried to work out how to control the damn thing. She still couldn't see anything.

"Rude, again," he replied.

Wait what? He could hear her too? Oh, Wrath. Could he see? She clamped a hand over the silk.

He chuckled. "She's working it out. Nice ceiling. Drameir looks drab, as ever."

"Go away," Suri replied.

"I'll go when you stop thinking about me. Did you get my note?"

Suri scowled. "Yes."

"Good," he said. "Did you like the song?"

She had liked the song. She had read it back a few times. It was sad and quite beautiful. For a pagan song, at least. But that's not what she said.

"Please just leave me alone, Kol."

He laughed again. "Quick tip, little thief, direct your thoughts to whatever poor soul you *actually* want to spy on, and I'll happily leave you alone."

Irritating. Man.

She grumbled and thought about how it was probably useless anyway. Perhaps Rasel had already found the silk she'd tucked into his cravat. Maybe he was laughing at her now.

As she pictured him, the image changed. She could no longer hear Kol's words, nor his breath in her ear. She focused in, imagining Rasel that day, him giving her the money. The image was unclear, obscured. A grey wall, half covered by a blackness. Her eye still stared up at the ceiling, but at the same time there was another picture, another place.

A door?

She realised she was seeing it, she was seeing through the silk. She closed her good eye and watched only the new lens, letting it pull into greater focus.

The black material that covered part of her sight must be the cravat. She could only get a partial visual from the piece of the silk that she'd tucked into it when he leaned in.

The door opened and behind it was a flight of stairs. This was the same flight of stairs she'd looked down before which Gill had stated led to the servant's parlour.

She heard a creak and her good eye darted open as she looked at the door to her bedchamber. Nothing. The creak wasn't here.

Yes, she heard Rasel's footsteps descending the stairs as she concentrated on the silken perspective.

The seeing silk could hear.

Kol had not told her that.

She was glad the silk was so often smothered by her foot at the bottom of her shoe. His attempts to spy on her should have largely been thwarted. She should have suspected there was some further trickery held in its magic. She was more glad than ever that she hadn't trusted him that day in the desert. His deal would have tied her up in unknown knots.

Rasel had reached the bottom of the stairs.

He stepped up to the second door on the left, knocking twice. Rasel entered.

The dark room was punctuated with only a small amount of weak purple light. There were no chandeliers or sconces, and the light appeared to be emanating from the liquid contents of glass vials and angular bottles. The various glowing containers were spaced and conjoined with tubing and a metal frame.

The cravat obscured the bottom of Suri's vision, and she couldn't fathom what she was looking at.

Rasel was not alone. In the light of the bottles was another man. A man Suri recognised. It was the footman, the one that had reluctantly allowed her entry to the castle and escorted her to meet the Queen.

He straightened from where he had been positioned, bent over the table staring intensely at one of the vials.

"No luck, then?" Rasel asked.

His voice swam in her head, muffled. As if her ear was also buried in that cravat.

The footman huffed. "She must have had them on her, they weren't anywhere."

"Perhaps you lacked the necessary... charm."

Suri heard, rather than saw, a clink of metal. Her sight remained locked on the footman and the space in front of him. The footman scoffed but moved around the table in no time at all look at something.

"She gave those to you," he said. His eyes were wide as he looked down at something.

"She traded them to me," Rasel corrected.

He looked up. "How does she know they are worth a damn?"

Suri's sight twitched from side to side. Shaking his head?

"She doesn't. She noticed I was interested and asked for a pittance in return."

A pittance. He was lying, surely. Even if she'd traded some of the finest jewellery in the Forgelands, five gold was a handsome sum. How could he truly dismiss it like that?

"She doesn't know what they are?" the footman asked.

"I don't think she knows much of anything, except how to deceive. I feel it around her. She must feel it too, but she's never acknowledged it."

Suri twitched an eyebrow. She wasn't ignorant to Him. He was everywhere with her now, but she had no one she trusted to make the slightest sense out of it.

She *had* to focus, and her focus was her sweet self. Always.

Rasel looked down, pitching Suri's sight to see the footman take the earrings from his palm. She noticed he had a large scar on the outside of his right wrist, slicing up. His sleeves were rolled up to halfway up his forearms, and she couldn't see where the scar ended.

The footman moved back to the sets of vials. Rasel followed, his slow steps not matching the eager speed of the scarred footman's.

"Let's test them," the footman said. There was something there, glee, or madness, Suri couldn't tell. Either way, she didn't trust it. Madness makes people unpredictable. Unpredictable people were nothing but trouble.

He twisted something, and a small blue flame leapt up from an iron nozzle. He placed the earrings in a small pan on top of the flame. Minutes passed, as the footman repeatedly tapped one finger on the table.

The metal began to melt, pouring down into three tiny puddles which linked into a dark metallic glob, which spread in liquid form across the base. Dotted around, unmelted and unmoving, were shards of something.

The footman picked up each shard and rinsed them in some kind of solution. Suri couldn't fathom their colour or origin in the dim light. Then, he took the bundle of clean shards and dropped them into a bottle of transparent liquid.

The effect was immediate, as the bottle started glowing.

"Would you look at that."

The light was instant and grew stronger as seconds passed. Brighter than all the dim bottles on the surrounding table. This one container emitted so much light that the edges of the room a few feet away were illuminated. She could see the marble walls, the wooden support beams, the counter filled with old plates.

The footman clapped. "She's right in its pocket then. Lera was right."

Whose pocket? It? The creature? She belonged to no one. How was the Queen involved in this? She didn't even know what *this* was. Her head spun with the questions she couldn't answer.

There, there, sweet Suri. We are one. You are you, I am you.

He eased her mind like a douse of cool water on a fevered brow. He was on her side, she knew that.

"The old bat tried to hide her," Rasel growled.

Her heart juddered in her chest at the words. The old bat. The earrings were given to her by Mother Edi. Was that who they meant? How did they know each other? Were they against her? Why would Mother Edi hide her?

Hush, Suri. They are all of us.

Suri tried to reassure herself. They believed her own name to be Edi. Surely that meant they didn't know Mother Edi, or they would have called her out on her fake name.

But still it seemed they knew of her, knew something of her world, her life, the Tangle. She thought that was hers. It was *supposed* to be hers; her den, where she knew she could hide from the world.

Her world now didn't make any sense.

The footman chuckled. "She's here now though... strolled straight in."

Her blood ran cold. Yes. She had walked right in.

The way they spoke. The glee at having her at their mercy. They wanted to exploit something in her. It showed her exactly why she needed to get away from this place as fast as her new gold would carry her.

23

I have run with the shrine folk to the Altar.
They believe me. They believe what I carry.
Diary of C. Aubethaan, est. early 8th century

The eleventh bell clanged through the walls of the Seat as Suri shoved two more practical dresses and a pair of shoes into a bag. She thought about taking everything, but she needed to travel light and disappear fast. She hadn't fully worked out where she would go, yet. Maybe North after all. If Geren could work out how to evade a blood bond, so could she.

Stay, Suri.

She tried to ignore the voice which tried to calm her, recalling the look in the footman's eyes. Even if she had no money to her name, she knew danger when she saw it. Now she had five gold, given freely. And no reason to stay.

They won't hurt you. They can help you.

She didn't want their help. She didn't want to listen to him. He helped her, but he was wrong about this.

The door opened.

It was Gill. The chambermaid walked into the room without knocking, her face looking distressed. She stopped dead when she noticed Suri standing by her bed.

She held a pan and a brush, likely for the ash. Suri found herself oddly disappointed there wasn't another letter.

"My sincere apologies, my lady. I thought you would be out."

Gill gestured to the window in explanation.

The view of the city outside was half-lit by an overcast sky. Suri supposed that Gill must have found it odd that she chose to remain in her room that day. She was grateful that she hadn't come in half an hour ago, when she had been lying on her bed with her bad eye covered in silk.

"It's fine. Do what you need to do," Suri replied.

Gill bobbed a curtsey before moving to the fireplace.

Suri stopped packing, hoping that Gill hadn't already picked up on what she'd been doing. Instead, she reached for the tea left with her breakfast tray and sipped the now cold liquid.

It was bitter and smelt weird, but it was something to do. She didn't know what ladies did.

Suri watched Gill sweeping at the fallen ash. It only took a couple of minutes for that same distracted distress to reemerge on her face. "Are you alright?" she asked, swallowing down the last of the horrid mixture with a grimace.

Gill whipped her head around, almost dropping the pan. "Of course, my lady."

Suri noticed how her hands trembled. "You can tell me."

Gill swallowed. "It's the priestesses, they haven't—"

Then she stopped, her blush growing beet red.

"Yes?" Suri prompted.

Gill swallowed again. "It's nothing, my lady."

Suri held her gaze, until Gill flicked her head back to her work. She worked hurriedly, likely hoping she could finish before Suri questioned her again. Suri shrugged and went back to packing her stuff up. Gill thought she was a guest of the Queen, a lady. Obviously, she wasn't going to tell her anything. Suri considered telling her the truth, to try to gain her trust.

But which truth would she tell?

Edi, Shadow Killer of the Tangle? The mysterious princess from the ball? A little mouse? A murderer? A kidnapper? Or her own truth. A survivor. An opportunist. A half-blinded thief. Would any of it recommend her to this girl? To anyone?

Instead, she finished the tea. It was gross. A knock came at the door.

Both Suri and Gill froze.

Suri realised it was her job to say something. "Um, yes?"

The door opened, revealing the footman she had spied on earlier that day. Suri's blood went cold. Then her pulse quickened, as she felt Him there again. He felt louder again. The shadowy tendril of Him, the imprint of a hand, pressed coldly to her shoulder. She could have sworn she felt a breath tickle her ear.

Hush, Suri. Calm yourself.

The footman smiled at her. Pleasant, but vacant. He ducked a bow. "Greetings, Edi."

Suri nodded as the darkness beside her whispered how sweet she was into her ear. "Good morning."

Her own voice was brittle. Guarded.

The footman looked at Gill, as if surprised she was still there. "Find something else to do, girl."

She scampered to her feet. "Yes, sir."

She curtseyed again to both him and Suri, then dashed past. He was worthy of a bow then. Perhaps 'footman' was not quite accurate. Housekeeper? Seatkeeper? Suri wasn't staying long enough to care.

The voice tutted at her.

The footman turned back to Suri and appraised her from the top of her hair to her half tied shoes. He glanced to the bed too, where the bag of clothes lay open. His expression didn't change. "The Queen requests your presence. In the Seat's gardens. If you would follow me."

How lovely, my sweet.

Rats, Suri thought. The Queen wanted to see her. Right now. Why? Had they noticed her spying? Or was this just a friendly chat?

Either way it fucked up her plans.

"I'll be down in just a moment," she replied.

He cocked his head. "My orders are to accompany you."

Shit. Well, that didn't give her any other option.

"Of course," she said.

She sat to tie her other shoe, wondering if there was any way she could get out of this.

She could think of none. If it were anyone else asking to see her, she could postpone and make a run for it. But she could hardly ask the Queen of Drangbor to stand around for a few hours.

At least the money was on her so, if this went pear-shaped, she could at least attempt to run off with just the bag of gold tied tightly around her thigh.

She could tell He wanted her to see the Queen. He was excited, and it was almost contagious. She found herself tying her shoe quickly, standing with a smile. She held in her sigh as she walked over to the waiting footman. The voice was right, she supposed. This was an honour.

The footman gestured for her to go before him, and she cast one quick longing glance back towards the bag before she exited.

Her steps felt light, and she made fast time down to the ground floor. The footman seemed surprised by her pace, and so was she.

Doors led into the gardens from four points around a courtyard. The gardens were refined, neat flower beds and low shrubs. The bushes were not like any plant she'd seen before. As opposed to the flowers she'd encountered across the rest of Drangbor, those sprawling green leafed bundles with the gorgeous bright purple flowers, these were different. The shrubs looked made of silver. She idly wondered whether the Queen had a team of scouts that she sent around every land to find the flora that matched her colour scheme. It didn't seem all that far-fetched.

The space was beautiful, but Suri was a little confused. A walk? She could walk straight through to the other side in around two minutes.

There were seven people in the garden. Two of them were her and the footman. Four of them were guards, stationed at each glass entryway.

The other was the Queen. She was alone, bent at the waist as she looked closely at a pink flower bud. She wore a pale green dress, and her wings bounced the colours of the flowers off the walls of the courtyard

The footman sighed. "Go on, then."

Suri looked at the impatient footman. How was she supposed to know that she was allowed to walk up to the Queen? Sometimes she needed an escort, sometimes she didn't. Sometimes they called her 'my lady' and fawned over her every request and sometimes, like right now, they tapped their feet derisively at her.

It was exhausting. They needed to make up their damn minds.

She walked over to the Queen with that same quick pace, stopping just before her.

"Your Grace," she said.

The queen straightened from her floral inspection and turned to her.

Realising only now that she was a whole ten years off mastering the curtsey, Suri thought, fuck it, and dropped into a bow instead. That was much easier. She remained bowed, gaze to the floor until the Queen spoke.

"Rise," she said. "Walk with me."

Queen Lera started to walk with tiny birdlike steps, her pace glacial. Suri tried to match her, but ended up moving ahead, then stopping, and trying to match again. If the Queen considered this walking, then Suri could see how it might take several hours to get anywhere.

The voice purred with mirth, but He mostly seemed happy they were together.

Before, it had seemed like there were two circles, her mind and the mind of Him. Two bubbles bouncing against each other. Now, it felt like one, with Him lingering over every part of her.

Suri cleared her throat after a minute or two. "The gardens are beautiful, your Grace. Are they like this year round?"

The Queen turned her face to Suri. They were matched in height. "My name is Lera. And you don't have to do that."

Suri floundered over how to reply. "I don't understand your meaning, your Grace."

The Queen stopped, which was a relief for Suri's half-squirrel step pace. It was strangely tiring. "Stop trying to be like us," she said, her calm and steady voice softening the words. "You're not, and I value you *because* you are not."

Suri swallowed. "Your Gra—"

"Do you know why I invited you to stay?" Queen Lera asked, interrupting whatever garbled crap was about to spill from the thief's lips.

Suri said nothing, waiting.

"I need people like you. People with drive, ambition, and natural power."

"Natural power?" Suri responded.

The Queen looked at her, really looked at her. "The very air around you is thick with the power of the Trio," she said. "You're a conduit."

A tendril of darkness swept across her collarbone and she was temporarily unable to breathe.

Suri, no last name, no title. Never once spoken of religion except to curse. The only wealth to her name strapped to her leg. A conduit of the Trio? What in Wrath's desert was a conduit?

She pictured the imagery of them, the carved stone Trio. It didn't *look* like the being of black tendriled rope that shadowed her, but she had no other rational explanation for the protector haunting her waking life. What did this make her? A priestess? Fuck that.

If this was the Trio, then surely the words were somehow divine? They didn't seem it.

Sweet Suri, the voice caressed her again with a laugh.

"This is wonderful," the Queen said, as if sensing her distress. "I only know a handful of priestesses where the feeling is this strong. Do you hear words? Messages?"

The cat was out of the bag then, if her reaction hadn't already given it away. "Yes."

The Queen nodded. "That is power. If you can tap into it, it is yours to wield."

Wield?

"I can't control it," Suri said. She flexed her fingers at her side, uncomfortable by her own admission of uselessness. Sometimes it felt like *it* controlled *her*.

The Queen didn't bat an eye. "I can help you with that."

Suri narrowed her eye. Help was rarely offered, and never free. "Why?"

The Queen started walking again, considering the thief's question. The same speed as before, drifting in tiny steps. Suri once again tried to match it with her own stubby-footed shuffle. She stopped by one of the bushes. "This is a Silverleaf bush. It is native to the Forgelands. Right up in the very North, by the mines."

Esra.

Thinking of him was a punch to the gut. It was a knee-jerk reaction. Anytime anyone mentioned the mines that blunt shock, just as it had that first day she'd found out.

Suri just nodded, trying instead to focus on the fact it confirmed her theory about silver and purple flower scouts.

"It was supposed to grow there, and only there. But it thrives here. My plants are in better condition here than they ever were in their natural habitat."

The thief sniffed, aware this was probably supposed to mean something, but was too tired of her short taste of this land to muddle through some weird analogy.

Queen Lera stopped again, staring directly at her.

"In the desert, the priestesses all came back. But one didn't. What happened to the High Priestess Manira?" she asked.

Suri didn't break her eye contact. Didn't hesitate, or fidget. "She died out there."

"Who killed her?"

"Scilla, or one of her guards. I'm not sure, it was all happening so fast."

The Queen broke eye contact, staring at one of her amefyre rings. She appeared to have two. Her voice was quieter when she spoke again, but the intensity had not faded. "My priestesses tell me that it was Lord Rasel that killed her."

Suri shrugged. "I don't know anything about that."

The Queen smiled. "You see the world as it is," she said. "You understand life and death. What we might want, against what we all need. We are the same, you and I."

The words hung in the air.

In a way, it was a salute. A gesture of respect.

Mostly though, it told her that the Queen knew nothing of her life. It told her, she doesn't understand. Maybe it could be said that they both understood power. Maybe it could be said that they both understood life and death. They might have the same understanding, but *how* Suri had reached that point had nearly killed her. Killed the parts of her willing to trust. She was never given the choice to see what else this world could be, and now half of her sight and her will to look for anything else, had been ripped from her.

Understanding came at no cost to the Queen. She could observe the workings of her people from afar. She could understand where the power lay, because she was the power. It was always with her. She had the glory of understanding, because she only had to look one way to see the tiers. Down.

If she had found her way to that understanding, it was by choice. Freedom of thought, freedom of will.

"Now tell me the truth, girl."

Suri cocked her head, intrigued at what truth she wanted to drag from her lips.

"Your earrings, the ones you gave to Rasel, when did you acquire them?" Queen Lera asked.

Suri tucked a loose strand of dark hair behind her ear. "They were a gift."

It was the truth. What she had asked for.

The Queen sighed. "It wasn't an accusation. Why were you given the first?"

Suri frowned. "I had nightmares."

There was an eagerness in the royal's tone when she replied. "Why? What happened?"

Suri considered lying, but then considered that she wanted to test the Queen's response. If they were the *same*. "I killed someone," she replied with no inflection.

The Queen nodded. "How old were you?"

Suri decided to lie here. Just a small one. She wanted to feel this Queen out. "Thirteen."

"Who did you kill? Why did you kill them?" The Queen questioned without pause. She didn't seem to notice the lie.

But there it was. The question.

The memory swept back unbidden. The flash of her knife into that orange shirt. The shock, the horror on Esra's face. How he'd told her it was alright, she hadn't killed him and then, when the guards had caught up to them later, how he'd taken the fall for it.

It wasn't his fault. It was hers. It was hers.

She *had* killed him. *She* had killed him.

There, there, my sweet.

It was Suri now who started walking.

Sweet Suri, I've got you.

She would not go there with the Queen, or anyone. Her memories were some of her finest belongings, often her only belongings. Suri didn't like to share. She had never been good at it and wasn't going to start with the Queen of Drangbor.

You have me, my sweet.

The Queen stepped with Suri, her eyes drifted over the spaces in and around her. A smile, perhaps the first real one Suri had seen, played on her lips. "The Trio clings to you like a shroud. I can help you harness it."

Suri swallowed. If the Queen meant to snatch her for a life at the priesthood, she couldn't say no. She couldn't tell her she didn't give two shits about the Trio, or that she just wanted the voice to leave her alone most of the time. "I don't know what any of it means."

The Queen dropped her almost wistful smile. "Did you know your earrings were amefyre?"

Suri spluttered. "Why? How did—how could that be?"

The pieces from the earrings, the shards they had dropped in that weird glowing liquid. Those were shards of amefyre? But why? How did she even get hold of the stuff?

"At least in part. Coated to look like regular metal, but inside..."

The Queen's voice had trailed off, as she stared at her own ring again, before looking back to Suri. "We make them here. I have a network in every realm, people whose job it is to spot those who seem to hold the capacity to engage with the Trio."

She tried to wrap her head around it, trying not to look like a rat caught in a trap under the solid gaze of the Queen. She tried to focus on what the Queen had told her. A network of spotters?

Suri's ears felt like they were ringing slightly. "So, the person that gave me my earrings..."

The Queen nodded. "They work for me."

Suri tried to keep her breathing steady. The pounding of the other pulse knocked her in a disjointed rhythm. "And the earrings?" she asked, her question breathy and unsure.

"To help dampen the raw strength of it, until you can be identified and taught."

A breath swept out of Suri's lungs and, for a moment, she couldn't catch another.

The metal disrupts the voices.

Mother Edi's voice whirled back to her. A stab of something—hurt, anger—betrayal. None of them, all of them, something else.

No.

Mother Edi... everything she had done, the gifts of the earrings...

All of it was to set her on a path to be found by Drangbor?

It couldn't be. She wouldn't believe it. Mother Edi wouldn't sell her out like that, sell her to the Queen. The earrings were to *help* Suri, to stop the nightmares, not to signal her to the powers that be as a potential recruit. But then her mind drifted to Ren. He'd had an earring, too. Just one, freshly pierced. And they'd taken him. Was that to be her fate too? Would Mother Edi have hobbled to the top of the stairs and waved her away in a silver carriage?

Suri's heart hurt. She didn't want to believe it. Mother Edi was the only person she had. Her brother had *told* her to trust Mother Edi, it was one of the last things... No. She couldn't think of it. Mother Edi was her friend. Her mentor.

She forced herself to focus back on the Queen, to keep her composure.

"You recruit us?" she asked, a strangled note in her voice.

The Queen gave another one of her diplomatic smiles. "We find those with potential, and we offer them a generous sum to live and study in Drameir as guards, priestesses, even scholars. Whatever befits their desires. It is a shame you were not found earlier, but you have found us now and that is what matters."

A shame...

They wanted to find her. They *wanted* to find *her*. Suri had never been sought out by anyone before. Not unless you counted people that wanted to kill her, which Suri chose not to.

It brought a strange wave of emotion over her.

Suri turned away from the Queen, nervous to show the flurry of feelings she couldn't suppress. They were seeking people like her. They would have *paid* her to come here.

She threw out a question in her mind, trying to speak to Him again.

Are you one of the Trio?

Suri stared at an unnaturally blue flower. This time, he replied to her.

I have many names, my sweet.

The Queen turned and stood next to her. "I would like you to come with us on our mission. The priesthood."

Is she lying? Are you a God?

"We will teach you how to channel the Trio," the Queen said. Suri tried not to jump at the feeling of a hand on her shoulder. "Prince Shaedon, Rasel, they have trained beneath me. Many have discovered true and unimaginable powers through worship. You could be one of them."

I am a watcher. I am powerful. I am everywhere. If that is a God, then that is one of my names.

More of nothing. The deep voice swayed her whole body, and she nearly stumbled. It was tiring trying to communicate with it. Every question was pushed through a mental wall in her mind, a wall seemingly made of thick mud.

Can I trust her?

Almost a laugh seemed to come back. *She is of us.*

Then the voice faded, and Suri couldn't grip back onto it. Her eye fluttered back open. It hadn't closed for more than a couple seconds.

The shadow spoke in cold riddles, but His parting inflection told her to trust in Lera. Wrath's bells, it wasn't like she could say no. She'd be stripped of everything she had and forced into exile yet again.

If the Queen was indeed trustworthy, then maybe Suri could string this along for enough time to escape. She allowed the hand to pull her back, and faced Lera.

"Do you know what amefyre does, Edi?" the Queen asked.

She still called her Edi. So perhaps Mother Edi worked for them, but wasn't important enough for the Queen to realise she'd stolen her name. Or maybe she suspected, and didn't care.

Suri wished she could reach out in her mind to Mother Edi and ask her. Who she was working for, why she'd given her the earrings. She wished someone else could tell her who to trust, who to become.

Esra had told her it was good to have allies, but he was gone now. They were all gone. She was alone, and it was her own fault.

She focused back on the question. "It powers the Gates?"

The Queen smiled. "And how does it do that?"

The question hung in the air. Suri didn't know the answer.

The Queen stepped closer, her eyes staring into Suri's single grey eye. There was a hardness in them, over a century of strength. "I can give you knowledge, teach you about the world, and teach you how to harness what burns within you. This is not a prison. This is what you've always wanted. Power."

Something flipped in Suri's stomach. Two feelings warred. First, how did she know? Was it that obvious? Then the second. Nothing was ever free.

"What do you want in return?" Suri asked.

The Queen smiled. Real? Or fake? Suri couldn't tell. "Only your loyalty."

Loyalty. For power. A pawn of the Queen, a speaker of a God, a priestess in training. Nothing she wanted to be, ever. Sure, there was power in those things, yet it was nothing more than Kol's offer. More cages, more restrictions. What was real power without freedom?

She didn't want to be beholden to anyone, or anything. The Queen didn't seem to want to hurt her. Instead, she would be used as a tool. For what purpose? Was this what Mother Edi wanted for her?

She swallowed and tried to think practically. It was an offer she didn't want to take. But it was better than an arrest for heresy. And that voice was so loud in everything. It swirled in her head, prickling at the faintest encouragement, stroking her skin inside and out.

Yes, my sweet girl. She is of us. Join us.

Suri found herself nodding.

24

The child grows, it is nearly time. I have no fear.
He will protect us all.
Diary of C. Aubethaan, est. early 8th century

"I didn't realise I had the joy of your company on this trip."

Suri glanced up at Rasel as he leaned against the doorway of the silver wagon. "The Queen invited me."

She mounted the carriage steps. He didn't move out of the way, and Suri shoved past him to get through the space with her bag.

Rasel reached out for her bag. "Did she now? She didn't tell me."

She let him take it from her, watching it as he set it down across the small central space. This was an identical sleeper carriage to the ones Manira and Rasel had travelled in before. Suri wondered if it was the exact same one.

"Maybe you're not her favourite anymore," she said, her voice distracted as she looked to the open door behind that led to a clean. empty bed.

She wasn't a morbid person, in general. Being morbid in the Tangle would be a full time job. But she did briefly wonder if this carriage was where the late High Priestess had spent her last night. Did she have any idea she would die out there? And by whose hand?

Rasel cleared his throat, and Suri turned back to him. "I figured you would be halfway across the country by now with my generous... patronage."

Suri almost choked. Luckily, he had turned to sit down, allowing her to compose herself. She shrugged, feigning nonchalance. "I considered it."

He raised a brow as he relaxed against a grey fur rug draped over a cushioned armchair. "But?"

If she was going to be locked into a chat with him, she may as well be comfortable. She sat down, across from him, on a couch with a thick, purple blanket. Part of her wanted to snuggle up underneath it, the winter's chill still biting inside the carriage. "I got another offer."

"A woman of few words as ever. This will be fun," he replied with a wink. "Tea?"

He swept his hand to the table next to him. A steaming glass teapot sat beside two perfect glass cups.

"Why not," she said, trying not to sound too eager. The stuff tasted grim, but at least it was hot. She wouldn't have to sit on her own damn hands if she could hold a warm cup instead.

She watched him pour the hot tea, admiring the wisps of white steam rising from the drink. "Where are we going?"

He smiled as he brought the tea over to her. "Oh, the Queen didn't tell you?"

She reached out her hands to take it from him. As her fingers touched the cup, she forced herself not to flinch. It was stone cold. Worse, it was almost ice to the touch.

Suri shook her head with gritted teeth. She realised then that the bite in the carriage was no error. Rasel was keeping the pipes ice cold. She could see the white frost clinging to them with her naked eye. The same action which had been the Trio's mercy in the Parched Lands, now told a very different story.

Rasel lounged back in his seat, watching her take a sip. She swallowed a large gulp of the near frozen liquid without a grimace. He didn't take partake, watching her suffer in silence.

He smiled. "A Gate is about to be born. A Gate for Drangbor."

The carriage jolted into movement as the words sank in. Drangbor had no Gate. The *birth* of a Gate.

Kol had been right.

"Since I've already stunned you back into silence, I'll take my leave," Rasel said, standing. "It's nearly a full day's ride. The blank wall in my chambers may be more interesting."

Suri blinked at him. As soon as he'd left, she put the cold cup on the table, grabbed the blanket, and moved into her own compartment.

It was immaculate. She scanned the room for any sort of obvious traps and saw nothing. The chest was empty but for a couple of books. One book on the medicinal uses of plants in Dramier and another silver-backed one, *Creatures of Greater Peregrinus.*

Manira had stayed here after all. Out of curiosity, Suri flicked through the tome. It fell open to a well-worn page, so frequently revisited that its exact location was broken into the spine. It was a page on harpies. An ugly creature with a woman's head and body, but whose hands extended into gnarled claws, with blackened bent wings. A faint line encircled part of the description;

these hideous beasts can be a product of breeding, or the affliction can be caused by a curse. But what drew Suri's attention was the alternate name of the creature. Its Old Tongue translation. *Vulturis.*

Asari ith vulturis.

Kol had said it meant try not to die. Rasel had said it meant beware the witch. What did it really mean, then? Witch, or harpy? Beware the harpy? Did the pagans have a lot of harpies in the desert? Was it some threat? Suri didn't know what any of it meant and didn't know why Manira seemed to care about them.

She closed the book and threw it back into the chest. Removing her eyepatch, she drew the curtains, lay on the bed, and slipped into sleep.

His voice brought her back to waking. *Suri.*

She didn't even have to look for Him, He sought her out, He came to her. Since she'd sold her earrings, He was in her ear and body every waking moment. She blinked her eye open. She couldn't tell how long it had been, the same level of light still peeking from behind the curtains.

Sweet Suri. Where's your revenge? Find your anger.

Suri's mind immediately went to Scilla. That sculpted face, not turning from Suri's own as the red hot, curved implement got closer and closer. She winced, remembering the pain, her stomach nauseous even now.

Yes, find its mark. You know what you need to do.

Then He appeared again, His shadowed form in the corner of the room.

She pushed back against the headboard with the heels of her palms, staring at where its face should be. Her knees bent as she rested her forearms against them.

He didn't scare her. Her heart thrummed, but it was anticipation that excited it, not fear. There was a tether there, like a string between her corporeal form and His ethereal one. She felt it coil and tighten inside her, as He moved closer.

He was vengeance. He was her own darkness mirrored. Her protector.

The shadow form stepped forward. Close enough that even in the low light, Suri could make Him out. He was tall, broad. The planes of His face were sharp, angular like the Fae. Smoke knotted and unknotted around His form, leaving gaps for a second before the tendrils moved again.

Open yourself to your desires.

The hand reached out and touched her forearm. She dropped it to her side instantly, as she shuddered, her mouth falling open in a soundless breath.

His touch.

It was temptation itself. It was powerful and debilitating. It didn't feel like skin, it felt like a caress of every imaginable sin. It was wrath. It was lust.

Hello, my sweet.

He touched the inside of one knee. Without thinking, her leg parted, dropping to the side. What he wanted. She belonged to him.

That's my sweet Suri.

Her breath hitched in her throat as she saw the tendril hand inching down.

A low chuckle reverberated inside her skull. It didn't sound like that body was making the noise, the voice of Him was everywhere.

He seemed to tut, pausing his movement at her thigh. *Jealous children...*

And then He was gone.

Someone knocked on her door, three hard raps against the thin frame.

She clamped her knee back up, breathing deeply, and tucked her dark hair behind her ears as she regained her composure. "Yes?"

Her voice sounded a little shaky.

Rasel pushed the door open, hitting it against the wall. He looked at her, eyes snagging for a couple seconds before he scanned the rest of the room. He looked at her again. "I thought I hea—"

Suri clucked her tongue. "He's gone."

Rasel pushed an errant lock of white hair back from his face. He furrowed his brow for a second, then his face transformed into his knowing look. It pissed Suri off.

"You see a male, then," he said with a smirk.

It took a moment for her to process what he was saying. He, the voice. Him. Him, Him, Him. Whatever He, it, they were. They also showed themselves to Rasel. Her first thought was confused. What, as a woman? As an animal? Something else entirely?

She wasn't alone. She wasn't crazy, even if Rasel's company wasn't the most reassuring. "What do you see? What does he sound like?"

Rasel smiled more, revelling in his moment of power where Suri wanted something from him.

Her temper flared. "I know you took the amefyre from my earrings."

Rasel's smile wavered. "And?"

Suri sat up more fully, crossing her legs under the blanket. She stared at him. "Are you using it to power the Gate?"

Rasel's eyes widened, and he breathed out in a whistle. "What a question."

"Well?"

Rasel thought for a second. "Yes," he said. "In a way."

Suri crossed her arms over her chest, waiting. She saw his eyes flick down, then back up to her face.

Rasel moved and sat on the edge of the bed. She could feel him looking at her other eye, the one that sat uncovered. "Do you know how the Old Gates used to work?" he asked.

Suri nodded. "They were Sotoledi's Gates. Death Gates. People would make barbaric sacrifices to him."

The prince smiled, looking down at his hands. "It was more than that. The first Gates themselves were built on the sites of historic battles, places where many people had died at one time. The more death, the greater the distance the Gate could power.

"The Forgelands Gate is at the site of the Four Year Revolt from a few hundred years ago. Many died. New Politan was built there *because* of the site of the massacre, not the other way around. Sure, they were kept ticking along by your 'barbaric' sacrifices of goats and odd old man, but they were founded in suffering already."

Suri felt like she remembered parts of this. The Priesthood had stopped all of that barbarism, discovering how to power the Gates with amefyre, not death.

Rasel didn't bother recapping that part. Instead, he sighed. "But there was a problem. We couldn't make new Gates. They require a lot of amefyre gems. We used nearly all of it in the forging of the last Gates, before the Wrath."

"The Forgelands mines ha—"

"Ran dry of amefyre twenty years ago." Rasel cut her off in a bored tone. "They've been mining for the barest scraps and supplementing their income with other gems."

Suri raised an eyebrow. That was new information.

He noticed her surprise. "Don't feel bad for them, their ruby supply is still obscene."

She snorted. As if she would feel bad for the nobility that stripped her of her home.

Rasel shrugged. "It's taken nearly a century to collect enough powered amefyre to forge a Gate. We have that now. The world of Seers, men of Blood and Souls and Time, that's over. It is time for new power. Ours."

He was clearly done with his history lesson, and Suri was surprised he'd given it at all. He owed her nothing.

She thought about what he had told her. "The amefyre in the Parched Lands. Were we really taking it back?"

"Does it matter?" he asked, lifting his head to stare at the thief.

"No, I guess it doesn't."

Rasel nodded. "Good."

Suri chewed her lip. "If you needed as much amefyre as you could get, why were you sending it around the land? Why was I given amefyre earrings as a kid?"

"The raw amefyre is only part of it," Rasel replied. "Did you notice a difference when you wore it?"

Suri nodded. "I couldn't hear... it was muted. Quieter."

"Numb."

"Yeah."

He trailed his hand over the end of the blanket, fiddling with the frayed edge. "The amefyre doesn't nullify... the voice. It absorbs. The pain, the death, her *comfort*, the amefyre claims it," he said. His voice was strained, and he paused for a breath. When he spoke again, his voice was lifeless. "It powers on the darkness in your soul. We needed powered amefyre for the Gate."

She smiled. "And who has more darkness in their soul than orphaned children on the street."

It was meant to be a joke, but the truth of it cracked through. The words fell flat into the air, but Rasel chuckled nonetheless. "Now you're getting it."

Suri blinked, the rage that was never far away swelling into her chest once more. "And you locked it into crappy metal jewellery.

Because we have nothing, so we would treasure even that and wear it all the time and not look any closer."

Rasel said nothing, only watched her as her voice rose.

"Then you track them down, bring the most fucked up ones down here, distill the darkness from their souls... and what?"

Her question shot out, an accusation of something, but she didn't know what. Once again, she was a tool in the wider machinations of the rich. Maybe she always had been.

"What? What do you think?" Rasel fired back. "We train them, Edi. Lots of them join the priesthood."

She forced herself to take two breaths, but that couldn't hold back the anger in her reply. "So, this is the real reason you took me then, back in the desert," she spat. "You knew from the earrings that I was one of those broken children. You knew you'd get the powered amefyre from me."

Rasel didn't even flinch. "Don't play the victim, Edi. It doesn't suit you."

She scowled at him.

"Your jewellery was a draw, sure." Then he winked at her. "But don't misunderstand. I'm a petty man. I got a kick out of helping the girl who'd tortured my sweet sis."

She spluttered. "I didn't-"

He held a hand up. "Don't ruin it. I'm just starting to like you."

Suri's mouth twitched in the ghost of a smile.

Rasel lifted his hand up and, after a second's hesitation, placed it on her covered knee. She prepared herself for a shock of cold that didn't come. His hand was full of human warmth.

He didn't meet her eye. "We hear it too. And whilst you were a useful tool in sponging up that darkness, you don't need to mute it anymore," he said, his voice barely more than a whisper in the dark room. "You can feel it, breathe it, let it sway you, move you. It speaks to us because it knows we are the power in this land, we are the ones strong enough to guide its plan. This is power. And you don't have to hide from it if you stick with us."

He removed his hand and stood.

She sat in the echo of his words until he reached the door, then cleared her throat. "The Drangborian Gate. Where is it?"

Rasel turned. "On the border of the Parched Lands. Why?"

Suri tried not to react. The border of Drangbor and the Parched Lands... wasn't that? She rolled her eye at Rasel, disguising herself as best she could. "I was hoping not to run into my least favourite person."

Rasel smirked and opened the door, letting in a shaft of light. "Don't worry, I'll be sure to give her a frosty reception."

Once he'd left, the door closed firmly behind her, Suri let her mind race.

The Great Altar was located on the border between Drangbor and the Parched Lands. It was where the Fae witch went, where she led the pagan ritual to Sotoledi. Birthing the infant Demon Lord of Death upon the Altar, scattering half the world to the ruin of his Wrath.

Rasel's words seared through her mind. '*The first Gates themselves were built on the sites of historic battles. Places where many people had died at one time.*'

It had taken them a century to get enough amefyre to build it.

A century of peace under the Priesthood.

What massacre could the new Gate link to?

Then the truth of it hit her.

Lera planned to channel the Wrath itself.

25

My sister has found me. I know not how. She
writes she is sorry. She wants to help. I tell her
she must come quick, the child is near.
Diary of C. Aubethaan, est. early 8th century

Rasel left the moment the carriages stopped, and she
hadn't been able to see where he went. She searched
his compartment though, the satisfying weight of a decorated knife strapped to her thigh. She waited, watching the
door of the finest carriage she'd ever seen, hoping that she
could at least track the Queen's leaving.

They had reached their destination, but there was little to
see. The world had once again transitioned from that carpet
of green, to sand and dirt.

She wanted to speak to the Queen or at least see her. She
didn't know what she wanted. But she thought that if she saw

the Queen, she would know her reaction. Trust it. Her gut had got her this far, more or less in one piece.

The moment she'd guessed at what the Queen's plans might be, she was conflicted.

She was curious. Could so much death be wielded? And where did they want the Gate to go? Plus, she reasoned to herself as she watched the space around her, she was trusted here. Respected, even. There were no binds to hold her, no guards to watch her. The Queen wanted her here. A Prince from the Pail was starting to *like* her. Sure, they had a use for her, but every relationship has its transactions. They had told her the truth, and that was more than most.

She had a bed, she had ample food. She had gold. They are of us, the voice had told her. They felt it too, the voice, the power. They didn't lie about it, they embraced it. Why *wouldn't* she be loyal to the Queen?

In that small gap underneath the storage carriage, on its far side, she saw feet silently drop onto the sand. More came out. There were four sets. Four sets of feet who had tried not to be seen exiting the storage carriage. Four sets of feet, one of which decidedly narrower and more feminine, now moving away, and disappearing, from the carriage.

Suri moved to the side of that carriage, ducking out of sight. She waited a few seconds to get her breath steady, before glancing around the corner. A couple of heads vanished behind a small tuft of land.

Why wouldn't she be loyal to the Queen? Because she had never been loyal to anyone but herself. To trust was to die. If these people were going to change that, they would have to prove it to her. Prove they were worthy of her. Because despite what Kol might say, she was far from worthless, far from nothing.

What were they worth when they didn't know she was watching?

At the lip of the hill, she crouched. It wasn't necessary. None of them looked back over their shoulders.

Carved into the half-hill, half-dune before her was a set of stairs. The four descended. The Queen was one of them. Even clad in a full cloak and hood, Suri only had to see the way she glided down the steps. Of the other three, two were clearly guards. The third man, Suri wasn't sure. Rasel, maybe?

When the four had disappeared, she approached the stairs. They went under the hill, the ground held up by stone supports. She peered down, but it was dark, and she was unable to see the bottom. She could hear in the distance the sounds of feet against stone, getting fainter.

She took her first step down, in her near silent slippers. Suri noticed then that the horizontal stone that lay across the stone support was not bare. Set into the stone was a carved symbol. One she knew. One she'd seen before. One she didn't expect to see here. A circle, with a triangle on the left and three dots to the right.

Diophage. The Old Life God.

And next to it, in darkened and long dried blood, half flaking off, another familiar symbol. Revenge.

The two in tandem again, like they had been in the study. *Diophage's Revenge.* Another pagan warning? Or something else?

Her body felt cold as she further descended into the darkness. At the bottom of the staircase, there was a short hallway with an arch leading into a hall. She could see the Queen even now. She was far away, at the end of the hall, but there was little to block her vision here. Suri sensed her about to turn, so she scuttled forward, standing with her back pressed against the wall next to the archway to the hall.

A male voice finished a question. "—last time?"

"It wasn't finished before, Lingyun," the Queen said. "It's full now. It'll work."

She glanced around her and saw no way out, bar the way she'd come in. Shit. She couldn't risk glancing around the archway. Four people, too good of a chance that one of them would look back her way.

"And if it doesn't?"

She was certain that was the footman's voice. Why was the Queen coming down into this dark underground stone hall to speak to him?

"Then we repeat the ceremony until it does."

"The priestesses are nervous."

Lingyun had a lot of nerve talking to his Queen like that.

"The priestesses are not your concern. Do you have any other objections?"

"None," he replied. Smart move. "The other lands have suspicions, but nothing more than whispers."

Suri didn't know what they were talking about. The Gate, she guessed. Why would the priestesses be nervous?

"Good. Are they ready for us on the other side?"

"Thanlas, Dellon, and Manthi have secured the area."

Dellon... that was the Food Guild envoy at dinner. The Gate was going to the Pail? That was days away. Maybe even a week, at the port of Lartosh.

"Isn't it beautiful?" asked the Queen.

Was the Gate in that very room? Her hands flexed against the stone at her back. She itched to take a look.

"The girl. You trust her?"

Lingyun's question sent a spike of fear down her spine. They spoke of her, surely. His implication was clear. He didn't trust her.

The Queen didn't respond for a couple of seconds, and Suri found herself leaning into the archway.

"She's been on the tea for days. She's *his* now."

The tea. She's been on the tea. They were drugging her.

No. The spike of fear blossomed into a deathly feeling of creeping horror. She's his. Whose?

The answer came in that whispering voice. *They are of us.*

The tendril of dark, the tendril of Him, swept across her body. It cooled her blood. They were amplifying Him? Making him louder, stronger.

Trust them, sweet girl.

"You're sure?" Lingyun replied.

Her heart pounded. She wanted to be angry. But that anger cooled, replaced by a wanting to listen to Him—to be his sweet Suri.

They had drugged her. Fucking *drugged* her.

But He wanted her to trust them. He had protected her. She dropped to the ground, clutching her knees as she rocked on the balls of her feet.

They had drugged her. They had helped her. Money, food, bed.

Him, Him, Him. *Sweet Suri.*

"She's a selfish creature. What I'm offering is her best option. She'll stay."

The words rang dully against her ears as she breathed in shallow breaths. Selfish. It was true, she *was* selfish.

"If the priestess can't channel it all, we can use her as a replacement conduit."

She tasted bile in her mouth and swallowed against the feeling of nausea. She was so *angry*. Until she wasn't. Until she couldn't be. It came and then went. She felt her rage as it was pushed down, stroked into submission.

They are of us.

No, they aren't.

Yes, sweet girl.

"Make sure you check all the girls again before they come in. Thoroughly. Even a stud could ruin it," the Queen said.

"Of course."

She heard then, the movement of feet moving back towards the end of the hall. Towards her. Oh shit, they were about to find her eavesdropping.

Fuck, fuck.

She had maybe a minute. Wrath's doors.

They might be of her, as he said. But if they found her here, it would be hard to explain. Even the tendril swirling around her seemed to understand that and let go of her.

Her one eye studied the room around her again. There was a small alcove in the stone, but it was higher than she could reach. There was a wooden support beam at head height, just shy of the alcove and, at one end, a diagonal brace curved down into the wall.

She hooked a hand over the brace and dug the side of her foot into the uneven stone face, hauling herself up to her waist as she reached and grabbed onto the horizontal beam.

Her body pushed flush into the alcove, just as the Queen and the footman moved through the archway. They did not look up, only forwards, as they left.

The two guards did not come after them.

Wrath.

She could leave now, pretend she hadn't heard anything. Pretend any tiny shred of trust she had in the Queen hadn't died in that room. Or she could escape. Take everything she had and run for it.

Stay.

His voice sang again, compelling her to stay with the Queen, to help the Queen. She cradled her head in her hands, as she struggled not to scream with frustration. She was caught between that dark ocean of calm He tried to wash over her, and a war that blossomed inside her head.

Damn. Damn. Damn.

Sweet girl.

Wrath. Death. Poison. Him Him Him. It was all *poison. He* was poison.

Suri...

No. No.

Amefyre. Amefyre numbs. She needed to be numb. She needed to think straight for once.

I can be your thoughts. Don't hide from me, sweet girl.

Suri dropped like a cat to the floor, smoothed her hair, made sure her dress lay flat, and walked into the hall.

The two guards, who had been leaning against the far wall, immediately bolted upright. They looked her up and down as she strode into the room.

"Who are you?"

In the centre of the room was a large rectangular stone block which seemed to be its natural centrepoint. At the end, however, was its new focus.

No, Suri.

The Gate.

Empty, closer to an ornate archway at the moment. It was only the amefyre that set it apart. It was different from the Northern Gate. The stonework spiralled in different, more undulating patterns, the top of the Gate carved in waves. Embedded into the stone were chunks of amefyre, with painted silver circles around them, the circles linked by painted silver lines to other circles holding amefyre. Most of these amefyre pieces were small, the size of a fingernail. Others were bigger, and if cupped in her palm, her fingers might not meet around them.

Every step was wading through thigh-high water. She pushed against the force, trying not to let Him speak, trying not to listen.

She stopped beside the Gate, her face hot with exertion.

Stop.

The two guards were poised, hands at the hilts of their swords. The grumpier one spoke again. "I said, who are you?"

Suri smiled. "I'm here to relieve you."

The guard scoffed, gesturing to her as if that alone made it plain. "As if! I've never seen you before. Who sent you?"

They wouldn't let her pass. She knew that.

She inhaled deeply and finally embraced the feeling of Him. He sought her out, He clung to her. But because of that, she knew exactly where that darkness sat in her. How to tap into it. She knew what it revelled in, how it praised her violence. When she spoke, the voice wasn't hers. It was His.

"I'm sorry, I didn't speak plainly." She unsheathed the knife from her thigh, her hand not feeling her own, her mind not knowing itself at all. "I'm here to relieve you of your lives."

26

The Altar is readied, I will birth there. The wildflowers bloom across the hills. The shrine-folk are gathered. My sister comes. My pains start under the morning sun.

Diary of C. Aubethaan, est. early 8th century

Suri retched into the sand. Nothing came up. She tried not to picture their bodies, but she couldn't shake it from her head. The piece of amefyre clutched in her fist steadied her somewhat. Simply holding it seemed to lessen that voice.

She could hear Him still, trying to coax her.

Go to her, she will explain. We are one. We are one.

It was much quieter though, a whisper easy to ignore.

She straightened from her hunched position and sat back on the half-dune. She'd left the Altar after slaughtering the two guards, stumbling a hundred yards from the encampment.

Clacker. Barsen. How many guards had she killed with His aid in the desert? Three? More? Now another two.

Before her twenty-first year.

She hadn't meant to kill them. She'd wanted to knock them out, move them somewhere until she'd left. But as soon as she'd pulled on Him, there was nothing but rage. She hadn't been able to stop. If there had been ten people in that room, she was certain she would have killed them all.

Suri wiped the blade in the dirt.

They had been drugging her. This is what they wanted her to channel. She wouldn't do it, she wouldn't become a conduit of a god that only wanted her to kill, of a Queen waiting to use her as a tool.

She wasn't a hero, but she wouldn't let them turn her into a monster.

She clutched the amefyre tighter in her hand. It was the most round one she could find, but it wasn't entirely spherical. She only hoped it would be good enough for her plan.

She checked around her to be certain no one was listening. She was downwind of them, so her voice shouldn't carry.

Then, she took off her eyepatch and attached the seeing silk in its place.

She thought of him, and the image appeared almost instantly. He strode down a lavish hallway with blue lanterns on either side. A moment later, he slowed to a more languid pace.

"Hello, again," Kol said under his breath. "Another happy accident in your new spying career?"

"Not this time."

Her voice sounded scratchy from all the retching.

Kol stopped. "Where are you?"

"Do you wear your silk all the time, then?" she asked, trying to work it out. She could only patch into Rasel through the silk she had tucked into his cravat. Was he wearing an eyepatch too?

"Where are you?" he asked again with an impatient edge.

"The Altar," she said. "You were right. Lera's got a Gate."

Kol's vision swung from side to side, then he ducked through the nearest door. It was a small dining room. Empty. "Is it working?"

"Not yet. The plan is to wake it tonight."

"Shit."

"I think they're trying to channel the Wrath itself."

Kol paused. "I think so, too. I was hoping they would take longer to gather the amefyre."

Suri played with the knife, idly dragging it in circles through the dirt. "Seems like they're all set."

Kol let out a strange noise. "Suri, I'm not close enough."

The sound of her name on his lips tugged at something in her. No one here knew who she was, they only knew the mask she wore. She'd only heard her name in *His* mouth and now that felt dirty and corrupted. This made her feel more real, more herself.

"There's something else. The Queen has Viantha."

Kol started pacing round the room. "Do you know where?"

"Storm Pan."

"Ah," he said, still moving back and forth.

"Yep," she replied.

There was silence for a moment, the only noise, his steps.

"I took a piece of the Gate," she said. "Do you think that will stop it?"

"It won't stop them trying, which is the bad part."

"Why is it bad?"

Suri knew that the Queen was an untrustworthy snake who wanted to use her as some weird god-vessel and channel a massacre, but she didn't understand why the Gate was itself bad. Did he know where it was going?

Kol stopped pacing, spreading his hands on the table in front of him. "Why did you contact me?"

Suri frowned at the question. "What?"

"You're choosing to tell me this. I want to know why."

Why? Because she was drugged. Because the Queen seemed to be hiding something. Because Lingyun gave her the creeps. "Because I am scared something bad is going to happen to the priestesses," she said. "And because I don't trust them."

"Do you trust me?"

Esra's words came back to her then, hitting her with a horrid weight. *'Is there anyone else you trust?'*

Suri swallowed. "I have to trust someone."

And she had picked him. The man who told her he wanted her dead. Somehow, still the lesser of two evils. He hadn't drugged her, lied to her, and tried to use her as a conduit of a vengeful god.

When he didn't reply for a while, she thought maybe her answer wasn't enough. That he needed more. But then he spoke. "Queen Lera is trying to start a war. Against me, but also against any of the guilds or lands that might side with me," he started. "This Gate is part of that."

"Why?" she asked.

"That is.... too big of a question. What you need to know right now, is that Gates cannot work off just amefyre and the power of the so-called Trio alone. That's horseshit. If Lera's channelling the Wrath, the Gate won't work anyway. But she will still try to open it, which means she needs a trigger of some sort. Do you understand me?"

"Why won't it work?" Suri replied.

Kol gripped the edge of the table. "Suri, she will try to sacrifice someone to open it. You need to be far away when that happens."

Suri dropped the knife handle.

A human sacrifice? But that was barbaric. That was what the pagans did.

"What? I can't—"

"Listen, I'm not close enough. I can't get there before tonight. But Scilla can, she's-"

"No."

Her voice was hard.

Kol's grip went rigid, his knuckles white on the table. "She can help. Get you away, I'll—"

"She's helped enough," Suri interrupted again. Enough for a lifetime.

A pause.

"Fine," he replied. His grip left the table, and he stood up.

"Thanks for the heads up about the sacrifice," she said. She stood up too, stretching her back.

He groaned. "Why does it feel like you're going to completely ignore me?"

Suri cracked a small smile. "Loud and clear. But I just killed two guards. I need to get them off my scent. I'll leave before it all starts."

Kol was quiet for a moment, before speaking again. "Try not to die, little thief."

"Tea?" Rasel opened the door to her compartment without knocking.

Suri spun to face him, checking her eyepatch was in place. She had just pulled a different dress over her head. This one was a burnt rust shade, with a square neckline and slit which made it easy to move in. The other, discarded across the room, was covered in guards' blood.

"Thanks," she said.

Rasel seemed to search her face for something. The quiet in her head was deafening. Then he brought in a cup and handed it to her. "It's nearly time."

She feigned taking a drink as he watched. "To power the Gate?"

"Exactly."

"I have something for you," he said.

Suri stared at him. "What?"

He wouldn't meet her eyes. Instead, he dragged an icy finger over the bust of Atrius in the corner. She only prayed he didn't look towards the back of the room, where her bloody dress was probably still far too visible. "I once told you that if we got out of the desert, I'd buy you something pretty."

She wasn't prepared for the shock. "Oh."

He glanced at her, before reaching into his tunic pocket and pulling out two dangling pieces of jewellery. The red gemstones caught in the beams of afternoon sun peeling through the window.

"Since I took your other earrings," he said, drifting off.

She instinctively held her hand out, and Rasel placed them in her palm. Each one held two round stones, which hung asymmetrically from the hook. They were gorgeous. She put them both in and felt their weight.

He looked a little uncomfortable. "It's firestone. You're Northern, right? We are the flame, and all that."

She hated his kindness. She didn't understand it. "Thanks," she said.

She also hated that she felt a bit guilty. She'd chosen to betray him, to tell Kol. Rasel had lied to her, lied about the earrings. Lied about so much. But there was something about him. He heard it too, he felt its pull. They were both His creatures, and they were both lonely.

"It's nothing."

He turned to leave.

"Rasel," she said. He swivelled, holding the door frame.

"If the Gate is powered by amefyre, why are the priestesses here?" It was the one question she still hadn't found the answer to, the only answer she wanted before she left.

Now she could think without all the noise, she could finally leave. It didn't—it couldn't—call on her to stay. If there was going to be some kind of summoning of the power of the fucking Wrath, she wanted to be on the other side of the damn land when it happened.

She assumed the priestesses were there for some kind of celebration or ceremony, or even just to spread the miraculous word of a new Gate. But after what Kol had told her, she wasn't so sure.

Rasel smiled. "You'll see. Come out as soon as you're ready."

Once he'd left, Suri waited until she heard him outside of the carriage.

No, she would not see.

She was going to follow Kol's advice and get out of there, right now. She might be caught, she knew that. She would choose death over the Queen's servitude, enslaved to the voice of their Gods. Leaving now, in the peak of their distraction, might be the best chance she could get.

She rechecked her small pouch of coins for the seventh time in the last half hour. All there. Nestled alongside the *seeing silk*. The golden keys to her new life. She'd find some way around the bond once she was far enough away. Maybe Kol could offer some cure as payment for her information. He dealt with Death and had an ancient blood witch in his lands. He must know something. Either way, she was gone.

She tied the drawstrings tight and pulled her dress up, fastening it to a thin sash she'd tied to her waist. It shouldn't move too much, and she could always feel it against her. She let the dress fall back down.

She picked up a cloak from the chest. Only two pockets in it. Honestly, tailors needed to learn what the people needed. Two pockets was poor.

She shoved a flask into one of them, before moving across to Rasel's compartment and trying the door. Locked. Damn. She'd cleaned and replaced the knife exactly where she had found it, not wanting a missing knife to link her to the two dead guards. And now there was no way into the room again.

Unarmed, then.

It wasn't a disaster, she could find another knife on the road. But it was pretty. Blue hilt with gold inlay. She'd liked the weight of it in her palm.

She opened the door of the carriage and stepped out into the night air. It was still firmly dark outside. The priestesses were lined up with the guards around them. They looked nervous, yes, but from what Suri could see it was more of a nervous excitement.

No one seemed to be looking at her.

She started walking away from the gaggle and had taken two steps before a voice called out.

"Edi, you take up the rear guard, back of the priestesses."

It was the damned footman. Lingyun.

Great.

She turned round, seeing his beady eyes on her near the back of the line of priestesses. Where had he come from? She swore she hadn't seen him there a moment ago. Shit.

She joined on to the back of the group of priestesses, as he moved towards the front of the line.

Rear guard? Fine. As soon as they were distracted, she could slip away.

Those at the front started moving towards the Gate. She couldn't see the Queen and soon the priestesses at the back were moving as she trailed behind.

If only she was a half decent horsewoman, or even likely to stay on, she could have made a much better run for it. But then, she figured, she gave them much more of a reason to come after her if she stole a whole damned horse. Maybe they'd leave her alone if she just left by herself.

"Did he say your name was Edi?"

The question knocked her out of her planning.

The priestess right at the back, just in front of her, was looking at her. Maybe only a couple of years older than her with a narrow, pretty face.

"Yes," Suri replied.

She smiled in return and her cheeks displayed dimples. "I thought so. I am Priestess Orienne."

Suri nodded, disinterested, about to look away. Wait? Orienne. That was a Northern name. And a New Politan accent. "You're from the Forgelands?"

Another dimpled smile. "Most of us are. I'm from the Tangle."

Home. An odd sense of kinship washed over Suri followed by disbelief. This girl. This girl had survived the Tangle? She seemed all innocence.

"Sorry to pry, but were you one of hers? Mother Edi's?" Orienne asked.

Suri gasped, checking to see no one was paying attention. "How did you—?"

Her grin widened. "I was, too. Before I was brought here."

She was one of Mother Edi's orphans, too. Orienne had sat in the same room, at the same dimly lit table. Maybe had her knee patched up in the same way. It was small but there was still something in it, some shared pain. A feeling of being less alone.

Yet with it, Suri felt that same stabbing feeling she'd experienced before. A feeling of betrayal. Was this the path Mother Edi intended her to tread too? She had sent Orienne here, and Ren, and now it was Suri's turn?

"Is that common?" Suri asked.

Orienne nodded eagerly. "Quite a lot of us end up here. Kalyn, second from the front, is one too."

So, Rasel hadn't lied. He had told her that they are brought here, that most of them join the priesthood.

Mother Edi's gift, those earrings, was just the first step in a long walk. A walk that would end here, as a piece in Drangbor's politics. Another conduit of the Trio found in the gutters of New Politan.

It wasn't like she thought Mother Edi loved her. She wasn't her child, she wasn't blood. But if she was to be sold down a river, she'd have liked to have known who was paying the fee. The anger twisted like a knife in the gut. She could have at least *told* her.

Suri thought she cared. That was the truth of it. She thought Mother Edi was one of the few safe places she had in the world. She thought—it didn't matter right now.

What mattered for the moment was surviving the day. Mother Edi, whether Suri even *wanted* to return to the Forgelands anymore, all of it could wait.

She suddenly realised that their conversation had brought them to the steps. At the front of the line, the priestesses were beginning their descent.

If she wanted to duck out unseen, now would be the time. Suri looked around her. No one was looking at her, even Orienne had turned her gaze forward trying to see down the stairs, her fingers shaking at her sides.

She could go right now.

She looked at the priestesses in front of Orienne, all glancing between themselves, biting lips, wringing hands, and folding their hair behind their ears for the seventh time.

Gill's words. '*It's the priestesses.*'

They were nervous. She just had to know why.

She would leave later, when they'd opened the Gate and all was well, or even in the middle of it once she'd got a flavour of it. She knew there was a greater chance of her being caught, but had to know what they were walking into.

At the foot of the stairs, Lingyun waited. He scanned all the priestesses as they passed. When the last had gone through, Suri nodded at the footman and moved to follow, but his arm shot out. "Arms up. Legs apart."

"What?" Suri asked.

Lingyun waved his hand down the procession of priestesses. "I need to check you. I've already checked the others."

Suri swallowed and followed his instructions. He searched her whole body as she tried not to flinch when his hands skimmed along her bare thighs. He checked her hands, neck, ears, even up into her hair. Perhaps Rasel had said something about her ring hiding place. He left her earrings in place, after checking them thoroughly.

And he didn't look under her eyepatch.

The relief of that was short-lived, for a moment later she felt his probing hands find her waist. "What's this?" he said.

No. That was her ticket. Her whole damned life.

"Take it out."

For a moment she scoured her brain, thinking of any single way she could refuse. But there were guards behind her. Fuck.

She did as he said, unfastening the pouch. His hand lay waiting, and he grabbed at it as her hand hesitated. "It's just my money," she said, staring at the pouch in his clutches.

He opened it, looking in. Thankfully, he didn't seem to care about the piece of black cloth. "Where does a girl like you get this much gold?"

Her entire world was being taken from her. "It's mine."

"Well, I'll hold onto it for now. After the ceremony, we can discuss it," he said. His smile was as cold as the grave.

Fuck him. Fuck this.

She scowled, watching him pocket her precious bundle.

He waved his hand towards the entrance.

She would go in, and she wasn't coming out again until she had her gold back.

27

We could not stop her. We could not stop the sister's knife. Diophage's revenge upon this land will sing forever more, as will her treachery.

Diary of C. Aubethaan, est. early 8th century

Suri descended the stairs, catching up to the back of the group as they moved into the antechamber. She looked to the places the guards had fallen. The sacks of flesh and their leaking trail of blood had been removed. She would not have guessed if it weren't for her own memory.

The room itself was mostly unchanged. The only addition was several candles of varying heights and widths, placed around the room. Instead of the warmth and comfort the candles used to evoke in the Tangle, here they cast flickering shadow puppetry on the curved ceiling. Suri suppressed a shudder.

The structure of the line had disintegrated, and the cluster of priestesses stood together at the start of the room, murmuring.

"Is that *the* Altar?"

"Where the Fae witch—?"

"—destroying it?"

"—incredible."

Lingyun's voice boomed out from behind them. "Keep walking."

The priestesses moved into the room, their excited voices echoing against the low curve of the ceiling, as they spotted the Gate at the end of the room.

"It's a Gate! A new one."

"There hasn't been a new Gate in over—"

Suri hadn't moved forwards as she tuned out the chatter. She hung at the back of the room, close to the archway, scanning the area. Guards. She counted four, half of those they had travelled with. Rasel leaned against the wall on the left of the room, his eyes firmly locked on the woman standing next to the Gate.

Once she followed his gaze, Suri could not tear hers away either.

The Queen was dressed in a black gown, so deeply black that it cast her fair skin in an almost luminous glow. The dress seemed to be constructed of iridescent onyx feathers, strapped in tight at her waist, spreading up to her collarbones, and then back down to the floor. Her eyes were lined with kohl, her face seeming more angular than before, the dim lighting of the room casting shadows under her cheekbones and narrow jaw.

Her wings were the same iridescent hue, but now picking up the warm ambers of the candles and refracting their light on the wall behind her.

She spread her palms out in greeting, and the priestesses fell silent.

"Welcome. You are honoured to be invited to the unveiling and reignition of the Drangborian Gate."

Not a sound was heard in the room, bar the single swish of the Queen's dress as she moved her arm to cup the air near the Gate.

"The Gate is powered by our own amefyre. We hope to bridge across lands and bring peace and prosperity to Peregrinus."

Suri looked away from the vision in black, and instead watched the awestruck faces of the priestesses. Each one of them was enraptured, any nerves replaced by some religious zealotry Suri could not understand.

The Queen smiled; a carefully placed, coercive smile. "The Three Gods need only the power of the Inverted Bone Ceremony to bring this Gate into perfect harmony."

A little chatter now from the Priestesses. Eager. Orienne's dimples were showing.

Lingyun moved through the priestesses, handing out small glasses of some pale, red wine. Twelve glasses for twelve priestesses.

Her skin prickled with that same distrust, but if it was simply the ceremony she had seen before, then she couldn't see that she needed to stay. She had only come this far to check. Check what though, she wasn't fully sure. To check that the priestesses would be alright, she supposed.

She chided herself for her own ridiculousness. Putting herself at risk to check on the Queen's favourite pets. Simply because one of them knew Mother Edi. It wasn't like she could help them.

She was no protector.

Suri glanced at the archway behind her. One guard stood by it. She was a guard herself, so thought it unlikely she would be stopped.

"First, a toast to the Gods!"

When the ceremony was in full swing, she would take her money back, duck out, and get away before anything happened. She watched as the priestesses drank. None of them fell dead, or choked. It was fine.

"Now, tether yourselves, signal your devotion to the Trio."

Suri watched on, distracted by her own desire for flight, as the priestesses huddled for a moment, then fanned out. It looked very similar to the ceremony she had seen before, at least in its formation. She took the time to take a couple steps back towards the edge of the room, towards the archway. Lingyun was halfway across the room.

The priestesses pushed back their hoods and pulled off their gloves.

In the centre, Orienne stood, holding a white-handled knife.

It was easier for Suri to see them as a mass when they were masked. Now looking around them, seeing their hair colours and textures, skin tones, even freckles, the reality of the individual was hard to ignore. She wondered which was the other from the Tangle.

It could have been any of them.

They seemed to be waiting for some signal.

Then Rasel started playing, irregular sweeps of sound that filled the room and swelled around her.

The other eleven priestesses started to move. In and around each other, and then every so often, one would take a step or two into the centre, and Orienne would lightly slice their palm with the blade of the knife. Then the two of them would twist around with their bloodied palms touching, and the first person would move back out again.

Before, she recalled it had been the person in the middle who would cut their own palm, sharing that wound with her fellow priestesses, and then swapping out. Here, it seemed Orienne stayed in the middle.

But still, a ceremony like one she'd seen before. Lingyun was making wide circles in the room with slow steps. Next time, his steps would lead him directly into her path.

Rasel kept the same pace, his movements of the bow against the string measured and slow. The Queen watched the priestesses with a smile.

They'd just completed the full cycle of all twelve of undulating in and out. Suri thought she might have missed her chance to leave, that the dance would end. She breathed a sigh of relief when the first priestess swelled back to the centre once more, the music continuing its peeling refrains. She needed to go soon but Lingyun was probably still a minute away. His steps were so damned slow.

She felt *Him* then. The echo of him, as it had been before when she'd been numb, with the earrings and Viantha's ring. It gurgled like nausea deep within her. It was an insistent voice. Not angry. It revelled. It praised. This, whatever this ceremony was... it wanted it. It fed on it.

She didn't like it. Her body itched to pull herself out of the room. She just needed her gold.

The priestesses kept going.

Moving in, getting cut a second time.

Moving back out.

She thought she saw Lingyun's lips moving, but she couldn't hear what he said over Rasel's instrument.

She saw the blood on the floor, the trails of it dropping from the priestesses' hands. More of it than she would have expected, their sleeves coated in it. The floor beneath their feet was a muddied ring of brownish red, carried and smudged underfoot.

And always Orienne in the middle. No dimples now. At first, she thought it was pure concentration. But her eyes looked glazed. She watched Orienne make the slice, watching her eyes not even seem to see the hand she pared open. She cut deep, from the end of the wrist to the start of the middle finger.

As ever, the priestesses kept moving, keeping the rhythm.

Rasel kept playing. Suri could not read his expressionless face. He did not look at her. He seemed to be watching the ceiling.

Lingyun circled closer, not twenty seconds away.

His voice rose in the gaps between Rasel's haunting melody, enough to know it was no language she understood.

Another priestess sliced. Her steps faltered, but she managed to keep herself from falling.

She needed to leave right now and start a new life. Be whoever she wanted. Free of the cages of *loyalty*.

Her eyes were locked on Orienne.

When Lingyun finally moved round, she tapped him on the shoulder and flashed a grin. He paused in his mutterings and moved next to her, and she leaned into him, brushing her arm against his. "This isn't like the last ceremony I saw."

He didn't return her smile, but that didn't alarm her. He was perpetually angry. He did watch the priestesses though, and she saw the corners of his eyes crinkle as another priestess nearly fainted. "No, I doubt it is."

"Is it nearly complete?" she asked, feigning nonchalance.

Lingyun shook his head. "She's the conduit. When she's channelled it all, that's when it ends."

Channelled it all. Channelled what? Blood itself?

"And then?" she asked, nudging him.

Her stomach flipped as the pocket she nudged was clearly empty. He'd moved her gold. Where?

"And then... she will go through the Gate and spark our new destiny."

He breathed the words, the words that seemed to ride the undercurrent of Him. The same praise, the claims to glory. *They are of us*, He had told her. But maybe *they* were all of *Him*. His playthings.

She was lucky Lingyun was even talking to her, his eyes seemed almost as glazed as the priestesses. Rasel and the Queen were caught in the same hazy rapture. She brushed into him again and still nothing. Where was it? Where was her gold?

The first priestess moved in for a fourth time, her red, curly hair bouncing as she hopped on unsteady feet into the centre. Orienne, her full arm and skirt drenched in blood, raised the knife and sliced.

The priestess dropped to the ground. As soon as she fell, Orienne's head whipped back, and she gasped.

There was a momentary pause, the music stilled, and the room seemed to tense.

And then it continued.

The other priestesses continued the dance around her and, when the next one moved in, she simply hopped over the body of her fellow priestess, as if it was just a lump on the ground.

"One."

Lingyun whispered it like a prayer and Suri covered her mouth, her head feeling foggy with sickness.

The hair of the girl on the floor splayed in an orange fire around her. Her skin was icy white, her eyes open and unblinking.

She was dead.

Suri pressed into Lingyun once more, feeling a knife. A frantic revulsion coursed through her veins. "They don't know what they're doing?"

She couldn't find it. She couldn't find the gold.

Something sick crept over his face. "They know to keep the ceremony going."

Then he moved away and started his counter-circling. His voice was louder, the chanting more repetitive. No. No.

She flicked the knife she had taken up into her sleeve. It wasn't enough. It wasn't five gold. That was supposed to be her new life. Now she was here.

This was how they were to start the Gate. They were going to let eleven priestesses die, and they were going to die drugged on wine, without understanding or choice.

They were doing it for *Him*.

Another priestess fell, as Orienne's head cracked back. Her legs crumpled on top of the first, but the others did not stop.

The words from earlier swept back to her.

'It's full now. It'll work.'

'And if it doesn't?'

'Then we repeat the ceremony until it does.'

She overheard the guards near her speak.

"The Gate isn't changing," one said.

"Maybe it's not working," the other replied.

She looked to the Gate, but it looked the same as she'd left it, stone and painted silver. No life or death seemed to be emanating from it. They didn't seem to notice it was missing a piece on its right hand side. A small half-sphere where amefyre had been, now sat empty.

She saw the Queen's pointed gaze still ever-fixed on the priestesses.

Lingyun kept chanting. Rasel kept playing.

The Gate wasn't working. It wasn't responding. Maybe she herself had broken it. But they weren't stopping. Suri fought the nausea, as the priestesses swirled with faltering steps, feet slipping in their own blood.

Again, the choice came back to Suri.

Two options.

Life and Death. Always life and death. Maybe Scilla was right.

Life. She could run. Leave. Maybe Kol would come. That could take hours, or it could never happen. All these priestesses would die.

Or option two. She could try to stop it.

Suri's ears pricked, as she heard something in the chant she recognised.

A name. Repeated.

And it was *His* name. She could tell it from the way He, even suppressed as He was, called out in response. He cried back. This ceremony was for Him, to call to Him, to evoke Him.

The name was *Sotoledi.*

The Old Death God.

It was heresy punishable by exile and murder to follow the pagan gods. The Queen of Drangbor, the leader of the Priesthood of the Trio, raised her hands in prayer to Him.

Sotoledi.

Again, He responded, and she felt the tug in her body. If it weren't for her secret weapon, she was certain she'd be enthralled. Lera had told her she had the voice of the Trio in her.

A lie.

She knew in her bones that this was who had been speaking to her all these weeks.

Sotoledi.

All those *years.* Since she had killed Clacker, and the nightmares had begun. Every earring to stop the nightmares had been to protect her from *Him.* He had spoken to her before she had even understood his words. The God of Death was the one who came to her, called to her to kill, to gain her revenge.

Kol's words came back to her. *You are death... If you're going to breathe death...* Had he known even then? That beat she'd felt around him, around Rasel? Was that Him? Was that Death?

Sotoledi.

This was how they had made the Gates before. This was why there hadn't been a new one since the Priesthood. They'd lied when they said they'd found a way to power the Gates through amefyre.

A sacrifice had to be made to tap into the site of the massacres.

And it was happening right here. Right now.

A third priestess crumbled into a heap on the floor. Orienne's head jolted back and, when it dropped again Suri could see her eyes were not just glazed over, but were black. Not just the iris, the whole space. Inky blackness.

'She's the conduit.'

She had made her choice when she followed the priestesses. She knew she might not leave this room alive.

And now she knew, if the Queen was happy to openly commit heresy, then no one would live to tell it.

Fuck.

She stared at Orienne, at where the dimples should have been. She waited until she had stopped in her most recent blood-soaked spin, watching her reach out to grab the arm of another priestess.

'She's channelling it all.'

She mentally apologised for what she was about to do. Then she threw the dagger.

It sunk deep into Orienne's heart. The priestess gasped, a slight rasping intake of breath.

The music screeched to a halt.

Orienne fell to her knees.

Queen Lera screamed. "No!"

It was the Queen herself that moved first, her black skirts whirling across the floor as she ran. Orienne collapsed on top of one of her fallen sisters, just as the Queen reached her.

Lingyun whipped around, fury blazing across his face, as he spat. "The exit!"

The guards snapped into action, blocking Suri's only escape route.

The Queen grabbed Orienne roughly, pulling her back, another scream falling from her beautiful face as she hauled the dead girl towards the empty Gate.

The remaining priestesses had fallen in dazed clumps to the floor.

Suri looked around her, scanning the four guards, working out if there was any way she could get past them.

Then she felt a jolt of extreme cold, a needle of frost lancing her heart. Her feet locked into place. No, not locked.

Frozen.

She looked across the room to see Rasel staring at her, his hand outstretched. His eyes were filled with hate. She couldn't move her feet, every shred of moisture in her foot wraps had frozen against the ground. She tried to pull her legs up, but she couldn't move.

The Queen dragged Orienne to the Gate's mouth, then moved around her and shoved her feet forwards, pushing her body through the archway.

Nothing happened.

Lera howled again.

Lingyun moved towards Suri, his fists clenched and his lip curled. She'd figured this would be how it would end. She'd fight though, tooth and nail to the bitter end. Lingyun stepped towards her. Rasel's cold deeper, locking into her joints and muscles, until she could barely move her limbs.

Not tooth and nail then. An execution as she stood in ice.

Lera stood half-hunched as she breathed in laboured breaths, staring at Orienne lying dead in the empty archway. She put her hand out for support and touched the Gate.

A moment later she dropped it, but Suri had seen.

In that single instance, the amefyre crown she wore went dull. Her skin went from luminescent pearl to ash grey. She sagged. Her face was still beautiful but contorted with overwhelming age. Her nails became talons. Her wings. The pale ethereal wings had morphed into stringy black monstrosities, heavy black corded lines with ragged flesh hanging down from their frame.

That was her true form. A harpy.

Asari ith vulturis. Beware the *harpy*.

Kol had warned her, back in the desert. Warned her against *Lera*.

Then her hand was gone from the Gate, and she was back to her usual form.

"Get her," Queen Lera said.

Lingyun reached into his pocket and realised his knife was missing. He glanced at Orienne, then back to Suri.

He shrugged.

"Live like a thief, die like a thief," he said, pushing his sleeves up.

Suri still couldn't move. Even breathing was hard, her breath like razors down her throat, as the very air inside her turned to ice.

Rasel did not smile. He did not stop.

Then a voice.

One she hadn't expected to hear.

Not here.

"Oh, fuck this."

From nothing, from what was a blank space, came a cloud of shadow and then a person.

Scilla.

She appeared in a moment, sweeping into existence.

Then she launched herself at Rasel.

28

Diophage has lain a harpy's curse on her body.
The child lives. We vow to protect him.
Diary of C. Aubethaan, est. early 8th century

The moment Scilla pounced on Rasel, the ice dropped from Suri's body. She could move. And move she did.

Lingyun turned his head to see the new disturbance and she moved forward, running at him, slamming her elbow deep into his gut.

Lingyun buckled over, stumbling back a couple of steps. Across the room, she saw Rasel dodge a fatal slice from Scilla's scimitar. Suri followed her elbow up with a kick to Lingyun's face, ripping the slit in her dress up to her hip.

As she twisted her leg back, he grabbed it. His face streamed with blood from his newly broken nose. His mouth twisted in rage as he pulled her leg with surprising force. She skipped forward and lost her balance, and he slammed into her side, knocking her onto her back.

He rammed his fist into her face, then clutched her face between his two hands and squeezed, raising her head and hitting it back against the stone.

She felt her head swim as she lifted her arms and broke his grip on her face. She twisted his wrists and Lingyun flinched backwards.

She swung her hips up, using his moment of disorientation to flip him. She straddled him, her head lancing with pain at the swift movement. He kept the motion rolling though, not letting her pin him, sweeping her back under him as he grabbed her wrists above her head.

Blood dripped from his lip onto her cheek. "How are you fighting me? You belong to *Him*."

Suri growled as she rammed her knee up as hard as she could. It was a cheap shot, his own fault, as he hadn't pinned her legs firmly enough. He squawked in pain, before using the loss of pressure from her hands to jerk them free.

She pulled herself out from under him, and kicked him in the face.

He twisted onto his side. She kicked him again.

She moved to kick him a third time, but he rolled out the way and hopped back onto his feet, turning to face her.

She spat at his feet and pulled off her eyepatch. "I belong to no one."

Lingyun's eyes widened. Underneath the patch was her salvation.

The only place she figured they wouldn't search... and she'd been right.

Glowing in the dead socket was a round gemstone. The missing piece of the Gate.

It numbed her. It brought her *back*. Away from *Him*. Amefyre.

If she hadn't been wearing it, she'd probably be standing with the guards, idly watching on. She might have enjoyed it, egged on by His voice. The numbness stopped Him from taking hold.

This was sick. They were all sick. The gem helped her see them more clearly than ever before. Amefyre was not holding her back from her power. It was protecting her from those that wanted to exploit it.

Lingyun came at her with everything. It was pure venom. The speed was nothing she had ever encountered before. She had experienced it when *He* had helped her and now it came at her.

He crashed his palm into her chest, and she was pushed off her feet by the force. The moment she hit the ground he was on her, punching her across the face.

Once.

So hard her skull rattled. Her vision eclipsed and then came back. She saw Rasel, running out of the room. She saw Scilla, rounding on the Queen.

Twice.

Her jaw had to be be broken. She tried to move—to do anything—but the pain was too much. When her vision returned, the Queen had disappeared.

A third time. The pain was everywhere, it was darkness. She couldn't see. She couldn't—

The fourth blow didn't come.

The weight was gone. A yell.

She blinked, her vision blurring and her head screaming.

Across the room, Scilla threw Lingyun into a stone post, hitting it hard. He slid down as if his bones were made of soup. His chest rose and fell, the only indication of life left in him, but firmly unconscious.

Suri sat up as Scilla stalked towards her.

"We're leaving, now."

Suri let herself be pulled to her feet. Her head swarmed with pain, and she nearly fainted on the spot. "The priestesses," she said, choking through a mouth filled with blood. She spat red on the floor and found her eye drawn to the pile of bodies. Some were still alive, breathing.

"I'm coming back for them. Let's go," Scilla said.

Suri moved towards the exit with small steps, unable to do anything else. Scilla sighed and grabbed her hand, yanking her forward. She barely had time to pull in a shocked gasp before she was enveloped in a dark cloud.

That same feeling of stepping through a Gate hit her. Weightless, yet weighted darkness swept across her body, tugging at her.

Scilla's grip dropped from hers, and she stumbled forward into the sand. She looked around wildly, noting the stone entranceway and the dunes around her. They hadn't gone far, only to the mouth of the stairs down to the Altar. Suri relaxed a fraction, allowing that horrible pain to threaten to consume her again.

Scilla stood above her, looking back at the stairway. Her hands twitched. Was she about to leave her?

"The Queen?" Suri asked.

If she was going to be ditched out in the desert again, she at least wanted to know she wasn't about to be recaptured a second later.

Scilla scoffed, something much stronger than annoyance flashing across that strong gaze. "We aren't the only ones who can move through shadow."

"You saved me," Suri said.

The words were said without affliction of confusion or gratitude. It was simply a statement; all Suri could manage.

Scilla rolled her eyes as the light of the moon bathed the smooth planes of her face. "It wasn't my decision."

Scilla's hands flickered again, then she was gone in a shadowed cloud. After a minute she was back, the limp body of a priestess in her arms. She put her down next to Suri and disappeared again. Suri watched the girl's shallow breathing.

Suri sat up. She tore her orange dress to pieces, wrapping one tightly around the girl's bleeding arm. The cuts were deep, and she'd lost so much blood already.

Scilla completed five trips and, when she appeared for the fifth time, laying the priestess down, she knew without having to ask. She could see it on her enemy's face. That was the last.

Only five.

Suri bandaged her as best she could. She swallowed, her head pounding. Pain everywhere. "You were there. The whole time. You let them die."

The general stared into the darkness. "So did you."

A choking feeling started in Suri's throat. "I took the gem from the Gate, I thought they would stop when they realised."

Scilla glanced down at her.

Suri pulled herself to her feet, staring straight into Scilla's unflinching eyes.

"You didn't know I'd meddled with it," she said. "All of them would have died, the Gate would have opened, and you would have done *nothing*."

Scilla raised an eyebrow. "Oh look. She cares about human life."

There was no venom in it, yet somehow that made it worse. It was a taunt, and it drew the wind from Suri's sails. She was right.

Scilla looked into the distance behind her. Looking over her shoulder, something swept over her face that she had never seen before. Something lighter.

Scilla flicked her eyes to Suri. "It was never going to open."

Suri fought back the rage, the misery, the guilt. "How could you know that?"

A noise from behind her. Wind and hooves. Suri span, as a giant horse slowed to a stop a few feet from them. Its rider, dressed all in black, swung off the back of the animal.

He pulled the sand guard down from his mouth and pushed the hood back over his curling black locks. His face was severe, his jaw locked, his eyes blazing with anger. He scanned the priestesses lying on the floor, then looked to his general, checking her.

Then his eyes pinned Suri. She could feel his red hot stare as he surveyed her torn dress, bloodied face, the amefyre blazing from where the grey eye should have been.

"Hey, little thief," Kol said.

29

Beware the harpy. Beware the harpy. Beware the harpy.

Diary of C. Aubethaan, est. early 8th century

S uri found her words stuck for a moment in her throat.

The giant horse pawed its hoof in the sand. Suri stumbled and touched Ruben's nose, his breath warming her fingers, his nostrils flaring.

"Lingyun's still in there," Scilla said with a sneer. "Rasel and the harpy got away."

Ruben huffed.

"Is he dead?" Kol asked.

Scilla shook her head. "Left him to you."

Kol's jaw hardened, and he nodded. With a flick of a wrist, he stepped into dark shadow and vanished. He was back before Suri had blinked.

He stared out into the dunes around them, scanning the horizon. "He's gone," he said, pulling a hand through his thick, dark hair.

Scilla gaped. "How? He was there a second ago. He wouldn't be strong enough to use the shadows."

Kol glanced down at Suri, then looked back to his general. "They're still close."

Ruben let out a nervous whinny.

Scilla shook her head. "Go. Take her."

"Are you strong enough?"

"Strong enough to move these," she waved her hands towards the priestesses, "to a safe place."

Kol stared at Scilla. There was so much in that gaze. Trust, fear. Love, even. Suri's head was still pounding, the blood rushing in and out of her ears.

Eventually, Kol nodded. "Then you'll come find us."

Scilla nodded. "Go."

She grabbed one of the girls and disappeared.

Kol reached his hand towards Suri. It was gloved in black leather, his palm was an offering, laid before her. Another choice. "Get up, now. They will be after us."

She swallowed.

"Where are we going?"

He tilted his head, a phantom smile on his lips.

"The City of the Damned."

He had come. They had helped her, and she was now too broken to run from those that were hunting her.

Maybe this was the lesser evil. Maybe this was what Esra wanted.

She took his hand and, even through the glove, she felt warmth there.

Kol stepped towards her, his eyes dark. He looked at her. A question. She nodded. Letting go of her hand, he used both of his to grip her waist, his hands almost circling it. He lifted her with ease up onto the saddle. She painfully moved her leg around to the other side, as he pulled himself up behind her.

His body was warm against hers, the strength of him pressing against her back.

Kol paused for a moment, watching his general crouched next to the five priestesses. Suri had to look away. Five. Only five.

Kol whistled. Ruben flew.

Suri was pushed back into Kol by the speed, and his arms encircled her, holding the reins loosely on either side, as she was pinned between him.

Ruben galloped like the wind itself, diving up and over the shallow dunes until they reached the cleared path. He knew the way, without movement or prompting, moving as he wanted to.

"He's a Roanhadham," she said.

It was a statement, but Kol answered it anyway. "Yes."

"Why did you offer him to me?"

"He knows his way back. Once you got to Drameir, I would have called him."

So, that part of the deal was a lie. Suri found she wasn't angry about it, but maybe she just couldn't fathom the rage right now.

She let herself be carried by the pummeling hooves. Her head was pounding, her chest screamed. Had she broken a rib? She felt confused and tried to distract herself from the pain by thinking of Kol.

She focused on the way his thighs were clenched around her own, his breath steady in her ear. She felt herself slipping a little and tried to grip the saddle in front of her, but her eye blurred and her hands couldn't grip. He reached down with one hand and pulled her back, tucking her more firmly against him. His arm stayed there, pinning her in place.

Her head lolled back against his shoulder. She felt faint—broken. Every pound of the horse's hooves ricocheted pain up her body.

"Suri—?"

Kol's question swirled around her. She couldn't answer.

"Who hurt you?" he asked.

She swallowed and tried to move. Her head felt so heavy, so she just gazed up at the sky. Dawn was near.

"Lingyun."

Kol's grip on her tightened. "That bastard." He whistled again, causing Ruben to go even faster. The cold night air made her eye well up, but she kept staring as dawn approached.

"How did you know?" she asked after a while. "That I was lying about my name."

The question had been swirling in her head for days.

Kol didn't reply for a while, and she stopped thinking that he would. She was almost asleep when he finally responded. "You gave your name as Edi. You had the earrings. I knew you were one of hers."

She blinked back into reality, letting his words sink in. "You know Mother Edi?"

He nodded. She hated the hope and vulnerability she'd heard in her own voice, hardening against it.

"Doesn't she work for the Queen?" she asked.

She said it as almost a statement, throwing out the worst possible version. Her blood sang for it to be denied, rebuked. Anything but a nod, for Wrath's sake.

Was he too involved in a plot to wrangle up amefyre? What new horror was she about to discover about the woman who had sheltered her?

Kol scoffed. "Everyone has to pay the piper. Edi was playing the harpy at her own game."

Suri had no idea what that meant, yet a feeling of profound relief washed over her. The way he spoke of her, it was more than approval. It was almost reverent.

Mother Edi wasn't one of the Queen's. She wasn't. She hadn't sold her out or, at least, maybe she had another reason. A good one, perhaps. Some constriction on Suri's heart loosened, just a fraction.

"She was one of the originals," Kol continued. "She carried me across this desert."

He was tense behind her. Suri whipped her head around to look at him, and he gazed at her with such intensity that she broke eye contact to look back at Ruben's mane.

One of the originals... carried him...

After the Wrath, she had been one of the pagans? *Mother Edi* had carried the Demon King in his infancy through the desert?

Why?

"She's not a pagan," Suri replied.

Kol laughed, tickling her ear. He laughed like it was the funniest thing he'd heard in a week. He coughed, half spluttering as he tried to stop himself, and Suri felt a twinge of embarrassment, a feeling of being left out of an inside joke.

"Are *you* a pagan?" he asked.

"Of course I'm not," she spat.

His voice held a trace of humour when he next spoke. "Then how did you survive the desert?"

Suri floundered for an answer. She'd stumbled through it barely alive for days, she'd hardly thrived. Sotoledi had given her the ability to kill. Did hearing Him make her a pagan? She had no belief in Him. "I walked, I—"

"Mother Edi taught you, didn't she?" he asked.

Suri quietened for a moment. She remembered walking miles without even a sip, but surely that couldn't have been right. "The beats."

"We call it life bonding."

The hooves juddered beneath her as she tried to make sense of his words. Mother Edi had taught her a pagan ability? Life bonding. The God of Life? *That* was the beats?

Kol breathed out. "The Wrath was not caused by the Death God. It was caused by Life," he said.

Suri said nothing, caught in her complete confusion.

He took it as a sign to continue. "My mother was murdered as she gave birth to me. She was a life priestess. Diophage took revenge. When he left, he took Life itself with him. Not just in the Parched Lands. He stripped that to nothing in his fury, but he also took life magic. Light, water, healing. They were corrupted, broken."

Suri's mind was whirring. She thought back to the symbols scrawled over that painting in the library. The mistranslated warning. Beware the harpy. Diophage. Revenge. "Who killed your mother?"

His arms tensed around her. "Guess."

"Queen Lera."

"Look at you go," he murmured in her ear.

Suri didn't know what to say to that.

Sotoledi's Wrath didn't destroy the world. Diophage's revenge did, sapping life from the world in punishment of the killing of a sacred priestess.

She tried to think about what that meant. About the witch, about Lera's story of the new gods, everything, but she was so tired, and couldn't hold all the threads of this new information in her head. So what. The result was the same. Whether you removed life or enacted death. Everyone, everything died.

Kol continued. "It's coming back now."

Suri remembered Mother Edi saying that, after the Wrath, those that used to be light manipulators were now confined to the shadows. And then discovering that Viantha could not only move water, but create it. But why was he telling her? How did any of it concern her?

"Is that why you didn't kill me in the desert?" she asked. "I lived, so therefore I must be friends with your pagan life god?"

"No," Kol replied, without hesitation. "Mother Edi has been teaching the beats for decades. That sort of basic life bonding has been working pretty well for a while. If I needed someone with that skill, I could find someone who'd be a lot less trouble than you."

Suri expected the rage to fill her, that bubbling thrum and voice telling her to kill him for it. But it didn't come. Sotoledi was nullified by that piece of rock in her eye, a piece of rock that was scraping, hurting. But less than the rest of her broken body at least.

"When I found you, I saw the plant," he said.

Suri twitched, curiosity making her crave asking him, stubbornness making her wait it out. She was eventually rewarded.

His voice was sombre when he spoke again. "That is the first plant I've seen grow in the Parched Lands in my entire existence."

Suri couldn't bite back her response. "And you think I had something to do with that?"

Kol sighed. "If you didn't... something did. As much as I wouldn't mind having you dead, I ought to rule you out first."

She barked out a laugh, despite herself, the action rattling her very bones.

"I've just found out that the literal embodiment of Death has been speaking to me for ten years," she said, feeling almost delirious. "And now you tell me that I might also have some weird ability to make tiny plants grow while I'm unconscious?"

He shrugged. "As you said, we don't know that."

She watched the desert floor beneath them fly under the ceaseless gallop.

"What does it mean?" she asked, half to herself.

Kol's voice was hard. "Today, it means I sent Scilla to bring you back alive. Whatever the cost."

She could tell from his tone, and how he tensed behind her, how badly that order had hurt him. He had risked Scilla's life, his general, in exchange for the dirty thief who had killed Barsen.

"And tomorrow?" she asked. She wasn't sure if she wanted to know the answer, but knew she needed it.

"We will see if you're worth it."

That was apparently all the answer she was going to get.

Mother Edi, not working for the Queen, and also a pagan? That was a question mark for another day. Her own abilities... Was it possible that she could have played some part in the existence of that plant? How? She hadn't done anything. She didn't remember doing anything.

All she could think about was how much everything hurt and how tired she was.

Not long passed before she found her eye drifting shut.

She blinked awake, as Ruben slowed to a canter. It couldn't have been long, the air was still cool, and the chill of the night hadn't been rushed off by the heat of the day.

Every part of her body screamed. She needed to lie down and rest. Maybe forever.

Around her was a city. Or at least, it looked like one.

Hundreds of buildings surrounded them. Ruben moved through a wide, empty sandstone street. The buildings were similar to that of the outpost.

These, however, were completely empty. It was a ghost town.

Surrounding the edges of the buildings, at the city's limits, were dusty cliffs and mountains, scaling high beyond the tallest roof.

This was the City of the Damned? Building after building of empty nothingness. Once it must have been the capital of Ucraipha, but now it was empty. For whatever reason, the Lord of Death had chosen not to fill the homes with his rabble of leftover people.

To Suri, it seemed like a massive waste. So many homes, where so many had none. Where did they live instead? The towers and ruthless dunes? At least here there were cliffs to protect from the worst of the elements.

Perhaps only ghosts were permitted to live in the City of the Damned.

They moved through empty street after empty street, Suri gazing into empty windows. Most of the buildings looked half finished, made in a rush and not cared for, dilapidated and worn by the storms, sand piled against walls.

Ruben turned down a narrower street, taking lefts and rights until Suri would not have been able to trace her way back.

Then the horse stopped. Kol slowly dismounted, holding onto her as he did, before pulling her from the horse and into his arms. They were huge, like branches.

She didn't push away from him and even if she had, she wouldn't have been able to pick herself up off the floor again.

"You were right. She was trying to channel the deaths of the Wrath for her Gate."

Suri looked up at him but said nothing, only able to concentrate on how the pain ricocheted with every movement. She tasted stale blood in her mouth.

Kol strode through the door of a building. It too was empty and dilapidated. There was nothing to set it apart from the rest. He went through a door and down a set of steps.

"And I knew it wouldn't work," he added.

It was a sandstone tunnel and, at its end, was a locked door. It was metal, heavy. Out of place.

Kol carried her to it, then placed her on her feet. He steadied her, then reached for a key slung around his neck. He clicked off the deadbolt, then pressed his palms to the door and closed his eyes. A few moments later, it unsealed.

He turned back to her. "Can you walk?"

She couldn't. Not really. "Yes."

He smiled and pulled the door open. "I knew it wouldn't work, Suri," he said, holding her hand and guiding her through. "Because I already did it."

A Gate stood before her. Plain, undecorated. Nothing more than a wall of sandstone, with a black void in the centre. He guided her forward and, together, they stepped into it.

Cold. Weightless. The echo of an echo of a scream. A small tug at her belly.

Then they were through.

Dappled moonlight danced on his black hair. The air was thick with moisture. A thick, green canopy blurred into view above her.

She knew this was a place she'd never been before. But there was something there, in his gaze, that made her guess she could trust him. For now.

The Lord of Death smiled. "Suri, welcome to the real City of the Damned."

AMEFYRE
BOOK TWO

A PROMISE OF BLOOD

R. A. SANDPIPER

A Small Request

If you're at this page having just finished this book... Hi stranger, congrats, another book under your belt, look at you being all cultured. Can I ask for a favour?

Please consider leaving a review.

It doesn't have to be a particularly good one. And I know you're busy. But reviews are everything for indie authors like me. Most of this author operation is a one-woman show, and the simple act of leaving a rating on Amazon or Goodreads is one of the best ways to make this become a genuine career for me.

Thank you for reading. You're pretty cool. Yes, I'm flattering you to provoke you to review. Is it working?

Acknowledgements

The first big thank you is to my beta and proof readers (formerly known as friends), for your valuable feedback and much needed validation. To those of you that read it more than once at my request, I am even more grateful. I'm going to thank my family here, too. I'm not sure they've yet read the full book, mostly because I wouldn't let them until it was the final version (hi, guys). Despite that, their support of me in all things has been indirectly incredibly helpful, and I know that if I *had* asked for help, they would have given it.

Another thanks to my colourfully named editors Elle W Silver and Stephen Black, I appreciate all the work that went into improving this book. Thank you to my fabulous cover designer, Saint Jupiter, who can currently find her on Instagram at this handle: saintjupit3rgr4phic. Thank you also to the artist who supplied the internal artwork for this book, Gurge Art, who you can find at gurge.art on Instagram. Finally, thank you to Alexa Donne, the Courtney Project and Sarra Cannon. I have watched more hours of your content than I would like to admit, and you deserve so much kudos!

Being an indie author is quite an isolating experience, and a lot of the burden falls on my shoulders. And yet, taking this book from conception to the hands of readers has required a village worth of support. I'm very happy with my little village and I'm so glad you're now a part of it, too.

Made in United States
Orlando, FL
04 February 2025